Into A Dark Realm

The Darkwar Book Two

Raymond E. Feist

W F HOWES LTD

This large print edition published in 2007 by
W F Howes Ltd
Unit 4, Rearsby Business Park, Gaddesby Lane,
Rearsby, Leicester LE7 4YH

1 3 5 7 9 10 8 6 4 2

First published in the United Kingdom in 2006
by Voyager

A CIP catalogue record for this book is available
from the British Library

ISBN 978 1 40740 150 8

Typeset by Palimpsest Book Production Limited,
Grangemouth, Stirlingshire
Printed and bound in Great Britain
by Antony Rowe Ltd, Chippenham, Wilts.

Into A Dark Realm

ALSO BY RAYMOND FEIST
FROM CLIPPER LARGE PRINT

FLIGHT OF THE NIGHTHAWKS
EXILE'S RETURN

ACKNOWLEDGEMENTS

As always, the many mothers and fathers of Midkemia, for giving me a world in which to tell stories.

To my children, Jessica and James, for keeping me grounded no matter how crazy the world around us gets.

To my mother for hanging in there.

To Jonathan Matson, again and always.

To my editors, in so many places, for caring about the work.

And to my readers; without you I'd be doing something a great deal less fun.

Raymond E. Feist
San Diego, CA July, 2006

*This one is for Janny, Bill, Joel, and Steve
For sharing their talents*

CONTENTS

NORTHLANDS

The Great Northern Mountains

Stone Mountain

The T

The HIG

THE LAKE OF THE SKY

Elvandar

Tyr-Sog

Yabon

LaMut   Loriél

Crydee

THE FAR COAST

THE GREEN HEART

The Grey Tower

Zûn

Hawk's Hollow

THE KINGDOM

Carse
Jonril

Walinor
Hush

Natal

Ylith
Queshon's View

Calastius Mountains

DIMWI

Sethanon
THE GREAT VEL

Tulan

THE FREE CITIES

Bordon
Port Natal

Queg

Sarth
SORCERER'S ISLE

Darkmoor

THE ENDLESS SEA

Margrave's Port
Lan   Palanque

THE KINGDOM OF QUEG

Krondor

Dorgin
Landreth
SEA OF DREAMS

THE STRAITS OF DARKNESS

LiMeth

Land's End

THE BITTER SEA

THE SCARLA

Durbin

Shamata

VALE OF DREAMS
(DISPUTED BORDER)

Elarial

Ranom

Caralyan

Trollhome Mountains

JAL-PUR DESERT

The Pillars of the Stars

THE EMPI

MIDKEMIA

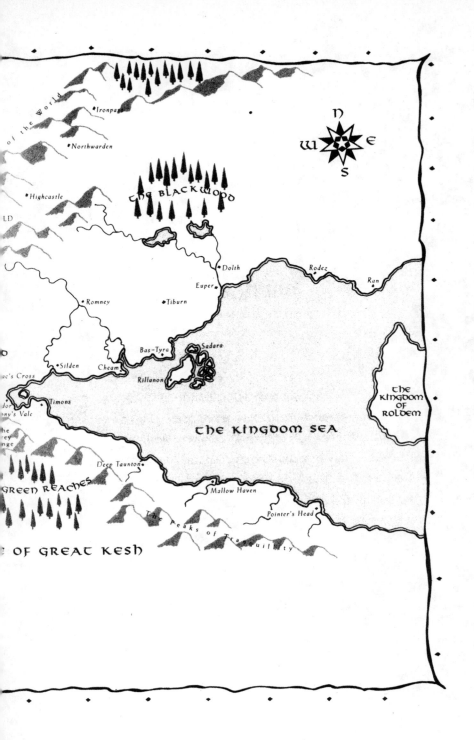

CHAPTER 1

CHASE

A woman screamed in outrage.

Three young men overturned carts and pushed aside shoppers as they crashed through the evening market. Their leader – a tall, rawboned youth with red hair – pointed to the retreating back of their prey and shouted, 'There he goes!'

Night approached the port city of Durbin as desperate men raced through the streets. Merchants pulled prized wares from tables as three young warriors shoved anyone and anything blocking their pursuit. In their wake they left consternation, curses and threats; all of which they ignored.

The summer heat of the Jal-Pur desert still clung to the walls and cobbles of the city, despite the slight breeze off the sea. Even the harbour gulls were content to stand idly by and watch for any morsel that might fall from a passing vendor's cart. The more ambitious among them would launch themselves into the air and soar for a moment or two, hanging languidly on the heat rising from the dock stones, then quickly return to stand quietly near their brethren.

The evening markets were crowded, for most of the inhabitants of Durbin had spent the blistering afternoon resting in the shade. The city's pace was leisurely, for these were the hottest days of summer, and men who lived on the desert's edge knew better than to struggle needlessly against the elements. Things were as the gods willed.

So the sight of three armed and apparently dangerous young men pursuing another, while hardly a remarkable experience in Durbin, was unexpected given the season and the time of day. It was just too hot to be running.

The man attempting to flee was, from his look, a desertman: swarthy and dressed in a baggy shirt and loose-fitting pantaloons, a midnight blue headdress and open robe, his feet clad in low-topped boots. Those who followed were led by a northerner, probably from the Free Cities or the Kingdom of the Isles. His ginger hair was uncommon in the Empire of Great Kesh.

His companions were also young men, one broad-shouldered and dark of hair, the other blond and of slighter build. They were all sunburned and dirty and had hard expressions that added years to their appearance. Their attentions were fixed on their quarry and their weapons were easily at hand. They were dressed in garb that marked them as men from the Vale of Dreams – breeches, linen shirts, riding boots and leather vests instead of robes and sandals. They were most likely mercenaries, a likelihood accentuated by their grim determination.

They reached a boulevard that led to the docks, and the man fleeing dodged between merchants, shoppers and dockmen heading home for the night. The leader of those in pursuit paused for an instant then said, 'He's heading for the grain-shippers' dock.' With a hand gesture he sent his blond-haired companion up a side street, then motioned for the darker youth to come with him.

'I hope you're right,' said the shorter man. 'I'm getting tired of all this running.'

With a quick glance that showed a grin, the leader said, 'Too much time sitting in alehouses, Zane. We need to get you back to the Island and Tillingbrook's tender mercies.'

Too out of breath to comment, the shorter youth just made a sound that clearly indicated he found that remark utterly lacking in humour, as he quickly wiped perspiration from his brow. He had to hurry just to keep up with his taller companion.

The inhabitants of Durbin were practised when it came to dealing with duels, brawling, gang wars, riots, and all other manner of civil disorder. By the time Jommy and Zane reached the corner around which they had seen their quarry vanish, the alarm had outstripped them, and the street leading to the docks was almost deserted. Passers-by, merchants, and seamen bound for nearby inns and taverns had sensed coming trouble and vanished into whatever scant cover they could manage. Doors closed, shutters slammed, and those that couldn't get inside did their best to find shelter.

As Jommy Killaroo kept his eyes on the tiny figure of their fleeing target, Zane con Doin glanced into every passed doorway, alley entrance or other cover for potential ambush. All he saw were citizens of Durbin hunkering down, waiting for the trouble to pass.

Jommy saw their man duck around a corner at the end of the boulevard, and said, 'Right towards Tad if he's as fast as he usually is!'

Zane grinned. 'He is. Suri won't escape.'

For a month Jommy, Tad and Zane had been on the trail of this man, an erstwhile trader named Aziz Suri, a desertman from the Jal-Pur who was reputedly an importer of spices and oils from the Free Cities. He was also reputed to be a freelance spy, broker in information, trader in secrets, and a close contact of the Nighthawks, the Guild of Death. One month earlier, at the Emperor of Kesh's Midsummer's Festival, a plot to destabi-lize the Empire and plunge it into civil war had been prevented by agents of the Conclave of Shadows, and now they were seeking out the remaining pockets of assassins, to put an end finally to their centuries' long reign of terror.

Zane struggled to keep up with Jommy. While he was able to run as far as the taller youth, he was not able to do so at his longer-legged friend's furious pace, and maybe Jommy was right: maybe he had spent too many nights in the alehouse. His trousers had been getting tighter of late.

As they reached the end of the street, they came

upon the grain-shippers' docks: a long series of stoneworks punctuated by three large derricks, fronting onto two massive warehouses. From the far end of the dock Tad ran towards them, shouting, 'In there!' and motioning that their quarry had slipped into the narrow passage between the two warehouses.

Jommy and the two younger boys took no pains to hide their approach, for after a month in Durbin they knew this area of the city fairly well: well enough to know that their prey had dashed into a dead-end alley. When they reached the narrow opening, the man bolted from it, heading straight towards the harbour. The setting sun glinted red off the sea, and he squinted and turned his head, raising his hands to shield his eyes.

Jommy reached out and got just enough of a grip on the man's arm for a second to turn him completely around. The man flailed his arms, tipping off-balance, as he vainly sought to keep his feet under him. Jommy reached out again, trying to grab the man's tunic, but only succeeded in causing him to stumble farther. Before anyone could get hold of any part of the slender trader, he slammed into the centremost derrick.

Stunned for an instant, the desertman turned, teetered, and then as he regained his wits, stepped off the edge of the pier.

A cry akin to a dog whose paw had just been stepped on filled the air as he vanished over the edge. The three young men hurried to the edge and looked over. Dangling from the derrick rope just above a loose cargo net was the little trader, hurling invective upward as he glanced down at the rocks below the jetty. The tide was out, so only a few inches of water protected the dangling man from serious injury below. All the shallow-draught barges used to ferry grain to the ships in the harbour were anchored out in deeper water. 'Pull me up!' he shouted.

Jommy said, 'Why should we, Aziz? You led us a nasty chase through the entire city of Durbin in this bleedin' heat—' he wiped perspiration off his forehead and flipped it with his hand at the man to demonstrate just how out of sorts he was, '—and all we wished for was a short, quiet chat.'

'I know you murderous cut-throats,' said the trader. 'Your chats get men killed.'

Tad said, 'Murderous cut-throats? I think he has us confused with someone else.'

Zane drew his belt knife. 'You're confusing us with a different bunch of murderous cut-throats is my brother's opinion. I'm not so sure.' Looking at his companions, he asked, 'If I cut this rope what do you think of his chances?'

Tad leaned over, as if studying the matter, then declared, 'It's no more than twenty feet to the rocks. I say it's better than even money he only breaks a leg or an arm or two.'

Jommy said, 'Depends on how he falls. Now, I've seen a bloke pitch backwards off a ladder once, only the bottom rung, mind you, and he

6

smacked his head against the ground and broke his skull. Took him a bit of time to die, then, but he was dead, in the end, and dead is dead.'

'I could cut it and we could see,' suggested Zane.

'No!' shouted the trader.

'Well, the evening tide's coming in,' said Tad to Aziz. 'If you hang there for another couple of hours, you should be able to just let go and swim over to those steps over there.' He pointed across the harbour.

'If the sharks don't get him,' said Jommy to Zane.

'I can't swim!' shouted the trader.

'Not a lot of opportunities to learn in the desert, I expect,' observed Zane.

'Then you're into it up to your neck, aren't you, mate?' asked Jommy. 'What say you we trade a bit? You answer a question, and if I like the answer, we pull you up.'

'If you don't like the answer?'

'He cuts the rope,' said Jommy, pointing to Zane. 'And we'll see if the fall kills you, or just ruins your life – whatever's left of it before the tide comes in and drowns you, of course.'

'Barbarian!'

Jommy grinned. 'Been called that more than a few times since I got to Kesh.'

'What do you wish to know?' asked the desertman.

'One thing only,' said Jommy, losing his grin. 'Where's Jomo Ketlami?'

'I don't know!' shouted the man as he tried to gain purchase for his feet in the dangling cargo net.

'We know he's somewhere in the city!' shouted Jommy. 'We know he hasn't got out of the city. And we know that you have been doing business with him for years. Here's the deal: you tell us where he is, we pull you up. Then we go find him, get what we want to know from him, and kill him. You've got no worries.

'Or you don't tell us and we leave you hanging. You might climb up to the top of this derrick, and get down from there somehow, but even if you do, we'll just start spreading the word you sold out Ketlami. So we'll just keep an eye on you, wait until he kills you, and we'll have him, anyway.' Jommy's grin returned. 'Your choice, mate.'

'I can't!' cried the terrified trader.

'Five imperial silvers he doesn't die when he hits the rocks,' said Tad.

'I don't know,' Zane replied. 'Seems like that's a bit better than even money.'

'What say you to my five against your four?'

Zane nodded enthusiastically. 'Done!'

'Wait!'

Jommy said, 'Yes?'

'Don't cut the rope, please. I have children to care for!'

'Liar,' said Zane. 'It's well known you tell the girls at the bordellos you're without a wife.'

'I didn't say I had a wife,' admitted the little man. 'But I do care for the handful of bastards I've sired.'

'You are the soul of generosity, mate,' observed Jommy.

'There are men who do far less for their get,' replied the dangling trader. 'I have even taken the eldest into my house to learn a craft!'

'Which?' asked Zane. 'Trading, spying, lying, or cheating at cards?'

'You know,' asked Tad, 'that as we stand here jibber-jabbing, the tide's coming in?'

'So?' Jommy looked at his friend with a narrowing gaze.

'Well, if we don't cut the rope soon, then the chances are he'll just drown, and that means the bet's off.'

'Can't have that,' said Zane. He flourished the large hunting knife he was holding, twirled it like an expert, and began sawing at the heavy rope that ran up through the block and tackle below the topmost pulley of the derrick.

'No!' shouted the panic-stricken little man. 'I'll talk!'

'So, talk,' returned Jommy.

'Not until you pull me up!'

Zane glanced at his companions. 'A reasonable request?'

'Well, I don't think he's going to be able to best all three of us,' said Tad. 'After all, he's an un-armed, skinny little fellow and we're, what did he call us?'

'Murderous cut-throats,' supplied Zane.

'Pull him up, then,' said Jommy.

Tad and Zed both gripped the heavy crank used to raise the netting, and turned it. Being well oiled, it moved freely and the little man quickly rose the dozen feet necessary to bring his head above the edge of the dock.

Jommy had his sword out and pointed to a spot on the dock. 'Put him there, lads.'

Tad and Zane ceased cranking, set the lock to keep the net from falling back, and then grabbed the long wooden arm used to swing cargo around. When they had the trader safely above the docks he let go of the net, dropping a few feet to the stones.

Before Aziz could think to flee again, Jommy had his sword's point at the man's throat. 'Now, you were going to tell us the whereabouts of Jomo Ketlami.'

With eyes downcast Aziz said, 'You must find him and kill him quickly, and those who serve him, for if any of those . . . murderers linger, my life is over.'

'That's our plan,' said Jommy. 'Now, where is he?'

'You were mistaken about him still being in the city. He has more ways through the walls than a sewer rat. There are caves in the hills above the beach a half-day's ride to the southwest, and there he has gone to ground.'

'And you know this how?' asked Tad.

'He sent word, before he fled. He has need of me. Without me, he has no way to send messages to his confederates in other cities on the Bitter Sea. I am to find my way to those caves in two nights, for he has messages he must send to his murderous brothers.'

'I think we should just kill him,' said Zane. 'He's in a lot deeper than we thought.'

'No,' said Jommy, putting up his sword as Tad gripped Aziz by the shoulder. 'I think we're going to take him back to the inn and have him sit down with your dad, and we'll let him decide this.' To the trader, Jommy said, 'It's all the same to me if you live or die, so if I were in your place, I'd put some effort into convincing us it's better for everyone involved if you stay alive.'

The man nodded.

'Come along,' said Jommy. 'If you're lying to us, your bastards will have to learn to fend for themselves.'

'On their heads, I will tell you only the truth.'

'No,' said Jommy. 'It's on your head, Aziz.'

As the sun vanished below the western horizon, the four men moved away from the docks into the pest hole of a city that was Durbin.

Armed men moved silently through the night. Before them lay a small cave, large enough to admit one man at a time, half-hidden under an overhanging cliff, where a knoll rearing up over the beach had been worn away by years of erosion. Above the cave two archers crouched, ready to fire down on anyone attempting to exit the cave without permission.

Mist rolled in off the Bitter Sea, and no moon was visible through the overcast. The night was coal-mine dark and the men surrounding the

11

cave could barely make out one another in the murk.

Caleb, son of Pug, motioned for his three boys to wait. Behind him his brother Magnus stood ready to answer any magical onslaught that might be forthcoming. A dozen other men were also moving to form a semi-circle around another exit to the cave a hundred yards down the cliff.

The two brothers bore a strong resemblance to one another. They were tall and slender yet strong, with hair to the shoulders, an almost regal bearing which they had inherited from their mother, and eyes that seemed to look through you. The one startling difference was in their colouring. Caleb had dark brown hair and eyes, while Magnus's hair was the palest blond, looking white in the sun, and his eyes were the palest blue. Caleb wore hunting garb, tunic and trousers, knee-high boots, and a floppy-brimmed hat, while Magnus wore simple black robes with the hood thrown back.

Caleb had spent most of the night before interrogating the trader Aziz with the help of his brother. Magnus lacked the special art to determine if the trader was telling the truth or lying, but the trader didn't know that, and after a simple demonstration of Magnus's magical ability Aziz was convinced the magician could parse falsehood from sincerity. Magnus came back with Caleb before dawn and the two brothers had employed their respective skills – tracking and magic – to ensure their quarry was, indeed, inside those caves. Just before dawn, two assassins had exited the cave and made a quick sweep of the surrounding terrain. Magnus had employed a spell of levitation to lift his brother and himself a hundred feet above the knoll, so there was no sign of them when the patrolling sentries reached the top of the knoll. In the dark even if they had looked straight upward there was little chance they would have been seen.

A single lookout had been stationed a short distance down the coast to ensure that no one had fled while Magnus had returned to the City of Kesh to get Chezarul, an erstwhile trader from the City of Kesh, who was one of the most trusted agents of the Conclave, and his most reliable warriors, returning within hours by magic. At dusk they had approached these caves and taken up position after nightfall.

Their best estimate was that Jomo Ketlami was holed up in a warren of caves with at least half a dozen assassins, waiting for Aziz to arrive so the fugitives could arrange safe passage out of Kesh. And given the events of the past month, these would be the toughest, wiliest, most fanatical survivors of the Nighthawks.

Since the attempt on the Emperor by the sorcerer Leso Varen, and his role in leading the Nighthawks, soldiers of the Empire, under direction from Keshian spies and agents of the Conclave of Shadows, had been rooting out every last hiding place in Kesh. By imperial decree, these men were under an order of summary execution.

Similar campaigns had been underway in the Kingdom of the Isles, as well as Roldem, Olasko, and several of the other larger cities in the Eastern Kingdoms. The Conclave was certain they had identified every last headquarters but one: the ultimate source of this murderous brotherhood, where their Grand Master sat like a giant spider in the centre of a web that stretched over an entire continent. And the man in the caves just a few dozen yards away knew where the headquarters for the Guild of Death was hidden.

Caleb signalled. A sentry standing behind the archers above uncovered a lantern and the men down the beach slowly entered the second cave mouth. Magnus had used every art he possessed to determine there were no magical snares waiting for them. He was less confident about more mundane traps. The dozen men entering the cave were among the most skilled agents of the Conclave in Kesh, and perhaps the most experienced hand-to-hand fighters in the Empire. They expected to give their lives if necessary, for they were committed to the undertaking of ridding the world of Midkemia of the Nighthawks for well and good.

Another half-dozen men took up positions before the second cave mouth, with another pair of archers poised above on the cliffs as well. The orders were clear: to defend their own lives, but Jomo Ketlami must be taken alive.

Caleb motioned for his men to move towards the mouth of the smaller cave, ready to receive anyone fleeing. With hand gestures, barely seen in the faint lantern light, he instructed them to stand ready, taking up their positions on either side of the cave. He motioned to the man carrying the lantern, who shuttered it again, plunging the beach into blackness once more.

Minutes dragged by slowly, the only sound being the rolling of the surf and the occasional distant sound of a nightbird. Jommy nodded to Caleb, who waited on the other side of the cave mouth, then turned to see how his two younger companions were doing. In the dark he could make out Tad and Zane huddled against the cliff face behind him, ready. In the months he had lived with them, he had come to feel a kinship, and he found himself adopting the role of eldest brother more often than not. Their family had welcomed him and made him feel at home – even though home was far from ordinary; but he had come to accept the extraordinary as a matter of course since meeting Caleb and his adopted sons. He knew he would die defending them, and knew in turn each would be willing to lay down his life for him.

Abruptly a shout echoed from within and the sounds of combat followed instantly.

The first assassin to bolt the cave was met with the flat of Caleb's blade across his face. Blood fountained from a broken nose as Jommy clubbed him on the side of his head with the hilt of his sword. Zane grabbed the stunned assassin by the collar and hauled him out of the way by main force.

A second assassin saw his companion fall, even if he couldn't see exactly what occurred in the dark, and hesitated before leaping forward, sword at the ready. Caleb barely avoided a thrust to his side, his parry ringing like an alarm. Jommy stepped forward to club the man on the head. He felt something tug hard at his tunic and realized he had almost been skewered by another assassin's blade as he crossed before the threshold of the cave. There was a burning sensation across his lower back as the swordsman pulled back his blade.

Ignoring the pain, Jommy slammed his hilt into the back of the head of the man facing Caleb, and in turn felt another burning cut as the swordsman behind him attempted to disengage his sword from Jommy's tunic.

Caleb reached out with his left hand, grabbed Jommy by the shirt front and yanked hard, pulling him away from danger. Zane hit the man trying to kill Jommy as another man leapt past him, attempting to run down the beach.

'Stop him!' shouted Caleb.

A sizzling sound, like a nearby discharge of lightning, filled the night and a bolt of energy sprang from Magnus's hand. Blinding blue light illuminated the cave mouth and beach for an instant as a sphere of energy sped after the fleeing man, overtaking him in an instant. The man screamed and fell, his torso contorting in pain as tiny bolts of energy danced over his torso, a sizzling sound punctuated by crackling adding a sinister note to the display.

Caleb and Magnus hurried to the fallen man, while the boys and the other agents of the Conclave subdued the remaining assassins.

'Coming out!' shouted a familiar voice, and a moment later Chezarul came out of the cave. 'How did we do?' he asked.

Jommy motioned towards the fallen man as Caleb reached him, shouting, 'Light!'

A pair of lanterns, one above them and another a short way down the beach, were uncovered, and they could see the form of a man writhing on the sand as the energy display faded from sight. Magnus said, 'Bind him before I release the spell. He is unable to use any poison secreted upon him. Search him well.'

Caleb looked down on the man for whom he'd been searching for weeks. Jomo Ketlami lay in agony, his face contorted. His fists flailed uselessly in the air, his elbows hard against his sides. His back was bowed and his legs kicked feebly against the sand. He went through the man's clothing quickly and found two poison pills and an amulet, the iron Nighthawk emblem they had come to know so well. He pulled a cord out of his belt pouch, turned the quivering man over as easily as he would a felled deer and trussed him up in the same manner.

'Check his mouth,' suggested Magnus.

'Get me a light.'

A lantern was fetched and held above Ketlami's face. Gripping his captive's jaw with his right hand, Caleb forced his mouth open and motioned for the lantern to be moved closer. 'Ah, what is this?' he said.

He held out his left hand, and a pair of iron tongs were placed in them. Caleb deftly reached into Ketlami's mouth with them and yanked out a tooth. The captive's whimpering increased but otherwise he was unable to react to the extraction. 'Hollow tooth,' said Caleb. He stood up and told Magnus, 'You can let him go, I think.'

Magnus released the spell and the captive fell limp for a moment, panting like an exhausted dog.

As they approached Ketlami, Chezarul said to Caleb, 'Two of them are dead, one will not live through the night, but three are unconscious and bound.'

Caleb nodded. 'Check them for poison, as well.' He glanced at Jommy, 'You're injured.'

'I've had worse,' said the young man with a grin. 'Last time I crossed swords with Talwin Hawkins he cut me three times, and he wasn't even trying.'

Caleb looked at the spreading bloodstains on Jommy's tunic. 'Get them bound, boy, or Marie will have my ears.'

Jommy winked at Tad and Zane as they joined the others in standing over their quarry. 'Your mum does look after me, doesn't she?'

Tad made a wry face. 'I think she likes you best.'

Zane nodded. 'I swear that's true.'

Jommy's grin widened. 'That's because you've been causing her grief your entire lives. I've only been annoying her for a few months. She'll get tired of me quick enough.'

Magnus said, 'No doubt,' as he cast a sidelong glance at the tall, redheaded youth. Jommy had quickly become well liked at Sorcerer's Island and had easily fitted in with Caleb's adopted family. In a few difficult spots, he had revealed himself to be tough, loyal and willing to risk himself for others, yet he never seemed to lose his sense of humour.

Tad moved to look at Ketlami who now lay motionless, moaning and cursing softly. 'What now?'

Caleb said, 'We need to take this one to Father.' To Chezarul he said, 'Take the three captives back to the city and get what you can out of them. These should be the last of the Nighthawks in Durbin, but against the possibility there are stragglers still at large, wring every drop of truth from them you can. Then see they plague the world no longer.'

Chezarul nodded once, then began issuing orders to his men.

Magnus pulled out an orb and said, 'Boys, stand close.' He stood directly over Ketlami, while Caleb reached down and gripped a handful of the man's tunic with one hand, and the hem of Magnus's black robe with the other. Jommy put a hand on Magnus's shoulder, while Tad and Zane each stood close behind Caleb.

Magnus depressed a switch on the orb and suddenly they vanished, leaving Chezarul and his men on the empty beach to clean up the last vestige of the Nighthawks in Durbin, and perhaps Great Kesh, if they were lucky.

CHAPTER 2

ORACLE

The prisoner glared defiantly.

Jomo Ketlami hung by shackles from the stone wall. His clothing had been cut away, leaving him no dignity, but Pug had judged it necessary as his dark body was tattooed with arcane symbols, black, white, red, and yellow, and some of these were wards.

He was a powerfully built man. To the three boys at the back of the room, he looked strong enough to rip the iron rings out of the wall. His head was completely shaved and glistened with perspiration. He had a wrestler's neck and shoulders, and his bare torso rippled with muscle. His black eyes showed no hint of fear. He snarled as he confronted his captors.

Half a dozen guards had been stationed outside the door and Magnus stood watch inside against any magical incursion, either to rescue Ketlami or to silence him. Caleb and the boys stood against the opposite wall, out of the way. Two men entered the room.

It was Pug, followed by Nakor.

Magnus asked, 'Where's Bek?'

21

'Outside, if I need him,' said Nakor. 'He doesn't need to see this.'

Magnus's glance at his brother communicated a silent question: *but these boys do?* Caleb nodded once. Magnus studied his brother's face then returned a single nod. The boys had proven themselves so far, showing iron will when needed and a fearlessness that was the hallmark of youth, but which was being rapidly replaced by a more sober appreciation of the real dangers they faced, youthful bravado becoming genuine bravery before Magnus and Caleb's eyes. But combat was one thing, and torture another.

No one spoke for a moment longer, then Ketlami shouted at Pug, 'You may as well kill me now, magician! I'm oath bound to take the secrets of the Guild to Lims-Kragma's Hall!'

Pug said nothing, but turned towards the door as two more men entered the small chamber. The boys moved to the left side of the rear wall, giving the newcomers room to make their way to where the prisoner waited.

One of the two men wore a black leather hood and a faded tunic covered in old stains. Tad glanced at his two companions and knew instantly they all concluded the nature of those stains. The torturer took up a position before the prisoner, while the second man came to stand beside Pug.

He was a nondescript man of middle height, with no distinguishing features and brown hair, and he wore the shirt and trousers of a trader or farmer. His feet were clad in modest leather boots. He stared at the prisoner, who suddenly turned and locked eyes with him. Ketlami's eyes widened. After a moment, he closed his eyes and an expression of pain crossed his face. More perspiration beaded on his forehead and he let out an animal growl, half pain, half aggravation. 'Get out of my head!' he shouted, then with an expression of triumph, he laughed and said to the newcomer, 'You'll have to do better than that!'

Pug glanced at the other man with an unspoken question. The other man looked at Pug, nodded once, then looked once more at Ketlami.

Pug said, 'Begin,' and the torturer took a quick step forward and drove his fist straight into Ketlami's stomach. He stepped back while the prisoner gasped, his eyes watering. After a moment, Ketlami sucked in a deep breath and said, 'A beating? What next? Hot irons and pincers?'

The torturer struck Ketlami in the stomach again, but this time it was two quick blows, and suddenly the contents of the victim's stomach emptied onto the floor.

Jommy's expression was grim as he looked at his companions. All three boys had been trained in hand-to-hand combat and an early lesson had been about double strikes to the stomach. A strong man could take a single blow and not miss a stride, but two quick strikes, the second coming before his stomach muscles could recover fully from the first, and he was doubled over, losing his last meal.

Magnus, Caleb, Pug and Nakor stood implacably, watching as Ketlami spat. The first indignity was but a start in slowly breaking the man down and learning what they needed to know, the location of the Grand Master of the Nighthawks.

Everyone remained silent as the torturer struck Ketlami across the face with the back of his hand. It was an insulting blow as much as a damaging one, and did nothing more than bring tears to the prisoner's eyes again and make him even more defiant. Caleb turned and whispered to the boys, 'It will be some time before he truly begins to feel hopelessness. He is a strong man: moreover, he's a fanatic.'

The three boys stood quietly, their grim expressions reflecting the proceedings they observed. The torturer was methodical and appeared to be in no hurry. He would strike the prisoner repeatedly, then pause, as if letting Ketlami catch his breath. He struck him in the face, the torso, the legs.

After nearly half an hour of this slow beating, Jomo Ketlami hung from his chains, unable to stand. He appeared to be on the verge of unconsciousness.

'Revive him,' said Pug.

The torturer nodded and moved to the far corner of the room where a table stood, upon which rested a variety of bags and instruments of his trade. He opened one of the bags and removed an item, a small vial. Stepping up to the limp form of Ketlami, he unstoppered the vial, holding it under the man's face. Ketlami's head jerked back and everyone heard his sharp intake of breath, followed by a faint groan.

'Where hides your master?' Pug demanded.

Ketlami raised his face to face Pug. Both his eyes were swollen nearly shut and his lip was split. He could barely speak for the swelling of his mouth, but he still retained a look of defiance. 'You'll never break me, magician. Kill me and get it over with.'

Pug glanced at the man standing next to him who shook his head slightly. 'Continue,' Pug said.

The torturer returned the vial to his bag and then came to stand before the prisoner. Ketlami glared at him. The man suddenly brought his knee up, brutally striking the Nighthawk in the groin. Ketlami collapsed completely, and hung for a moment from his chains, gasping for air.

And the beating continued.

Well into the second hour, Tad appeared to be on the verge of collapsing himself. With each repeated blow he would wince visibly. Caleb observed his adopted son's behaviour, then motioned him to leave the room with him. With a wave of his hand, he instructed Jommy and Zane to stay.

Outside the door, in a long corridor with guards on either hand, Ralan Bek was hunkered down with his back against the wall. The strange and dangerous youth had been given over to

Nakor's supervision and seemed content with the situation.

'Are you all right?' Caleb asked Tad.

Tad took a long breath and let it out slowly. 'Not really,' he replied. 'I've seen a few fights, as you know, but this . . .'

'It's different,' finished his step-father.

Tad took a deep breath. 'I know what he is, but . . .'

Caleb looked Tad in the eyes. 'It's brutal. It's evil, and it's necessary. You know what he is: he would kill you without a thought; kill me, your mother, anyone, and then sleep the night like a baby after doing so. He is not worthy of your conscience.'

'I know, it's just that I feel as if . . .'

Caleb, in an uncharacteristic act, suddenly put his arms around Tad and hugged him close. 'I know; believe me, I know.' He released his step-son. 'Something is lost by this, and it is something I doubt any of us can earn back.

'But those who oppose us mean naught but ill for those we love and they must be stopped. Now, this is going to take a while longer. If we didn't have the resources we do, it might take days. But this man will give up what we wish to know in another hour or two. If you wish, you may remain out here.'

Tad thought it over for a moment, then shook his head. 'No. Some day I may have to do this myself.'

Caleb nodded, knowing that both Jommy and

Zane would have missed this aspect of the lesson. 'Yes, more's the pity.'

They returned to the room and found the torturer reviving Ketlami again. Caleb and Tad resumed their place alongside the others, and Zane whispered, 'Surely he can't last much longer?'

Caleb whispered in return, 'You will discover that men are a great deal more resilient than you think if they believe strongly in their cause. This man is a depraved animal, but he thinks he serves a higher cause, and that makes him very difficult to break. Talk to Talwin Hawkins—' as he remembered his own father's stories of his years in a Tsurani labour camp, '—or your grandfather about what men can endure. You'll be surprised, I wager.'

For almost another hour the punishment was meted out, then suddenly the torturer halted. He glanced at Pug, without a word, and the magician nodded. Pug then turned to the man next to him who made a noncommittal gesture.

Pug said, 'Give him water,' and the torturer complied, giving the prisoner a long drink from a copper cup. The drink seemed to restore Ketlami a little and he spat in the torturer's face. The implacable man in the black hood merely wiped away the spittle and looked at Pug for instructions.

Pug asked again, 'Where is your Grand Master?'

'I'll never tell you,' said Ketlami.

The man next to Pug reached over and gripped his forearm. 'I have it,' he said in a low voice.

'You're certain?' asked Nakor.

'I am certain,' replied the man.

Pug took a deep breath, then looked at Ketlami, whose distorted features couldn't hide the malevolence of his expression. Pug said quietly, 'Finish.'

With a quick, unhesitating motion, the torturer drew a sharp blade from his belt and made a single downward cut, sliced through an artery which fountained blood into the air. Ketlami's eyes widened in shock for a brief instant. 'What—'

Then his mouth filled with blood and his head fell forward.

Nakor turned to the three boys. 'Sever the blood-flow to the head and he loses consciousness before he even understands he's been cut. It looks like butchery, but it's kinder than any other cut I know of.'

Jommy whispered, 'Kind or not, dead is dead.'

Pug motioned for everyone to depart as the torturer began to take Ketlami's body down.

Seeing everyone leaving the room, Bek stood up and said to Nakor, 'Can we go now? I'm bored.'

Nakor nodded. 'We will have some bloody work to do soon enough.' He turned to Pug. 'We will meet you upstairs,' he said, leading Bek away.

The room where the torture had taken place was in the cellar of one of Chezarul's warehouses on the edge of the City of Kesh. The now dead Nighthawk had been transported there by Magnus against the threat of any agents lingering in Durbin. They were nearly certain the Conclave had destroyed the Nighthawks in Great Kesh, but nearly certain wasn't absolutely certain.

Pug turned to the man who had stood next to him and said, 'Where?'

'Cavell Keep.'

Pug's expression turned thoughtful, as if he was trying to recall something. 'I remember,' he said, finally. 'Thank you,' he told the man, and motioned for him, and the guards, to depart. After a moment only Magnus, Caleb and the boys remained in the hallway.

'Who was that man, Father?' asked Caleb.

'Joval Delan. Though he is not one of our community, he is someone who owes the Conclave a favour or two. He's the best human mind-reader I've ever encountered, but rather than use his ability for a cause, he hides it except when he exploits it for profit.' He glanced at the back of the retreating man. 'A shame. He could teach us much. He knew Ketlami would have strong wards to prevent his mind being read, but that eventually he couldn't stop himself from thinking about what he wished to hide.' Glancing at the three boys, he added, 'That was the reason for the beating. Remember the child's game where you say, "Don't think of the dragon in the corner?"

'You can force yourself not to think of something for a great deal of time if you have the training, and the physical and mental resources, but if you're beaten down enough, what you are trying to hide does eventually come to the surface of the mind.' To his son he said, 'Which is why we now know the Grand Master of the Nighthawks hides at Cavell Keep.'

'Cavell Keep?' asked Caleb. 'I know Cavell Town, north of Lyton, but a keep?'

'Abandoned,' said Pug. 'High in the hills above the highway. From the distance it blends into the rocks; you'll only notice it from the road or river if you're looking for it. It's up a draw from the town. You have to want to find it.

'The last Baron Corvallis refused to live in it . . . it's a long story. I'll tell you about it some other time, but what I know is that the ancient keep used to guard a fair portion of the trade route between Lyton and Sloop. Baron Corvallis's daughter married a man from Lyton, a commoner I believe, and the King let that title fall vacant. The Earl of Sloop was given that area to rule, despite it being closer to Lyton.

'In any event, the old keep was linked to Nighthawk activity nearly a century ago, and it was one of my students, Owyn Belfote, and Prince Arutha's man James who ended that particular threat to the region.'

Pug tapped his chin with his forefinger and considered for a moment. 'They must have decided enough time has passed for them to utilize the place again, and it's a smart choice: no one goes there, even the villagers, because of superstition, and it's an inconvenient place to visit by any measure. As long as people think it's deserted, why bother?'

Caleb said, 'Shall we go to Lyton?'

'No,' said Pug. 'I'm going to give this to Nakor. He's close to Duke Eric and the Kingdom should handle this final confrontation.' He looked at Magnus. 'I'm sending you along with Nakor, though, just to make sure Eric has enough protection against any magic the Nighthawks might still muster, and you know I'm only moments away if you have need of me. I'll ask your mother to visit the Assembly and see what progress is being made with the Talnoy.'

Magnus nodded, smiling wryly. 'We know how much the Great Ones of the Empire enjoy that.'

Pug smiled, the first time he hadn't looked grim in days. There was some amusement in his tone as he said, 'They still have trouble with women magicians in general, but your mother . . . I'll tell her to mind her manners.'

Magnus's smile broadened. 'And Mother began doing what you tell her to . . . when?' Pug's wince showed that his son's barb had hit home. 'Shall I tell Nakor to make ready?'

'Nakor is always ready to travel; it's a legacy of his gambling days. Meet me upstairs in a few minutes. I want a word with Caleb and the lads.'

Magnus departed and Pug turned to the boys. 'That was bloody work,' he said.

Jommy glanced at Tad and Zane. 'It was, but he deserved it.'

Pug put his hand on Jommy's shoulder. While not properly an adopted grandson like Tad and

31

Zane, Pug had grown fond of the brash red-head and treated him as he did the others. 'No man deserves such treatment, Jommy.' He glanced at Zane then Tad then returned his gaze to Jommy. 'Some men deserve death for what they've done, but causing suffering, that harms you rather than the man you make suffer.' He looked from face to face. 'What makes us better than those we oppose is that we know when we are doing evil. And it should sicken us. Even if we justify it by saying we serve a larger good, or that it's necessary.' Glancing at the door where the torturer was getting Ketlami's body ready for disposal, he added, 'It's the price we pay and while it's necessary, it does diminish us.' He looked at each boy in turn. 'Your only solace is knowing that if you were not part of this, those you love would be at that much more risk.'

He turned to Caleb. 'I'm thinking you and Marie have not had much time alone since you've been wed.'

Caleb smiled ruefully. 'A fact she has reminded me of from time to time, although she hardly complains, Father.'

'Things are under control for a while. I've got Kaspar down in Novindus with Rosenvar and Jacob, and Nakor and Magnus are going to the Kingdom to deal with the Nighthawks. Right now, we don't need you.'

Caleb fixed his father with a questioning expression and said, 'And . . .?'

'Why don't you return home and have your mother give you the orb we use when we travel to our own little retreat? It's not much – an island in the Sunsets – but there's a small hut, well provisioned, and you can be alone for a few days.'

'Sounds lovely. What about these three?'

Pug smiled. 'Send them along to Talwin. They can guest at the River House, earn their keep for a week or two, and improve their swordsmanship.'

Zane grinned. 'The River House!'

Jommy patted his friend hard on the stomach. 'I thought you were going to lose that?' The River House was the finest restaurant and inn in Opardum, and arguably the finest dining establishment in the world. Zane had developed an appetite for fine food since his mother had married Caleb and he had had the opportunity to sample better fare than he had known as a child.

'I'll work extra hard, trust me,' answered the stocky young man.

'Well, I'm sure Talwin and his wife will find ample work for you.'

'What of you, Father?' asked Caleb.

'I have a journey I must make, a short one, but one long overdue. Tell your mother I'll be home in another day or so, but not to wait for me; she should go to Kelewan and see what the Assembly is doing with the Talnoy.'

They embraced, and Pug waved goodbye to the four of them, and vanished.

Jommy shook his head and sucked in his breath. 'Crikey, I'll never get used to seeing people just vanish like that!'

Caleb laughed. 'You'll get used to a lot of things before you're done, my lad.' He pulled an orb out of his tunic and said, 'We're off home: then you three are going to Olasko!'

Glancing at the door into the torture room, Tad said, 'I'm glad we're done with this part of it, that's for certain.'

Without another word, each put a hand on the next man's shoulder, while Caleb activated the orb, and they vanished as well.

A vast presence was veiled in darkness, its form barely recognizable in the faint light emanating from a single lantern set within a sconce on the opposite wall.

A voice spoke without sound: *Welcome, Pug of Crydee.*

Pug smiled as he said aloud. 'I haven't been called that in years, m'lady.' He knew the presence required no honorific, and that the one he chose was barely appropriate, yet he felt the need to convey respect.

'As you wish, magician,' said the deep voice. 'Do you wish more light?'

'That would be agreeable,' Pug replied.

Suddenly the room was ablaze in light, as if the sun shone through glass walls. Pug glanced around, for he had not visited this chamber in years. It was a cavern, deep beneath the city of Sethanon, where Tomas had bested a conjuration of the Dragon Lord Drakin-Korin, and Pug and others had battled to seal a rift that threatened to destroy all of the Kingdom, if not the world of Midkemia.

The being before him was the body of the great dragon, Ryath, but the mind housed in it was that of an ancient being: the Oracle of Aal. In that epic struggle, the dragon had given everything in defeating a Lord of the Dread, and it had taken magic of unmatched power and skill to keep a spark of life in the body after the mind and spirit had fled, so that the Oracle could find a living host. The dragon's natural scales had been obliterated and a makeshift solution had turned the creature into a being of unsurpassed magnificence. The great Dragon Lords' treasure secreted below the city ages before had provided gems used to repair the damaged scales, forming a creature unmatched in majesty and power in this world, a great jewelled dragon. Light danced off the facets of thousands of stones and the creature seemed to glitter as if moving, even when she rested, motionlessly.

'The cycle of renewal has ended well?' asked Pug.

'Yes,' answered the Oracle. 'The cycle of years has passed and again I possess all my knowledge.' She sent out a mental call, and a dozen white-robed men entered the room. 'These are my companions.'

Pug nodded. These men had come to understand the nature of the great dragon of Sethanon,
and had volunteered to give up their freedom in
exchange for a lifespan many times normal, and
the honour of serving a greater good.

For the Oracle was more than a simple seer. She
possessed the ability to see many possible
outcomes that might result from a given choice,
as well as alert those she trusted to the approach
of grave danger. And she trusted no one in this
world as much as she did Pug. Without his inter-
vention, the last of the race of Aal – perhaps the
eldest race in the universe – would have perished
a century before. Pug inclined his head in greeting
to the Oracle's companions and they returned the
honour.

'Do you know why I'm here?' asked Pug.

'A grave threat approaches, faster than you think,
but . . .'

'What?' asked Pug.

'It is not what you think it to be.'

'The Dasati?'

'They are involved, and are the primary cause
at this point, but there is a much larger danger
behind them.'

'The Nameless?'

'More.'

Pug was stunned. From his perspective, there
could be nothing 'more' in the universe than the
Greater Gods. He gathered his wits. 'How can
there be a greater threat than the Nameless?'

'I can only tell you this, Pug of Crydee: across the expanse of time and space the battle between good and evil transcends all else.

'What you perceive is but the smallest part of this struggle. It is ageless, begun before the first of the Aal rose from the mud of our homeworld, and it will endure until the last star is extinguished. It is part of the very fabric of reality, and all creatures struggle within that conflict, even if they are unaware of it.

'Some beings live their entire lives in peace and security, while others struggle without let. Some worlds are virtual paradises while others are ceaseless wretchedness. Each in its own fashion is part of a much larger balance, and as such, each a vital battle ground in this struggle. Many worlds are in balance.' The Oracle paused for a moment, then said, 'Some worlds are teetering on the brink.'

'Midkemia?'

The great dragon head nodded. 'Your lifetime is long compared to other mortals, but in this struggle, what will come to this world occurs within the blink of a god's eye.

'Midkemia has been too long without the influence of the Goddess of Good. What you and your Conclave have begun has blunted the Nameless One's efforts for a century and more.

'But he lies sleeping, and his minions are but dreams and memories, powerful by your measure, but nothing compared to what would be faced should he awaken.'

'Is he waking?'

'No, but his dreams are more fevered, and his cause is embraced by another, a being even more powerful and deadly.'

Pug was stunned. He could not imagine any being more powerful and deadly than the God of Evil. 'What sort of being could possibly . . .' He could not finish the question.

'The Dark God of the Dasati,' said the Oracle.

Pug materialized in his study. He took one quick glance around the room to see if he was alone, for his wife often curled up in the corner to read in peace when he was absent. He was shaken by what the Oracle had told him. He had thought himself a man of experience, one who had faced calamitous events and survived, one who had seen countless horrors and endured, one who had confronted Death in her very hall and returned to the realm of life. But this was beyond any ability he had to comprehend, and he felt overwhelmed. More than anything at this moment he wished to go somewhere quiet and sleep for a week. Yet he knew such feelings were only the result of the shock he experienced, and would soon pass once he began grappling with the problems at hand. Ah, but there was the rub, as the old expression ran: where to begin? With a problem as immense as the one now confronting the Conclave, he felt like a baby asked to move a vast mountain with his tiny hands.

He went to a cabinet in the corner and opened it. Inside were several bottles, one containing a strong drink Caleb had brought to him the year before. Kennoch whisky: Pug had developed a fondness for it. He also had a set of crystal cups given to him by the Emperor of Kesh recently, and he poured a small dram of the drink.

Sipping the pungent, yet flavourful and satisfying drink, he felt its warmth spread through his mouth and down his throat. He closed the cabinet and moved across to a large wooden box sitting upon a bookcase. It was simple in design, yet beautifully carved, acacia wood, dove-tail and glue, without a single nail of brass or iron. He set aside his drink and lifted the top, putting it aside, and looked into the box, wherein rested a single piece of parchment.

He sighed: he had expected to find it there.

The box had appeared one morning, years before, on his desk in his study in Stardock. It had been warded, but what had surprised him wasn't that it had been warded, but that it had been warded in a fashion he quickly recognized. It was as if he, himself, had warded the box. Expecting a trap, he had transported himself and the box a great distance away from the Island of Stardock and had erected protective spells around himself; then he had opened the box, easily. Three notes had been contained within.

The first had said, 'That was a lot of work for nothing, wasn't it?'

The second had said, 'When James departs, instruct him to say this to a man he should meet: "there is no magic".'

The last had said, 'Above all else, never lose this box.'

The handwriting had been his own.

For years Pug had kept the secret of this box, a device that allowed him to send notes to himself from the future. Occasionally he pondered the device, studying it at leisure, for he knew eventually he must unravel its secret. There could be no other explanation than that he was sending himself messages.

Eight times in the intervening years he had opened the box to discover a new message inside. He didn't know how he knew, but when a message arrived he sensed it was time to open the box once more.

One message had said, 'Trust Miranda.' It had arrived before he had met his wife, and when he first encountered her, he realized why he had sent the message. She was dangerous, powerful and wilful, and at the time, an unknown.

Yet even now he still didn't completely trust her. He trusted her love for him and their sons; and her commitment to their cause, as well. But she often had her own agenda, ignoring his leadership and taking matters into her own hands. For years she had agents working for her in addition to those working for the Conclave. She and Pug had endured several heated arguments over the years, and several times she had agreed to keep her efforts confined within the agreed upon goals and stratagems of the Conclave, yet she always managed to do as she pleased.

He hesitated. Whatever was in that parchment was something he needed to know, yet something he dreaded knowing. Nakor had been the first person he had told of the messages – just in the last year – though the box was still known only to Pug. Miranda thought it merely a decorative item.

As he began to unroll the parchment Pug wondered, and not for the first time, if these messages were to ensure that a certain thing happened, or to keep something terrible from happening. Perhaps there was no distinction between the two.

He looked at the parchment. Two lines of script in his own handwriting greeted him. The first said, 'Take Nakor, Magnus, and Bek, no others'. The second said, 'Go to Kosridi, then Omadrabar'.

Pug closed the box and sat down behind his desk. He read the note several times, as if somehow he might discern a deeper meaning behind those two simple lines. Then he leaned back, sipping at his drink. Kosridi he recognized as the name of the world shown in a vision to Kaspar of Olasko by the god, Ban-ath; it was one of the worlds upon which resided the Dasati. Where lay Omadrabar, he had not even an inkling. But he knew one thing: somehow he had to find a way into the second realm of existence – to the plane of reality to which no one from this reality, to the best of his knowledge, had ever ventured. From there, somehow, he and his companions must make their way to the Dasati world of Kosridi, and from there to this Omadrabar. And if he was certain of nothing else, he was certain that this Omadrabar would be the most dangerous place he had ever visited.

CHAPTER 3

AFTERMATH

Kaspar reined in his horse.

He fought back worry. This was a hard land and he felt a stab of apprehension as to what might be waiting for him. He had considered the little farm something close to a home for months after beginning his exile in this land, and Jojanna and her son Jorgen had been as close to family as any people he had known.

It had taken no more than a glance for him to know the farm had not been inhabited for some time, at least a year from the look of things. The pasture was overgrown and the fence was knocked down in several places. Before Jojanna's husband, Bandamin, had disappeared they had raised a few steers for the local innkeeper. The corn patch and small wheat field were both choked with weeds and the crops had gone to seed.

Kaspar dismounted and tied off his horse to a dead sapling. The tree had been planted after he had left, but had since died from neglect. He glanced around out of habit: whenever he considered the possibility of trouble, he always made a survey of the surroundings, noting possible places of ambush and escape. He realized there probably wasn't another living human being within a day's walk in any direction.

Entering the hut, he was relieved to see no sign of struggle or violence. All of Jojanna's and Jorgen's personal belongings, scant though they may have been, were gone. The departure had been orderly. He had feared bandits or wandering nomads might have done harm to his . . . what? Friends?

Kaspar's life had been one of privilege and power, and many people had sought him out, currying favours, begging protection, or seeking some advantage, but until he had been deposited in this distant land by Magnus, the former Duke of Olasko had few he could name 'friend,' even as a child.

He had terrorized Jojanna and Jorgen for two days before he could make them understand he had not come to this little farm to harm them; he was merely a stranger in need of food and shelter and he worked hard to pay for his keep. He had negotiated a more favourable trade with a local merchant on their behalf and had left them in a better situation than he had found them. When he departed to begin his long journey home, he thought of them as friends; possibly even more than friends . . .

Now, three years later, Kaspar was back in Novindus. He had been watching the secret cache of Talnoy, providing a sword against more mundane threats to the ten thousand apparently sleeping killing machines, if indeed a machine slept. Two magicians – an older man named Rosenvar and a youth named Jacob – were investigating some aspect or another of their nature, following instructions left by Pug and Nakor.

Nakor had briefly returned with his companion, Bek, to inform the magicians he would be absent longer from his pet undertaking, finding a safe means of controlling the army of Talnoy. Kaspar found the magical aspect of these discussions mind-numbing, but he had greeted the news of the imminent obliteration of the Nighthawks with anticipation.

When Nakor made ready to depart, Kaspar asked him to request someone come to guard the two scholars as he had some personal business he wished to take care of in Novindus before returning to Sorcerer's Isle. Nakor had agreed and as soon as another had been dispatched to guard the magicians, Kaspar had begun his journey southward.

Lacking the magical devices employed by other members of the Conclave, Kaspar had to endure two weeks' travel. The closest town to the caves where the Talnoy were hidden was Malabra, and from there the road south became more well travelled. He rode his horses to near exhaustion, trading mounts twice in the towns along the way. Twice more he had outrun bandits and three times he had endured the scrutiny of local soldiers, two of the encounters ending in bribery.

Now he felt a sense of futility. He had hoped to find Jojanna and Jorgen, though he was unsure of what he wished once he found them. He had been exiled to Novindus as punishment for his part in the destruction of the Orosini people and his plots against his neighbouring nations. He had somewhat redeemed himself in the eyes of his former enemies by bringing word of the Talnoy to the Conclave, and had been fully forgiven after his role in foiling the Nighthawks' plot against the throne of the Empire of Great Kesh. But he had a lingering sense of obligation toward Jojanna and Jorgen, and to Kaspar an unpaid debt was a canker that became more inflamed as time passed. He wanted to see that the pair of them were safe, and leave them with enough wealth to ensure they'd live well for the rest of their lives.

The small purse of coins he carried made him a wealthy man in this land. He had travelled the roads of the Eastlands before, on foot and by wagon, and had seen the conditions lingering after the great war of the Emerald Queen, a land still struggling to recover even thirty years after the war. Coins of copper were rare, silver almost never seen, and even a single gold coin was worth a man's life. Kaspar had enough gold on him to hire a tiny army and set himself up as a local noble.

He left the hut and considered what to do next. He had ridden straight through the village of Heslagnam as he made his way to the farm, and it was on his way back to the Talnoy cave. He would reach it after sundown – it had taken them two days and half a morning to walk there the last first time he had journeyed there from the farm – and while the inn was nothing worth noting, it was serviceable, and he had slept in far worse over the last three years.

He pushed his horse and arrived at the village of Heslagnam shortly after darkness had fallen. The ramshackle wooden inn was as he remembered it, though it looked as if it might have had a new coat of whitewash; in the dark it was difficult to tell.

When no one appeared as he rode into the stabling yard, he un-tacked his horse and rubbed it down. By the time he was finished, he was tired, irritated and in sore need of what passed for a drink in this part of the world.

Kaspar walked around to the front door of the inn, and pushed it open. The inn was unoccupied save for two villagers who sat at a table opposite the fireplace and the owner of the inn, a thick-necked man by the name of Sagrin, who stood behind the bar. Kaspar walked up to the bull-necked man who regarded him closely.

Sagrin said, 'I don't forget faces, even if I can't recall a name, and I've seen you before.'

'Kaspar,' answered the former duke, removing his gloves. 'I've got a horse out the back. Where's your lackey?'

'Don't have one,' answered Sagrin. 'No boys in town. All dragged off to serve in the war.'

'What war?'

'Who knows? There's always a war, isn't there?' He hiked his thumb over his shoulder, in the general direction of the stabling yard. 'You can shelter your horse for free, seeing as I've got no one to care for it, but you'll have to buy your own feed at Kelpita's store across the way in the morning.'

'I've oats in my pack. I'll care for the horse before I turn in. What have you to drink?'

'Ale and some wine. If you know wine, take the ale,' said the innkeeper.

'Ale, then.'

The ale was produced and Sagrin squinted a bit as he eyed Kaspar. 'You were here, what? Two years back?'

'Closer to three.'

'Can't quite place it . . .'

'If you sit on the floor and look up at me, you might remember,' said Kaspar. He took a drink. The ale was as he remembered it, thin and without much to recommend it, but it was cool and wet.

'Ah,' said Sagrin. 'You're the bloke who came in with Jojanna and her kid. Dressed a fair bit better these days.'

'Right,' said Kaspar. 'Are they around?'

Sagrin shrugged. 'Haven't seen Jojanna for over a year.' He leaned forward. 'The boy run off and she was nearly frantic and went looking for him, I guess. Sold off her cattle and mule to Kelpita, then found a trader heading south – said he'd take her on for a fee.' Sagrin shrugged, but his tone was regretful. 'She's probably buried under some rocks a day or two south of here.'

'Jorgen ran off?' asked Kaspar. He knew Jojanna and her son well enough to know that the boy was devoted to his mother, and he couldn't imagine any reason why Jorgen would run away from home.

'Some crew came through and word got back to the farm that the boy's dad was serving with a company of soldiers out of Higara – seems Bandamin got himself impressed by a company of . . . well, they'd be slavers no matter what they called themselves, but as they were selling those who were captured into the army of Muboya, they called themselves "recruiters".'

Kaspar remembered a relatively pleasant supper with a general of a brigade who was cousin to the Raj of Muboya. If Kaspar could find him he could . . . what? Arrange to have him discharged?

'How goes that war?' asked Kaspar.

'Last I heard Muboya had forced Sasbataba to surrender, and was now battling some bandit lord named Okanala for control of the next bit of land he wants.

'I'll give the boy Raj credit though: after his army leaves, the lands left behind are almost as quiet as they were before the Emerald Queen's war. Wish he'd send some of his lads up this way to calm things down between here and the Hotlands.' Seeing Kaspar's mug was empty, Sagrin said, 'Another?'

Kaspar pushed himself away from the bar. 'In a

while. First let me feed my horse and make sure there's adequate water.'

'Staying?'

Kaspar nodded. 'I'll want a room.'

'Pick any one you like,' said Sagrin. 'I've got lamb on the spit and the bread was baked yesterday.'

'That'll be fine,' said Kaspar. He left the common room.

Outside the night air was cool; it was winter in this land, but he was far enough north and close enough to the Hotlands that it never got truly cold. He went to the stable and got a bucket, filled it at the well, and made sure the trough was full. He put a nose-bag on his horse and took some time to inspect the animal. He had ridden it hard and he wanted to make sure the gelding was sound. He saw an old currying brush sitting on the shelf next to some worthless old tack, and he picked it up and started brushing the horse's coat.

As he curried, Kaspar became lost in thought. Part of him had wanted to return here, to build a new personal empire; but these days the stirrings of ambitions were muted in his heart. But they were never gone entirely. Whatever effect the influences of the mad sorcerer Leso Varen had been on Kaspar, the former ruler of Olasko's basic nature was still ambitious.

The men who were bringing order out of chaos on this continent were men of vision as well as desire. Power for its own sake was the height of greed; power for the benefit of others had a nobler quality he had only just begun to appreciate as he observed men like Pug, Magnus and Nakor, men who could do amazing things, yet only sought to make the world a safer place for everyone.

He shook his head at the thought, realizing that he had no legal or ethical foundation for building an empire here; he would just be another self-aggrandizing bandit lord carving out his own kingdom.

He sighed as he put away the currying brush. Better to find General Alenburga and enlist in the Raj's service. Kaspar had no doubt he would quickly win promotion and have his own army to command. But could he ever take service in another man's army?

He stopped, and started to laugh. What was he doing now? He was serving the Conclave, despite the fact he had never taken a formal oath of service with any of them. Since bringing Pug and his companions word of the Talnoy and the threat Kalkin had shown him of the Dasati homeworld, Kaspar had been running errands and carrying out missions for the Conclave.

Still chuckling as he reached the door to the inn, Kaspar decided that he was serving this land, as well as the rest of the world, and his days as a ruling lord were over. As he pushed open the door he thought: at least life was interesting.

Ten days later, Kaspar walked his horse through the crowded streets of Higara. The town had changed in the last three years; everywhere he saw the signs of prosperity. New construction was turning this town into a small city. When he had last passed though Higara, it had been a staging area for the Raj of Muboya's army as they readied an offensive southward. Now the only men in uniform to be seen were the town's constables. Kaspar noted they wore colours that resembled the regular army's, a clear indication that Higara was now firmly part of Muboya, no matter its previous allegiances.

Kaspar found the very inn where he had spoken to General Alenburga three years previously, and saw it had been restored to its former tranquillity. Instead of soldiers everywhere, a boy ran out of the stable to take charge of Kaspar's horse. The boy was roughly the same age as Jorgen had been when Kaspar had last seen him, reminding him of why he was making this trek. Putting aside a growing sense of futility in finding one boy and his mother in this vast land, Kaspar handed the boy a copper coin. 'Wash the road dirt off and curry him,' he instructed. The boy grinned as he pocketed the coin and said he would.

Kaspar entered the inn and glanced around. It was crowded with merchants taking their mid-day meal and others dressed for travel. Kaspar made his way to the bar and the barkeep nodded. 'Sir?'

'Ale,' said Kaspar.

When the mug sat before him, Kaspar produced another copper coin and the barman picked it up.

He hefted it, quickly produced a touchstone, struck the colour of the coin, then said, 'This will do for two.'

'Have one for yourself,' said the former duke.

The barman smiled. 'Little early for me. Maybe later. Thanks.'

Kaspar nodded. 'Where's the local garrison these days?'

'Don't have one,' said the barman. He pointed in the general direction of the south road. 'There's a garrison down in Dondia, a good day's ride. They pulled all the soldiers out of here when Sasbataba surrendered. We get a regular patrol up here once a week, and there's a company of town militia to help the constables if needed, but frankly, stranger, things around here are quiet to the point of being downright peaceful.'

'Must be a welcome change,' said Kaspar.

'Can't argue about that,' said the barman.

'Got a room?'

The barman nodded and produced a key. 'Top of the stairs, last door on the left. Got a window.'

Kaspar took the key. 'Where's the local constable's office?'

The barman gave Kaspar directions and after finishing his ale and an indifferent lunch of cold beef and barely warm vegetables, Kaspar headed to the constable's office. Walking the short distance, he was assailed by the sounds and sights of a bustling trading centre. Whatever the previous status of Higara, it was now clearly a regional hub for the expanding territory. For a brief moment Kaspar felt a twinge of regret; Flynn and the other traders from the Kingdom would have found the riches they sought in such a place as this. The four traders from the Kingdom of the Isles had been responsible for Kaspar coming into possession of the Talnoy, each of them dying ignorant of the part he had played.

Thinking of that infernal device, Kaspar wondered if he should set himself a limit on how long he'd look for Jojanna and Jorgen.

He found the constable's office easily, and pushed open the door.

A young man wearing a tunic with a badge looked up from a table that served as a desk. With the air of self-importance that only a boy recently given responsibility could manage, he said, 'What can I do for you?'

'I'm looking for someone. A soldier named Bandamin.'

The lad, good-looking with light brown hair and a scattering of freckles, tried to look as if he was thinking. After a moment, he said, 'I don't know that name. Which company is he with?'

Kaspar doubted the boy would have any idea where Bandamin was even if Kaspar knew that. 'Don't know. He was living outside a village up north and got pressed into service.'

'Pressed man, huh?' said the youngster. 'Most likely he's with the infantry south of here.'

'What about a boy? About eleven years of age.' Kaspar tried to judge how much Jorgen would have grown since he had last seen him, and held up his hand. 'Probably about this high. Blond hair.'

The young constable shrugged. 'There are lots of boys coming through the city all the time, caravan cooks' monkeys, luggage rats, homeless boys, runaways. We try to keep them off the streets as much as we can – some of them run in gangs.'

'Where would I find such a gang?'

The young man fixed Kaspar with what the former duke assumed was a suspicious expression, but all it did was make the lad look ridiculous. 'Why do you seek this boy?'

'His father was pressed into the army; the lad came looking for him. And his mother is looking for both of them.'

'And you're looking for the mother, too?'

'All of them,' said Kaspar. 'They're friends.'

The youth shrugged. 'Sorry, but we only notice those that are causing trouble.'

'What about the gang of boys?'

'You'll usually find them down near the caravanserai or in the market. If too many of them gather, we chase them away, but they just gather somewhere else.'

Kaspar thanked the young constable and left the office. He looked up and down the busy street, as if seeking inspiration, feeling like a man crawling across a battle field seeking one specific arrow among the tens of thousands that had fallen. He glanced skyward and fixed the hour at approximately half-way between noon and sundown. He knew that the markets here were busy throughout the day, with no cease in the afternoon for rest as it was in the hotter parts of Great Kesh. Here the markets were thronged with buyers and hawkers until shortly before sundown, then there was a frantic bustle of activity as the merchants finished for the day. He had approximately two and a half hours before sundown.

He reached the market and glanced around. The market was haphazardly organized across a sprawling plaza created more by happenstance than design. Kaspar assumed that originally there had been one major road through town – the north-to-south highway that dominated this region. Somewhere in years past circumstances had shifted the route a hundred yards or so to the east, and at that point buildings had been thrown up all around. As a result, a half-dozen lesser streets and a handful of alleyways led off from this area; the empty space in the middle served as the market.

Kaspar saw a fair number of children, most helping their families in booths or tents. There was little order to the market in Higara, save by common agreement it appeared no one was permitted to erect a tent, booth, or table in the centre of the square. There a single lamppost reared up, equidistant from the intersections of side streets forming the square. Kaspar wandered over to it and saw that it had a usable lantern hanging from the top, so he assumed it was lit by some townsman each night, perhaps one of the constables. This was the only lamppost he had seen in Higara, so he assumed the office of lamplighter was hardly likely. He noticed faint writing carved into the post: somewhere back in antiquity a ruler had decided a direction marker had been necessary at this point. Kaspar ran his hand over the ancient wood, wondering what secrets of ages past it had overheard whispered below its single lantern.

Leaning against the post, he surveyed his surroundings. Like the practised hunter he was, he noticed little things that would have escaped the attention of most others. Two boys hung around by the entrance to an alley, apparently discussing something, but clearly watching. Lookouts, Kaspar decided. But lookouts for what?

After nearly half an hour of watching, Kaspar had some sense of it. Every so often one boy, or more often a pair, would exit from or enter the alley. If anyone else approached too closely, a signal was made – Kaspar assumed a whistle or a single word, though he was too far away to hear. When the potential threat moved past, another signal was given.

Curiosity as much as a desire to chase down information about Jorgen and his mother impelled Kaspar through the market to the distant alley. He approached, but halted just shy of where he had seen the lookouts.

He waited, observed, and waited some more. He could sense as much as see that something was about to happen, and then it did.

Like rats erupting from a flooding sewer during a sudden downpour, the boys came roiling out of the alley. The two lookouts just ran, in seemingly random directions, but the dozen or so after them were all carrying loaves of bread – someone must have found a way into the back of a bakery and handed out as much fresh bread as he could before the baker cried alarm. A moment later shouts echoed across the square as merchants became aware that a crime was in progress.

One boy of no more than ten hurried right past Kaspar, who reached out and snagged him by the collar of his filthy tunic. The boy instantly released his bread and threw his arms straight up, and Kaspar realized he was about to slip right out of the rag he wore as a shirt.

Kaspar grabbed him instead by his dirty long black hair. The youngster yelled, 'Let me go!'

Kaspar hauled him away down another alley. When he was out of sight of those in the market, he hiked the lad around and inspected him. The boy was kicking, trying to bite and strike him with surprising strength, but Kaspar had grappled with an assortment of wild animals all his life, including one unforgettable and nearly disastrous encounter with an angry wolverine. Hanging on to that creature's neck with an iron grip and holding its tail had been the only thing between Kaspar and being eviscerated, until his father's master of the hunt could come and dispatch the animal. He still carried an assortment of scars from that encounter.

'Stop struggling, and I'll put you down, but you have to agree to answer a few questions.'

'Let me go!' shouted the dirty boy. 'Help!'

'You want the constable to come and talk to you?' asked Kaspar as he held his struggling prey high enough that the boy had to dance on his toes.

The boy ceased struggling. 'Not really.'

'Now, answer some questions and I'll let you go.'

'Your word?'

'My word,' answered Kaspar.

'Swear by Kalkin,' said the boy.

'I swear by the God of Thieves, Liars and Tricksters I'll let you go when you've answered my questions.'

The boy ceased his struggles, but Kaspar hung on. 'I'm looking for a boy, about your age I'm thinking.'

The young thief fixed his eye on Kaspar and said with a wary tone, 'Just what sort of boy did you have in mind?'

'Not a sort, but a particular boy, named Jorgen. If he came through here, it would have been a year or so ago.'

The boy relaxed. 'I know him. I mean, I knew him. Blond, sunburned, farm lad; came from the north, looking for his pa, he said. Nearly starved to death, but we taught him a thing or two. He stayed with us for a while. Not much good with thievery, but a stand-up boy in a fight. He could hold his own.'

'"Us"?' asked Kaspar.

'The boys and me, my mates. We all hang together.'

A pair of townsmen turned into the alley, so Kaspar put the boy down, but held tight to his arm. 'Where did he go?'

'South, down to Kadera. The Raj is fighting down there and that's where Jorgen's pa went.'

'Did Jorgen's mother come after him?' Kaspar described Jojanna, then released the boy's arm.

'No. Never saw her,' said the boy; then before Kaspar could react he darted off.

Kaspar took a deep breath, then turned back towards the market. He'd look to a good night's rest, for tomorrow he would be moving south again.

Another week saw Kaspar leaving the relative prosperity of what, he had learned, was now being called the Kingdom of Muboya. And the young Raj had taken the title *Maharajah*, or 'great king'. Again he was riding through a war zone, and several times he had been stopped and questioned. This time, he found little hindrance because at each stop he simply stated he was seeking out General Alenburga. His obvious wealth, fine clothing and fit horse, marked him as 'someone important', and he was motioned on without further question.

The village, he was told, was called Timbe, and it had been overrun three times, twice by the forces of Muboya. It was a half-day's ride south of Kadera, the Maharajah's southern base of command. After riding in at dawn, Kaspar had been told that the General had come to this village to inspect the carnage the last offensive had unleashed.

The only thing that convinced Kaspar the Muboya army hadn't been defeated was the lack of retreating soldiers. But from the disposition of those forces still in the field and the destruction visible everywhere, Kaspar knew the Maharajah's offensive had been halted. At the very best, the Maharajah had achieved a stalemate. At worse, there was a counter-offensive coming this way in a day or two.

Kaspar had little trouble locating the commander's pavilion, situated as it was on top of a hill overlooking what was likely to be the battlefield. As he rode up the incline, he could see positions to the south being fortified and by the time he was approached by a pair of guards, he had no doubt as to the tactical situation of this conflict.

An officer and a guardsman waved to Kaspar and the officer asked, 'Your business?'

'A moment with General Alenburga.' Kaspar dismounted.

'Who are you?' said the officer, a dirty and tired-looking young man. His white turban was almost beige with road dust and there was blood splattered on his leggings and boots. The dark blue tunics of both men did a poor job of hiding the deep red stains of other men's blood.

'By name, Kaspar of Olasko. If the General's memory is overwhelmed by the conflict below, remind him of the stranger who suggested he leave the archers at his rear outside Higara.'

The officer had appeared inclined to send Kaspar on his way, but he said, 'I was part of the cavalry that rode north and flanked those archers. I remember it being said an outlander gave the suggestion to the General.'

'I'm pleased to be remembered,' said Kaspar.

To the guard, the officer said, 'See if the General has a moment for . . . an old acquaintance.'

After a moment, Kaspar was bade to enter the pavilion's main tent. He gave the reins of his mount to the guard and followed the officer inside.

The General looked ten years older instead of three, but he smiled as he looked up. His dark hair was now mostly grey, and combed back behind his ears. His head was uncovered. 'Come back for another game of chess, Kaspar?' He rose and extended his hand.

Kaspar shook it. 'I wouldn't have expected to be remembered.'

'Not many men give me a brilliant tactical plan and beat me at chess in the same day.' He motioned for Kaspar to take a canvas seat near a table covered with a map.

Then the General signalled for his batman to fetch something to drink. 'Could have used you a few times along the way, Kaspar. You have a better eye for the field than most of my subcommanders.'

Kaspar inclined his head at the compliment, and accepted a chilled cup of ale. 'Where do you find ice around here?' he said as he sipped.

'The retreating forces of our enemy, the King of Okanala as he calls himself, had an ice-house in the village we liberated a few days ago. They managed to haul off all the stores and destroy anything else that might have been helpful to us, but somehow I guess they couldn't work out a quick way to melt all the ice.' He smiled as he took his drink. 'For which I'm thankful.' He put his cup down. 'Last time I saw you, you were trying to take a dead friend home to be buried. What brings you this way this time?'

Kaspar glossed over what had happened after the last time they had met and said, 'The occupant of the coffin got to where he was intended to be, and other duties have overtaken me since then. I'm here looking for friends.'

The General said, 'Really? I thought you said when last we met you were merchants. Now you have friends this far south?'

Kaspar understood the suspicious mind of a general who just lost a major battle. 'They are from the north, actually. A man by the name of Bandamin was pressed into service quite far up north – I believe he was taken by slavers, actually, who were most likely illegally doing business outside of Muboya with your press gang.'

'Wouldn't be the first time,' said the General. 'During a war, it's harder than usual to observe the niceties.'

'He had a wife and son, and the son got word that his father was with your army and came south looking for him. The mother followed the boy.'

'And you've followed the mother,' said Alenburga.

'I'd like to get her and the boy back home to safety.'

'And the husband?' asked the General.

Kaspar said, 'Him, too, if possible. Is there a buy-price?'

The General laughed. 'If we let men buy their way out of service, we'd have a very poor army, for the brightest among them would always find a means. No, his service is for five years, no matter how he was enlisted.'

Kaspar nodded. 'I'm not particularly surprised.'

'Feel free to look for the boy and his mother. The boys in the luggage-train are down the hill to the west of here, over by a stream. Most of the women, wives as well as camp-followers are nearby.'

Kaspar drank his ale, then stood. 'I'll take no more of your time, General. You've been generous.'

As he turned to leave, the General asked: 'What do you think?'

Kaspar hesitated, then turned to face the man. 'The war is over. It's time to sue for peace.'

Alenburga sat back and ran forefinger and thumb along the side of his jaw, tugging slightly at his beard for a moment. 'Why do you say that?'

'You're recruited every able-bodied man for three hundred miles in any direction, General. I've ridden through two cities, a half-dozen towns and a score of villages on my way here. There are only men over forty years of age and boys under fifteen left. Every potential fighting man is already in your service.

'I can see you are digging in to the south; you expect a counter-attack from there; but if Okanala has anything left to speak of, he'll punch through on your left, roll you up, and put your back to the stream. Your best bet is to fall back to the town and dig in there.

'General, this is your frontier for the next five years, at least, ten more likely. Time to end this war.'

The General nodded. 'But our Maharajah has a vision, and he wishes to push south until we are close enough to the City of the Serpent River that we can claim all the Eastlands are pacified.'

'I think your ambitious young lord even imagines some day he might take the city and add it to Muboya,' Kaspar suggested.

'Perhaps,' said Alenburga. 'But you're right on all other counts. My scouts tell me Okanala is digging in, as well. We're both played out.'

Kaspar said, 'I know nothing of the politics here, but there are times when an armistice is a face-saving gesture and times when it is a necessity, the only alternative to utter ruin. Victory has fled, and defeat awaits on every hand. Have your Maharajah marry one of his relatives off to one of the King's and call it a day.'

The General stood up and offered his hand. 'If you find your friends and get them home, Kaspar of Olasko, you're welcome in my tent any time. If you come back, I'll make a general out of you and when the time comes we'll push down to the sea together.'

'Make me a general?' said Kaspar with a grin.

'Ah, yes, I was the commander of a brigade when last we met,' said the General, returning Kaspar's grin. 'Now I command the army. My cousin appreciates success.'

'Ah,' said Kasper shaking his hand. 'If ambition grips me, I know where to find you.'

'Good fortune, Kaspar of Olasko.'

'Good fortune, General.'

Kaspar left the pavilion and mounted his horse. He walked the gelding down the side of the hill towards a distant dell through which wandered a good-sized stream.

He felt a rising disquiet as he approached the luggage wagons, for he could see signs of battle all around. The traditions of war forbade attacking the luggage-boys or the women who followed the army, but there were times when such niceties were ignored or the ebb and flow of the conflict simply washed over the non-combatants.

Several of the boys he saw bore wounds, some

minor, some serious, and many were bandaged. A few lay on pallets beneath the wagons and slept, their injuries rendering them unfit for any work. Kaspar rode to where a stout man in a blood-covered tunic sat on a wagon, weeping. A recently-removed metal cuirass lay on the seat next to him, as did a helm with a plume, and he stared off into the distance. 'Are you the Master of the Luggage?' asked Kaspar.

The man merely nodded, tears slowly coursing down his cheeks.

'I'm looking for a boy, by the name of Jorgen.'

The man's jaw tightened and he dismounted slowly. When he was standing before Kaspar he said, 'Come with me.'

He led Kaspar over a small rise to where a company of soldiers were digging a massive trench, while boys were carrying wood and buckets of what Kaspar assume was oil. There would be no individual pyres for the dead; this would be a mass immolation.

The dead were lined up on the other side of the trench, ready to be carried and placed atop the wood before the oil was thrown over it and the torches tossed in. A third of the way down the line the man stopped. Kaspar looked down and saw three bodies lying close together.

'He was such a good boy,' the Master of Luggage said, his voice hoarse from shouting orders, from the battle dust, the day's heat, and strangled emotions. Jorgen lay next to Jojanna, and next to her lay a man in soldier's garb. It could only be Bandamin, for his features were similar to the boy's.

'He came looking for his father almost a year ago, and . . . his mother soon after. He worked hard, without complaint, and his mother looked after all the boys as if they were her own. When their father could, he would join them and they were a joy to know. In the midst of all this—' he waved his hand in an encompassing gesture, '—they found happiness in just being together. When . . .' He stopped and his eyes welled up with tears. 'I asked for the . . . father to be detailed with the luggage. I thought I was doing them all a favour. I never thought the battle would spill over to the luggage-train. It's against the compact of war! They killed the boys and the women! It's against every rule of war!'

Kaspar took a moment to look down at the three of them, reunited by fate and fated to die together, a long way from home. Bandamin had been struck a crushing blow in the chest, from a mace perhaps, but his face was unmarked. He wore a tabard in the blue and yellow of Muboya. It was faded and dirty and slightly torn. Kaspar saw the man Jorgen would have become in his father's face. He had an honest man's face, a hard-working face. Kaspar thought Bandamin had been a man who had once laughed a lot. He lay with eyes closed, sleeping. Jojanna appeared unmarked, so Kaspar suspected that an arrow or spear point had taken her in the back, perhaps as she ran to protect the boys. Jorgen's hair was matted with blood and his head rested at an odd angle. Kaspar felt a tiny sense of relief that it must have been a sudden death, perhaps with no pain. He felt an odd, unexpected ache; the boy was still so young.

He stared at the three of them, looking like nothing so much as a family sleeping side-by-side. He knew the world spun on, and no one but he, and perhaps one or two people in the distant north, would note the passing of Bandamin and his family. Jorgen, the last scion of some obscure family tree was dead, and with him that line had ended forever.

The luggage-master looked at Kaspar as if he expected him to say something. Kaspar looked down on the three bodies for another moment, then put heels to his horse's sides, turned the gelding and began his long ride northward.

As he cantered from the battlefield, Kaspar felt something inside him turn cold and hard. It would be easy enough to hate Okanala for violating the strictures of 'civilized' warfare. It would be easy to hate Muboya for taking a man from his family. It would be easy to hate anyone and everyone. But Kaspar knew that over the years he had issued certain orders, and because of those orders hundreds of Bandamins had been taken from their homes, and hundreds of Jojannas and Jorgens had endured hardships, even death.

With a sigh that felt as if came from deep within his soul, Kaspar wondered if there was any happy purpose to existence, anything beyond suffering and, at the end, death. For if there was, at this moment in his life he was sorely pressed to say what it might be.

CHAPTER 4

NIGHTHAWKS

The soldiers moved quickly.

Eric von Darkmoor, Duke of Krondor, Knight-Marshall of the King's Army in the West, and Warden of the Western Marches stood behind a large outcropping of rocks, observing his men moving slowly into position. Silent silhouettes against rocks bathed in deep shadows cast by the setting sun, they were a special unit of the Prince's Household Guards. Erik personally had designed their training as he ascended through the ranks of the army, first as a captain in the Prince's army, then as Commander of the Garrison at Krondor, then Knight-Marshall.

The men were once part of the Royal Krondorian Pathfinders, a company of trackers and scouts, descendants of the legendary Imperial Keshian Guides, but now this smaller elite company was called simply the 'Prince's Own', soldiers whom Erik called upon in special circumstances, such as the one that confronted them this night. Their uniforms were distinctive: dark grey short tabards bearing the blazon of Krondor – an eagle soaring over a peak, rendered in muted colours – and black trousers with a red strip down the side tucked into heavy boots, suitable for marching, riding, or as they were employed now, climbing rocky faces. Each man wore a simple, dark, open-faced helm, and carried short weapons – a sword barely long enough to deserve the name, and an estoc, a long dagger. Each man was trained in a specific set of skills, and right now Erik's two best rock-climbers were leading the assault.

Erik let his gaze move up to the top of the cliffs opposite his position.

High above them sat the ancient Cavell Keep, looking down upon a path that diverged from the main draw, a path known as Cavell Run. A small waterfall graced the rockface near the keep, landing in a pool in an outcrop halfway up the cliff, then falling again to the stream that had originally formed the run. As such things are wont to do, the course of the stream had changed over the years, and some event, geological or manmade, had forced the stream bed down the other side of the draw, leaving the original creek bed dry and dusty. That pool was their destination, for if the intelligence Erik possessed from nearly a hundred years ago was valid, behind that pool existed a secret entrance, the keep's original bolt-hole.

Erik had brought his soldiers into Cavell Town before dawn, quickly hiding them as best he could, a difficult task in a town so small, but by noon the townspeople were about their business as best they could be with armed men hiding in every other building. Erik was unconcerned about Nighthawk spies in the town, for no one was allowed to leave Cavell that day; his only concern was for someone observing from up high, in the hills above the town, and he was convinced he had taken every precaution possible.

Magnus had aided the effort with an illusion spell, and unless any observer was a highly trained magic-user, the few minutes it took to get a hundred men into the town would have passed uneventfully. At sundown, Magnus had again cast his enchantment and the men quickly broke up into two companies, one heading to the main entrance up Cavell Run, and the other under Erik's personal supervision heading to the rear of the keep.

The old soldier stood motionless, his attention focused on the deployment of his men. He was nearly eighty-five years of age, yet thanks to a potion given him by Nakor, he resembled a man thirty years younger. Satisfied that things were as they should be, he turned to his companions, Nakor and Magnus, who stood nearby, while the Knight-Marshall's personal bodyguard stood uneasily to one side; they were not entirely comfortable with their commander ordering them to stand away, as it was their personal mission to protect him at all costs.

'Now?' asked Nakor.

'We wait,' said Eric. 'If they have any concerns about this approach to their citadel, they should have seen us coming, and if so, they'll either do something inhospitable or they'll attempt to flee through the other escape route.'

'Your best guess?' asked Magnus.

Erik sighed. 'I'd hunker down and pretend there was no one at home. If that didn't work, I'd have a very nasty reception in mind for anyone attempting to enter the keep.' He waved absently with his hand as he said, 'We have old records, which even then were not entirely accurate, but what we do know is that Cavell Keep is a warren, and there are many places to lie in ambush or leave behind some nasty traps. It's going to be no walk through the meadow going in there.'

Nakor shrugged. 'You have good men.'

'The best,' said Erik. 'Hand-picked and trained for this sort of business, but I still hate to put them at risk needlessly.'

Nakor said softly, 'There is need, Erik.'

'I'm convinced of that, Nakor,' said the old soldier. 'Or I would not be here.'

'How does that sit with the Duke of Salador?' asked Nakor.

'He doesn't know I'm here.' Erik looked at Nakor. 'You picked a hell of a time to give me this to worry about, old friend.'

Nakor shrugged. 'We never get to pick our moments, do we?'

'There have been times when I think that I might have been better off if Bobby de Longville and Calis had hanged me that cold, bitter morning, so long ago.' His eyes looked off into the distance, as the sun disappeared behind the rocks there. He turned to Nakor. 'Then there are times that I don't. When this is over, I'll know better what sort of time this is.' The old man smiled. 'Let's go back and wait a while.'

He led Magnus and Nakor down a narrow path between high rockfaces, passing lines of soldiers quietly waiting to assault the keep on the rocks above. At the rear lackeys stood ready with the horses, and behind them waited wagons with supplies. Erik waved to his personal squire, who had stayed behind with the boys in the luggage.

The squire produced a pair of cups and filled them with wine from a skin. Nakor took one, eyebrow raised. 'Serving wine before a battle?'

'Why not?' said the Duke, drinking deeply. He wiped his mouth with the back of his gauntlet. 'As if I didn't have enough to worry about, you send me off halfway across the Kingdom to dig out murderers.'

Nakor shrugged. 'Someone has to do it, Erik.'

The old warrior shook his head. 'I've lived a long life, Nakor, and one more interesting than most. I'd be a liar if I told you I would welcome death, but I would certainly be glad to be free of my burdens.' He fixed Nakor with a narrow gaze. 'I thought I was until you appeared that night.'

'We need you,' said the Isalani.

'My King needs me,' said Erik.

'The world needs you,' said Nakor, lowering his

voice so that those nearby would not overhear. 'You are the only man of rank in the Kingdom Pug still trusts.'

Erik nodded. 'I understand why he chose to separate himself from the Crown.' He took another drink of wine, and handed the empty cup to his squire. When the lad made to fill it again, Erik waved him away. 'But did he have to embarrass the royal personage of the Prince of Krondor in doing so? Publicly? In front of the army of Great Kesh?'

'Old business, Erik.'

'I wish it were so,' said Erik. He lowered his voice further. 'You will know this if you don't already. Prince Robert has been recalled.'

'This is bad,' said Nakor, nodding.

'We've had three princes in Krondor since I gained rank, and I am only Duke because King Ryan took Lord James with him to Rillanon. My temporary position has lasted nine years, and if I live long enough, will probably last another nine.'

'Why was Robert recalled?'

'You have a better chance of uncovering the truth than me,' said Erik. After a long moment of silence during which he watched the evening sky darken, the Duke said, 'Politics. Robert was never a popular man with the Congress of Lords. Lord James is a western noble, which rankles with many of those who wished to be first among the King's advisors; James is a shrewd man, almost as shrewd as his grandfather.' He glanced

76

at Nakor. 'There was a name to conjure with, Lord James of Krondor.'

Nakor grinned. 'Jimmy was a handful before he became a duke. I know.' He glanced up at the soldiers who were now ready, waiting for his signal to begin the climb. 'Still, we tend to remember the greatness and forget the flaws; and Jimmy made his share of mistakes. If Robert will not serve, then who?'

'There are other cousins to the King more able . . .' He looked at Nakor and his expression was sad. 'It may come to civil war if the King's not careful. He's directly descended from King Borric, but he has no sons of his own, and there are many cousins, most of them with a valid claim to the throne if he does not produce an heir.'

Nakor shrugged. 'I've lived a long time, Erik. I've seen kings come and go in different lands. The nation will survive.'

'But at what price, old friend?'

'Who is to be the new Prince of Krondor?'

'That is the question, isn't it?' said the Duke, standing up and signalling to his men to make ready. The sky was sufficiently dark: it was time to begin the assault on the keep. 'Prince Edward is well-liked, intelligent, a good soldier, and someone who could forge consensus in the Congress.'

'So the King will name someone else,' said Nakor with a chuckle as Erik started forward along the draw.

Erik said nothing, but gestured once and two

men hurried out from behind rocks below the keep, both with loops of cord around their shoulders. They started to climb the rockface, using only their hands and feet.

Nakor watched closely as the two men disappeared into the gloom above. They moved silently like spiders crawling up a wall. Nakor knew how dangerous it was to make that ascent, but he also knew that it was the only way to get a rope down for the soldiers below.

Turning to Nakor, Erik said, 'I'm thinking Prince Henry will get the nod, for he can be easily enough replaced if Queen Anne bears a boy. If Edward sits in Krondor for any length of time, the King may not be able to replace him with a son in . . . a . . . few years . . .' His voice trailed off as he watched the men reach the lip of the pool.

Nakor said, 'Odd place for a bolt-hole, over a hundred feet above ground, isn't it?'

'I imagine the Nighthawks did some work around here some years back. My men report tool marks on the rockface. There was probably a path down to the floor of the run that was demolished.' He sighed. 'It's time. Where's your man?'

Nakor nodded behind them. 'Sleeping, under the wagon.'

'Get him, then,' said Erik von Darkmoor.

Nakor hurried back to the luggage wagon, where the two boys responsible for looking after the stores from the town waited. They spoke in hushed tones, understanding how dangerous this mission was; even so, they were only boys and the waiting was making them restless. Underneath the wagon lay a solitary figure, who roused quickly when Nakor kicked lightly at his boots.

Ralan Bek wiggled out from under the wagon, then unfolded himself to tower over Nakor. The youth was six inches over six feet in height, and he loomed over the diminutive gambler. Nakor knew he was possessed by some aspect of the God of Evil, a tiny 'sliver' as Nakor thought of it; an infinitesimal portion of the god himself, and that made Bek extraordinarily dangerous. The only advantage Nakor possessed was years of experience and what he thought of as his 'tricks'.

'Time?'

Nakor nodded. 'They'll be up there in a moment. You know what to do.'

Bek nodded. He reached down and picked up his hat, a hat he had claimed as a prize from a man he had killed before Nakor's eyes, and he wore it like a badge of honour. The broad-brimmed black felt hat, with its single long eagle's feather hanging down from the hatband, gave the youth an almost rakish air, but Nakor knew that beneath the young man's convivial exterior seethed a potential for harm, as well as preternatural strength and speed.

Bek trotted over to the face of the cliff, and waited. A coil of line was dropped quietly from above, followed a moment later by another.

Soldiers quickly tied heavier rope to the lines, and this was pulled up. When the first rope was made secure, Ralan Bek unbuckled his scabbard belt and tied it over one shoulder, so that his sword now rested on his back. With powerful ease he pulled himself up the rope, feet firmly on the rock-face, as if he had been climbing this way all his life. Other soldiers followed, but Bek's speed up the rope was unmatchable.

Erik watched him ascend into the darkness. 'Why are you so insistent he goes first, Nakor?'

'He may not be invulnerable, Erik, but he's a lot harder to kill than any of your men. Magnus will look out for those guarding the main entrance to the keep, but if there's magic on this back door, Bek has the best chance of survival.'

'Time was I would be the first one up the rope.'

Nakor gripped his friend's arm. 'I'm glad to see you've got smarter over the years, Erik.'

'I notice you're not volunteering to be up there, either.'

Nakor just grinned.

Bek waited, running his fingers over the door's outline. It was a rock, like the others, and in the darkness he couldn't see the crack his finger-tips told him marked the edge of the entrance to the bolt-hole. He let his senses drift, for he had discovered early in life that sometimes he could anticipate things – an attack, an unexpected turn of the trail, the mood of a horse, or the fall of the dice. He thought of it as his 'lucky feeling'.

Yes, he thought. There was something just beyond this door, something very interesting. Ralan Bek did not know what fear was. As Nakor had suggested to him, there was something very different, even alien, about the young man from Novindus. Glancing down to where the little man waited with the old soldier, he found he could barely make them out in the dark. 'Lantern,' he whispered, and a soldier behind him handed him a specially constructed, small, shuttered lantern. He pointed it at Nakor and Erik and opened it and shut it again quickly. That was the agreed-upon signal to proceed cautiously.

Not that Ralan truly understand caution. It was as alien to his thoughts as fear. He tried to understand a lot of things Nakor talked to him about, but sometimes he just nodded and pretended to understand the strange little man in order to keep him from repeating himself endlessly.

Ralan continued to run his fingers along the seam until he determined that the door was designed to be opened only from the inside. He shrugged. 'Bar,' he demanded, and a soldier stepped past him and inserted the crowbar where he pointed. The soldier struggled for a moment, until Bek said, 'Let me.'

With preternatural power, he forced open a crack, and the door swung suddenly wide with a protesting sound of twisting metal as an iron bar was ripped from its restraining mechanism. With a loud clank it hit the stones and instantly Bek had his sword out and was through the opening. Unconcerned about the noise, Bek turned towards the soldiers and held up a restraining hand. 'Wait!' he said in low tones, and then he entered.

The soldiers knew their orders. Bek would enter first and they would only follow when he gave the order or ten minutes after, whichever came first. One soldier turned over an hourglass bearing markings, red lines drawn to indicate demarcations of ten minutes. Erik's hand-picked men hunkered down before the entrance, along the edge of the pool, listening to the sound of the waterfall in the darkness.

Bek moved cautiously, ignoring his lack of sight. He stepped lightly as he progressed, not putting his full weight down until he knew he wasn't stepping into a pit, or triggering some sort of trap. He knew he could take a lot of damage – he'd been wounded several times in his short life – but he had no more appetite for injury than the next man. Besides, if what Nakor said was true, there should be some fun ahead.

Thinking of the little man caused Bek to pause a moment. Bek didn't like him; but then again Bek didn't like anyone; he didn't dislike anyone either. His feelings towards other people were fairly predictable: they were either allies or opponents – or they were inconsequential, like a horse or some other animal, sometimes useful, but mostly not worth the attention. But the little man stirred some strange feelings in Bek, feelings he couldn't put a name to. He didn't know if it was familiarity, or enjoyment or what. His pleasures tended to the intense: watching men bleed and scream, or rough coupling with women. He knew he liked fighting. The crashing of steel, the clamour of voices, blood and . . . death. He liked watching things die, he had decided some time before. It fascinated him to see that one moment an animal or a man might be alive, aware, moving, and the next it was lying there, just so much meat. Not even useful meat if it was a man.

Bek expected to kill some very dangerous men, and looked forward to it.

A faint sound from ahead caused him to forget Nakor and his confusion over things the odd gambler said all the time. Someone was moving at the far end of a tunnel and Bek's entire body quivered with anticipation.

He was supposed to go back, but he had lost track of time – how long was ten minutes, anyway? The other soldiers would come in after him, and besides, Bek was anxious to be about some slaughter. It had been a very long time since he'd enjoyed a good fight. Nakor had done something to him, and often his head hurt when he tried to think about things. But Nakor had said it was all right for him to kill anyone who was hiding up in this old keep, except for more of the old soldier's fighters who might be coming in from the other side.

Ralan Bek found his head swimming, so with a grunt he shoved aside all thoughts except finding the author of the noise he had heard in the darkness. He picked up his pace, and almost fell face forward into an open pit. Only his 'lucky feeling' caused him to pull back at the last instant.

He took out a small cylinder Nakor had given him, and pulled off the top. Inside was a bundle of sticks, one of which he pulled out. He recapped the cylinder and put it back in his tunic, then waved the stick rapidly in the air, and after a few seconds a tiny flame erupted from the end. As Nakor had promised him, after the total darkness of the tunnels, he'd be surprised at the amount of light the small burning stick could provide.

Bek looked down at a pit that yawned at his feet, and couldn't see the bottom. He was glad he hadn't fallen, not because he feared injury, but because he would have had to wait at the bottom until the old soldier's fighters caught up with him. He didn't know if they'd even notice until one of them fell in and he didn't relish the notion of one of them landing on top of him; and he didn't know if they'd bring enough rope to haul him out.

He took two steps back then with a powerful stride launched himself above the pit and landed easily on the other side, a dozen feet away from his take-off. He dropped the flaming stick to the floor, grinding it under his boot heel.

He paused to see if anyone might have heard his landing, and when he was certain he had gone unnoticed, he continued down the hall. For an instant he wondered if he should have left something to warn the soldiers behind him of the pit. Then he wondered where that thought had come from; why should he worry if one of the old soldier's men fell into the pit? This was too difficult to consider now: it was something Nakor would understand. He had no time to dwell on it.

Ahead he could hear faint voices, and he knew mayhem awaited.

Magnus studied the sky and judged that it was time to move, so he signalled to two guards to accompany him up the long entryway to the ancient keep. The road appeared to have not been in use for years, but Magnus had secretly inspected it at dawn and saw by tiny signs that the 'disuse' had been artfully forged. Someone had been using this road recently, but endeavouring to keep that fact a secret. That as much as anything convinced him that his father's faith in Joval Delan, the hired mind-reader, had not been misplaced. Some local bandit, smuggler, or gang of errant youths would not have the means or inclination to do so thorough a job.

The soldiers had been creeping up the draw known as Cavell Run, which was the only obvious approach to the ancient keep. Magnus was not the student of things military his father and brother were, but even he could imagine what a lethal prospect attempting to storm this keep would present. Only the rumours of demonic possession and a curse, followed by nearly a century of peace in the region would have kept such an obvious military asset unused.

Still, he had other concerns, the first of which was to ensure that the men with him went undiscovered for as long as possible. Magnus was still young compared to most powerful practitioners' of magic, and he had inherited certain abilities from his parents. His mother had always possessed a finer instinct for detecting the presence of magic than his father, though Pug was better able to determine the nature of a spell or device once it was uncovered. Magnus had the happy fortune to have inherited both abilities. And so he sensed and understood at least four magical traps located between the floor of the Run and the ancient gate at the top of the ramp.

With the deft moves of a master of his craft, Magnus countered each spell quickly, allowing the soldiers from Erik's command to approach on silent feet. If there was a lookout above he would have been hard pressed to notice the darting grey figures hunched over, moving along the edges of the roadway in the night's gloom. Small moon didn't rise for another hour and its light was faint even on clear nights. Tonight was overcast.

With hand signals, the officer in charge motioned

for his men to make ready. An ancient drawbridge had once covered a gap between the top of the roadway-ramp and the keep's gate. Now it hung by a single chain, dangling uselessly on the other side of the gap, an open space too wide for any man to leap. Signals were passed and from the rear two pairs of men ran forward, carrying scaling ladders that would serve as bridges across the chasm. Magnus used his skills to elevate himself and float above the breach.

He watched the men calmly walking on the ladder rungs, heedless of the yawning space below their feet. A misstep would send a man tumbling to his death. Magnus admired their discipline.

Now Magnus cast his senses forward, attempting to seek out more magic entanglements or lures, and found none. The warder of this keep had been content to trust to the snares left along the roadway to alert the residents of the keep to any unwelcome company. He strode forward, unmindful of any physical danger, for he sensed something in the distance that caused the hair on his arms and neck to stand up.

He held up his hand and a faint light shone from the palm, illuminating the killing ground between the now-fallen outer gate, where once a drawbridge and a portcullis had provided the first barrier, and the inner doors, which were shut and, Magnus supposed, barred from within. The soldiers behind him assembled silently. In the eerie mystical illumination Magnus's pale hair and height gave him an almost supernatural appearance, but whatever discomfort the soldiers might have felt being given over to the command of a wizard was not in evidence as they waited for his instructions.

Magnus closed his eyes to better aid his concentration and envision the large wooden doors. He reached out with his senses and ran mental fingers over the surface of the wood, then pressed slowly through until he could feel the other side. As he did so a picture as clear as if he were using his eyes appeared in his mind, and he saw the large wooden bar set in two wooden brackets. He inspected every inch with his mental touch, then opened his eyes and stepped back. 'There's a trap,' he said softly to the officer who stood to his right.

'What do you suggest?' the young knight-lieutenant asked.

Magnus said, 'Find a way through that door without lifting the bar.'

He extended his hand and a faint humming could be heard by those standing closest to him. Suddenly, there was a hole in the bottom of the gate, large enough for a man to pass through on hands and knees. 'One at a time,' said Magnus, 'and have no man touch the gate or the walls on either side.'

The officer passed the word and quickly each man in turn made his way through. Magnus got ready to control the magic that would be unleashed should any man falter, but the preparation proved needless. Each man did exactly as he was instructed.

Then it was Magnus's turn and he crawled through awkwardly, finding his robe an unexpected impediment. Halfway through the hole he was forced to lift first one knee, then the other, pulling the fabric ahead of him, so he could get through without falling on his face.

Chuckling as he stood, he said, 'There are times, and this is one of them, when I feel the need to question my father as to why magicians are expected to wear robes.'

The lieutenant revealed himself to be a man of little humour as he asked, 'Milord?'

Magnus sighed. 'Never mind.' He faced the soldiers. 'Stay behind me unless I tell you to move forward, for there are forces here that are more than the bravest man can face without my arts.

'Any man you see who is not Ralan Bek or one of your own, kill on sight.'

Then he turned and walked forward into the darkness, the light from his hand bobbing like a swinging lantern's.

Bek walked as if strolling down a street, mindless of the darkness. There was light coming from several distant rooms at the ends of tunnels which crossed the one he had chosen, but he ignored them, and kept going straight ahead. He didn't know how he knew, but he sensed that he needed to move straight from the secret entrance at the rear of the keep to the innermost chamber, which was probably some ancient great hall or throne room.

He felt positively buoyant in anticipation of the coming fight. He liked some of the things Nakor made him do, but he hadn't been in any sort of combat for far too long. He'd bashed a few skulls in a tavern or two, but there had been no serious bloodletting since he'd killed that emperor for Nakor the year before. That had been fun. He almost laughed aloud thinking of the stunned expressions on the faces of everyone looking up at where he stood, his sword thrust straight though the old man's back.

A man wearing black armour but no helm walked around a corner and before he stopped moving, Ralan Bek had run his sword point into the man's throat, which was exposed above the cuirass. The man dropped with a fairly loud noise, but Bek didn't care. Less than a hundred feet ahead light beckoned and he was anxious to bring havoc.

He strode down the last length of shadowy hall into a high-ceilinged chamber. It was an old-style keep hall, where in the dead of winter the family and close retainers of the original ruler of Cavell Keep would sleep during winter's coldest nights. Once magnificent, the great hall had fallen into drab disrepair.

The vaulted roof was still supported by massive wooden beams so ancient they were as hard as steel, but the once whitewashed walls were now dark grey and high in the darkness above Bek could hear bats fluttering. No tapestries hung on the walls to shield the inhabitants against winter's chill in the stones, nor were there rugs on the floor. But a fire burned in the massive fireplace to the left of the door through which he entered. Sword drawn and with a maniac's grin in place, he surveyed the two dozen men resting before the fire.

In the centre of this group sat two men, both in large chairs made in an older style – a 'u' of wood set on top of another to make the legs, with a wooden back nailed across the upper half, stuffed with cushions or furs. The rest sat on camp stools or on black cloaks spread on the floor. All were dressed in black armour, the hallmark of the Nighthawks, except for the two men in the centre. One wore a tunic of finely woven linen and trousers and boots worthy of a highborn noble, though his clothes hung loosely on this frame, as if he had lost a great deal of weight lately; the other wore the black robes of a cleric or magician. The man in the tunic wore a heavy amulet of gold around his neck, identical to the black amulet Bek had been shown by Nakor. The robed man wore no jewellery whatsoever. He was thin and there wasn't a hair on his face or head.

A moment after Bek appeared the eighteen seated men were scrambling, two blowing bone whistles that sent a shrieking alarm throughout the keep.

The man with the gold around his neck looked harried, and his eyes were wide as he pointed at Bek screaming, 'Kill him!'

As the first swordsman raised his sword, Bek gripped his own weapon with two hands, his eyes narrow slits, focusing with keen anticipation on the coming slaughter. But the robed man shouted, 'No! Halt!' His eyes locked onto Bek's in wonder.

Everyone, including Bek, froze as the man wove between the swordsmen. He passed the man closest to Ralan Bek, and came straight towards the young warrior. Bek sensed some strange power in this man, and his lucky feeling told him something unusual was about to happen. He hesitated, then began to swing at the man in the robe.

The man held up his hand, not in defence, but in supplication. 'Wait,' he said as Bek hesitated again. He reached out slowly, almost gently, and put his hand on Bek's chest, and said again, 'Wait.'

Then slowly the robed man went to his knees and in a voice that was little more than a whisper, he said, 'What does our master bid us?'

The man with the amulet looked on in mute astonishment, then he too went to his knees, followed moments later by every other man in the room. Another half a dozen men ran into the hall from other parts of the keep, answering the alarm. Seeing their brethren on their knees, their eyes lowered, they followed suit.

Bek's sword lowered a little. 'What?'

'What does our master bid us?' asked the robed man again.

Bek tried to puzzle out what to say next, from what he had overheard Nakor, Pug and the others say at Sorcerer's Isle. At last he said: 'Varen's gone. He's fled to another world.'

'Not Varen,' said the robed man. 'He was highest among our master's servants.' The man slowly reached out and touched Bek on the chest. 'I can feel our master, there, inside you. He lives within you; he speaks through you.' He raised his eyes to Bek's again, and asked once more, 'What does our master bid us?'

Bek had been ready for combat, and this was beyond his ability to comprehend. Slowly, he looked around the room, rising frustration in his voice as he said, 'I don't know . . .' Then suddenly, he raised his sword and brought it down, shouting, 'I don't know!'

Minutes later Magnus rushed into the room with a company of Erik's soldiers at his back, and more Kingdom soldiers entered through the same door as Bek. All of them stopped at the scene before them. Twenty-six corpses littered the floor, but there was no sign of a struggle. Twenty-six head-less bodies lay in a wash of blood. Heads still rolled on the crimson stones and blood-soaked cloaks.

The fire crackled. Bek stood beside it, covered

in blood. His arms were crimson to the elbows and gore was smeared across his face. He stood like a fiend possessed by madness. Magnus could see it in his eyes. He was trembling so much he looked like a man about to go into convulsions.

Finally, Ralan Bek threw back his head and gave out a howl which rang off the stones high above. It was a primal burst of rage and frustration, and when even the echoes had passed away, he looked around the room, then directly at Magnus. Like a petulant child he pointed to the corpses, and said, 'This wasn't fun!'

He wiped his sword on the tunic of a nearby corpse, and sheathed it. Then he picked up a bucket of water which had been set near the fireplace to heat and lifted it, letting it wash down over his head, without even bothering to remove his hat, and then picked up a relatively clean cloak to use as a towel. Cleaning himself off as best he could, Bek said in a more controlled tone, 'It's not fun if they don't fight back, Magnus.' He looked around the room and then said, 'I'm hungry. Anyone got anything to eat?'

CHAPTER 5

PREPARATION

Miranda shouted.

'Are you mad?' she cried far louder than was necessary in the small room.

Magnus watched his mother with guarded amusement as she strode away from her husband's desk for as far as she could in the small study, then turned with a dramatic frown. She often would vent loudly over matters that eventually would end up exactly as his father wished them to be. But Pug had over the years come to understand that his wife's often volatile nature required a physical expression of her frustrations.

'Are you mad?' Miranda shrieked for the second time.

'No more than you were to spend almost a half-year shadowing the Emerald Queen's army down in Novindus,' said Pug, calmly, as he rose from behind his desk.

'That was different!' shouted Miranda, still not through venting. 'There was no Pantathian snake priest who could find me, let alone challenge me, and I'm the one who can transport herself without a Tsurani sphere, remember?'

Magnus saw his father begin a comment – probably on how Nakor, Pug, and Magnus were all becoming adept at the skill – but think better of it and say nothing as Miranda continued.

'You're talking about going to an alien world! Not only an alien world, but one in a different plane of reality! Who knows what powers you may have there, if any?' She pointed her finger at Pug. 'You don't even know how to get there in the first place, and don't tell me you're going to use the Talnoy on Kelewan to anchor a rift there. I know enough about rifts to know that you could find yourself swimming at the bottom of some poison sea, or standing in the middle of a battlefield or any other number of deadly places! You'd be going in blind!'

'I won't be going in blind,' said Pug, holding up his hands in supplication. 'Please, we must learn more about the Dasati.'

'Why?' demanded Miranda.

'Because I've been to see the Oracle.' He didn't need to tell either his wife or son which oracle.

Miranda's anger leeched away as curiosity took over. 'What did she say?'

'They're coming. There are too many uncertainties for her to say more, now – I will return to her later as events draw closer. But for now we must learn more of these people.'

'But the Talnoy down in Novindus are warded, as motionless and without magical presence as they were for the countless years they lay hidden,' countered Mirada. 'If they're warded, how could the Dasati find us?'

Pug could only shake his head. 'I don't know. The Oracle is rarely wrong when she speaks of certainties.'

Magnus sensed an argument coming and deftly changed the subject. 'And again I ask, as I have many times before,' he said, like a patient school-master, 'who put them there?'

Pug knew the question was rhetorical, since they had several theories and no facts, but he thanked his son silently for diverting his wife's ire. Their first thought had been that one of the Valheru, a Dragon Lord of fabled antiquity, had brought the Talnoy back, but there was no proof of that. Tomas, Pug's boyhood friend, was imbued with the memories of one of the ancient Dragon Host, and had no recollection of any of his brethren returning from their ill-fated raid on the Dasati homeworld with a single Talnoy as a trophy. They had been too busy trying to keep those fiendish creations from destroying them; several dragon-riders had fallen during the incursion into the Dasati realm. In the end, there was only one inescapable conclusion.

'Macros.'

Miranda nodded in agreement. Her father, Macros the Black, had been an agent of the lost God of Magic. 'Every time we turn around we bump into one of Father's schemes.' She crossed her arms, getting a far-away look as she seemed to remember something. 'I remember . . . once . . .' She looked down at the cavern floor, her face revealing flickering emotions as if what she recalled was painful. 'I spent so many years being angry with him for abandoning me . . .'

Pug nodded sympathetically. He had been with his wife when she had last been reunited with her father and remembered her poorly-hidden anger at seeing him after years of estrangement. He also remembered her grief when he had been swallowed up in the rift that closed around him as he held the Demon Lord Maarg, giving his life in a desperate act that saved this world.

Pushing aside her memories, Miranda said, 'But we do end up with another of his bloody messes, don't we?' Her tone held a hint of affectionate humour, as well as some bitterness.

Before his mother could get back into another black mood because of his grandfather, Magnus spoke. 'We know that Grandfather had a hand in warding off the Dasati rifts from the one Talnoy we found, and his wards are still in place around the others.'

Both parents regarded their eldest son and Miranda said, 'This we all know, Magnus. What's your point?'

'Grandfather never did anything without a reason, and everything you have both told me about him leads me to conclude that he knew, somehow, that the day would come when one or both of you would discover the Talnoy, and that leads me to believe he also knew there would be a confrontation with the Dasati.'

Pug sighed aloud. 'Your father,' he said to his wife, 'knew more about time travel than anyone. Gods, all of us combined probably know only a hundredth part of what he knew. What he did with Tomas and the ancient Valheru, Ashen-Shugar, his ability to understand the time trap sprung on us by the Pantathians at the City Forever, all the rest of it. I've struggled to learn as much as I could about what he did, but most of it remains a mystery. However, in this I agree with Magnus. He left things as he did in Novindus for a reason, and I believe that reason involves the Conclave.'

Miranda looked unconvinced, but said nothing.

Magnus said, 'Mother, if Grandfather had not wanted the Talnoy found he had the magic to bury that cave under a mountain which it would have taken millennia to uncover. Something vast and dangerous is moving out there.' He made a sweeping gesture. 'And this thing is coming no matter what we do.'

'What we can do is try to understand our enemy's nature, to see his face,' said Pug.

'Well, I'm not ready to agree this is a good plan,' said Miranda. 'But obviously you two have your minds made up. So how do you propose to get to the Dasati world, stay alive, and bring back the information, or are those details too trivial to worry about?'

Pug was forced to laugh. 'Hardly trivial, my love.

I plan on looking for someone who has been to that realm and can, perhaps, guide us there.'

'And where do you expect to find such a person?' asked Miranda. 'Is there anyone in this entire world who has visited the second circle of reality?'

Pug said, 'Probably not. But I'm not going to be looking on this world. I plan on visiting Honest John's.'

Miranda froze for an instant at the mention of the establishment at the heart of the Hall of Worlds. Then she gave a sharp nod. 'If there's anywhere to find such a one, that is where I'd start looking, too.'

Magnus said, 'Who will go with you, Father?'

Pug threw a warning look at his son, knowing that this was certain to set off another round of complaints from Miranda, who even now was regarding her husband with an expression of curiosity. Pug took a breath, then said, 'You, Nakor and Bek.'

Instead of the anticipated eruption from Miranda, she merely said, 'Why?'

'Magnus because he is ready and I need someone as powerful as myself with me – and you need to stay here and conduct the business of the Conclave, as well as visit the Assembly and see to their progress with the Talnoy.' He waited, and when she said nothing, he continued, 'Bek because . . . something tells me he is important; and Nakor because he is the only one who can control Bek. Besides, if anyone can get us out of an impossible situation it's Nakor.'

Miranda said, 'You've planned this all out, so I suppose there's no point in continuing to argue about it. I'm not even sure you can find a safe means to visit the second plane.'

'Still, we must try.'

'When do you leave?' asked Miranda.

'For the Hall? Tomorrow. I still need to do a few things around here before I go.' To Magnus he said, 'Why don't you see how the boys are doing in Roldem, then be back here in a day or so to let your brother's wife know how her boys are?'

Magnus nodded. 'What about the Talnoy down in Novindus?'

Pug paused at the door of the study. 'Rosenvar and Jacob will keep an eye on things. If anything out of the ordinary occurs, Nakor or myself can be back here quickly enough. It'll be some time before we leave for the Dasati world. I am going to make one more quick trip to Kelewan and see if there's any hint of Varen's presence there.'

'You think he'll be foolish enough to reveal himself?' asked Magnus.

'He's a clever man,' said Pug. 'Brilliant in a twisted fashion, but he's also driven. His madness has made him more impulsive over the years. The duration between his attacks lessens each time. He will either do something rash over there, or he will return to Midkemia. Either way, eventually we will find him out, and this time he has no easy way to seize a new body.'

'What about a hard way?' asked Miranda.

'What do you mean?'

'You said he has no easy way to take over a new body. I understand that, since you destroyed his soul jar, but he still has the knowledge of how to inhabit another's body, and might there not be other means, perhaps less convenient, but equally effective?'

Pug said, 'I hadn't thought of that.'

Miranda could barely constrain her smug expression.

'Then we must be both meticulous and stealthy,' said Pug, ignoring his wife's superior expression. 'I shall make enquiries of some less than high-born sources in Kelewan, while you see what you can find out in the Assembly while I travel to the Hall. Trust only Alenca.'

'How can I trust anyone?' asked Miranda. 'After taking possession of the Emperor of Kesh, I think it safe to argue that Varen can be anyone on Kelewan, including their Emperor.'

'I think not,' said Pug. 'Consider how he placed his soul jar in the sewers near the Emperor's palace. I suspect location has much to do with who he can reach. In any event, without the jar, I think he had to leap blind and inhabited the body of whoever was closest. As his "death rift" acted in many ways like normal rifts, I would expect it propelled him to a point near the Assembly, if not within its halls. As he would have been a disembodied spirit, the Assembly's usual defences would have been useless – that's the reason, by the way, I think it unlikely he would ever be able to occupy a high level cleric on either world; wards against spirits are common in temples.'

'Very well,' said Miranda. 'I'll speak with Alenca when I go. Now, one more question.'

'Yes?' said Pug, obviously impatient to be underway.

'If you're going to visit Kelewan without the Assembly being aware, just how do you propose to go through the rift without being noticed?'

Pug smiled, and years seemed to fall away from him. 'A trick, as Nakor would call it.'

He left the room and Magnus started laughing at the consternation on his mother's face.

Miranda glared at her older son. 'That annoying little man is such a bad influence around here!'

Magnus laughed even harder.

Pug crept down a side street, his face hidden beneath a deep hood. Beards were rare in the Tsurani Empire among freemen, being worn for the most part by those of Midkemian birth and a few rebellious youths. Being out late at night and sporting facial hair was likely to mean being stopped by any patrolling city watch, and while his rank as a member of the Assembly of Magicians meant instant obedience from any soldier or constable, Pug wished to avoid drawing attention to his clandestine visit.

The domicile he sought was modest, off a side

street in a section of the city of Jamar that was only a slight improvement over the slums and docks. The houses here were modest, the whitewash traditional to the Tsurani home kept somewhat clean, and the streets not too littered with refuse. There was even a street lamp some way behind him.

Pug reached the desired house and knocked loudly on the wooden door. From within a voice said, 'Come in, Milamber.'

Pug pushed his way into the small house, which was barely more than a one-room hut, and said, 'Greetings, Sinboya.'

The old man sat on a rush mat on the floor behind a small, low table upon which rested a single lamp, its flame barely illuminating the room. A small wood stove in the corner provided heat for cooking – the weather in the Empire rarely got cold enough for anyone to worry about heating the house. A curtain sectioned off a sleeping pallet, and a rear door led to what Pug knew to be a small vegetable garden and an outhouse.

The old man behind the table was rake-thin, looking every minute of his eighty-plus years of age. His wispy hair was white and his blue eyes were covered with film, yet Pug knew his wits were as sharp as they had been thirty years before when they had first met.

'You knew I was coming?' asked Pug.

'I may lack your prodigious powers, Milamber,' he said, using Pug's Tsurani name, 'but I am a master of my craft, and my spells of warding are second to none. I can detect the approach of friends as well as enemies.' There were two porcelain cups on the table and he poured hot water out of a precious metal pot. 'Chocha?'

'Thank you,' replied Pug.

'Then sit, please.'

Pug sat upon the floor, arranging his travel clothing, a nondescript light blue robe, over which a hooded cloak had been thrown.

The old man's eyesight was failing, but he was still alert enough to take notice of Pug's manner of dress. 'Travelling incognito?'

'I do not wish others of the Assembly to know I'm here,' Pug replied.

The wizened magician chuckled. 'You have a colourful history with the Assembly. I believe you were even once cast out and branded as a traitor to the Empire.'

'Nothing quite that extreme, but there is a matter of grave concern that places me at a disadvantage with the Assembly; in short, I can't trust any member of it.'

'What can I do to help you, old friend?'

'There is now loose within the Empire a fugitive from my world, a magician of exceptional cunning and danger, and he may be impossible to find.'

'Already you paint a grave picture,' said Sinboya. 'If *you* can't find him, he will be very difficult to find, indeed.'

Pug nodded, taking a sip of his hot drink. The

four years he had abided with the Assembly, being trained as a Great One of the Empire, had given him a fondness for the bitter brew, which tasted like nothing so much as a very bitter tea found in Novindus. 'He has the power to possess another's body and it will be hard even for those closest to the host to detect him.'

'Ah, a possessor. I have heard tales of such, but so often such tales are nothing more than that: stories without any truth.' Sinboya was a magician of the Lesser Path, much like Pug's first teacher, Kulgan, a magic that Pug was never suited for by temperament until much later in his education. Pug was conversant in all forms of magic, but unlike Sinboya he was not a specialist in this area. 'I assume this visit, then, is not so much for the pleasure of my company, but for what device or trinket I can fashion for you?'

'I apologize for my failure to stay in touch.'

'Not necessary. If half of what I hear about you through rumour is true, you are a man in need of twice the hours in the day.'

Pug said, 'I need something to detect necromancy.'

The old magician sat quietly for a moment. 'It is forbidden, as you know.'

'I know that, but some men are driven by more than the fear of being discovered.'

'It is true that the lure of the dark arts can be powerful. Animation and control of the dead, the use of others' life energies, and the creation of false life are abominations in the eyes of every temple; and magicians at the time of the Assembly's founding feared such men.' The old man chuckled. 'You'll never hear a Tsurani Great One admit this, but those of my "lesser" calling can reach levels of power terrible to contemplate. It takes time to learn either path, but the Greater Path is the quicker path to power. What few know is that the Lesser Path is the slower path to greater power. I can create devices, given enough time and materials, that can do things none of the Greater Path – with you being the possible exception, Milamber – can duplicate. Give me what I need, and I can build a box that will hold great storms until opened, or a flute that can command obedience in a thousand animals at once. There are many things we of the Lesser Path can accomplish that are often overlooked by the Assembly.

'What do you wish this device to do?'

'I need something that will identify any significant manifestation of necromancy, say the seizing of a soul or the animation of the dead.'

The old man was silent for a few minutes, then he said, 'Difficult. These are subtle manifestations to detect if you're talking about a single life taken, or a single body animated.'

'Can it be done?'

Sinboya was contemplative. At last he said, 'Of course it can, but it will take time and I will need help.'

Pug stood. 'I will have someone contact you

within a day, and he will provide you with every-thing you need. Set your price for the work, and you will be rewarded, as well.

'The man I seek may be the herald of the gravest danger the Empire has encountered in its long history.'

The old man chuckled. 'No disrespect, my old friend, but there have been many grave dangers in our history.'

Pug leaned closer. 'This I know, for we of the Greater Path study the Empire's history as part of our training. I do not exaggerate this, Sinboya. This may be the unleashing of the Eater of Souls.'

The old man sat silently as his guest left. The Eater of Souls was a being of extraordinary power, one of the foundation myths of Tsurani religion. It was written in the temples that in the last days, before the destruction of the world of Kelewan, a being known as the Eater of Souls would appear and begin to harvest the unworthy before the gods unleashed their final war in the heavens.

As the door closed behind Pug, Sinboya felt an unexpected need to visit the temple of Chochocan, the Good God, to say a prayer and make a votive offering, an impulse he had not experienced in fifty years.

As Pug left Sinboya's modest home, he felt a strange sense of familiarity, a sort of deja vu. He hesitated, looked quickly about, and after seeing nothing amiss in the darkness, hurried along.

He had cast a rift from a deserted spot on Sorcerer's Island to a place he knew near the City of the Plains, where the original Tsurani rift into Midkemia had existed, almost a century past. He had then employed a trick he had mastered in reaching the Eldar under the polar ice cap of Kelewan years before: simply transporting himself by line-of-sight, a method which was occasionally tedious, but ultimately effective.

He needed no such trick to return to the world of Midkemia, only a deserted place where he might depart undetected. He moved quickly along the dark street, looking for an alley into which to disappear.

From around the corner, a figure emerged from deep shadow, watching as Pug vanished from sight. The stocky man in the black robe waited for a minute, then sighed. 'What were you doing in that little house, Pug?' he muttered under his breath. 'Well, best go find out, hadn't I?' The man walked purposefully, using a large staff to bear a little of his weight when he stepped forward with his right leg. He had hurt his knee a while back, and found the walking staff a comfort.

Without knocking, he pushed open the door and stepped inside.

CHAPTER 6

HONEST JOHN'S

Pug retreated.

He could see the caravan wending its way along the Hall of Worlds and knew from experience that anything was possible here. The Hall was the great thoroughfare between worlds, a place where a mortal man could walk between planets if he knew the way and possessed the necessary skills, or power, to survive. He glanced at the doors nearest his position, but none offered a convenient place into which he could vanish. Two led into worlds he knew were inimical to human existence, with poisonous atmospheres and crushing gravity, and the other two led to very public places of disembarkation. Unfortunately he lacked the means to anticipate local time for places where appearing in the public square at noon was a bad idea.

He had no choice but to stand his ground, for advance guards had already espied him and were hurrying forward, weapons drawn, in case he was some sort of threat – which he would be should they give him cause.

The guards were human, or at least appeared to

be from a distance, and they came to a position about half-way between the lead wagon – pulled by something that looked somewhat like a purple needra, the six-legged beast of burden familiar to Pug from his years on Kelewan. Four guards were dressed in plain grey uniforms, with small turbans of the same colour, their only armour golden-coloured chest-plates. They bore black shields and wicked-looking scimitars. Two of the guards carried some sort of projectile weapon, Pug judged, for they pointed long cylindrical tubes mounted on shoulder stocks at him.

Pug stood his ground.

After a moment in which neither side made a move, a short man dressed in light blue robes and a white turban came forward and stood behind the guards. He looked at Pug then called out a question.

Pug did not understand the language. The Hall of Worlds apparently gave access to and from every planet in the universe, or at least that was the theory. No one had ever found the end of the Hall and news of new worlds being found was constantly filtering back to Honest John's, Pug's intended destination. As a result, denizens of hundreds of thousands of nations could be encountered, all speaking different languages.

There were basically three types of individual one encountered in the Hall of Worlds, denizens, sojourners, and the lost. The last were hapless souls who had somehow blundered into an entrance to the Hall on their homeworlds, lacking any knowledge of what had happened to them, or how to return. Often they were victims for the more predatory inhabitants of the Hall. Most who travelled the Hall were, like Pug, sojourners: merely using it as a means of quick access across a vast distance. But an entire culture had arisen in the Hall formed by those who chose to live in it. These were not just humans but all manner of intelligent species, and they had developed, if not rules, then conventions.

One of these conventions was the Trading Tongue. Pug spoke that language with some skill and he answered in that: 'Could you repeat your question, please?'

The little man glanced back at a figure sitting on top of the first wagon, then returned his attention to Pug. 'I asked,' he began in the Trading Tongue, 'where are you going?'

Pug pointed ahead. 'That way.'

The little man looked perplexed, then said, 'Where are you from?'

Pug pointed back over his left shoulder with his right hand. 'That way.'

'What is your business?' demanded the little man.

Pug was growing weary of the exchange. He was only five doorways away from the closest entrance to Honest John's and he was impatient to be on his way. Trying his best to hide his annoyance, he answered, 'My own.'

'You walk the Halls alone, yet I see no weapons. You are either a man of great power or a fool.'

Pug stepped forward, and the guards' weapons rose slightly. 'I have no need of weapons. Now, do you intend to bar my passage?'

'My master seeks only to ensure we move amongst one another with the least amount of difficulty,' answered the little man with a toothy grin.

Pug nodded. Sweeping his hand across his chest he said, 'Then go that way, and I shall go this way.'

'How are we to know you will not turn and attack us once we've let you pass?'

Pug let out a breath of exasperation. 'That's enough.' He waved his hand and a ripple that was visible in the air swept forward, knocking the six guards and the little man over. He started to walk past when one of the guards leapt to his feet, drew back his sword and struck downward. Pug raised his hand and the sword struck an invisible barrier that sent a shock up the guard's arm as if he had struck a bar of iron.

One of the men holding the tube device pointed it and released a mechanism, sending a rapidly expanding net at Pug. He had expected a missile of some type and the netting caught him by surprise. Suddenly entangled, he had to pause long enough for other guards to reach him. He closed his eyes and used the transporting skill Miranda had taught him, coupled with what he had learned years before from the Tsurani Great Ones, and picked a place on the floor a dozen paces farther along the Hall. One moment he was entangled in the net with a half-dozen guards attempting to pull him to the ground, and the next he stood twelve paces away looking at the confusion.

Pug turned to the obvious master of the caravan, a richly-dressed fat man sitting atop the lead wagon who blinked in astonishment as Pug walked towards him, and said, 'If you would rather I reduce you to smoking ash, I can do that.'

'No!' shouted the man, holding up his hands in supplication. 'Do us no harm, stranger!'

'Do you no harm?' asked Pug in an exasperated tone. 'I'm just trying to walk that way.' He pointed. 'What's the boggle?'

Seeing that the robed man was not continuing the attack, the caravan master lowered his hands and said, 'My agent acted, perhaps, in haste. He shall be rebuked. He sought, perhaps, another item of merchandise, thinking you, perhaps, of some value.'

Dryly, Pug said, 'Perhaps.' He looked down the length of the caravan, a dozen wagons and a line of individuals following them. 'You're a slaver?'

'Only in the sense, perhaps, you might say . . . yes.' He spread his hands palms up and then said, 'But it is a minor sideline, perhaps a source of some small income, but not my major trade.'

'And that would be?' asked Pug. He disliked slavers, having spent four years as a slave on the

Tsurani world before his magical ability had been detected. But there was an unwritten law in the Hall that you troubled no man's trade without cause. Granted he had been attacked, but from any slaver espying an unaccompanied individual in the Hall, it was only to be expected.

The man said, 'I deal in items of rare antiquity, unique magical devices, and holy relics. Perhaps you are seeking something of the sort?'

'Some other time. I must be off,' said Pug. He looked at the fat trader consideringly. 'But you might be able to sell me some information.'

Putting his right hand over his heart, the man smiled, bowed, and said, 'Perhaps.'

'Have you traded with anyone who knew the way to the second plane?'

The man's face became a mask of confusion. 'Perhaps I do not speak the Trading Tongue adeptly enough, stranger. The second plane?'

'The second circle. The second realm. That which lies below?'

The man's eyes widened. 'You are mad, but if such a one exists, seek him at John's Without Reproach. Ask for Vordam of the Ipiliac.'

Pug bowed slightly. 'I was going to John, but thank you for the name.'

'Perhaps we shall meet again . . .?'

'Pug of Midkemia. Also called Milamber of Kelewan.'

'I am Tosan Beada. Of the Dubengee. Perhaps you've heard of me?'

'Sorry,' said Pug, as he resumed his walk. 'Good trading, Tosan Beada of the Dubengee.'

'Good travelling, Pug of Midkemia also called Milamber of Kelewan,' answered the trader.

Pug gave scant attention to the wagons and forced himself to ignore the slaves. At least fifty were chained together in a coffle, looking universally miserable. Most were human, and the rest were sufficiently human-like to be able to move as one with the humans as they marched. Pug could have freed them, but at what cost to his scant time? And what would he do with them? Most would have only the local name for their world, and the chances were good that none would have even the remotest idea of where their home-world's door would be found. Pug had learned a long time ago that when entering the Hall, it was best to leave all ethical and moral imperatives at home.

Pug easily reached the nearby entrance to Honest John's. He hesitated for an instant, for no matter how many times before he had done this, stepping off the Hall floor between doors always gave him a second of near-panic. He recognized the glyphs above the doors on either side and knew he was in the right location. Still, no one knew what happened if one stepped off between doors – no one had ever done so and returned to talk about it. He ignored the sudden twinge in his stomach and stepped down, as if descending a staircase.

Suddenly he was in an entryway, a small room with a false door behind it. He knew the door was only painted on the wall, but it served to reassure a certain percentage of the clientele at Honest John's.

A large creature, around nine feet in height, looked down at him with enormous blue eyes. It was covered in white fur and bore a slight resemblance to an ape, save for the face which was more canine in a appearance than anything else. Black patches on the fur would have given the creature an almost jolly appearance, if it wasn't for its huge claws and teeth . . . 'Weapons?' asked the Coropaban.

'One,' said Pug, producing the dagger he had secreted in his robe. He handed it over and the creature motioned for Pug to enter. Pug stepped into Honest John's.

The saloon was immense: more than two hundred yards across, and a quarter mile deep. Along the right wall ran a single bar, with a score of barmen. A pair of galleries, one above the other, overhung the other three sides of the hall. The galleries were cluttered with tables and chairs, offering vantage points from which those above could gaze down upon the main floor.

There, every imaginable game of chance was underway, from cards to dice to games involving wheels and numbers; there was even a small sandpit for athletic contests and duels. The customers were of every race and species Pug had ever encountered, and any number that were new to him. Most were bipedal, though a few had more limbs than usual, including one creature that looked oddly like a man-sized, skinny dragon with human hands at the end of its wing-tips. The serving staff hurried though the throng bearing trays covered with a variety of pots, platters, cups, buckets, and bowls.

Pug wended his way through the press and found the inn's proprietor at his usual table. John of Unquestioned Ethics, as he was known on the world of Cynosure, sat at a table by the near end of the bar which provided him with an excellent view of the entrance. Seeing Pug approach, John stood up. His face was unremarkable: brown eyes, an average nose, and a gambler's smile. He was wearing a suit of shining black cloth. The trousers broke without cuffs at the top of shiny black boots with pointed toes. The jacket was open at the front, revealing a white shirt with ruffles, closed by pearl studs and sporting a pointed collar, set off by a purple cravat. This ensemble was topped by a wide-brimmed white hat with a shimmering red silk hatband.

He extended his hand. 'Pug! Always a pleasure.' He glanced past him, 'Miranda not with you?' They shook hands and he indicated that Pug should take the seat opposite him.

'No,' said Pug, taking the seat offered. 'She has other business occupying her at the moment.'

'It's been a while.'

'As always,' said Pug, sharing the joke. Time

didn't pass in Honest John's. Those who resided in the Hall were somehow spared the ravages of time's passage. In this place without days, weeks, months or years, time was measured in hours, one passing after another, endlessly. Pug wagered that John had the means to tell him exactly how long it had been since Pug's last visit, but he suspected it had nothing to do with the man's memory.

'It's not that I'm unhappy to see you again, but I suspect there's a purpose to your visit. How may I be of service?'

'I seek a guide.'

John nodded. 'There are any number of competent guides in my establishment as we speak, and a far greater number who could be here swiftly if I summon them, but which is appropriate to your needs is determined by one question: where do you want to go?'

'The Dasati homeworld, in the Second Realm,' Pug said.

John was a man of ageless experience. He had heard almost everything imaginable during his years in the Hall. For the first time, he sat speechless.

Miranda walked slowly beside an elderly man in a black robe through the garden on the south side of the great Tsurani Assembly of Magicians. It was a beautiful afternoon with a light breeze coming down from the distant mountains to the north, tempering the usually hot Tsurani day.

The massive Assembly building rose up to

119

dominate the island, but the shore across the lake had been left untouched and provided a soothing vista for Miranda's troubled mind. She hated it when Pug was absent.

The elderly magician said, 'As happy as I am to see you, Miranda, you'll understand that many of my brethren are still . . .'

'Old-fashioned?'

'I was going to say "traditionalists".'

'In other words they dislike taking advice from a woman.'

'Something like that,' said Alenca, the most senior member of the Assembly of Magicians. 'We Tsurani have endured a lot of change in the last century starting, coincidentally, with our first encounter with your homeworld; and yet more thrust upon us by your husband, but we are still a hidebound bunch.' The old man's face was a collection of crags and ridges, lines and age spots, and only the wispiest echo of white hair graced his pate, but his eyes were a vivid blue and sparkled when he talked. Miranda liked him a great deal.

'This business with the Talnoy has become something of a bone of contention between various groups among us, and word of it has made it all the way to the Imperial Throne in the Holy City.'

'Someone's tattled to the Emperor?' Miranda raised an eyebrow.

The old magician waved a dismissive hand. 'With something as potentially dangerous as the Talnoy on this island, you didn't think it was going to remain a secret from the Emperor for long, did you? Remember, our first mandate is still to serve the Empire.'

Miranda looked out across the garden at the still waters of the lake. 'I am not surprised, really. My reason for being here is to see if you've made any progress.'

'I assume then that Milamber and Magnus are away on some business that prevents them from coming themselves?'

Dryly, Miranda said, 'You forgot to mention Nakor.'

The old man laughed. 'That fellow amuses me no end.' He took a deep breath. 'I believe he may know more about the Greater Art than I do, though he insists there is no such thing as magic and we all do . . . tricks.'

'Nakor is a constant source of amusement, yes, but let us go back to the topic at hand: has the Emperor made any comment about the Talnoy?'

'Other than wanting it gone from our world, no.'

Miranda crossed her arms even though the breeze off the lake was warm. 'Has he made that a command?'

'Had it been, the Talnoy would have been returned to you already,' said Alenca. He rubbed his hands together as if in anticipation of a task. 'Many of our brethren are convinced we are at an impasse, and the rising occurrences of random rifts are a cause for concern. One of us is already dead as a result of one.'

Miranda nodded. 'Pug told me: Macalathana. But I don't know what happened.'

'Some little creature or another came through and, as I understand it, exploded! If you can believe that.'

'I can believe a lot.'

'Wyntakata, who was with him, was so distraught that he retired to his estates in Ambolena for nearly a month before returning to us.' Lowering his voice, Alenca added, 'He hasn't seemed quite right since then, if you ask me.'

'Is the Assembly going to request we remove the Talnoy?'

'If you can't work out a way to stop these damned rifts, yes,' said Alenca.

Miranda was silent for a moment. She had only visited Kelewan and had no particular affection for it: the men were too stiff-necked in their attitude towards women – especially those who wielded magic – the weather was always too hot, and the cities were too crowded. She gazed out across the lake to the distant shore and majestic peaks of mountains – the High Wall – beyond. On the other hand, she had to admit that the landscape was magnificent. After a long moment of contemplation, she asked, 'How long was the Talnoy here before the reports of rifts began to reach you?'

'Why, several months, I believe.'

'Then we should take the Talnoy back to Sorcerer's Isle,' said Miranda.

'Why?' asked Alenca.

'Because the rifts are either following the Talnoy to this world for some natural reason; or some intelligence is manipulating it. If there is some intelligence behind it, it may take months for it to find the Talnoy back on Midkemia.' She looked at Alenca. 'I wonder if we might just drop it on some uninhabited world Pug knows of, and study it there.'

Since this seemed to be a rhetorical question, Alenca did not comment.

'You said one of your members was destroyed by a creature exploding. Pug was vague on the details; what can you tell me?'

From behind them a voice spoke. 'Better I tell you, Miranda.'

Miranda turned to see a stocky man in a black robe, carrying a staff – which was unusual for a Tsurani Great One – approaching across the garden. He had obviously overheard some of the conversation as he neared. Miranda didn't recognize him, but the man said, 'It is good to see you.'

'Have we met?' she asked. She was not in the habit of using the honorific 'Great One', as was common in this society, since she was also a magic user of great skill.

The man hesitated only for a second; then he smiled. He wore his grey-shot black hair unusually long, almost to his shoulders, and his face was cleanly shaven in the Tsurani fashion. 'No, I believe we have not, but your reputation precedes you. Perhaps it would have been better if I had said, "It is good to meet you".' He inclined his head, slightly, in deference. 'I am Wyntakata. I was witness to Macalathana's death.'

'I would count it a courtesy if you would tell me what happened,' said Miranda.

'We received a report of a rift sighted by a needra herder a half-day's journey to the north-east of the city of Jamar, in the centre of the great grasslands of Hokani Province. We arrived and found a rift no larger than two hands' span floating perhaps a half-hand's span above the ground. A small creature stood motionless in front of it. I advised caution but Macalathana was impatient to examine it; I suppose he judged it posed little threat because of its size.

'As he reached a point before the creature, it erupted in a powerful blast of light and flames, incinerating a fair amount of grass around him. The rift was gone. I returned at once to the Assembly with the grave news and others returned to collect Macalathana's body.'

Miranda asked, 'Did you get any opportunity to study the creature?'

'No, I'm sorry to say. I saw it only for a few moments, just enough to see that it was tiny, stood on two legs and did not wear garments or carry artefacts. It could perhaps have been some sort of wild creature that blundered through the rift from the other side.'

'That is our current thinking,' said Alenca.

124

'Unless these Dasati beings tend to explore in the nude,' he added with a chuckle.

'We have very little information about them,' Miranda said ignoring the old magician's chuckle. 'But I think that's highly unlikely.' To Wyntakata, she said, 'Alenca and I were just discussing the possibility of removing the Talnoy back to Sorcerer's Island.'

'Oh, that is premature,' said Wyntakata.

'Really?' asked Miranda.

'We've had some reports of rifts, true, but I have personally undertaken to investigate as many of the reported sightings as anyone here—'

'That is true,' Alenca interjected.

'—and I can say with some certainty that most reports have been inaccurate – sightings of things no more magic than weather disturbances or a child's kite! The one additional rift I did manage to find was only the size of my fist, and it endured only for a few minutes once I arrived.

'I am convinced these small rifts are natural by-products of the Talnoy being here and that there is neither intelligence behind them nor that they are being utilized by any agency seeking the way to Kelewan. I think we may soon be able to tell you a great deal more about this Talnoy and to curtail our investigation now would be a great waste of the time already invested.'

'I'll relay that to my husband,' said Miranda. Smiling at Wyntakata, she said, 'I must bid you good day, and return to my home.' To Alenca she said, 'Would you mind escorting me to the rift?'

The old man inclined his head, and Wyntakata hesitated a moment before bowing slightly and departing in another direction. As they left the garden, Miranda asked, 'Wyntakata has, to my ear at least, a somewhat strange accent.'

'His childhood was spent in Dustari Province, across the Sea of Blood. They tend to crush certain vowels when they talk, don't they?'

Miranda smiled. 'I have another question.'

'What, my dear?'

'Have you come across any rumours of anyone practising necromancy in any part of the Empire?'

The old magician's step faltered. 'Why, that's forbidden! It's the one practice that even in the old times, when our word was as law, could bring a Great One down. Any hint of it meant a death sentence.' He turned to look at Miranda as they walked. 'Why?'

'Pug has reason to suspect that you may have one come recently to the Empire from our world, a necromancer of vast power. He's a grave threat, and he may be hiding anywhere. But his nature is such that he can not overlong avoid the practice.'

'I'll ask around.'

'I would prefer it if you didn't,' said Miranda. 'Pug is concerned for many reasons, which I will leave for him to recount another time. But he trusts you, and you alone. And the one thing you need to know is that this person – Leso Varen – has the power to occupy the body of anyone. We do not understand the mechanism by which he does this, save it involves necromancy and requires a great many deaths, the more hideous the better for his dark arts to work. We think he may be trapped here. If so, we must hunt him down and finally put an end to him.'

'You think he might be here?' Alenca looked around, as if suddenly fearing that someone might be watching them.

Suddenly Miranda realized she had made an error. 'Perhaps not. His choice of people to possess appears to be haphazard, but he last masqueraded as a man of great power. I only ask that you keep this concern quiet until Pug returns to speak with you at length. Will you?'

'Of course,' he answered as they entered the massive main building of the Academy. 'We shall continue our work on the Talnoy – and please tell Nakor when you see him next that I'm still waiting for that idea of his about how to control this thing without the madness-inducing ring.' He patted her arm and whispered theatrically, 'I'll let you know if I hear any rumours . . . about the other thing.'

Miranda allowed the familiarity. She wasn't overly fond of Tsurani Great Ones, but she made an exception for Alenca.

They entered the room set aside for the rift to Midkemia – Pug had adjusted the Tsurani rift machine so that it could now pick any of half a dozen Midkemian destinations, not just Stardock any more. She chose Sorcerer's Island and the two magicians who were detailed to operate the device quickly made the incantation.

Miranda sighed. Just a few short years ago, as she counted such things, rift magic had been largely unknown. The study her husband had conducted for the four years he lived in this very Assembly, as well as work he'd done in the decades since, had reduced her astonishment to that of hailing a public carriage in Roldem for a ride from the docks to the River House.

As she stepped into the rift, she thought it really wasn't surprising: she had rather more sense of wonder left to her in contemplating an invading horde of warriors from the second circle of hell.

Pug walked along the upper gallery of Honest John's, seeking out the merchant whose name he had been given. John had confessed he had no idea who might be able to breach an entrance into the Second Realm, as Pug had come to think of that circle of reality, but he suggested there might be someone who might know someone who in turn might know someone and so forth . . .

The merchant was named Vordam of the Ipiliac, a Delecordian, the trader mentioned by Tosan Beada. Pug knew Delecordia solely by reputation. The only remarkable thing about that world was its location. It was as far from Honest John's as any civilized world, and as such had contact with even more remote worlds and races that had as yet not become commonplace in the Hall.

Pug found Vordam's place of business, and as soon as he stepped across the threshold into the modest shop he knew something was amiss.

Pug had visited two places in the universe that were in it, but not a part of it. The first was the City Forever, a legendary place built by no one knew who, which was vast to the point of seeming limitlessness; and the Garden, which was linked to the City without being part of it. The other was the Hall, and by extension, Honest John's.

This shop was another, for while it was located within Honest John's, it also was somewhere else. No sooner had Pug assimilated these impressions than a being came into the shop from a curtained door at the rear. He seemed to speak, but Pug realized this also was something illusory, for there were no words, merely the impression of words.

Magic was a rare thing in Honest John's: there was too much potential for mischief if magic was left unchecked. There were wards throughout every part of the establishment to prevent the casual use of magic. This kept the games of chance honest, the negotiations among merchants above-board, and bloodshed to a minimum. The exceptions were spells contrived by John, or others on his behalf: one to let all denizens of the establishment understand one another (although there were always a few of the more alien guests whose frames of reference were so different from the mainstream of sentient beings that only fundamental or rudimentary comprehension was possible). Another spell provided a hospitable environment for everyone, despite a diversity of races that counted a wide range of conditions desirable. The last was a defensive spell that would, Pug imagined, unleash breathtaking damage on anyone attempting to harm John or any of his staff. An occasional brawl might erupt, but no serious conflict had occurred in the Hall in the memory of the oldest living customer.

But there was something magical about this shop, something beyond Pug's experience, and his experience was far from limited. The creature repeated his interrogative, and Pug nodded. 'A moment, please,' he said. The being was human in general appearance. It was taller than most and more slender, with arms and legs that were a bit longer than one would expect on a human. The face comprised a single mouth, a nose above, and two eyes; but the cheekbones were exaggerated compared to any human Pug had encountered; and the creature had excessively long fingers. There was a faint greyish-purple hue to its skin and its hair was a luxurious black with a violet sheen.

Pug sent his senses quickly outwards, extending them like a mystic vine that touched the vibration of the room, sensing the difference between it and the rest of Honest John's. For a moment it was oddly familiar. Pug struggled to recognize it, then suddenly he remembered: it echoed the traps set for Tomas and him, decades ago, as they searched for Macros the Black.

Pug stared at the merchant. 'I seek Vordam of the Ipiliac.'

The creature, dressed in a plain grey robe with a single white cord around its waist, pressed its hand to its chest, bowed slightly and said, 'I am he.'

Pug was silent for a moment as he drank in the harmonics of the vibrations he felt running through every inch of this shop. At last he understood. He fixed Vordam in his gaze and said, 'You are Dasati!'

CHAPTER 7

DEATHKNIGHT

The sword slashed downward.

Fifty armoured Riders of the Sadharin shouted and beat steel gauntlets on their breast plates. The roar echoed off the vaulted ceiling of the ancient stone Hall of Testing, and the wooden seats surrounding the sandy floor shook from the demonstration.

Lord Aruke's only surviving son looked down at the man he had just killed, and for an instant was visited by an alien thought, *What a waste*. He closed his eyes for a moment to clear his thoughts, then turned slowly to acknowledge the cheers.

Valko of the Camareen, nursing three serious cuts and an uncountable number of bruises and minor scrapes, nodded four times, once to each group of the gathered riders seated above him along each of the four walls. Then he looked down at the fighter he had killed and nodded again; a ritual recognition of a fierce struggle. It had been a close thing.

Valko spared a quick glance at the father of the slain warrior, and saw that he was cheering, but without conviction. Lord Kesko's second son lay at Valko's feet: had the boy prevailed, two living sons would have earned Kesko great honour and a higher place in the Langradin. Kesko's only acknowledged son stood next to his father, and his celebration was sincere; Valko had eradicated a possible claimant to his father's favour. Then Valko turned to see two lackeys putting down his varnin, a neutered male he had named Kodesko, after the great crashing surf at the Point of Sandos in the westernmost holdings of his father, where Sandos jutted into the Heplan Sea. His opponent's varnin had died during the fight, when Valko had cut deep and severed its neck artery. That blow had given Valko the match, for the faltering varnin had distracted the rider's attention for the brief moment it had taken for Valko to inflict the wound that had finally proved the difference.

A healer from the Hall of Attenders – a First Rank Master – hurried over with his assistants, and began to treat Valko's wounds. Valko knew he'd lose consciousness soon from blood loss if they didn't staunch the flow, but rather than show weakness before his father and the assembled Riders of the Sadharin, he pushed aside the Attender, and turned to his father. Removing the massive black steel helm, he took a deep breath and shouted, 'I am Valko, son of Aruke of the House of Camareen!' It took all his strength to raise his sword above his head with his right arm, cut as it was below the shoulder, but he managed to produce an acceptable salute before he let the blade fall to his side.

His father, Lord of the Camareen, stood and pointed at his son, then slammed his gloved fist against his own armoured chest. 'This is my son!' he cried loud enough for the assembly to hear it.

Again the Riders shouted their approval, a short, deep 'ha! and then as one they turned and bowed to their host. Valko knew that a few of the most trusted among them would stay to dine with Aruke and his household, but the others would be on their way back to their own strongholds, rather than risk being caught on the road by rivals or outlaws.

As his mind began to wander, Valko focused long enough to shout, 'Lord Kesko. This *thing* could be no son of yours!'

Lord Kesko bowed to the compliment paid him by the victor. He would be the first to leave Castle Camareen, for while there was no shame in having a would-be son killed in combat, it was also nothing to cause rejoicing.

The Master Attender whispered, 'Bravely done, young lord, but should we not strip away your armour, you'll soon lie next to the one you killed on the rendering table.' Without waiting for permission, he instructed his assistants and the leather straps and buckles were quickly unfastened and the armour removed.

It didn't escape Valko's notice that while doing so, the Attenders were providing him subtle support, so that he could remain on his feet as his father slowly made his way through the riders who lingered to offer further congratulations. The young warrior was tall by the measure of his race – a full half-head taller than his father, who stood a full four inches taller than six feet. His young body was powerfully muscled and his arms were long, providing him with a deadly reach with a sword, one he had put to good use against the smaller opponent. He was by the standard of his race a fair-looking man, for his long nose was straight and not too wide, and his lips were full without looking feminine.

Aruke stopped before him and said, 'Sixteen times before you claimants to my house's name have come. You are only the third to survive the blade challenge. The first was Jastmon, who died at the battle of Trikamaga; the second was Dusta, who died defending this very keep eleven years ago. I am pleased to name you their brother.'

Valko looked directly into the eyes of his father, a man he had never laid eyes on until one week ago this day. 'I honour their memory,' said Valko.

Aruke said, 'We will have quarters prepared for you, near my own. As from tomorrow you will begin your training as my heir. Until then rest . . . my son.'

'Thank you, Father.' Valko studied the man's face and could see nothing in it that reminded him of his own. While Valko's face was long and unlined, noble by the standards of his people, his father's face was round and creased with age lines and a strange mottling of spots on the left of his brow. Could his mother have lied to him?

As if reading his thoughts, Aruke said, 'What was your mother's name?'

'Narueen, a Cisteen Effector assigned to Lord Bekar's demesne.'

Aruke was silent for a moment, then he nodded. 'I remember her. I took her for a week while guesting at Bekar's keep.' He glanced down at Valko, who was clothed only in a loincloth while the Attenders cleaned and dressed his wounds. 'She had a thin, but pleasing body. Your height must have come from her family. Does she still live?'

'No, she died in a purging four years ago.'

Aruke nodded once. Both men knew that anyone who was foolish enough to be outdoors at the first hint of a purging was weak and foolish, and no loss. Yet Aruke said, 'Unfortunate. She was not unpleasing, and this house could use a female's touch. Still, now that you're acknowledged, some ambitious father will seek to throw his daughters at you soon enough. We shall see what fortune provides.' Turning away, he added, 'Go and rest now. I will have you at my table tonight.'

Valko managed a slight bow as his father departed. To the Master Attender, he said, 'Quickly, now. Get me to my room. I'll not faint before the servants.'

'Yes, young lord,' answered the Master Attender,

and he signalled for his helpers to assist the new young lord of the Camareen to his quarters.

Valko awoke when a servant gently shook his bed cover, not daring to actually touch the young scion of Camareen. 'What?'

The servant bowed, 'Master, your father requests you join him at once.' He motioned to a chair upon which clothing had been draped. 'He bids you wear these garments, fitting of your new rank.'

Valko got out of bed, barely hiding a wince. He glanced to see if the servant had noticed his hint of weakness, and saw a blank expression. The man was young, perhaps a little older than Valko's seventeen years, but clearly he was very practised in his role as servant in a great house. 'What is your name?'

'Nolun, master.'

'I will need a body servant. You will do.'

Nolun almost grovelled when he bowed. 'I thank the young master for the honour, but the Reeve will assign a body servant to you, soon, master.'

'He already has,' said Valko. 'You will do.'

Again Nolun bowed. 'Honour you do me, master.'

'Lead me to my father's hall.'

The servant bowed, opened the door, let Valko move through it, then hurried ahead to guide him to the central hall of his father's keep. As a claimant to paternity, Valko had been taken straight to the 'poors', the quarters reserved for the powerless and those of low enough rank that offending them was unimportant: useful merchants, Attenders, entertainers and very minor relatives. Those rooms were little more than cold cells containing mattresses stuffed with straw and a single lantern.

Valko already missed his new bed, the softest upon which he had ever rested. In the years of Hiding, he had rarely slept on anything better than what he had found waiting for him in the poors.

As they rounded a corner, Valko hesitated, then said, 'Nolun, wait.'

The servant turned to see his new young master gazing out of a large window overlooking the Heplan Sea. Beyond the city of Camareen and its docks the water sparkled in the night, the energy of the motion giving rise to a play of colours across its surface the boy had never seen before. His mother had taken him into the mountains for the Hiding, and he had only glimpsed the ocean on his way to the city during the day. The size of this body of water had been impressive when seen from the peaks and passes of the Snow Wardens, as the mountains were called, but nothing had prepared him for the sheer beauty of the sea at night.

'What are those small bursts of colour, there, and there?' he asked, pointing.

Nolun replied, 'A fish called shagra, young lord. It leaps from the depths . . . for no reason anyone can ascertain, perhaps simply for the joy of it, and the leap disturbs the pattern of the ocean.'

'It is . . . impressive.' Valko had almost said beautiful, but it would have been unmanly to use such a word. He realized Nolun was regarding him. Shorter than Valko by more than a foot, he was a youth with a burly build: with a barrel-chest, thick neck and short, heavy fingers on huge hands. 'Do you fight?'

'When needed, young lord.'

'Are you good?'

For an instant something flashed behind the servant's eyes, then he lowered his head and said quietly, 'I still live.'

'Yes,' said Valko with a chuckle. 'You do. Now, to my father's hall.'

As they reached the great hall, two armoured guards saluted the new heir to the mantle of Camareen. Valko ignored the pain in his arm, shoulder and left thigh and strode across the hall to stand before his father. Aruke sat at the centre of a long table which was placed before a huge fireplace and. 'I am here, Father.'

Aruke motioned to an empty chair. 'This is your place, my son.'

Valko walked around the table, taking note of those already seated. Most were, by dress and badge, functionaries. To his father's left hand sat a beautiful woman, no doubt his current favourite. Gossip he had overheard the day before led Valko to believe his father's most recent companion before this one had vanished, almost certainly a Hiding.

Two other men Valko recognized, though he had no name for them; they were Riders of the Sadharin, Deathknights of the Order like his father. These would be trusted allies, bound by mutually beneficial alliances and trust, or they would have been gone from this hall long before the sun had set in the west.

Aruke said, 'Bid welcome to our guests, Lord Valin and Lord Sand.'

Valko said, 'Welcome to my father's guests,' and passed behind them to reach his seat. That neither man turned to watch his passing was an acknowledgement of trust. A servant pulled out the large wooden chair to the right of Lord Aruke and Valko sat down.

The Lord of the Camareen said, 'Sand and Valin are my closest allies. They are two of the three legs of power upon which rests the Sadharin.'

Valko nodded to acknowledge this.

Aruke waved a hand and servants hurried forward to load the table with their lord's bounty. A whole kapek, head and hooves intact, was carried in on a spit, sizzling fat cracking through the tough hide, and the two burly servants who bore its weight looked barely up to the task. As it was deposited on a large wooden platter in front of him Aruke said, 'Tonight is a good night. A weakling died and a strong man survived.'

The others at the table nodded and muttered words of agreement, but Valko said nothing. He breathed slowly and tried to keep his mind focused.

His body ached, the wounds throbbed, and his head pounded. He would just as soon have slept the night through, but he knew that his actions over this night and the few days that followed would be critical. Any misstep and he might just as easily find himself tossed off the battlements as being escorted to the Heir's Ceremony.

As the meal wore on, Valko found some of his strength returning. He partook only a little of the fine Tribian wine, wishing to keep his wits and not fall asleep at the table. From the course of conversation it could be a long night of story-telling.

He knew little about the company of warriors. Like most young males he had endured the first seventeen years of his life in the Hiding. His mother had prepared well, so he had no doubt she had planned on bearing the son of a powerful noble. His education had also shown her to be a woman of ambition, for Valko could read, do arithmetic, and understand things most warriors left to Effectors, Attenders, Mediators, Mongers, Facilitators and the other, lesser castes. She had made sure he was practised in all manner of study: history, language, and even the arts. She had driven home one thing above all: beyond the power of the sword arm lay the power of the mind, and more was needed to succeed than merely obeying the instincts of the race. His nature told him to be merciless with the weak, but his mother taught him there were uses even for the weak, and that by cultivating the weakest rather than destroying them, some measure of benefit could be discovered. She had said more than once that the TeKarana was supreme ruler of the Twelve Worlds for one reason alone: his ancestors had been smarter than everyone else's.

His mother had told him many stories of the great feats held in the great hall of Lord Bekar where she had been selected by his father to warm his bed. She had obeyed the strictures of the law, and had made clear to the visiting noble she was able to bear young, and in a cycle to conceive. She had ensured that her name was clearly given to at least three witnesses and had then joined him in his bed chamber.

Suddenly, the meal was over, and Valko realized he had fallen into a reverie. A quick glance at his father reassured him that he had not been detected. Drifting off in thought was dangerous; he might not hear something critical, and he might be thought inattentive.

Aruke rose and said, 'I am pleased tonight.'

This was as close as any warlord could come to giving thanks to anyone without revealing weakness. Lord Sand and Lord Valin stood and nodded to their host, and almost in unison said, 'It was my pleasure to be here.'

Quickly the hall emptied until Aruke and Valko were alone, save for a handful of servants. Seeing Nolun at Valko's elbow, the Lord of the Camareen asked, 'Are you claiming this one?'

Valko said, 'I claim him as my body servant.'

It was a very slight challenge, one which could serve as an excuse for a fight – and Valko knew that despite his youth his father was still powerful and had years of experience – but he was correct in assuming that his father was merely observing form; he would hardly kill a surviving son over such a trivial issue.

'Then I acknowledge the claim,' said Aruke. 'Come with me, and have your thing follow. I wish to speak with you of matters between fathers and sons.'

Aruke did not wait to see if he was obeyed; he assumed Valko would be a step behind him as he turned and walked from the table to a large wooden door in the left wall. It was highly polished and in the dim light, Valko could see that it pulsed with energy. It was an open warning: this door was magically warded and only certain people could open it without injury or death.

The lord of the castle put his hand on the door and it opened to his touch. 'Wait outside,' he instructed Nolun. He removed a torch from a nearby sconce and led Valko through the door.

Once through, Valko saw they were in a short hallway, at the end of which waited another door, also warded. Aruke said, as he opened the second door, 'It is foolish to hide the wards, for I am not setting traps, and the spellmongers demand ridiculous prices for such niceties.'

At the mention of spellmongers Valko felt a

familiar tightening of his stomach. It was weak, he knew, to harbour fears from childhood, but stories of evil spellmongers and the mysterious sand wizards had been the common fodder for night tales before sleep, and his mother had ingrained in him a healthy distrust of those who could fashion things from air, by making incantations and waving their fingers in mystic patterns.

The room was simple, though beautiful, if that word could be safely used. Beauty was always something to be suspicious of, his mother had told Valko. It gulled fools into not knowing the true worth of a thing, for often beauty adorned worthless things . . . or people.

Aruke had furnished this room with two chairs and a chest. Even the stone floor had been left devoid of any item of comfort: no furs, woven rugs, nor quilt warmed the room. But it was beautiful: every stone facet had been polished and whatever this strange stone might be, it had the property of reflecting the torchlight as if a treasury of gems had been crushed and applied to the surface; every hue at the edge of the visible spectrum raced across the surface in scintillating sheets of colour. It hinted of alien energies.

As if reading the boy's mind, Aruke said as he put the torch in a sconce, 'This room has but one purpose. It is where I keep that which is most valuable to me.' He waved Valko to the chair nearest the single window. 'I come here to think, and find the colours of the walls . . . refreshes me. And sometimes I come here with a few others with whom I wish to speak plainly.'

Valko said, 'I think I understand, Father.'

'It is about being your father I wish to speak.' He sat back and for a moment seemed to relax.

Valko knew it might be a ruse, a ploy to lure him into an early assault, for it was not unheard of for a newly-named heir to attempt to seize power. In some ways that made sense to Valko: this man might be his father, but until a few days earlier he had been a total stranger, a shadowy figure whom he could not imagine even after asking his mother countless questions.

Valko waited.

Aruke said, 'It is our custom to prize strength above all else.' He leaned forward. 'We are a violent people, and we honour violence and power above everything else.'

Valko said nothing.

Aruke regarded him. After a while he said, 'I remember your mother vividly.'

Again Valko remained silent.

'Have you had a woman?'

Valko appraised his father, attempting to discern if there was a correct answer. Finally he said, 'No. My Hiding was in an isolated—'

'I do not need to know where,' his father interrupted. 'No father should know where his surviving son was hidden and raised. It might be tempting to eradicate such a place in the next Purging.' Then softly he added, with something close to a chuckle, 'And if it is a place where a strong son was raised, that might . . . be wasteful.'

Valko blurted, 'As wasteful as killing another man's son who was only beaten by the scantest margin?'

Aruke's face was impassive, but there was a faint tightening around his eyes. 'Such a question borders on blasphemy.'

'I mean no disrespect to His Darkness, nor His Order, Father. I just wondered: what if the youth I killed today was a better warrior than one who was victor in another match, in another keep, within the Order? Isn't that a waste of a fine warrior to serve the Order?'

'Mysterious Are His Ways,' intoned his father. 'Such long thoughts are the thoughts of the young. But it is best to keep them to yourself, or to speak of them only with those under the seal of silence: your priest, an Attender, or . . .' He laughed. 'Or an Effector like your mother.'

Aruke stared out of the window for a moment at the roiling surface of the distant sea, and the ripple of scintillating colours that played across its surface. 'I have been told that there is a realm in which the sun shines so brightly that without a spell or ward a warrior would burn up within hours from the heat of it. And that those who live there can't see the splendours we take for granted.' He looked at his son. 'They see only colours, but not high hue or low hue. They can only hear waves

146

of sound in the air, but not the thrum of the God Speak in the heavens or the vibration of the Whole beneath their feet.'

'I saw a blind man once, serving an Attender.'

Aruke spat and made a ritual sign. 'In such a one's care is the only way you'd see such weakness. I'm sorry you had to see such a thing at so young an age.

'The Attenders have their uses, His Darkness knows, and he also knows I would not be sitting here speaking with you had they not ministered to me after battle. But this thing they have . . . this caring for weakness . . . it disgusts me.'

Valko said nothing. Rather than feeling disgust, he was fascinated. He wanted to know why the Attenders kept such a one alive. He had asked his mother, and all she would say was 'they find him useful, no doubt'. How could a blind one be useful? He realized this must be another of what his father had just called his 'long thoughts', and he had best keep his own counsel.

Aruke sat back. 'A woman. We must get you one . . .' he pondered. 'But not tonight. You held up well and made me proud, but I've seen enough battle cuts to know you've lost too much blood to do aught but sleep tonight. Perhaps in a day or two.

'Your mother was the one who . . .' He seemed to get lost in thought. 'She spoke of things. As we lay side by side after coupling, she'd muse about . . . all manner of things. She had a unique mind.'

Valko nodded. 'Even those other Effectors I've met during my Hiding were nothing like Mother. One said she saw things that weren't there.' Aruke's eyes widened, and Valko knew he was treading close to a disastrous mistake; even a hint that his mother was gripped by the madness could cause his father to order his immediate death. He quickly added, 'Possibilities.'

Aruke laughed. 'She often spoke of Possibilities.' He gazed out of the window. 'Sometimes what she spoke of bordered on . . . well, let's say it wouldn't have been good for her to be heard speaking by any of the Hierophants. A Soul Priest would have cautioned her and bid her repent, praying for her darkness within to assert itself, but there were things to her moods and natures that I found . . . appealing.' Looking down at his hands, clasped before him, he said, 'She once wondered aloud what would happen were a child to grow up at his father's knee.'

Valko's mouth dropped in astonishment, then he shut it. 'Such thoughts are forbidden,' he whispered.

'Yes.' With a sad smile Aruke added, 'Yet you would know more than I of your mother's ways. Of all those I have coupled with who have declared before witnesses to bear me an heir, it is she I recall . . . most often.' He stood. 'I have often wondered what you would be like, whether you would share some of your mother's nature.'

Valko also stood up. 'I will confess she made me think about things at times, in odd ways, but I never

148

strayed from His Teachings and . . . I ignored much of what she tried to teach me.'

Aruke laughed. 'As I ignored my mother during my Hiding.' He put his hand on his son's shoulder. Squeezing it firmly, he added, 'Stay alive, son of mine. I've fifty-four winters behind me, and while other sons will appear in years to come, they will be fewer and fewer. And I would not be displeased if you were the one to take my head at the end, just as I took my father's. I still remember the pride in his eyes as I swung down at his neck, while he lay on the sand of the pit.'

'I will not disappoint you,' said Valko. 'Yet I hope that day is years away.'

'As do I. But first, you must stay alive.'

'Stay alive,' repeated Valko in an almost ritual tone. 'As He wills it.'

'As He wills it,' repeated Aruke. 'What is discussed in here is never repeated. Understood?'

'Understood, Father.'

'Now go and have your thing escort you to your quarters, and sleep. In the morning you begin your training to be the future Lord of Camareen.'

'Good night, Father.'

'Good night, Valko.'

Valko left and Aruke returned to his chair. He stared out at the sea and the stars, fascinated by what he knew of them, and curious about what he didn't know. He saw the star light pushing through the thick air of Kosridi. He thought of his third journey to the Capital to present his son to the Karana, to have him swear allegiance to the Order and the TeKarana who sat upon an ancient throne worlds away. He thought of his third day of enduring the Hierophants and their long incantations as Valko dedicated himself to His Darkness and the Way.

Then Aruke rose and removed a single, very old scroll from the chest. He opened it and read slowly, for reading had never been one of his better skills. Yet, he knew every word by heart. He read the words on this scroll twice, and put it away, wondering as he had, twice before, if this son was the one in the prophecy.

CHAPTER 8

NEW DIRECTIONS

Pug waited.

After a pause, the merchant said, 'No, sir, but you are not far from the truth.' He waved Pug over to a small table and two chairs of sufficient proportion to provide comfortable seating for humans as well as himself. When he was seated, Vordam went on, 'An understandable misapprehension; we of the Ipiliac are related to the Dasati.'

Pug was not sure he could read the alien merchant's expressions, but he thought he saw something akin to surprise on his face. 'I must confess I never expected to find anyone here at the Inn who would ever have heard of the Dasati let alone be able to recognize one on sight.'

'I heard a vivid description,' said Pug, choosing to hide his ability to sense the differences between the vibrations in this room and the rest of Honest John's. 'For reasons I'm reluctant to discuss at the moment I would rather not go into why I need information, just that I need information.'

'Information is always among the most prized commodities.' The merchant clasped his hands before him and leaned forward on the table, a very human gesture. 'As to the reasons for your enquiry, that remains your business, but I feel compelled to informed you that I am bound by several oaths of privilege regarding the business I do with my clients here in the Hall.' He nodded once. 'It is, you understand, essential for staying in business.'

'What is it you do, exactly?'

'I procure hard to find items and other . . . things: rare artefacts, unique devices, lost people, information. If you have something you wish to find cheaply, I am most certainly not your first choice. If you have something you are desperate to find, I am almost certainly your final choice.' He regarded Pug and the magician discovered he was beginning to understand the Ipiliac's facial expressions. The merchant was curious.

'I need to find a guide.'

'Guides are plentiful, even the good ones. You must need a special guide if you seek me out. Where do you wish to go?'

'Kosridi,' said Pug.

Pug had no doubt that the expression he read on Vordam's face was one of surprise, for the merchant's eyes were wide, his mouth slightly open.

'You can't be serious.'

'I am. Very.'

For a long moment the merchant sat appraising him, then he said, 'May I ask your name?'

'Pug of Midkemia.'

A slow nod. 'Then perhaps . . .' Vordam considered his choice of words, then said, 'Perhaps it is possible. Your reputation in the Hall has grown, young magician.'

Pug smiled. It had been some years since anyone had called him 'young'.

'I knew your mentor, Macros.'

Pug's eyes narrowed. No matter what occurred in his life, he found signs that his father-in-law's hand was in it somewhere. 'Really?'

'Yes, he had occasion to do business with me, several centuries ago. When you first arrived in the Hall, in his company and with two others, your passing was not unnoticed. Tomas of Elvandar caused quite a stir, you see, as he appeared at first glance to be a returned Valheru, a potential cause of great distress to several races on many worlds. The young woman, though remarkable by all reports was, and remains, unknown to us.'

To the best of Pug's recollection of their travelling back to Midkemia through the Hall, after rescuing Macros from the Garden in the City Forever, they had encountered no other person along the way. 'Apparently, you have very acute sources of information,' said Pug. 'Did you know Macros well?'

The trader sat back further, allowing his left arm to hang over the back of his chair in a relaxed pose. 'Did anyone? I have not met another like him, however.'

Pug realized that the merchant was holding something back, something he was unlikely to divulge until he was ready, so he moved back to the reason for his visit. 'The guide?'

For a moment the merchant was silent. Then he said, 'It is very difficult.'

'What is?'

'For any being from this plane of reality to journey to the Dasati realm.'

'Yet you are here and claim kinship with the Dasati.'

Vordam nodded, then looked towards the door, as if expecting someone. Slowly, he said, 'Understand . . . great thinkers and philosophers from myriad worlds have grappled with the nature of reality. How to explain the existence of so many worlds, so many sentient races, so many gods and goddesses and, most of all, so many mysteries.' He looked at Pug directly. 'You are not a man to whom I need describe the nature of curiosity. So I have no doubt you have often spent time considering these and other imponderables.'

'I have.'

'Think of everything, I mean *everything* as an onion. Each layer you peel away has another layer below. Or if you could start from the centre, each layer another above. Only it's not a sphere, this "everything", but, well . . . everything.

'I know you to be a man of keen perception, Pug of Midkemia, so forgive me if I sound like a tedious lecturer, but there are things you *must*

154

understand before even considering a journey to the Dasati realm.

'Above and below this universe we inhabit exist discrete realities, those we have knowledge of only indirectly. Much of what we know is filtered through mysticism and faith, but most scholars, theologians and philosophers hold that there are other dimensions, the seven higher and lower levels.'

'The Seven Hells and the Seven Heavens?'

'So many races call them,' answered Vordam. 'There are probably many more, but by the time one reaches the seventh level of either the Heavens or Hells there are no frames of references beyond them that . . . well, that make enough sense to bother with. The Seventh Heaven is a realm believed to be so blissful, so joyous that mortal minds cannot encompass even the concept of it. The Sixth Heaven is populated with beings whose brilliance and beauty would bring such wonder and joy to us that we would die, overwhelmed by happiness from merely being in their presence.

'According to some accounts,' said Vordam, 'you've had dealings with the demons of the Fifth Circle, the Fifth Hell.'

'One of them,' said Pug with a grim expression. 'It nearly cost me my life.'

'The Fifth Heaven is its opposite. Those beings are concerned with matters beyond our ability to apprehend, but they mean us no harm. Yet to see them would be dangerous in the extreme, so intense is the state of their being.' He paused. 'Beyond the so-called Spheres, or Planes, lies the Void.'

'Wherein dwell the Dread,' Pug supplied.

'Ah,' said Vordam. 'Your reputation is not over-stated.'

'I have had dealings with the Dread.'

'And live to speak of it. My respect for your abilities grows by the second. The Dread are anathema to both the Heavens and Hells, as the Void surrounds them, and would devour them if it could.'

'You speak as if the Void has awareness.'

'Doesn't it?' Vordam asked rhetorically. 'Directly above us, so to speak, is the First Heaven, as the First Hell is seen to be below us.' He looked into Pug's eyes and said, 'Just so we have no misunderstanding, Pug. That is where you wish to travel. That is the Dasati realm of which you speak. You're asking for a guide to take you to Hell.'

Pug nodded. 'I think I understand.' His expression was a mixture of curiosity and apprehension. 'At least in the abstract.'

'Then let me provide you with a less abstract image. You can't breathe the air or drink the water for more than a little while. The air may act like corrosive gas and the water like acid. That is an analogy, though the truth is likely to be far more subtle, for their air may not be corrosive nor their water contain acid.'

'I am . . . confused,' Pug admitted.

'Think of water running downhill. The higher up the realms we climb, from the lowest hell to the highest heaven . . . all energy, light, heat, magic, everything, burns brighter, is hotter, is more powerful; and therefore, all energies flow down from the highest to the lowest. The air and water of Kosridi world would literally drag all the energies from your body: you would be like a handful of dry straw thrown onto a low fire. It would burn brightly for a while, then fade.

'The inhabitants of that realm have an equally difficult time in your realm, though their problems would be different; they would become blissful as they drank in all the abundant energies surrounding them, but after a while, they would be like men who have had too much to drink and eat, and be overwhelmed by drunkenness and gluttony, barely able to move until excess caused their death.'

'How then can you, kin to the Dasati, exist here in the Hall?'

'Before I explain that, might I suggest you select your companions who wish to accompany you and return here with them?'

'Companions?' asked Pug.

'You may be willing to risk going to the Dasati world, but only a madman would venture there alone.' The merchant regarded Pug with an expression that could only be called calculating. 'I'd suggest a small party, perhaps, but a powerful one.' He stood. 'I will explain the rest of this to

157

you once they've arrived. While you are away, I shall set about finding you a guide, who will also be your teacher.'

'Teacher?' asked Pug.

With what Pug could only call a smile, an expression another might regard as a fearful-looking grimace, Vordam said, 'Return here in one week by your calendar, and all will be ready for your instruction.'

'What instruction, Father?' asked Valko.

Aruke sat back in his chair. They were once again in the room where he had taken his son to speak after their first supper together. 'There is a place maintained by the Empire in which we train our sons.'

'Train? I thought *you* would train me,' Valko said, preferring to stand by the window rather than sit opposite his father. 'You are an excellent warrior, one who has ruled his house for twenty-seven winters.'

'There is more to ruling than the ability to lop off heads, my son.'

'I don't understand.'

Aruke had brought two large flagons of wine into the chamber. Valko's sat untouched on the floor next to his chair. The Lord of Camareen drank from his. 'I remember emerging from my Hiding. I was at a disadvantage compared to you, for my mother was not as clever as yours. I knew how to fight. No one survives living in the Hiding without that, but the ability to knock someone down and take what you need is only part of it.' He studied his son. In the few days he had been living here, Aruke had come to feel a sense of pleasant expectation at seeing the boy. They had even gone hunting two days earlier and he had found the lad able, if not polished. Yet he had stood fearlessly before a charging tugash boar defending his sow and their litter, decapitating the animal with a deft move that prevented the creature from killing him. Aruke had been visited by an odd notion: that had the beast killed Valko he would have felt a sense of loss. He wondered whence that alien emotion had arisen, and if it was a sign of that weakness which came with age: sentiment?

'This place is called a school. It is not far from here so you will be able to return to visit from time to time. It is a place where Facilitators and Effectors will show you the things you will eventually need to know if you take my head and rule after me.'

'That will be years away, Father, and I hope when I do you will welcome it.'

'If you spare me weakness and prove my line is strong, no man can ask for more than that, my son.'

'What will I be learning?'

'First of all, the ability to learn. It is a hard concept: sitting for hours listening to Effectors and watching Facilitators can numb the mind. Secondly, to hone your fighting skills. I remember how I learned, as a child, with wooden sticks at first, battling the other boys who were Hiding. Then the forays into a neighbouring village at night, to steal what we needed, eventually trading with Facilitators for enough gold to buy armour from a monger.' He sighed. 'It seems so long ago.

'But no amount of scuffling with older boys, not even your defeat of Kesko's son, means you're a skilled warrior. You have raw talent, but it needs refinement before you're fit to ride with the Sadharin.' Aruke sat back, sipped his wine, and then added, 'And, as unpleasant as it may sound, a ruler has to know how to deal with the Lessers.'

'Deal with them? I don't understand. You take what you need, or they are killed.'

'It's not that simple. The Effectors will teach you just how complex things can be, but do not worry; you appear intelligent enough to understand. And the Facilitators will show you how to implement what the Effectors have taught you.'

'When do I go to this school, Father?'

'Tomorrow. You will leave with a full escort, as befits the heir to the Camareen. Now, go and leave me to my own thoughts.'

Valko rose, leaving his untouched drink sitting by the chair. As the door closed, Aruke wondered if the boy had somehow guessed the drink was poisoned or just hadn't been thirsty – he never would have let him die so early in his education, but a little writhing in pain was a good point-maker, and an Attender had been standing close by to administer the antidote.

As the door closed behind him, Valko smiled slightly. He knew that right now his father must be wondering if he had known the drink was poisoned. His smile widened. Tomorrow he would start the serious education his mother had told him about. He looked forward to the day he could send for her and tell her all that she had taught him had been not wasted. What she had told him about his father had been true, and what she had told him about school would certainly be true. Perhaps then she would tell him the truth about why she had him lie to Aruke about her death. He put that thought inside, and instead re-membered her parting words: *Always let them underestimate you. Let them think they are more clever than you. It will be their undoing.*

'Instruction?' asked Jommy. 'What for?'

'Because,' answered Caleb, who had just arrived from Sorcerer's Island.

Talwin Hawkins added, 'Pug says you need it.'

Tad and Zane exchanged glances. They knew that Jommy was in a mood to argue and when he did, he became as stubborn as a mule with its hooves nailed to the floor. The boys had been enjoying a long stretch of city life, and all had been both delighted by the distractions and amusements offered by Opardum, capital of the

161

Duchy of Olasko, now part of the Kingdom of Roldem.

They sat in the empty main dining room of the River House, the restaurant Talwin had opened after returning to Opardum. So successful had the endeavour been – people waited for hours to gain seats – that he had been forced to expand. He had just purchased the building next to his and would enlarge his seating capacity by half again. Lucian, who had been Tal's personal cook in Roldem before joining him in Opardum, had elected to call himself *chef*, a Bas-Tyran word for a master cook. He and his wife Magary were celebrated throughout Olasko. The boys worked as cleaners in the kitchen, occasionally lending a hand as servers. The best part of the work was the food: there were all manner of wonderful dishes, and at the end of the day Magary often kept aside special desserts or other treats boys of their station would never usually experience, for she had developed a fondness for them.

The boys had come to regard Talwin as something of an uncle, the one who let you have fun when your father didn't. But that father, Caleb, had arrived the night before after having spent a few weeks alone with Tad and Zane's mother, then another week running some errand for his father.

And the boy who had become something of a cousin to them sat quietly trying not to live up to his name. Laughter-In-His-Eyes Hawkins, as precocious a seven-year-old as any of them had encountered, was failing miserably at hiding his glee. Named for his grandfather, the boy was the eldest of Hawkins' two children, the second being a delightful baby girl named Sunset-On-The-Peaks.

Jommy shot the boy a black expression, and it tipped the balance: Laughter could not contain his amusement any longer. 'What's so funny, Laff?' asked Jommy.

'You're going to school!' whooped Laughter. He had his mother's reddish-blond hair and his father's features, and his blue eyes held an evil glint as he grinned at Jommy.

At last Tad said, 'Don't think me stupid for asking, but what exactly is a school?'

Caleb said, 'You're not stupid for not knowing something. You're only stupid if you don't ask. A school is a place where students go to study with a teacher. It's like having a tutor for a lot of boys and girls at the same time.'

'Ah,' said Zane, as if he understood. He obviously didn't.

'In Roldem they have schools,' said Tal. 'Lots of them, most run by the various guilds. It's different from in the Kingdom or Kesh or here in Opardum.' Glancing at Jommy, he added, 'and very different from anything you knew down in Novindus.'

'We've got schools where I came from,' offered Jommy with a hint of defiance in his voice, which made it clear he had never heard of a school before in his life. 'Just never saw one, that's all.'

Their lives since arriving at the River House had been equally divided between hard work, which none of them minded, and hard play. In the time the three boys had been together a bond of brotherhood had formed that had conspired to keep them constantly on the edge of trouble when they weren't undertaking tasks for the Conclave. When they were, it was usually under the direction of their stepfather, or one of Pug's appointed agents. But when left to their own devices the lack of super-vision was decidedly noticeable. On more than one occasion, Tal had had to intercede with one city official or another on their behalf.

'It'll be good for you,' said Caleb. 'Tal tells me you country boys seem to find a little too much trouble in the city for my liking. So, beginning tomorrow you will no longer be working here, but students at the University of Roldem. You will seem to leave by ship for the benefit of the thugs and tarts you socialize with, but later tonight Magnus will take to you Roldem where you will appear to have arrived by a ship before dawn.'

'Roldem!' said Tad, suddenly enthused. It was, as Talwin opined, the most civilized city in the world, and as he had undertaken their education for the last month, his opinion on the matter counted for much with the boys.

'I thought you said we'd be going to a school,' said Jommy, no longer hiding his confusion.

Tal laughed. 'It *is* a school. It's a school where they try to study everything, hence the name. You will be taught alongside the sons of Roldem's nobility and those from other nations surrounding the Kingdom's sea.'

'Sons?' asked Tad. 'No daughters?'

Tal shook his head sympathetically.

Caleb said, 'Father's view on educating women is . . . distinctive, perhaps unique. No, you'll be lodging with boys, most of them a few years younger than you, but some your own age.'

'Lodging?'

'Yes, you'll be living at the university with other students under the supervision of the monks.'

'Monks?' asked Zane, his tone showing what the others revealed in their expression. 'What monks?'

Hawkins feigned a cough to hide his smile. 'Why, the Brothers of La-timsa.'

'La-timsa!' shouted Tad. 'They're . . .'

'Strict?' supplied Caleb.

'Yes, they are that,' agreed Talwin.

'Very strict,' responded Caleb, glancing at his friend.

'Some might say a little too strict, though I've never heard of a student dying from too much discipline,' said Tal.

'They don't drink anything but water,' whined Zane. 'They . . . eat coarse bread and hard cheese and . . . boil their beef.' He cast a longing look at the kitchen door.

'Who's La-timsa?' asked Jommy. 'I get confused by all the different names up here.'

Tal said, 'I'm not conversant with the names they use down in Novindus . . .' He looked to Caleb and shrugged.

Caleb said, 'Durga.'

'Durga!' shouted Jommy. 'They're celibates! They beat each other with canes for penance! They take vows of silence that last for years! They're celibates!'

Tal burst out laughing, which set his young son off into gales of hilarity.

'Get whatever you think you need together, then you've got an hour to go out and say your good-byes,' said Caleb, laughing with the others. Then his voice turned serious. 'I'm saying this now, so be clear. The day will come when you will be standing where Talwin and I stand now, at the heart of the Conclave. You will not be soldiers, but generals. That is why you're going.'

He left and the three boys looked at one another with a shared expression of resignation. After a minute, Tad said, 'Well, it is Roldem.'

'And they can't keep us locked up in this university all the time, can they?' asked Zane.

Jommy's black expression suddenly lifted and he grinned. 'Well, they can bloody try, can't they?' He slapped Tad on the shoulder. 'Come on, we need to pack, and then there's this one girl I want to say goodbye to.'

'Shera?' asked Zane.

'No,' said Jommy.

'Ruth,' supplied Tad.

'No.' Jommy started walking towards the kitchen

behind which their quarters and belongings waited.

'Milandra?'

'No,' said Jommy as he walked though the door.

Zane grabbed Tad's arm. 'How does he do it?'

'I don't know,' said his foster-brother, 'but it's going to stop once we get to Roldem.'

Zane sighed. 'I already miss Opardum.'

Pushing aside the door, Tad said, 'You mean you miss the food.'

CHAPTER 9

ROLDEM

The boys circled slowly.

Jommy, Tad, and Zane waited as more than a dozen university students approached them. The three foster brothers had walked from the docks where they were expected to have arrived, though they had been transported by Magnus at Pug's request to a Conclave warehouse. They were appropriately dirty and rumpled, so the story that they had spent a month or more on a caravan and then a week at sea would pass muster. Each wore a plain tunic and trousers, and had a travel-sack slung over his shoulder.

They watched as the students fanned out, forming a rough half-circle before them, looking them up and down as if examining livestock. They ranged in age from approximately twelve years to roughly the same age as the three newcomers – though Jommy suspected he'd turn out to be the oldest student in sight at nearly twenty years of age.

All the students were dressed in the official garb of the university: a black felt beret wore tilted to the left, a pale yellow shirt, over which a long blue tabard with white trim along the edges hung, tied front to back on both sides; yellow trousers and black boots. Each student carried a black leather pouch in their left hand. From their dark complexions, several students appeared to be Keshian; from the varied accents, many were from other nations.

One of the older boys, with dark hair and eyes, his smile bordering on a smirk, walked up to Jommy and looked him up and down. He then turned to a disdainful-looking fair-haired youngster at his side and said, 'Who's this, then?'

'Country lads, obviously,' replied his friend.

'You can tell from the smell of manure.'

Jommy put down his travel bag. 'Look, mate. We just got off a ship after some rough seas, and before that had a long wagon ride, so let's say we're not in the best of tempers. So why don't we start the "making life hell for the new boys" tomorrow? How'd that be?'

The dark-haired youth said, 'This bumpkin wants to postpone our welcome, Godfrey. What do you think?'

'I think he's being presumptuous, Servan.'

'So, it's presumptuous to want to be friendly?' asked Jommy, rhetorically.

Servan's dark eyes narrowed as he feigned deliberation. After a second he said, 'No. I don't think so. Let's begin now.' He poked his finger hard into Jommy's chest. 'Why don't you put down that bundle so I can start your education right now, peasant, beginning with not speaking back to your betters!'

Jommy sighed. He took off his bundle slowly, saying, 'So, it's going to be like that, then, is it?' He put the pack down, and grinned as he stepped forward. 'See, as a rule I'm as easy going as the next fellow, but I've been around enough to know that everywhere you go, regardless of nationality or rank, time of the day, or month of the year—' and he suddenly threw a straight right punch to Servan's jaw which caused his eyes to roll up in his head as he collapsed to the ground, '—you find idiots!'

To the blond-haired boy he said, 'You want any of this, then?'

'No,' said the now-shocked boy.

'Then be kind enough to tell us where the new students go.'

'Brother Kynan's office.' Godfrey pointed at the main entrance to the university. 'In there, to the right, second door.'

'Thanks, mate,' said Jommy with a smile. 'And when your friend awakes, tell him no worries. I believe everyone's entitled to a mistake now and again. So, we can start over fresh tomorrow. But next time he tries to lord it over us "country lads" I'll really lose my temper.'

Godfrey just nodded.

Jommy picked up his travel-pack and said to his companions, 'Off we go, then.'

They started across the large courtyard between the main gate and the huge building that was the Royal University of Roldem, leaving a muttering group behind as they gathered around their fallen classmate. A younger student hurried to Jommy's side, looking up with a ferocious grin and said, 'I'll show you the way!'

'That's a lad. What's your name?'

'Grandy, what's yours?'

'Jommy. These are Tad and Zane.'

The boy looked no more than twelve or thirteen years of age, and had an infectious smile. His face was freckled and his head was crowned with a thatch of dark brown hair. His expression bordered on the gleeful.

'You always this happy?' asked Tad.

Grandy shook his head. 'No, only on days when someone hits Servan in the mouth.'

'Happen a lot?' asked Zane.

'No, today was the first time, but I'll come and watch any time you want to do it again.'

'Bit of a pain, is he?' asked Jommy, as they mounted the wide steps leading to the massive double doors.

'More than a pain. He's a bully and . . . he's just mean. I don't know why; he's got everything anyone could want.'

'I'm surprised no one's punched him before,' said Jommy.

'That's probably because his uncle's the King,' said Grandy.

Jommy stopped so suddenly that Zane stepped hard into him, tripping and landing in a heap. Tad stared at Grandy, his eyes blinking like an owl surprised by a lantern.

'His uncle, the King?' said Zane, getting quickly to his feet.

'Not properly,' said the boy in a bright tone. 'His father's some sort of cousin, a nephew to the King's father, the old King, if you see—' his grin got wider, '—but he refers to the King as his "uncle" and no one's willing to argue about it. Because he's still a prince and all.'

Jommy stood motionless, then said, 'Stepped into it that time, didn't I?'

'What are you going to do?' asked Tad.

'Well, as I see it, I've either got to make him my new friend, or I've got to beat him so badly he'll be afraid to tell anyone.'

Grandy laughed aloud. 'I don't think either's going to work. Who's your patron?'

'Patron?' asked Zane. 'What do you mean?'

'Who got you in to the university?' asked the active boy as they entered the vestibule and moved towards a large hall running to the right and left. 'My father's a former captain in the royal fleet, and my grandfather was the old king's – what the people call the current king's grandfather – admiral of the Southern Fleet. Both went here, so they had to take me, as a legacy. When I'm done here, I'm going for the navy, too. So, who's your patron?'

Tad tried to remember what Caleb had told them to say should anyone ask this question, and said. 'Well, we're from the Vale of Dreams, so we know people in both the Kingdom of the Isles and Great Kesh—'

Zane cut him off, saying, 'Turhan Bey, Lord of the Keep, Chancellor of Great Kesh.' The boys had only met the man once, briefly, less than a year earlier, when the plot against the throne had been thwarted, and it was unlikely the Lord of the Keep of Great Kesh could pick them out of a street gang, but Pug had close ties with the man and he apparently had agreed to act as sponsor without looking too closely at Pug's reasons.

Grandy laughed. 'Well, that's a high enough personage that Servan will at least think twice before he complains to his father, or maybe if he does, his father will think twice before he has someone cut your throat. Here we are.' Now they stood before a large wooden door to the right of the hall with a small viewing window in the middle. 'Knock three times, then wait,' said Grandy. 'I'll see you later.' He scampered off and the three newcomers exchanged shrugs.

Jommy knocked three times and they waited.

After a moment the cover on the viewing window moved aside. They saw a brief glimpse of light and what appeared to be a man's eyes, then the viewing window closed. The door swung open wide and a monk of La-Timsa stood in the doorway. He was tall, broad of shoulder and chest, and wore a light brown robe which reached the floor. The robe's hood was currently thrown back to reveal an equally massive head, clean shaven in the style of his order. 'Yes?'

Jommy glanced at his companions whose

expressions made it clear they expected him to do the talking, so he said, 'We were told to come here . . . sir.'

The monk said, 'It's "Brother" not "sir" Enter.'

When the three boys were in the room, he said, 'Close the door.'

Zane closed it and the monk sat down behind a large table. 'I am Brother Kynan, Reeve of this university. You will address all monks as "Brother", and any priest you meet as "Father". Is that clear?'

'Yes . . . Brother,' said Tad. The others echoed him a moment later.

'Who are you?'

Jommy said, 'I'm Jommy, and this is Tad and Zane,' he indicated which was which. 'We're here from—'

'I know where you are from,' said the monk. His head was dominated by a massive brow ridge and deep-set eyes which gave the impression that he was constantly glaring. Or perhaps, thought Zane, he *was* glaring. 'You are not what I expected when we received a request from the Imperial Court in Kesh to admit three "promising young men" in the middle of the year.' He fell silent as he regarded them.

Jommy was about to say something, when Brother Kynan cut him off. 'You only speak when you are spoken to, is that clear?'

'Yes, Brother,' said Jommy. His expression showed he was not happy being addressed in this fashion.

'You will have to work harder than the others,

174

to catch up. Our education is the finest in the world, so consider yourselves privileged to be admitted to the university. Here you will study many things: history, the arts, the revealed truth as given by La-Timsa to her chosen, as well as military strategy and tactics. Roldem's finest young nobles study here, preparing to serve the nation in the navy, the marines, or the royal court, as it is the duty of all who finish their studies to spend ten years in service before returning to their families. Many remain in service to the Crown their entire lives.'

Tad and Zane exchanged worried glances, for no one had said anything about service to Roldem. What they knew about the Conclave didn't preclude Pug ordering them to spend years in the royal court, or fighting Roldem's enemies on land or sea; but it would have been less of a shock had someone mentioned it to them. As if reading their thoughts, Brother Kynan said, 'Those of you who are not citizens of Roldem are not given the privilege of serving, but rather are required to pay a large sum in gold.' He looked Jommy up and down. 'Your looks belie your station, but that is not at issue. Shortly, you will go see Brother Timothy, who will take those garments from you and store them. You will henceforth wear the university's uniform every day from now until you depart. There is no rank among the students, so no titles are permitted. You will address one another by name only, and the brothers and fathers by both their title and name. Our rules are strict and we do not tolerate disobedience. Now, strip off your tunics.'

The boys exchanged quick glances, then dropped their bundles and shed their tunics. 'Kneel before the table,' said Brother Kynan. Again they glanced at one another. 'Kneel!' shouted the large monk, and the boys did so.

Brother Kynan strode to the corner of the room and returned with a long wand of dark wood. 'This rod,' he said as he showed it to them, 'is the instrument of correction. Any infraction will earn you strokes from it. The number of strokes will be determined by the severity of the infraction.' Suddenly, he lashed out, taking Jommy across the shoulders, then Zane, then Tad. All three boys winced but none of them cried out. 'This is so you know what you face. Are there any questions?'

Jommy said, 'One, Brother.'

'Speak.'

'What is the punishment for striking another student?'

'Ten strokes.'

Jommy sighed then said, 'Well, then, I suppose you'd best lay on, Brother, as I hit a chap named Servan a few minutes before getting here.'

'Good,' said the monk. He delivered ten hard strikes across Jommy's back as Zane and Tad stayed on their knees wincing every time the wand fell. When he had finished, he said, 'Rise and put on your tunics.'

They did as instructed and then Brother Kynan said, 'You're more intelligent than you look, Jommy. The punishment for not reporting yourself is double the lashes. You would have had twenty had someone else told me of your striking Servan.'

Jommy just nodded.

'Go down the hall and at the last door on the left you'll find Brother Timothy. He will see to your needs.'

Tad and Zane put on their shirts with some signs of discomfort but Jommy just yanked his on, picked up his bag and left the room. In the hall, Tad asked, 'Doesn't your back hurt?'

'Of course it hurts,' said Jommy. 'But I had worse from my dad back when I was younger than Grandy, and I don't like giving his type the satisfaction.'

'What type?' asked Zane.

'There are two types of men who give out punishment, old son. Those who know it's necessary and those who enjoy it. Brother Kynan's the sort who enjoys it. The more you show how much it hurts, the more he enjoys it.'

They reached the door and knocked three times. A voice from within said, 'Don't just stand out there in the rain! Come in!'

Zane glanced around. 'Rain?'

Jommy laughed and opened the door. Inside they found another room, larger than Brother Kynan's office, but instead of being an austere workplace it was a veritable warehouse. Along the wall to their left shelves ran from floor to ceiling and on each rested small wooden boxes, each with a name and number carefully painted on it. There must have been hundreds of them, for the room stretched away behind row upon row of shelves that rose up from the floor to block their view. Two narrow paths ran between the shelves and the bare right wall and one between the shelves on the left wall and the shelves they faced. The only other feature in the room was a small table and chair, occupied by a monk. The wizened little man was perhaps the tiniest human being any of the boys had ever seen; the average dwarf would have seemed to tower over him. His head was shaved like Brother Kynan's, but he sported a full red beard streaked with grey. The man's eyes were a vivid blue and his face seemed to be frozen in a perpetual smile. 'New boys!' he announced with glee. 'I heard we were to have some new boys! That's just splendid!'

Tad said, 'Brother Kynan told us to come here. Are you Brother Timothy?'

'Yes, I am, indeed, that's who I am.' He continued to chuckle. 'Well, then, let's begin. Off with your clothes.' He stood and scurried down the left aisle, leaving the boys looking at one another in surprise.

'Perhaps we get uniforms,' said Zane.

'No,' said Tad. 'Really?'

Jommy winced slightly as he pulled off his tunic, and by the time Brother Timothy returned, carrying three wooden boxes in a stack that threatened to overbalance with each step he took, the boys stood naked.

Tad said, 'Here, Brother, let me help you,' as he grabbed the topmost box.

'That's fine,' said the monk. 'You each take one.' When they each stood holding a box – inside which were tunics, trousers, hats and boots, as well as white linen small-clothes – he said, 'Well don't just stand there like fools, Get dressed. If something's too big or too small, we'll sort it out.'

It took only a minute to realize the uniform handed to Jommy was too small and the one Zane had far too large. They swapped and discovered both had decent fits. The boots were a different matter and it took the diminutive monk several trips to the rear of the storage room to find boots that fitted them. But in the end each of them stood wearing the identical costume they had seen the others wearing.

Tad suddenly laughed, and Jommy said, 'What?'

'I'm sorry, Jommy, but . . .'

'You look ridiculous,' finished Zane.

'Well, neither of you look as if you'll be impressing the girls around that fountain in Kesh where I met you any time soon.'

Tad laughed even more.

'Girls,' said Brother Timothy. 'Can't be talking about girls, now. It's not allowed.'

All three stopped laughing and Tad said, 'No girls?'

'No,' said the monk. 'We know how young boys

179

are, yes we do. Just because we're a celibate order doesn't mean we don't remember, though it's not a good thing to remember too much. Why, when I was a lad, before I got the calling . . .' He let the thought finish itself. 'No, no girls. You must study, yes, study, and practise, practise a great deal. Yes, but no girls.'

The odd little monk seemed to have reached the point of utter confusion on the subject and Jommy said, 'Brother, what next?'

'Next?' asked the monk.

'What do we do next?' Jommy elaborated.

'Oh, what do you do next!' said the monk, returning to the amused state the boys had found him in. 'Why, you study, and you practise.'

Tad rolled his eyes, while Zane decided to clear things up. 'He means, what do we do right now; are we finished here?'

'Yes, yes. You come here when you need supplies, and if you tear a garment or need new boots – though the Father doesn't like it if you wear out boots.'

'What sort of supplies?' asked Tad.

'Oh, supplies!' exclaimed the little monk and he was off to the back of the room once more. A moment later he returned with three of the odd leather pouches they had seen all the other students carrying. 'Here are your supplies. These are student purses. Look inside!'

The boys discovered that the purses were basic-ally two soft leather skins sewn together, one bigger than the other so it created a flap which folded over, keeping the bag's contents inside. Inside they found a small knife, a small squat jar with a stopper, a half-dozen quills, and a sheaf of paper. There were other items wrapped in paper that was treated with some sort of oil or wax, as well as a small box.

Jommy started to extract the box, but Brother Timothy said, 'Later. You can look later. I just wanted to make certain I didn't give you an empty purse. Now, learn to write small.'

'Small?' asked Zane.

'Makes the paper last longer,' replied Timothy.

'Where do we go now, Brother?' asked Jommy.

'Go to the hall of residence. Ask for Brother Stephen; he is the Proctor.' With a wave of his hand, he said, 'Now, go away!'

'Brother,' asked Tad as they moved towards the door, 'where is the hall of residence?'

'The residences are in the other wing of this building. Go back down the hall to the right and at the last door on the left you'll find Brother Stephen. He will see to your needs.'

They left the room and went back down the hall. At the end of the hall they came to a room with no door. It was an immense hall, and along each wall a row of beds jutted out. At the foot of each a wooden chest rested.

Walking down the aisle between the chests was another monk, this one with no beard. 'You are the new boys.' It was a statement, not a question.

'Yes,' answered Zane, quickly adding, 'Brother.'

'I am Brother Stephen, the Proctor. I am in charge of all the students when they are not at class, prayer or otherwise tasked by another monk or priest. Follow me.' He turned and led them to the farthest end of the hall. He pointed to a single bed on the right, and said, 'One of you will sleep here.' He then pointed to two beds on the left side of the room. 'Two of you will sleep there.'

The boys quickly looked at one another, shrugged, and Tad and Jommy went to the left, while Zane took the right-hand bed. As Zane started to sit down on it, the monk said, 'Do not sit!'

Zane snapped upright. 'Sorry, Brother.'

'Look inside the chest.'

They did and in each chest they found a boot brush, a comb and a large coarse linen cloth, as well as a razor and a cake of hard soap. Zane started to reach into the chest to examine the comb, and the monk said, 'Touch nothing!'

Zane's expression was one of pain. 'Sorry, Brother . . . again.'

'Look at how each item is arranged. Each morning you will rise and make your bed, and go to the bathroom. There you will bathe, clean your hair, shave your face, and afterwards give your towel to a servant who will give you a dry one. You will then return here. Your clothing will have been folded the night before and placed in the chest. You will get dressed, then replace the other items exactly as you see them. If any item is incorrectly replaced, you will receive five strokes of the cane. If any item is missing, twenty strokes. Is that understood?'

'Yes, Brother.'

'You may not sit on your bed until after the evening prayers, for one hour, before you sleep. If you are found sitting on a bed before then, you will receive five strokes of the cane.' He looked at the three and said, 'Now, find the provost and he will further instruct you. His office is on the other side of the entrance.'

Zane lingered for a moment, staring down into the chest, then he lowered the lid. As he turned to leave, Brother Stephen said, 'Which of you struck Servan?'

Jommy turned with a look of regret. 'It was me, Brother.'

Brother Stephen just looked at Jommy for a long moment, said, 'Hmmm,' then turned and walked away.

As they left the dormitory, Tad said, 'Zane, what were you staring at?'

'I was trying to memorize where everything went. I have no appetite for that cane.'

'You get used to it,' said Jommy. 'Besides, you'll have an hour before we sleep tonight to stand and stare down in to it.'

'Oh, right,' said Zane unenthusiastically.

The three boys wondered what it was that their foster-father had got them into.

CHAPTER 10

PURGING

Valko readied himself for violence.

The warrior who faced him was old, his scars looking like badges of honour, and his bearing revealed he was no elder waiting for a son to dispatch him to the Dark God's final service. There were many battles left in this man.

He stood in the centre of a large room, laid out in identical fashion to the fighting floor in the Hall of Testing in Valko's father's castle, but many times larger. Five hundred riders could sit in the gallery and a dozen combats could be waged at the same time. Valko glanced right, then left, and saw other Dasati youth also ready to fight.

The old warrior was dressed in the armour of the Scourge, almost identical to that worn by the Sadharin: a dark grey open-faced helm, breastplate, bracers and greaves, but rather than the tall plume sported by the Sadharin, his helmet was topped by a spike trailing two long ribbons of blood-orange cloth. He spoke and his voice was commanding, though he did not raise it. 'You are going to die.' Several of the other youths tensed and a few hands gripped their swords. 'But not today.'

He walked slowly before the sixteen young warriors who stood in a semi-circle, looking each in the eye as he spoke. 'You come to me, here, because you have survived your first testing. Survival is good. You cannot serve the TeKarana if you are dead. You cannot father strong sons and clever daughters unless you survive. And you want strong sons who will some day stand here to begin their training, and clever daughters who will hide your grandsons until they are ready for their testing.

'Such is the way of the Dasati.'

'Such is the way,' the young warriors repeated ritually.

'The second most glorious thing you can do is to die bravely for the Empire, when all else has failed. The most glorious thing you can do is make the Empire's enemies die for us. Any fool can die stupidly. Stupidity is weakness. There is no glory in dying a fool.

'Such is the way of the Dasati.'

'Such is the way.'

The old warrior continued. 'I am Hirea, a Rider of the Scourge. Some of you are sons of the Scourge.'

Several of the young warriors shouted.

'No longer,' said Hirea, his voice rising just enough to communicate his displeasure at the display. 'You are no longer Scourge. You are not sons of the Sadharin. You are neither Kalmak, nor Black Thunder; no Darkrider, Bloodtide, or Remalu stand here. Whatever you thought you

185

were when you arrived is past. You are mine now, until I judge you fit to return to your fathers, or you lie dead on the sand beneath your feet.' He pointed to the sand for emphasis. 'Here you may claim your heritage as true Deathknights, serving your fathers or the Dark God. I will send you to either with equal pleasure.' He looked from face to face. 'Each of you will be paired with another. You will share quarters. From this moment, that warrior will be your brother. You will gladly give your life for him, and he for you. If your fathers are enemies, it does not matter. He is your brother. That is your first lesson.

'Now,' he pointed quickly to the two young warriors at each end of the semicircle. 'You and you, step forward.' They did so and he pointed to each. 'Your name!'

Each warrior stated his name and Hirea said, 'You are now brothers until you leave this place. After that you may feel free to kill one another, but until then you will die for one another.' He motioned over his shoulder. 'Stand behind me.'

He repeated this with the next two youths, and the two after that, until he came to Valko. He was paired with a son of the Remalu, by the name of Seeleth, son of Silthe, Lord of the Rianta. Valko said nothing as the remaining warriors were paired up, but he was dubious about his new 'brother'. The Remalu were known throughout Kosridi as fanatics. Many of their youth gave up the way of the sword to become Deathpriests. To serve the

Dark God was an honour, and no one would say otherwise, but many felt it a less manly path. Priests died of old age and had no sons they could acknowledge. Any son of a priest was doomed to be a Lesser. Any warrior would prefer death to having a child survive to become a Lesser. Let the Lessers breed their own kind.

Rumour also told that they counted many among the Order of Deathmages. They were related to powerful lords on other worlds, and were kin to advisors to the TeKarana himself. Among the families on Kosridi the Remalu were most hated, as well as the most feared and distrusted.

Seeleth whispered, 'Many of these will die soon, my brother.'

Valko said nothing, returning only a single curt nod.

When eight pairs of brothers stood before him, Hirea nodded and pointed at the first pair, then let his hand sweep in an arc as he addressed all of them. 'Each of you has been given a room with two beds,' said Hirea. 'Those of you who were on my left when I called you out, move your belongings to the room your brother occupies. Dine at the zenith, then return here for your first training combat. Go!'

The young warriors moved in orderly fashion and soon Valko found himself alone in his quarters watching Seeleth put his few belongings in a chest at the foot of the second bed. Valko noted these contained quite a few mystic items, the sort given to a son by a worried mother. Perhaps

Seeleth's mother had come out of the Hiding to take a place of honour in his father's court, or had given them to him before he left the Hiding. But a few of the items looked to be of much darker aspect than mere trinkets and had the feel of magic to them. Wards? Charms for good fortune?

Seeleth grinned at Valko as he sat on his bed. To Valko he resembled a hungry zarkis – the feared night hunter of the plains. 'We are going to do great things, Valko,' Seeleth whispered.

'Why are you whispering?'

'Trust no one, my brother.'

Valko nodded, once. *If that is the case,* he thought, *why should one trust a 'brother' who will only be that until we leave?* Seeleth was apparently a peculiar type. The more he thought about it, the more Valko thought he might be the sort to become a Deathpriest. 'Let us go to the zenith meal,' said Valko, rising.

Seeleth stood as well, but stepped close and looked his new 'brother' squarely in the eyes. This was either an act of confidence or challenge. As no weapons were drawn, Valko assumed Seeleth was confiding in him. 'We shall do great things,' he whispered. 'Perhaps we shall be the ones to find and destroy the White.'

'The White are a myth,' shot back Valko. 'To imagine such beings is . . . madness!'

Seeleth laughed. 'Such distress over a myth!'

Valko felt his anger rising. 'We are here to train, *brother*. I care not for the ambition of a son of the

Remalu, nor do I waste time in fanciful visions of glory quests; they are for children playing in the Hiding.

'My father commanded me to be here, so I am here. Hirea instructs me to call you brother, and to die for you if needed. I obey. But don't vex me with your mind games, *brother*, for I will kill you.'

Seeleth laughed again. 'You answer as would any proper Dasati warrior,' he said, then left the room in the direction of the eating hall. Valko stood perplexed for a long moment, wondering what the purpose of all that had been. The White was an obscene concept, a blasphemy even, something not spoken of by anyone who wished to survive the harsh reality of Dasati life. To admit that the White might exist was to admit the Dark One was not omnipotent. Yet, if such a thing did exist, and if somehow one could be the warrior to end it, greatness would surely follow. But how could the White exist unless the Dark God was not supreme? The very question was an affront to logic. Was it offensive enough that he could justify taking Seeleth's head without having to defend himself against Hirea? To kill a Remalu would earn him standing with his father. He pondered it but an instant, then pushed aside the question and followed Seeleth to the zenith meal.

It had been a tiny mistake, but one that left a young warrior lying on the sand with his blood flowing unceasingly through the fingers that clutched his wound.

Hirea strode over and looked down at the wounded youth. His training opponent looked down as well, his face an unreadable mask. Hirea turned to the victor in the match and said, 'Go stand over there.' He pointed to a spot at the edge of the training floor.

Hirea was silent for a moment. Then he asked, 'What do you need?'

The wounded young warrior could barely speak as he lay curled on the floor, clutching his stomach. Finally he said, 'End it.'

Hirea's hand shot to the hilt of his sword, and before the other young warriors could even fully comprehend the motion, the sword came down and ended the young man's life. Then several of them started to laugh at his misfortune; Valko and Seeleth were not among them. Looking up at those laughing, Hirea said, 'He was weak! But not so weak as to ask for an Attender.' He glanced down. 'This is not funny. It is not worthy of regret, but it is not funny.' He motioned with his free hand for the boy's body to be removed, and the two Lessers standing nearby hurried to pick up the now-lifeless thing and carry it away to the Death Room, where the Renders would take apart the corpse and harvest all that was useful. The rest would be mixed in with the livestock feed. In that tiny way he would still serve.

'Does anyone here not understand?' When no

one spoke, Hirea said, 'It is permitted to ask a question; you will not learn if you stay silent.'

A warrior on the other side of the room said, 'Hirea, what would you have done had he asked for an Attender?'

Hirea put up his sword. 'I would have watched him bleed to death slowly. His suffering would have been reward for his further weakness.'

Seeleth said, 'Now, that would have been funny.'

Hirea overheard him and turned. 'Yes, that would have been.' He gave out a single laugh, a harsh barking sound, then shouted, 'Return to your places!' To the opponent of the dead man, he said, 'I shall be your partner in the drill until another dies, then he who makes the kill will be your new brother.' He faced off against the youth who had just mortally wounded his brother and said, 'Good kill.'

The youth nodded, not venturing a smile and his nervous expression showed that he now wondered if he would survive the rest of the day's training.

The young warriors were roused in the dead of night by the servants. The Lessers were cautious in rousing the warriors, entering each room quietly, whispering to the young men then prudently stepping away lest a suddenly awakened young warrior vent his ire on the nearest target. Yet the message was heeded: *Hirea says to be ready to ride at once.*

The warriors slept in dark nightshirts in

Dasati fashion, but with their weapons at hand. Quickly servants returned to each room to aid the young fighters, quickly stripping off the nightshirts, helping them to don a simple loincloth, foot and ankle wraps and a light undershirt. Then came padded pants and a light jacket, then armour. Each warrior who survived training would find a complete wardrobe of garments suitable for every occasion when he returned home, but during training this was the sum of their wardrobes: battle dress and a nightshirt. Even during their lessons with the Eflectors and Facilitators did they wear their armour.

The young fighters hurried to the stable where lackeys had already saddled the waiting varnins. The mounts pawed the ground and snorted in anticipation of a hunt. Valko went to his mount, a young female who had not yet bred, and patted her hard on the neck before springing into the saddle. The varnin's massive head bobbed slightly in acknowledgement that her rider was there then she snorted as he took the reins, yanking once, hard, to let her know he was in command. Varnins were stupid animals, and one had to remind them constantly who was in control. Great riders chose males for their aggressiveness, but most riders were on geldings and young females.

Valko waited while the remaining warriors mounted – ten in all from the original sixteen. The six who died all deserved their fate, Valko knew, but something about the death of the last, a youth named Malka, troubled him. He had been sparring with Seeleth and had suffered a minor wound, merely a cut to the fleshy part of the forearm, and hadn't even dropped his sword. As with such wounds, he was permitted the opportunity to dress it himself. Valko had seen him signal to Seeleth for a pause, and Seeleth had stepped away, acknowledging the cessation. Malka began to shift his sword from right hand to left and Seeleth had waited, then when Malka was least able to defend himself, the son of the Remalu had struck, a single blow to the neck which killed him instantly.

Nothing had been said. Valko could not imagine Hirea hadn't seen the kill, for nothing escaped the old warrior's sight. Yet he had done nothing. Valko had expected Seeleth to be chastised, even killed, by the old teacher for breaking the rules of the combat, but Hirea had merely turned his back as if he had seen nothing.

Valko was troubled, but not enough to ask a question. Questions when they were not expected were dangerous; too many questions meant a warrior was unsure of himself. Lack of certainty was weakness. Weakness was death.

Still, he remained troubled; rules were not followed, yet no punishment was forthcoming. What could be the lesson here, Valko wondered? That victory negated rules?

Hirea stood up in the stirrups on the back of an

old male, as veteran and battle-scarred as he was. He signalled and the riders left the stabling area and reined in at the portal of the stabling yard. Hirea held up his hand for order and then spoke. 'A warrior must be ready to answer the call at any moment of the day or night. Now we ride!'

The young warriors followed their instructor as he led them down the long winding road from the old fortress that was now their training home. In ages past the fortress had belonged to a chieftain of an ancient tribe, its name now known only to archivists. The shifting sands that were the foundations of Dasati society had swallowed up another family. Perhaps a group of families had switched allegiances, abandoning an allied family to a harsh fate while seeking a more powerful patron. Perhaps a patron had been deserted by clients who sought more power by forming new alliances.

Valko realized he would never know unless he took the time to seek out an archivist, something for which he had little time and even less inclination. Valko let his senses attune to the night. He preferred the night: the lack of visible light was more than compensated for by his ability to see heat and, to a lesser degree, sense motion. Like all his race he could easily adapt to most environments; even deep, cold tunnels and caves. As he had spent most of his days of Hiding in such, Valko had developed an exceptional knack of judging distances and shapes, no matter how faint, by echoes.

He drank in the landscape as they rode down the trail – the blank, rolling fields, the distant hills almost imperceptible save for being slightly darker than the surrounding air. All was a panorama of gloom, except where tiny hot spots revealed vermin and their predators. A distant pack of zarkis could be seen chasing a swift prey animal, perhaps a loper or darter, across a distant field. Dangerous for one man, the zarkis pack would give eleven riders a wide berth. Years of being killed by the Dasati had bred a healthy fear of armed riders into them. But there were other night predators to be wary of: keskash, the two-legged ambush-hunter of the woodlands who would rush from concealment and snap a rider off his mount with jaws strong enough to shred armour. Its hide secreted a film of moisture that evaporated rapidly, hiding its heat form until it was almost upon its prey.

In the air the night-pouncers circled, their tiny intellect turned completely to calculating chances of survival as they struck down various prey, for nothing on this world surrendered its life without a struggle. Their heat images were hazy, for their large membrane wings dissipated heat quickly, hiding them from detection, both from those they sought to consume and from the flying claws, the powerful flyers who drifted high above them. The claws soared in the upper atmosphere, at times miles above the surface, until they expelled the gases from their bowels that gave them buoyancy;

then they would swoop down on unsuspecting targets in the sky or on the surface. Their large wings would snap open with a crack like thunder as they turned their stoop into a sudden glide, their hollow pointed claws seizing their prey. Their powerful wings would beat as they climbed higher into the sky while they sucked fluids from the bodies of those they clutched in their talons. Before they reached their soaring altitude, they'd let go of a dried carcass that would tumble slowly back to the surface. The claws were powerful enough to seize a varnin and lift it, and those talons could punch through a breastplate. It was rare, but not unheard of, for a rider to be snatched from the saddle and carried off.

Valko revelled in the night. Like most of those on this ride, he had slept days most of his Hiding, venturing out after sunset to steal what he needed. His mother had told him that once he had sought out and won his place at his father's right hand, he would come to appreciate the daylight. He never doubted his mother; she was a woman of powerful intellect and keen perception, and he had yet to discover that she was wrong on any subject, but he wondered if he would ever feel completely comfortable in the harsh day after the concealing night.

He wondered why they were making this sudden night ride, but knew better than to voice any question. Hirea would tell them what they needed to know when they needed to know it. The Dasati way was predicated on a complex set of relationships, and when it was time for blind obedience, any question would almost certainly get a young warrior killed.

His varnin was huffing as they crested another hill, for these creatures were bred to charge over short distances at high speed, not for endurance rides. But no draught varnins had been stabled at the old castle. Each youth knew the more sedate creature was a poor steed in battle, but they were preferable for longer rides. Valko concluded that either dire circumstances had led Hirea to call out the young riders or he just didn't care if the animals were incapacitated. Valko didn't care if his mount suffered; he just didn't like the inefficiency of seeing a good war mount ruined and had no desire to walk back to the castle if it should fail.

As they started down the hill, Hirea motioned for a halt. Several varnins were huffing with flaring nostrils and trembling as they fought to catch their breath. Idly Valko wondered if the varnins and draught varnins could somehow be bred, resulting in a steed with both endurance and the requisites needed for ferocity in battle. He took a moment to save the question to ask a breeder at his father's demesne. Such a steed would gain the Camareen power, raising their status in the Sadharin, and perhaps even bringing them closer to the Karenna's court and the Lagradin, for such a beast would be of great value to the Empire.

Then Valko sensed it. Familiar as his mother's voice, the sense of being near a Hiding. His mind

197

struggled with conflicting thoughts and feelings. He saw other young riders also looking agitated and confused.

Mere weeks ago he would have been among those seeking shelter from the night riders, trying to blend in with the shielding countryside.

He forced himself to think. Why would there be a Hiding here, in low farmland hills running with zarkis, keskash and other dangers? He willed his mind to be free from the conflicting desires to hide and to hunt. There! He saw it. A stream that had cut deeply enough into the wash below that it was not visible from the road. It would be leading down from the hills to the east. Whoever was concealed nearby had been driven down from the mountains above, perhaps a local lord had caught wind of the Hiding on his land and had been clumsy in hunting down the fugitives. Or perhaps the fugitives were relocating as a matter of practice, as his mother had done many times during his childhood – though his mother never would have led him and the other children into any position this exposed.

There was a natural wish in Dasati warriors to destroy any potential young male rivals or females too young or too old to breed. As his mother had taught him, if warriors were too successful, the race would perish. Yet if they did not earnestly try to purge the weak, the fate of the race would eventually be obliteration. His mother was a remarkable teacher, always giving Valko subjects to ponder. On more than one occasion she had observed that intelligence had not been a useful gift from the Dark One and that animals who are more in balance with the natural order survive at better rates than the Dasati. Only one child in five survived into adulthood, which is why breeding young had been such a drive.

Even abstract thinking about breeding while in the middle of a hunt made Valko's body start to ache. If there was a suitable breeding female nearby he would take her this night, even if she was a Lesser! It had been those first such yearnings that had forced his mother to send him to his father, for once he was able to breed, he was ready for the testing; moreover, he was a deadly danger to every immature Dasati in the Hiding. Valko wondered where his mother might be. He knew that as soon as he had departed, she and the other mothers in Hiding would have moved to another safe location, perhaps to one of the villages of Lessers in the high peaks.

Valko shook his head to clear it. This was madness, dwelling on the past while a purging was commencing! He saw Hirea watching him, for he, alone among the riders had regained his perspective. He didn't hesitate, but spurred his still-breathless varnin down the bank towards the stream. As he suspected, there was someone hunkered below the sheltering overhang of rocks there. As soon as his varnin's hooves struck the water, they were off.

He couldn't see features clearly in the dark, but as they moved the concealing wet mud started to fall off their upper bodies and was washed off legs and thighs by the water in the stream. There were half a dozen young and three adult females. He drew his sword and charged. One female ushered the young ahead of herself while two turned to challenge him. Suddenly he wished it was day, for he could not tell from their heat-shape if they were armed. He knew the desperate females would defend the young with nails and teeth against armour if they must, and two adult Dasati females were not to be taken lightly by a young warrior.

He was anxious to kill. The demand for blood on his sword pounded in his ears like an ancient chant, and he realized it was the sound of his own heart he was hearing.

It would be rash to go straight in, either attacking the first female with his varnin, while striking at the second with his sword. But he also knew that whichever one he attacked, the other would almost certainly leap at him, attempting to pull him from the saddle.

As if coordinating by thought alone, the two females spaced themselves evenly, forcing him to choose one over another. A the last instant, Valko took his varnin to the edge of the bank, away from one female and beyond the reach of the second. He didn't waste a second trying to cut at her from below, for he knew she would most certainly try to duck under the sword blow, and might grab his boot and unseat him.

He feigned with his sword and as she started to stoop, kicked her in the face. Then he leapt down from his mount, landing with his boot heel on her throat, crushing it. He was close enough to hear the deadly snarl of the second female who almost certainly knew she was about to die, but who would do so willingly to save her young. She crouched, and in her right hand she held a blade.

Valko could hear other riders finally coming down the bank, and he knew that in a moment they would be past him, attempting to overtake the other female and the young. His anger at not being in on the killing of the children fuelled his already considerable bloodlust, so he looped a lazy blow towards her head, as if he had no regard for how dangerous she could be with a large dagger. As he expected she ducked easily underneath it and thrust her dagger at the spot where his neck was unprotected by his breast plate; but he had only feigned the blow. At the last moment he turned his blade down, catching the female across the shoulder, and rather than trying to use force to sever her head from her neck, he just pulled back hard on the blade, opening up a deep wound in her neck that started a fountain of blood. She took a staggering step towards him, then collapsed to her knees.

Without waiting to see her fall forward, he dodged around her. Other riders sped past him.

He reached his varnin, mounted it and was about to put his heels to its sides when Hirea's voice shouted, 'Valko! Wait here!'

The young fighter reined his mount around, the need to kill still pounding in his chest. He sat trembling, but obeyed as Hirea said, 'Hold.'

Hirea came to his side, their mounts facing in opposite directions so they could speak face-to-face. 'How did you know?'

Valko couldn't catch his breath.

'Deep slow breaths, and turn your mind away from killing. You are not an animal. You are Dasati.'

Valko found it difficult. He wanted nothing more than to ride after the others, find those in Hiding and slash and hack until the stream ran orange with their blood. He gritted his teeth.

'Think!' shouted Hirea, one of the rare times he had raised his voice. 'Do not let any part of you overwhelm your mind! Your mind, Valko! Always the mind first. You are not an animal. Now, think!'

Valko forced his attention to his hand, the one holding the reins of his varnin. He then concentrated on the trembling he felt in the reins, as the animal waited for his next command, ready to answer the call to hunt, excited by the smell of blood in the air. He felt his mind expand from the attention he paid to the animal, the stream, their surroundings, to Hirea himself. Finally, he slowly sheathed his sword.

'We had received a message from a trader that

he had seen smoke on the wind at sunset. I was guessing as to the most likely place they might hide from that tiny piece of information. But you found their exact location. We should have ridden past and they should have reached that distant woodland. How did you know?'

Valko spoke slowly, his voice thick with emotion. 'I knew they were down there.'

'But how? I didn't smell them, for the mud masked the scent, and I couldn't see them.'

'It is where I would have hidden,' said Valko. 'It is what I would have done.'

Hirea's old eyes studied the young face, not seeing the features clearly, but sensing the pattern of blood as it pulsed under the skin. Valko knew his face must have looked like a burning mask in the night when Hirea had come to his side.

'You were overwhelmed by the conflict between your training to hide and your desire to kill, yet you regained control faster than any youth I have trained.'

Valko shrugged. 'I just did.'

'Ah,' said Hirea. He leaned over and said, 'Listen, young lord of the Camareen. The Scourge have little concern for the youth of the Sadharin, but you have . . . potential. It is not in your best interest or that of your family to make that potential too widely known too early in life. You must learn to walk the thin line between strength and weakness, the balance that will keep you alive until you find your own place in the order of the Dasati.

'You have two kills tonight, both adult females in their prime. This is not an insignificant achievement for a youth. It earns you merit.

'But for you to have overtaken the others and killed more this night . . . that would have been . . . remarkable. And being remarked upon is something you do not wish right now.' Hirea turned his mount slightly, motioning for Valko to bring his varnin alongside. 'Come, let us see how the others are doing.'

Valko fell in beside his teacher.

'I can smell the blood and breeding lust in you, young Camareen. If I'm a judge of such things you will soon be back at your father's castle.' He leaned over and again dropped his voice. 'But not too soon, as that would also be remarkable.' He pointed, 'The others are over there. If any of those children escaped, I will have them walk back to the keep, leading their mounts, and if they have to fight a pack of zarkis, so be it.

'I am rewarding you,' said Hirea. 'I will send a female Lesser to your room when we return. You reek of breeding need. I will have her teach you the Games of Tongues and Hands, but do not couple: you would displease your father should you begin breeding, even with unacknowledged Lessers, before I have judged you ready to establish your place in his house.

'But you deserve acknowledgement for being the first to find the Hiding, and for the first kill. Share the female with your brother or not as you wish, but remember, what you did this night was remarkable.'

Valko nodded, realizing that soon he might have to kill this old man.

CHAPTER 11

DELECORDIA

The vista was amazing.

Pug, Nakor, Magnus and Bek had exited a doorway from the Hall of Worlds, after following detailed instructions by Vordam and were now standing upon a peak overlooking the city of Shusar, on the world of Delecordia. As he had warned them, the doorway used was the less travelled of the three doors known to connect Delecordia to the Hall, and it was the least used for an obvious reason; for it exited onto a windswept ledge with barely enough room for the four men to stand, and only a single narrow pathway down to safety.

Pug didn't worry about falling; he had enough magical skill to protect himself and the others, though none of them would likely need his help. Magnus was better able to levitate and fly than any student in the history of Sorcerer's Island, Nakor always had a 'trick' at hand, and while Bek couldn't fly, everything he had revealed about himself gave Pug the distinct impression it would take more than a tumble down a small mountain to kill the young warrior.

'Look at that,' whispered Bek. 'That's interesting.'

Nakor was forced to agree. 'Yes, very interesting.'

The sky contained colours they had never experienced, scintillating rushes of hues across the spectrum that pulsed and glowed for brief instants, never staying still quite long enough for the eye to apprehend them. It seemed that every gust of breeze or movement of a cloud above was outlined in these alien colours. Pug was quiet for a moment then said, 'I've seen colours like that once before.'

Magnus glanced at the steep mountainside sweeping downward from where they stood. 'When was that, Father?'

'When I was a boy. During the ride with Lord Borric, when Tomas and I were travelling with him to warn the Prince of Krondor of the Tsurani invasion. Beneath the dwarves' mountains we encountered a waterfall with colours like those. The rocks bled minerals that were made luminescent from the churning energy of the water, and the light from our lanterns. I've not seen those colours since, and never this vivid.'

'I like it!' shouted Ralan Bek, as if the point needed to be emphasized by volume.

Nakor said, 'Really?' Nothing in his experience with the young man had prepared him to consider he possessed any aesthetic appreciation.

'Yes, Nakor.' Bek looked heavenward, a near rapt expression on his face. 'It's nice. I like the flashes and the way you can see the wind.'

'You can see the wind?' asked Magnus.

'Yes. Can't you?'

'No,' Magnus admitted.

Nakor squinted. 'Ah, now I can see . . .' He turned to the two magicians. 'If you try to see through the air, to the space behind it you can see the pressure of the wind, like water rippling across a smooth sheet of rock. Try.'

Pug did and after a moment he began to gain a sense of what the two men had seen. 'It's like heat shimmer on the desert,' he said at last.

'Yes!' said Bek. 'Only it's more. You can see it behind itself.'

Pug's eyes narrowed questioningly as he looked at Nakor who merely shook his head. 'He sees deeper than any of us.'

Pug decided not to pursue the matter for the moment. The wind was chilling and the air had a bitter tang. In the distance, they could see their destination, the city of Shusar. 'Look at the size of it,' he said.

He had spoken at length with Kaspar about his vision on the mountains called the Pavilion of the Gods, and asked him questions about every detail. One thing Kaspar had been emphatic about was the enormity of the Dasati cities.

Pug tried to calm himself, but the entire experience of entering Delecordia was taking its toll. 'I think this will take some getting used to.'

'We'd better start down, Father,' said Magnus. 'Vordam's instructions are helping, but I can feel myself beginning to feel ill. We must reach Kastor soon.'

Pug agreed with a nod and started walking down the path. 'As soon as we are able, I'll try a small jump to a visible site, but I suspect I may not be able to focus my mind correctly. It feels as if I've been given a sleeping draught.'

Nakor nodded. 'It's interesting here, but not good. We need to find this Kastor fellow, yes.'

As he had predicted, Pug was unable to effect the spell he used to travel short distances, willing himself to any place he could see. Nakor watched him struggle and said, 'Yes, yes, it's as I thought. Stuff here is different than back home. It's twisted . . . wrong.'

'What do you mean?' asked Magnus as they continued to trudge down the long trail to the road that led to the city.

'I don't know,' said Nakor. 'It's how I think of it. Stuff has rules. It acts a certain way when you do things do it. You push on the right side, and it goes left. You push down and it goes down. This world's stuff . . . it's as if you push on it and it pushes back, or you press down and it wants to go left.' He grinned as he added, 'Interesting, and if I had time, I think I could figure out how to work it.'

Pug said, 'If Kastor can take care of us as Vordam said he could, we should then have time for you to learn, Nakor. Magnus and myself as well.'

Bek pointed, his hand sweeping in an arc,

indicating the entire vista. 'This is a wonderful place, Nakor. I really like it.'

Nakor looked at his young companion. 'How do you feel?'

Bek shrugged as he walked at Nakor's shoulder, down the narrow trail. 'I feel fine. Why? Don't you?'

Nakor said, 'None of us feels well here, but you do?'

'Yes. Is that wrong?' asked the powerful youth.

'Apparently not,' said Magnus.

The trail broadened as it reached the lower hills. After nearly two hours of steady walk, they reached the verge of a wide road, almost a highway, that led to the city. A cart pulled by something that looked a great deal like a horse, but had broader shoulders and a shorter neck rolled by, the beast snorting as the driver in the high seat behind prodded it with a long stick, apparently the item of control. As the cart passed them, the driver gave them a glance; but if he was surprised to see four humans standing on the roadside, he didn't reveal any change of expression.

'I wonder how he gets it to stop,' said Pug.

Nakor said, 'Maybe he just stops prodding it and it stops out of gratitude?'

Magnus laughed just loud enough to cause Pug to turn. His elder son rarely displayed any sense of humour and on those rare occasions when he did, it always surprised his father.

They turned up the highway, staying on the

verge, as vehicles were a steady feature of this thoroughfare. Pug had visited other worlds, had lived on Kelewan with the Tsurani for eight years, and had spent time with non-human sentient beings, but there was something about this place that fascinated him more than anything he had ever encountered. This place and these people were alien in a way he had never imagined possible.

Vordam had been quite precise in all his instructions, and he had answered a few questions, but only those pertaining to Pug and his friends reaching the merchant Kastor quickly and efficiently. He had deferred many questions to Kastor, as if Vordam had reasons for being cautious that were not apparent to Pug.

The city was magnificent. As they trudged along the road, getting closer by the minute, Pug could see the stones of the dark wall were slightly reflective, giving off hints of colour as if light had been broken into a spectrum, like oil on water. Were there minute crystals in the stone? Pug wondered.

As they neared the vast city gates, the wonders increased. The stones were fitted so closely the walls appeared seamless. They towered eleven or twelve storeys by human standards.

'What sort of enemy were they expecting?' said Pug.

'Oh, maybe they just like really tall things,' replied Nakor as he drifted over to the left side of the massive entrance to the city. 'Now this is interesting,' he observed.

There were no gates in the traditional human fashion, but rather a massive portion of wall was retracted inside, swinging on hinges of unimaginable design. Nakor laughed. 'They haven't had to use them in a while.'

A tree of some sort had grown up alongside the wall, blocking the segment that was retracted. 'That would make closing the gate problematic,' said Magnus with a smile.

'I think they'd figure out a way,' offered his father as they entered the Ipiliac city of Shusar. 'That they're peaceful is welcome news.'

'Or they killed all their enemies,' Bek offered.

Pug spared the youth a backward glance and saw him looking around at everything as if his head was on a swivel, his eyes wide and his face a grinning mask. 'I like these people, Nakor,' Bek said. 'This is an interesting and wonderful place.'

Pug didn't have Nakor's appreciation of the way this odd boy thought, but he knew him well enough to know that this was as close as Bek could get to exhibiting what others would call joy. Bek lived in a heightened state of existence, it seemed, his pleasures coming from anything that offered an emotional peak, be it sex, violence or beauty. Pug wondered, and not for the first time, why his future self had insisted on the lad being in this company. Now tiny pieces of a very complex puzzle were falling into place; of all of them, Bek was the least disoriented and least troubled by coming to this realm. He actually seemed to be enjoying it while his three companions were experiencing mounting discomfort and illness.

If their presence caused any alarm in the Ipiliac they masked it well. In fact, Pug noticed, most barely spared the four humans a glance.

He was forced to admit that once the alien aspect wore off, the Ipiliac appeared to be a handsome race: tall, almost regal, their movements fluid and graceful. The women were striking if not obviously attractive by human standards. They moved with even more grace than the men, motion that had an almost seductive quality to it, yet they appeared unselfconscious as far as Pug could see. There were apparently playful moments as men and women in the market joked with one another and shouted greetings. By any measurement Pug could apply, these seemed a happy people.

By the time they reached the plaza Vordam had described, Pug was feeling a tightness in his chest, a shortness of breath, and he was starting to cough. The others, apart from Bek, were also labouring. Pug halted before a fountain, one which astonished him because of its beauty, a crystal thing with lights within, and water tumbling in sheets to strike harmonious sounds each time drops splashed on a crystal face.

'There,' said Pug, pointing. 'The shop with the red door.'

A company of mounted riders was coming through the plaza, all wearing black tunics trimmed with purple, each with a shield of white on his back. Each man wore a hat that looked to be made of some felted material and boots that reached the knees with a high flap folded down in front. The dashing look was heightened by each man sporting a small chin beard.

They were riding the odd horse like creatures at a posting trot and Bek laughed like a child. 'Ha! I wonder if they can fight?'

Pug looked at once to see if he intended to test the question, but was relieved to see him merely watching in open-mouthed admiration. He motioned for the others to follow him and they moved towards their destination. Pug spared a look up and down the streets, more to gauge how the local populace approached these shops: whether they knocked then entered, were admitted, or were just entering.

Seeing that shops were being entered and left without issue, he pushed open a shop door. Inside they found nothing that resembled a human shop: no counters, no shelves, no apparent inventory or even images of products for sale. Instead there were cushions strewn across the floor around a large device with several hoses of woven fabric leading from it. A large bowl topped this apparatus.

An Ipiliac came through a beaded curtain, tall and thin even by this race's standards. He wore a rippling robe of rainbow colours that shifted hue as he walked. He paused for a moment, looked from face to face, then spoke a phrase in an alien tongue. When they didn't respond, he tried another language, one Pug recognized.

'We are not from that world,' he said. 'We are from Midkemia.'

In Keshian, the entrepreneur said, 'Welcome to my establishment. I rarely get human clients. You must be the ones Vordam spoke of. How may I be of service?'

'We seek a guide to the world of Kosridi.'

Now Pug saw surprise on the merchant's features.

'You seek a way into the next realm?'

'Is it possible?' Pug asked.

'Yes, but difficult. However, Vordam would not have sent you had he thought it impossible. You are beings of considerable strength to have reached this shop without the aid of powerful magic.'

'Which doesn't seem to work here,' Magnus responded. 'And it is getting difficult to breathe.'

Nodding, Kastor said, 'I can help.' He vanished into the rear of his shop, then returned with a small pouch and deposited the contents into the bowl of the device. Then he added a liquid and almost at once a light mist appeared above the bowl. 'If you would inhale this mist, through these hoses I think you will find your breathing difficulties will be ameliorated.'

Bek said, 'I don't need to.'

The Ipiliac studied the young man for a minute, then softly said, 'I think you are right.'

Pug hesitated for an instant, as Nakor and Magnus began inhaling from their small hoses. It was pointless to worry: they had no other choice; they were here and had to trust this being. Pug inhaled deeply, fighting back a cough as the pungent mist started to affect his lungs. After several deep breaths, his discomfort eased.

After one long deep inhalation, Nakor said, 'This is very good.'

Kastor said, 'Forgive me for being direct, but you will discover time is against you should you decide not to continue onward with your quest.'

'We have no intention of turning back.'

'So you say, but there are many things about the place you seek I am certain you do not understand, and I will not agree to help you until I am certain that you do.'

Pug nodded.

'The Dasati will kill you on sight. Simply for existing. They are a race akin to our own, but driven by realities you can only begin to imagine, let alone fully comprehend. Everything that is a potential threat is to be destroyed, utterly, and anything not understood is a threat, and therefore destroyed.

'In the history of those people, twelve worlds have come under their dominion. Of these, five were inhabited by other races. In each case, that world was completely cleansed of its native race: today every animal down to the lowest insect, every plant, every form of life, is from the Dasati home world: Omadrabar.'

Pug recognized the name from his own note to himself, but said nothing. He wanted to meditate on why he must not only do this nearly impossible thing, but go to the very heart of the most dangerous threat faced by his own world.

'I take your caution,' said Pug. 'The Dasati are fearsome and deadly.'

'Implacable, my friend. You will never get one to speak with you, let alone negotiate. So, I must first tell you that to survive for more than a few minutes on Kosridi will be a far more difficult undertaking than merely preparing your bodies to endure the state of life on that world.'

'Vordam has touched on the subject,' said Pug. 'He likened it to throwing straw on a flame.'

'More like a combustible oil,' replied Kastor. 'Analogy aside, let us argue that you have been trained to endure the state of existence, but you still must survive the Dasati. To do so will require magic of staggering proportion, for you will have to appear Dasati in every imaginable way, not only in likeness, but to senses beyond your own. For example, they can see your body heat, as I can, and you burn brighter than they do. So many details must be considered, down to your body odour and the pitch of your voice. Moreover, this spell must endure not for mere minutes or hours but for weeks, perhaps even months. In addition you must learn their language, culture, and behaviour in order to blend in. And you must be of sufficient importance to avoid . . .' He threw up his hands. 'It is impossible.'

Pug regarded him. 'I think not. I think you know how we can do such things. You just don't see the profit in it.'

'Not true. For this training I shall demand a price which would appal a king on your world.' He narrowed his gaze. 'Vordam would not have sent you had you been without means to pay such.'

'I can provide payment,' said Pug.

Nakor said, 'I am curious. What manner of payment?'

Vordam said, 'The usual. Metals of value: gold from your realm is especially useful given its non-reactive qualities. Silver for the opposite reason. Certain gems, again for their utility as well as beauty. Like many other races, we enjoy items that are unique, or at least distinctive, objects of art or curiosity.' He looked at Nakor and said, 'Most of all, I prize information.'

'Reliability and improbability,' said Nakor.

'Yes,' agreed Kastor. 'You understand.' He looked at Magnus. 'Do you?'

'Probably not,' said the younger magician, 'but I am my father's son, and I go where he goes.'

To Bek, Kastor put the same question. 'And you, young fighter. Do you understand?'

Bek just grinned, and Pug was struck how young he looked at times. 'I don't care. Just as long as

I can have fun. Nakor said this would be fun, so I'll go with him.'

'Very well,' said the Ipiliac, rising. 'We begin at once. Before anything else, we must conspire to find solutions for a myriad problems, but none so pressing as your ability to breathe the air of Kosridi, drink its water, and keep your life's energy inside your bodies.'

He motioned for them to follow and led them through the beaded curtain. In the rear of the building they discovered a hallway that led to a much larger building: a warehouse filled with row upon row of shelves.

After passing through the warehouse, he led them into a hallway with doors on either side. At the end of the hall he indicated two doors, one at each hand, and said, 'Here you will stay. Within the hour I will return with several draughts, potions, and powders for you to ingest. Without these you will soon sicken beyond anyone's ability to help you. Despite these measures, you must be prepared to endure great discomfort for many days to come. When you have been fully acclimatized to our world we will begin on four courses of action: we shall prepare you for your journey to the second realm, which will seem as if you're starting the entire process over again; we shall begin a reorganization of thought so that your understanding of magic will allow you to practise your arts of magic; we shall begin your appreciation of the Dasati, their language, and beliefs and how to contrive to be like them, so that they will not kill you; and we shall come to fully understand why you are undertaking a task of such monumental stupidity.'

Saying nothing else, he departed, leaving the four men alone in the hall. After a moment, Pug opened one of the two doors, indicating to Magnus that he should join him, and left Nakor and Bek to enter the other.

After two weeks, the food began to taste normal to them, and the air smelled sweet. The bouts of stomach cramps, coughing fits, malaise, and sudden sweating passed. Kastor had arranged for a series of instructions from an Ipiliac magician, a being named Danko who instantly fascinated Nakor and who seemed to reciprocate the little gambler's interests. After an exercise had been concluded, the two would wander the city, Bek trailing behind, while Pug and Magnus considered other problems to be anticipated.

Taking advantage of the others' absence, Pug and his son sat talking about the one question Pug had yet to explain to anyone's satisfaction: why had they undertaken this journey?

He said, 'Truth to tell, son, I do not know.'

Magnus sat on a sleeping pallet, his legs crossed beneath him, and smiled. 'Mother would rejoice to hear such an admission.'

Pug had weighed for months whether to tell his

family about the notes from the future, but caution always prevented it. He sighed. 'I miss her more right now than I can tell you, son. I'd endure one of her tantrums just to hear her voice.'

Magnus smiled broadly. 'I can only imagine what you'd hear if she heard you call them tantrums.'

Pug laughed. Then his face returned to an expression of concern. 'Magnus, all I can tell you now is that I know it is imperative we travel to the Dasati homeworld, to the very heart of their empire, and that we must do it via a particular world – where I suspect we shall find the cause of these incursions into Kelewan and the origin of the rifts – and then we must do whatever we discover needs doing to save our world and Kelewan.'

'But what I don't understand is why should we be at risk at all? The Talnoy is safely contained in the Assembly and no more rifts are troubling Midkemia. Why not destroy the Talnoy? Tomas's memories of the Dragon Lords say they are not impervious to all harm. Or at least remove it to some other place, perhaps a deserted world?'

Pug sighed. 'I have considered all that, and more. If we can learn anything valuable from the Assembly's study of the device it is worth the risk. I am unwilling to disturb any of the Talnoy still hidden from the Dasati by the wards in Novindus. If needs be, the Assembly can remove the Talnoy back to Midkemia via a rift to our island, and your mother knows what must be done should that be necessary.'

Magnus stood up. 'Let us go for a walk. I feel the need for a change. My stomach no longer bothers me and this room has become confining.'

Pug agreed and they left the merchant's quarters. They were expected to be there at sundown when Danko was due to join them for another exercise in magic. Nakor's observation about 'stuff' in this world behaving differently had proven apt; once the Ipiliac magician had begun his tutoring, Pug quickly recognized that everything in this realm followed different laws of behaviour and required new rules of operation for magic to work. It was, as Pug had observed after the first lesson, like learning a new language.

In the plaza they encountered another of the Ipiliac festivals in progress. Pug had been amused to discover that these people had many such events, some commemorating holy events or dates of historic significance. This one seemed to have something to do with food, as small cakes were being thrown to the crowd from those in the procession.

Pug snatched a muffin-sized confection out of the air and nibbled it. 'Not bad,' he observed, handing half to Magnus, who held up his hand to decline the offer.

They walked the plaza, venturing a little way down the main boulevard, still amazed at the scale of the Ipiliac city. Buildings rose up a dozen storeys, all smoothly faced with matching stone. There was nothing of this city that remotely resembled any human city that either father or son had visited, none of the slap-dash construction seen in the Kingdom, nor the accommodations to the weather seen in the Hotlands of Kesh, where houses were squat dark havens from the day's heat; nor Kelewan where buildings were uniformly painted white to reflect the sunlight, and manors were built with wood and paper, sliding walls to accommodate breezes, and many fountains and pools.

Down one side street a small parade approached: a woman of wealth riding in a sedan carried by burly – by Ipiliac standards – bearers. Magnus and Pug stepped aside as the regal woman passed, bedecked in what could only be called a provocative fashion: a slender girdle studded with jewels from which hung the lightest of skirts, leaving very little to the imagination, and a top consisting of complex beadwork which shifted and moved with tantalizing glimpses of bare skin beneath. Her black hair, the most common hue among these people, was piled high on her head and gathered in a ring of gold, falling down the back of her head like a horse tail, and she wore gems on every finger.

As she moved away, Magnus observed, 'This acclimatization we are undergoing has an interesting effect, Father. I found that female attractive.'

'They are a handsome race, once you get used to their alien appearance,' observed Pug.

'No, I mean attractive in a way that I might find a human woman arousing. Which is strange.'

Pug shrugged. 'Perhaps, perhaps not. I found the elf-queen to be beautiful by any standard, yet it was not a genuine physical yearning; but Tomas was smitten long before he transformed into what he is today.

'Maybe it has something to do with the changes we are subjecting ourselves to, or maybe it is merely a case of you having a more encompassing view of beauty than your father.'

Magnus said, 'Perhaps. I wonder who she might be. Were we in Kesh, I would think she was a member of the nobility or a minor royal. In Krondor, a courtesan to some man of wealth.' He shook his head in resignation. 'Here? Can we learn enough about the Dasati in . . . anything approaching a reasonable time to survive a visit to their world?'

Pug sighed. 'I think I can say with some conviction we will, but as to how I come to believe that . . .' Once again he wondered about telling his son about the messages from the future. 'Let us say I believe this journey is less dangerous than it looks.'

Magnus was silent for a minute, then he said, 'You have to stop treating me like your son, Father. I am, and have been for years, your most gifted student. I am nearly as powerful as you or Mother in several skills, and I suspect I may some day outstrip you both. I know you're trying to protect me—'

Pug cut him off. 'If I was trying to protect you, Magnus, I'd have left you back on the island with your mother and brother.' He looked around, as if trying to frame his thoughts and choose his words carefully.

'Don't ever claim that I'm trying to protect you, Magnus. I've kept silent a dozen or more times when you've gone in harm's way and every fibre in me screamed to send someone else. You may be a father some day and when you are, you'll understand what it is I'm saying. If I merely wanted you to be safe, you wouldn't be here.

'You lost a brother and sister you never knew, but I lost children I loved as dearly as I love you and Caleb.'

Magnus stood with his arms crossed and stared down at him, and for an instant Pug saw his wife in his son, both in his stance and expression. At last Magnus sighed. He looked Pug in the eye and said, 'I'm sorry, Father.'

'Don't be,' said Pug, gripping his arm. 'I appreciate your frustration. There isn't a day that goes by when I don't recall my own as I grew into my power, and I will remind you that your growth has been far more easy than my own.'

Magnus smiled warmly. 'I realize that.' He knew that his father had struggled while training under his original mentor, the old Lesser Path magician Kulgan, because at that stage in his life, Pug had been a natural adept of the Greater Path, a distinction which was no longer significant, but had very much been so when he was a boy. And after that came four years spent as a slave, then another four training with the Assembly of Magicians on Kelewan. By comparison, Magnus's training had been positively idyllic.

'Still,' continued Pug, 'it remains to be seen exactly how we are going to survive the coming journey.'

A voice from behind, speaking unaccented Keshian, said, 'Exactly the question you should be asking.'

Pug and Magnus had not noticed the speaker approach, so they both reacted quickly, assuming positions that could be only called defensive: weight distributed evenly, knees slightly bent, and hands near the daggers in their belts. Neither felt competent enough to attempt a magical defence yet.

'Be at ease. If I wished you dead, you would both already be dead,' said the speaker, a tall Ipiliac with the most human-looking face either had seen so far, made so in part by deep-set eyes and a heavy brow of bushy black hair. He wore his hair down to his shoulders, another unusual feature among these people as most men trimmed theirs at the nape or higher. His face was lined, suggesting his age to be past his prime, but his eyes were alert, his gaze scrutinizing, and his bearing and clothing could only be called a warrior's: quilted gambeson jacket, a crossed leather harness bearing several weapons, and breeches and boots, suggesting he was a rider.

'I am Martuch,' he said calmly. 'I am your guide. I am of the Dasati.'

CHAPTER 12

ENEMIES

Miranda threw a vase.

Exasperation overcame self-control and she needed to vent her frustration. Instantly regretting the act – she liked the simple but sturdy pottery – she reached out with her mind and stopped the ceramic vessel scant inches before it reached the opposite wall, preventing it from shattering. She willed it back to her hand and replaced it on the table where it had stood a moment earlier.

Caleb entered just in time to witness the display. 'Father?' he asked.

Miranda nodded. 'I miss him, and it makes me . . .'

Caleb grinned, and for a moment she saw her husband's smile. 'Impatient?' he offered.

'A wise choice of words,' she said. 'Is there news?'

'No, not from Father or Magnus, nor do I expect any soon. But we do have a message from the Assembly requesting your appearance at your earliest convenience.'

Miranda did a rough calculation in her head and

realized it was mid-morning on both worlds, for the uneven days caused long periods where mid-afternoon on one would be the middle of the night on the other. 'I'll go now,' she told Caleb. 'You're in charge until I return.'

Caleb held up his hands. 'You know many of the—'

'Magicians don't like it when you're in charge,' she finished. 'I know. And I don't care. This is your father's and my island, and that makes it your island when we're not around. Besides Rosenvar is still in Novindus with the Talnoy, Nakor and your brother are with your father, so that means you will just have to cope with any petty annoyance that comes along. If a dispute arises, settle it, or at least postpone resolution until one of us is back.

'Beside, my son, I may not be long on Kelewan.'

'I can only hope,' said Caleb.

As his mother walked away, she turned and said, 'Any word from the boys?'

Caleb shrugged. 'They don't have the ability to communicate quickly, Mother. I've asked a couple of our agents in Roldem to keep a watch when they can, but how much trouble can they be in surrounded by an entire university of La-Timsan monks?'

'You are in *so* much trouble,' said Zane.

'So much,' echoed Tad.

Jommy shot them both black looks as he stepped

out onto the practice floor. The students were training with swords, and while Jommy knew how to club a man with the hilt, cut his throat after kicking him in the groin, and every other dirty trick Caleb had been able to teach him, this was tournament sword fighting, with rules, a Master of the Sword to observe they were followed, and his opponent was Godfrey, Servan's closest ally, and from the way he held his weapon, he was no stranger to the practice floor.

Jommy tugged at the tight collar of his jacket as the Master of the Sword motioned for the two opponents to come together at the centre of the floor. The rest of the class watched quietly, all of them under the supervision of half a dozen monks.

The Master of the Sword spoke just loudly enough for his voice to carry over the muttering of the boys without yelling. 'This practice is to demonstrate the counter-strike.' He turned to Jommy and said, 'As Godfrey is the more experienced with a sword, you shall launch an attack. You may choose any line, high, middle, or low, but light or no contact only. Is that clear?'

Jommy nodded and returned to where his two foster-brothers stood. Tad handed him the helmet, a basket face-mask sewn to a cloth back. He lowered it over his head and took the starting position.

'Start!' commanded the Master, and Jommy hesitated, then launched a high blow, attempting as best he could within the rules to take Godfrey's head off.

Godfrey easily beat aside the strike, extended his arm, and delivered a hard touch to Jommy's chest; then as he withdrew his sword, with a flick he struck the only exposed part of Jommy's body, the back of his hand.

'Ow!' Jommy shouted, dropping his sword, to the obvious delight of the other students who laughed loudly.

'Pick up your sword,' the Master said.

'He did that on purpose,' Jommy said accusingly as he knelt to pick up his weapon.

Godfrey removed his helm and grinned at Jommy with contempt.

With disdain, the Master of the Sword said, 'It's a poor swordsman who accuses an opponent as a means of disguising his own shortcomings.'

Jommy stared for a long moment at the Master of the Sword, then said, 'Right. Let's do it again.'

He removed his own helm, walked to Zane and handed it to him, ran his hand through his damp hair, then nodded once as he retrieved his head-gear. Putting the helm back on, he turned to face Godfrey.

Tad said, 'I don't like that look.'

'Remember what happened the last time we saw it?'

'That tavern in Kesh?"

'Yes, where that soldier said that thing to the girl—'

'The one Jommy had taken a liking to?' Tad finished.

'That's the one.'

'That wasn't good.'

'No, it wasn't,' agreed Zane.

'This can't be good,' said Tad.

'No, it can't,' agreed Zane.

Jommy walked to the centre. The Master said, 'Again,' and directed the two combatants to their position. 'On the last pass,' he said to the observing students, 'this lad—' he pointed at Jommy, '—over-extended his attack, putting himself off balance, off-line, and leaving himself open to a simple beat from his opponent's sword, which put him further off-line and left him open for the counter-blow.' He glanced at the two opponents and said, 'Begin!'

Jommy came in, exactly has he had last time, repeating every move until the moment when Godfrey beat aside his blade. Rather than extend his arm fully, Jommy circled his blade around Godfrey's so his hilt was inside the other boy's, forcing Godfrey to try his own circling move, attempting to catch Jommy's blade, and again force it to the outside.

But instead of making another circle, Jommy raised his blade as if saluting, an unexpected move that caused Godfrey to falter. That was all the time Jommy needed. But instead of retreating a step to give himself room and re-establish his right-of-way, required before a touch could be claimed, Jommy just cocked his elbow and drove his sword hilt into Godfrey's face with as much force as possible.

The practice helms were designed to ward off a sword's tip or edge, not withstand a full-on blow from an angry youth of considerable size and strength.

The face-mesh folded and Godfrey went to his knees, blood flowing from under the mask. 'Foul!' cried the Master of Swords.

'Probably,' said Jommy. 'But I've seen worse in a fight than that.'

The Master of Swords looked at the senior monk in attendance, Brother Samuel, who managed to control any impulse to laugh that visited him. A soldier in the Army of Roldem before receiving the call to La-Timsa's service, Samuel was in charge of the students' martial training. Jommy, Tad and Zane had taken an instant liking to the man, and he seemed to enjoy their rough-edged approach to the subject. While the three boys might be far behind the others in matters of history, literature, philosophy and the arts, it was clear their previous 'education' had included a fair amount of hand-to-hand combat and swordplay. They might not be duellists, but they were fair brawlers. Brother Samuel tilted his head and arched his eyebrows, as if to say to the Master of Swords, 'you're in charge: you deal with it.'

'This is the *Masters' Court!*' he said, as if that explained everything. 'These lessons are to perfect the art of swordsmanship.'

'Then I won,' said Jommy.

'What?' The look on the Master of Swords' face was one of incredulity.

'Certainly,' said Jommy, putting his own helmet under his right arm so he could gesture with his left hand.

'That's outrageous!' shouted Servan.

Jommy took a deep breath, and in a tone used by those talking to little children or very stupid adults he said, 'I *knew* you wouldn't understand, Servan.'

To the Master of Swords he said, 'My opponent was trying to establish a line of attack that would make me step back while trying to disengage his blade, correct?'

The Master of Swords could only nod.

'So, if I did that, he'd have pushed my blade to the outside and lunged, and unless I was a lot faster than him – which I'm not – he would have touched me and I'd have lost. Or he would have beaten it to the inside, made a quick follow to re-establish his line and probably get right-of-way before me, and another touch. One more touch, he wins the bout.

'On the other hand, if I punch him in the face, and he can't win off a foul, we have to start again, and maybe this time I win.'

'This is . . .' words seem to fail the Master of Swords.

Jommy looked around the room and said, 'What? Isn't that the way it's supposed to work after a foul?'

The Master of Swords shook his head. 'The bout is finished. I declare Godfrey the victor.'

Still nursing his bloody nose, Godfrey hardly looked the winner. He glared at Jommy who merely smiled at him and shrugged.

Brother Samuel instructed the boys to change back into their uniforms: today's lesson was over. Servan whispered something into Godfrey's ear while the injured boy glared at Jommy.

Brother Samuel walked past each boy in the class in turn, offering an observation or two on their fighting styles and when he got to the three boys from Sorcerer's Island, he said, 'Tad, well done. Quickness is a good advantage. But be a little more cautious in trying to anticipate your opponent's next move.' He looked at Zane and said, 'You need to anticipate more. You're too cautious.'

Then he looked at Jommy and said, 'I'd never take you to a tournament, boy, but you can stand on my left at the wall, any time.' He winked and walked away.

Jommy smiled at his foster-brothers and said, 'Well, it's nice to know someone appreciates my better qualities.'

Zane looked past Jommy to Servan and Godfrey. 'He may be the only one.' He dropped his voice. 'You're on your way to having a couple of very powerful enemies, Jommy. We're not always going to be at university and a relative of the King may have a very long reach.'

Jommy sighed. 'You're right, but I can't help

myself. It's like those Bakers' Boys down in Kesh – bullies just make me want to start cracking heads. Probably comes from being the smallest lad in my family.'

Tad's eyes widened. 'You were the smallest?'

'Downright puny,' said Jommy as he pulled his uniform tunic on over his head. 'My older brothers, they were big: strapping fellows.'

Zane looked at Tad. 'It boggles the mind.'

'Come on,' said Jommy as he finished dressing. 'We need to get back to the others.'

The students followed Brother Samuel back to the university, where they returned to their other classes. For the three boys from Sorcerer's Island, that meant returning to the modest study room put aside for them in which to meet their tutor, Brother Jeremy, who was attempting to give them a fundamental grounding in mathematics. Zane took to it naturally and couldn't understand why Jommy and Tad seemed to have such difficulty with something he found surprisingly simple.

After two hours of maths tutoring, it was time for the evening meal, a meal that was conducted in silence, as the students dined with the monks, and occasionally one of the priests of La-Timsa. Breakfast and the midday meal were noisy and as lively as a hall full of boys could be, but the only sounds to be heard during the evening meal were the clatter of dishes being moved around the table, and the sound of knives and spoons against crockery.

Jommy couldn't speak, but nothing prevented him from nudging Zane, who in turn nudged Tad. Jommy indicated with a slight tilt of his head that someone special was sitting at the head table. The man was a tall, older cleric: from his robes a priest of some important rank. His eyes seemed fixed on the three boys from Sorcerer's Isle. The cleric's stare made Jommy very uncomfortable and he quickly dropped his gaze to his plate.

At the end of the meal, the students had specific duties until their free hour before they turned in, but rather than go to the kitchen where they were required this week, the three boys were approached by Brother Stephen. 'Come with me,' he said, turning his back and walking away without waiting to see if they followed.

The boys followed the Proctor until they reached his office. Entering it, they found the cleric who had sat at the head table, waiting. He motioned for them to shut the door; then he sat behind Brother Stephen's desk. He inspected each boy in turn, then finally said, 'I am Father Elias. I am the abbot here at the university. While it may not appear such, this school is, in fact, an abbey.

'You three have managed to somehow get on the wrong side of some very powerful people. I've been fielding many enquiries about you, including one from a deputy to the King himself, regarding the reasons why you're here, why a Keshian noble of considerable influence with the Emperor and his brother would sponsor you, and a host of other, difficult and awkward questions. Suffice it to say I've had some very annoying exchanges of messages over the few weeks since you've arrived.'

Jommy looked about to speak, then remembered he wasn't permitted to without permission. The abbot saw this and said, 'You have something to say?'

'Yes, Father.' He felt silent.

'Then say it, boy.'

'Oh, well, then . . .' Jommy began. 'Father, we didn't come here looking for trouble. It was waiting for us when we got here. I don't know if it's just one of those things, or if someone decided it was fair game to start in on us before we'd even set foot inside this building, but the truth is we'd have rather walked in, made ourselves known to Brother Kynan, and obeyed the rules as best we could.

'But Servan has decided that it's his life's work to make our every day miserable, and while I'm inclined to be easy-going, I just don't see how I can ignore this for . . . however long it is we're supposed to be here.'

'How long you remain here is one of the things we're going to talk about.' The abbot's dark eyes narrowed slightly as he studied each face. 'Tell me what you were told to expect here?' he asked, directing the question at Jommy.

Jommy said, 'Father, truth is, we weren't told very much, just that we were to come here from—'

'I know you came from Olasko, that colourful tale about the caravan from the Vale of Dreams notwithstanding. I also know you didn't come by ship.'

'—from Olasko,' Jommy continued. 'We were just told to get ready, come here, and learn whatever it was we were taught.'

The abbot was silent for a minute, drumming his fingers on the table in an absent-minded gesture that set Jommy's teeth on edge. Finally, Father Elias said, 'We have a special relationship with your . . . mentors.' Again he studied their faces. 'While we don't entirely accept that all their aims are in concert with our own, we do accept that they are an agency for good, and as such are to be given the widest possible latitude in matters of trust.' He sat back and stopped drumming, for which Jommy was grateful. 'I suspect if I were to mention a man named Pug, you boys would never have heard of him.'

Tad shook his head as did Zane, while Jommy said, 'Can't say I have, Father.'

The abbot smiled. 'Very well. We'll continue with the charade, but like so many things involving the man you've never heard of – whom I believe to be your adopted or foster grandfather if I have the story right – we'll continue to let things remain shrouded in shadow.

'But here is what he should have told you, or at least Turhan Bey should have told you: this is the finest institution of its kind in the world, in many ways unique, and here we train the sons of Roldem, and the rest of the world, to be leaders. Most of our young men enter the navy – we are an island people – but some enter service in our army or in other capacities. We do not discriminate against boys who are not from Roldem. Some of the finest minds serving nations who at one time or another were our enemies have studied here. We teach them because people do not fear things they are familiar with. We are certain that over the years powerful men have been sympathetic to Roldem because of the time they spent here, and that has tipped the balance in our favour against war, or simply made them more prepared to listen to us.

'Toward this end, you will be given the same education as the other boys, and no matter how long you are here – a week, a month, or a year – you will master the subjects before you each day. Moreover, you will cease this endless hostility with the other boys. So, I am making some changes. You will all be moved into senior boys' quarters. Three to a room is the usual rule.'

The news surprised them. The senior boys were the ones who were expected to end their studies within the coming year, or promising younger lads, like Grandy, who were thought to benefit from spending time in the company of older students. They grinned at each other; but their joy was to be short-lived.

'You two,' Father Elias said to Tad and Zane,

'will share quarters with Grandy.' Zane exchanged glances with Tad.

'And you, Jommy,' the abbot went on, 'will be joining Servan and Godfrey in their quarters.'

Jommy could barely suppress a groan. 'Father, why not just hang me?'

The abbot smiled slightly. 'You'll adjust. You all will, because as of today, if one of you earns punishment, all six of you will be punished. If one of you is to be given the cane, all of you will. Is that clear?'

Jommy couldn't speak. He just nodded.

'Good, then be off and move your possessions. Your new assignments are in Brother Kynan's hands, and he will not brook your being late.'

The three boys nodded, said, 'Yes, Father,' and left the room. In the hall, Jommy took two large strides, stopped, put out his hands and looking upward made a sound of pure aggravation. 'Argghhh!'

Jommy pushed open the door and saw three faces look up in surprise. Grandy grinned, Godfrey scowled, but Servan jumped up as if he'd sat on a blade and said, 'What do you think you are doing?'

With an insolent grin, Jommy said, 'Seeing if this is the right room.' He made a show of looking around and said, 'Yes, it is.'

Grandy looked over his shoulder at the two older boys, seeing their distress at the intrusion, and his grin broadened. 'Hello, Jommy. What are you doing?'

'Moving in,' Jommy said, turning and hauling in his own trunk. 'You're moving down the hall with Tad and Zane. Better get a shake on.'

Grandy said, 'Really?'

'On whose authority?' shouted Servan.

Jommy pulled his trunk across the threshold. 'Father Elias, I believe was the name. You met him? He's in charge.'

Servan said, 'Who?'

'Father Elias, Abbot of this—'

'I know who he is!' shouted Servan, jaw jutting forward as he strode in Jommy's direction.

'Now, now,' said Jommy, raising his right hand. 'Remember the last time?'

Servan hesitated and stopped. 'I'll go see about this.'

'Have a good time,' said Jommy cheerfully as the young nobleman pushed past his new roommate.

'Better get going,' said Jommy to Grandy.

'Wait,' ordered Godfrey.

Grandy hesitated, and Jommy said, 'Get along. It's all right.'

Grandy started to get up to grab his trunk, when Godfrey said, 'I told you to sit down!'

Jommy took one menacing step toward Godfrey and said, 'And I told him it was all right!'

Godfrey sat down, his eyes widening.

Grandy dragged his trunk from the foot of his

bed and out of the door, and Jommy pulled his into the now-vacant space. He looked at Godfrey and said, 'So bed-sitting is all right in this room?'

Godfrey jumped up as if burned. 'Only when the door is closed!'

Jommy grinned. A few minutes of silence was ended by Servan's return. He pushed past Jommy and said to Godfrey, 'We're stuck with him.'

Jommy closed the door, walked over to what was now his bed, sat down and said, 'Fine, then. What do you want to talk about?'

Miranda walked purposefully down the hall, ignoring startled Tsurani magicians as she swept past them. Reaching the door leading into the room where the Talnoy was kept for study, she walked in to find four Great Ones of the Empire studying the device.

'You broke it?' she asked unceremoniously.

Alenca turned with a wry smile. 'Miranda! How lovely you look.'

'You broke it?' she repeated.

He waved his hands slightly. 'No, we didn't break it. My message said it suddenly stopped working.'

Miranda moved past the old magician and his three companions to the bier upon which the Talnoy rested. She didn't need to touch it to know that something about it had changed. It was a subtle change, imperceptible except to the keenest magical sensitivity, but it was . . . as if something wasn't there.

'It's empty,' she said. 'Whatever was inside before is now . . . gone.'

'That is our conclusion,' agreed Wyntakata. He gestured with one hand while holding his staff with the other. 'We were trying a new set of wards – constructed by a group of the most gifted Lesser Path magicians in the Empire – and gave the creature a simple instruction so that we could see if the ward shielded it . . . and it didn't move. Every test we can apply says that whatever the motive power was before, it's now absent.'

'The soul is finally gone,' said Miranda softly.

Alenca looked doubtful. 'If, indeed, a soul was the power within, then it is gone.'

Miranda said nothing of the other Talnoy still motionless in a cave in Novindus. She sighed, as if disappointed. 'Well, one good thing; I suspect we can now stop worrying about rifts from the Dasati world to here.'

'Would that this were true,' said Alenca.

A magician Miranda knew only by sight – Lodar – said, 'We had a report this morning, after we had discovered the Talnoy was inert, and we sent two of our members to investigate, as we usually do.'

Alenca said, 'They returned telling of a terrible sight; a portion of woodlands was . . . bare, every last living thing sucked into a newly-established rift. We had to send Matemoso and Gilbaran to close it. They were tested to the utmost before they could shut it down.

'But the most perplexing thing was that it was a rift back to the Dasati world, and the energy being sucked through the rift – which was about the size of your body – was a wind fierce enough to topple a grown man.'

'No,' said Miranda slowly, 'that's not what's perplexing. What's perplexing is how a rift *from* here to the Dasati world could open. Because the original one usually comes from there to here, not the other way around. Which means it's half of a pair . . .' She turned and gripped Alenca by the shoulder. 'There's another one that you haven't found, and it's out there somewhere. You must find it!'

CHAPTER 13

CHANGE

Valko struck hard.

His opponent staggered backwards, off balance, and Valko lunged. He got both arms around his opponent's waist, picked him up, took two quick steps and slammed him into the wall, driving his shoulder into the helpless man's stomach. Air exploded out of the trainer's lungs and Valko thought he heard ribs cracking.

He let go, stepped back, and as his opponent began to fall to his knees, Valko brought his right knee up hard and fast and struck him full in the face, shattering what was left of an already bloody nose.

'Enough!' shouted Hirea.

Valko halted, fighting down the urge to step on his opponent's neck, crushing it and taking the young man's life. He looked at the remaining warriors, who were watching him in cool appraisal. He knew what each and every one was thinking, even his 'brother', Seeleth: *Watch closely; you may have to kill this Valko some day.* The fight had been taxing, though the outcome had been in no doubt from the start; Valko had known he was faster and stronger, and after the first minute, he had known he was smarter. For the briefest of instants, now, he felt a sudden fatigue, a fatigue beyond what was to be expected from this sort of exertion.

Hirea came to stand next to him. 'This is training, not the arena. He may be a *vashta* at this moment, but he's an experienced enough brawler to teach most of you a thing.' He glanced around at the other nine riders, each waiting his opportunity to grapple with the chosen opponent. 'That will be enough for today. Retire to your quarters and contemplate your errors. Take no pleasure from your successes. You are still children.'

The remaining nine warriors rose from their kneeling positions around the combat grounds and as Valko moved to join them, Hirea said, 'Wait a moment, Valko.'

When they were alone he said, 'When Faroon put his hand on your upper arm, you did something to break the hold. Show me.'

Valko nodded and waited. Hirea grabbed the young fighter's left arm, and not gently, and without thought Valko reached up with his left hand, taking a very painful handful of skin on the back of Hirea's right arm, pulling down forcefully. With his right hand, Valko formed a dagger of fingers and jammed them hard into the right side of Hirea's neck, stepping behind Hirea's left leg with his own, and suddenly the old instructor was on the sand, looking up at a cocked fist pointed at his face. 'Hold!'

Valko stepped back. Hirea said, 'No new warrior has ever come to us knowing fast-hand combat techniques, and even those who I've trained for years in the Scourge cannot do what you have done so quickly and easily.' The old fighter got up to his feet, and demanded, 'Who taught you?'

'My mother,' said Valko. 'She made it clear to me there could be times during the Hiding when a warrior might come across me while I had nothing to defend myself with but my open hands.'

Without warning, Hirea drew his sword and swung a looping overhand swing that would have taken Valko's head from his shoulders, had the young fighter not stepped inside the blow. Had he stepped away or tried to duck, the strike would have crushed his shoulder or head. Valko hooked his left arm up under Hirea's shoulder, stepped behind his right leg with his own, and slammed the palm of his hand into the older fighter's throat as hard as he could, driving him to the ground. Valko knelt as Hirea went down and at the last instant, as his knee touched the sand, he stood up and put his left foot on Hirea's sword hand. With his right, he raised it to crush the old man's throat.

'Hold!' Hirea managed to choke out, holding up his left hand, palm up in a sign of supplication.

Valko hesitated, then forced himself to speak calmly as he nearly hissed his words. 'Why? There is training, old man, and there is killing. Why should I not take your head now? Are you weak and begging for *mercy?*' He spat out the last word for the obscenity it was.

'No,' said the old man. 'But if you wish to live, hear me out.'

Valko reached down and took the sword from Hirea's hand. He put the point to the old man's throat and with his left hand, motioned him to rise.

'There are only a few in the world who could have done what you did. Name your mother.'

'Narueen. A Cisteen Effector.'

Hirea ignored the blade at his throat. 'No, she was not.' He looked around to ensure no one could hear them. 'What I tell you means both our lives are forfeit should any other hear us. Your mother, whatever her true name might have been, was Bloodwitch. Only a handful of people can teach what you've learned, and only one band of women in the Twelve Worlds are counted among those: the Orange Sisterhood.'

'They are a myth . . .' Valko studied the old man's face, and added, 'like the White.'

'Many truths are hidden by myths, young warrior.' Hirea glanced around one more time. 'Now, heed me closely. Speak of this to no one. There are secrets you may not even know you know, and there are those who would peel your skin from your body in tiny strips to get to those secrets.

'I will send you to your father, soon – you could have taken my head today; there is nothing more I can teach you – but we shall speak of this again before you go; there are things I must ask you and things I must tell you.' He turned away, ignoring the sword at his throat. 'Should anyone, especially Seeleth, ask why I kept you behind, just tell him we were correcting a flaw in your footwork. Now, go to your quarters and clean up.' He pointed to the prone figure of his still-unconscious training assistant and said, 'Faroon may be as stupid as a vashta, but right now you smell like one.'

Valko reversed the sword and returned it to his teacher. 'I'll say nothing of any of this. But it was hard not to take your head, old man.'

Hirea laughed. 'You may still get the chance. I have no living son, and some day, soon perhaps, I may seek you out to put me down: my bones begin to feel the cold and my vision isn't as keen as when I was young. Now go!'

Valko obeyed. Hirea might have been his victim today, but he was still his teacher and as such must be obeyed. But what he had said troubled the young fighter, who walked slowly back to his quarters, wondering if the old man had been right about his mother. She was certainly unlike other women, and many of the things they had spoken of when alone were forbidden. Could she have been Bloodwitch? That fabled sisterhood had been banned by the TeKarana himself. Every member was to have been hunted down and executed without hesitation. They were declared blasphemers by His Darkness's Highest Priests, and their teachers were declared an anathema.

Suddenly, very tired, Valko thought, *Mother, what have you done?*

'Caleb, what have you got us into?' Tad said as they clung to the side of the cliff face.

'I don't think he can hear us,' shouted Jommy over the wind.

Zane said nothing as his teeth were chattering and he hung on to Tad's tunic to keep him from falling.

'Move up!' shouted Servan. 'You've got to go up, first, then down!'

Jommy nodded, and said just loud enough for only Tad and Zane to hear, 'I hate that he's right.'

'Well, stop worrying about that, and start worrying about getting Grandy down,' said Tad.

Jommy nodded then climbed over Tad's position on the narrow ledge, and came down between him and Zane, who moved slightly to let him get settled.

Six boys were perched upon a mountain a half-day's ride from the city of Roldem. The exercise had been designed to train them to work as a group in difficult circumstances, in this case climbing to the top of a rocky crag without the aid of ropes or tools. They were just a few yards shy of the peak when an unexpected squall blew out of the north, unleashing torrential rains and a brutal wind.

Five of the six boys were in reasonable situations, hunkered down against the rock face, in a good position to wait out the storm, which should pass within an hour or two, but Grandy was in trouble.

The smaller boy had been nearly blown off the face of the mountain by a sudden gust of wind as he traversed along a ledge in their attempt to get back down the mountain. He had slid down to a shelf of rock a few yards below the others, and now he clung to it with the tips of his fingers and terror-inspired determination.

Servan had quickly organized the others. 'Jommy, lie flat against the rock face, then let Zane, Tad and Godfrey lower you down to where Grandy can grip your hands!'

'Why are you the only one standing around?' shouted Jommy.

'Because of the four of us, I'm the weakest,' Servan replied: which was true. A very good swordsman, he lacked the physical strength of even Godfrey, who was a good deal weaker than the three robust young men from Sorcerer's Isle.

Jommy was left with no reason to complain: Servan was being honest and putting his personal vanity aside in trying to get Grandy to safety.

A hundred feet below them, two monks were desperately trying to get up the face of the wet rocks to aid them, but they were having even less success than the six boys, since they were wearing sandals and long robes.

Jommy half-slid, and was half-lowered down the rock, water sheeting along the surface and granting him little to hold on to. 'Hang on tight!' he shouted to Tad and Godfrey.

Godfrey and Tad each held a leg, while Zane, the stockiest and strongest of the three, lay back with his full weight while he hung on the backs of their tunics. Jommy reached down and got one hand on Grandy's shirt, and shouted, 'I'll pull you up!'

'No!' shouted Servan. 'Grab him, hang on tight, and we'll pull *you* up!'

The odd chain of boys inched back up the mountainside, when Grandy was gripped by sudden panic and tried to climb up Jommy's arm. Jommy felt his grip on the boy's shirt loosen, and he tried to turn, not realizing he was only barely being held by Godfrey and Tad. Their grip on his legs began to slip, then failed; first Tad lost his hold, then Godfrey. Within an instant, Grandy was climbing up to a place of relative safety while Jommy twisted in place, his legs swinging past his head, and found himself suddenly sliding down the rocks, feet first, clawing for any handhold. Servan sat down hard and let himself slide after Jommy, then he rolled, ignoring cuts and bruises from the rocks, and turned himself head first, nearly diving down the side of the rocks. He managed to reach out and grab Jommy's tunic collar.

Zane managed to grab Servan's leg as he slid past. The boy shouted in pain as his hip was almost dislocated by Zane's actions. Jommy reached up blindly and found his hand seized by Servan. 'Don't let go!' he shouted.

Servan said, 'I won't!'

Forcing himself to calmness, Jommy shouted to Servan, 'What now?'

Grimacing in pain, the royal cousin's eyes never left Jommy. 'I can't move. Use me like a rope and climb over me.'

Jommy used all the strength in his left arm to heave himself up. He reached with his right hand, grabbing the belt on Servan's trousers. Feeling, around with his right toe he got a scant purchase in a crevice and hauled himself up. Then he let go with his left hand and reached high to get a strong grip on the fleshy part of Servan's right thigh, pulled once more and felt Godfrey's hands on his shoulders, helping him to the ledge.

As soon as he was safe, Jommy turned and helped Zane pull Servan back up to the ledge. The six boys sat panting with exertion, terror and pain, freezing in the driving rain on the ledge. Jommy looked at Servan. 'You're mad, mate, you know that?'

Servan said, 'I don't like you, but that doesn't mean I want to see you dead.'

'I don't like you either,' said Jommy. Servan's face was cut, his cheek swollen and from the way he rubbed at his right shoulder, he might have dislocated it. With the rain pelting down Jommy couldn't tell, but he thought Servan's eyes swollen from tears, probably from the pain. 'But I owe you my life.'

Servan managed a faint smile. 'A bit of an awkward situation, isn't it?'

Jommy said, 'Doesn't have to be. I don't know why you felt the need to lord it over us when we first arrived, and right now I don't care. You saved my life: I was sliding down this mountain and there was no way I was going to stop till I hit the bottom. So, if anyone asks, I'll be the first to say you're no coward. A madman, maybe, but no coward.'

Suddenly Servan smiled. 'Well, I couldn't let you fall after you almost killed yourself getting my cousin.'

'Cousin?' asked Tad. He looked at Grandy. 'He's your cousin?'

Grandy, teeth chattering with cold, said, 'Yes. Didn't I mention that?'

'That makes you another of the King's nephews?' asked Tad.

'No,' said Servan. 'That makes him the King's son. Grandy's older brother is Crown Prince Constantine of Roldem. Which means that some day he's going to be the younger brother to the King.'

'Damn me!' said Jommy. 'The people you meet.'

Suddenly, Servan started to laugh. The sound was so genuine – a release of tension and fear – that the other boys could not help themselves, and joined in.

Brother Thaddeus, the monk who was attempting to reach them, found a safe ledge a dozen yards below them and shouted, 'Wait there! Brother Malcolm is hurrying back to the university. He will bring Brother Micah back. Stay there and hang on!'

The boys huddled closer in the rain. Micah was not properly a monk of the Order, but a Lesser Path magician who resided on the grounds of the university. His many talents included control over the weather.

By the time Micah arrived, the boys were thoroughly miserable, shivering uncontrollably and hardly able to move. Micah chanted a spell to lessen the severity of the storm, creating a large pocket of more clement weather around the boys. The sphere of the spell was nearly a hundred yards in all directions, so that within it the rain fell like a gentle spring fall, rather than this unexpected squall.

With the torrent abated for a few minutes, Brother Thaddeus clambered up the rock face so he could help the boys get down to the wider ledge below. From there it was a relatively easy trail down to the foot of the mountain, a mere three hours' walk under normal conditions. As they made their way down the slippery trail,

Jommy turned to Grandy and said, 'Why did you never mention you're the King's younger son?'

Grandy, shivering and looking the worse for his ordeal, said, 'If you've noticed, no one at the university talks much about family. It's considered rude. We're all students.'

Jommy nodded, though he didn't understand. In the time he had been at the La-Timsan university a few idle remarks had been made about this student or that student being the son of a noble or rich merchant, but as he thought about it, he realized no one had come out and said whose father was whose. Grandy had been the exception when he mentioned that Servan was a cousin to the King's family.

Jommy felt confused. Exhausted, battered, and totally confused. From the look on the faces of his foster-brothers, he could tell that Tad and Zane were feeling equally out of their depth.

He saw horses waiting at the bottom of the trail. At least they wouldn't have to walk back to the city. And when they were there, there would be dry clothing and hot food.

As they reached better footing down the trail, they picked up speed, and when they were near enough to smell the damp scent of horse hair and the pungent smell of the wet woods, Jommy looked again at Servan. He was in no frame of mind to puzzle out exactly what kind of fellow the young royal really was, but he was determined that things would not return to how they had been before. He saw Godfrey limping, and without saying a word, he slowed a little, moved in next to him, and slipped the boy's arm over his shoulder, helping him take the weight off his injured ankle.

Valko stood silently with the other nine surviving young warriors as Hirea and another older warrior motioned for the youngsters to line up. When everyone was in place, Hirea said, 'There is more to bringing honours and glory to your empire, your society and your father's name than being a mindless killer.

'Good killing is an art and nothing brings more pleasure than watching an artful killer dispose of a weakling. Nothing, that is, save the art of mating.'

A couple of the young men laughed.

Hirea said, 'I do not speak of lying with a female, you stupid tavaks!' The field animal he called them was well known for being both sexually active and incredibly stupid.

Now several of the warriors looked confused. A few had taken females while in the Hiding. It was one of the signs that a young male was nearing the time of testing. When the competition among the boys in the Hiding became too violent, their mothers attempted to get them back to their fathers' domains.

Hirea laughed. 'Are there any among you whose

mothers have returned with you to your father's keep, castle or estate?'

Two young warriors held up their hands.

He pointed at those two. 'They are fortunate. They have clever mothers, as well as strong fathers. Their mothers were unforgettable. Their fathers wanted them to return, perhaps to sire another son.

'Some of you had to remind your fathers just who your mother was.' He shook his head as he looked down. 'It is the nature of the Dasati that ideal pairings are rare, but they are desirable, not only for the chance for superior offspring, but because an ideal pairing makes a man's life more bearable, more pleasurable.'

He motioned to the man at his side. 'This is Unkarlin, a rider of the Bloodguard.' He turned to him and asked, 'How many surviving sons and daughters are in your household?'

'I am the third son, and fifth of seven children.'

'From the same mother?'

Unkarlin inclined his head in assent, and several of the young warriors made noises of astonishment. Two, even three offspring from the same parents was not unheard of, but seven! It was heroic!

'Thus are dynasties born!' shouted Hirea. 'When your sons kill their enemies and claim spoils, then riches, then estates, Lessers and more riders come into the family! This man's family is partially responsible for the Bloodguard's power and success. Consider your fathers and how many kinsmen ride with him. How many uncles and cousins count you in the Sadharin, Valko?'

In the weeks he had spent with his father before coming to Hirea for training, Valko had learned these details. 'My father is eldest in the Sadharin, Hirea! He counts a younger brother, and four lesser cousins in the riders. From them I have twenty-seven cousins and sixteen lesser cousins.'

'How many riders in the Sadharin?'

'Ninety-seven, fifty lords.'

'Out of fifty lords of the Sadharin, Valko counts forty-nine as kinsmen!' He looked around the room. 'You can hardly have stronger ties than that!

'But to breed that sort of strength, to have that power to call upon, you must pick wisely who you bed, young fools! There are women you will desire until your body aches for them, but they are a waste of your time and seed. Even if you have a powerful son with a Lesser, he is still Lesser born. If you have a son from a warrior family, but it is a weak family, without strong patrons or blood-ties, what do you gain? Nothing. They gain by joining your line, but it drags you down.

'You need to seek out equals, or if you are clever enough, if you have something unique in you—' here he seemed to stare directly at Valko, '—then you breed upward. Any man who can bed one of the female kin of the Karana, no matter if she is the ugliest female you have ever beheld, then do so, and if you keep her until she is with child, pray that child is a warrior of the first renown, for then shall you have ties that will make your enemies tremble at the very thought of you.

'Then can you rise above the politics of your nation, even the politics of your world, and become a force within the Twelve Worlds.' He paused as he saw he had each young warrior listening raptly.

'But it all begins with having the sense to know that mating is an art.'

Now the warriors were ready to understand their next task, thought Valko. He had appeared as interested as the next student, but nothing Hirea had said was new to him. His mother had spoken with him on such topics for hours.

He knew that to waste time with a female of any rank less than his own was the height of foolishness, unless it was to bind a vassal, perhaps a lord with no surviving sons, for lands and livestock had more value than sons from lesser houses. But he would focus on trying to rise in status. He knew that his mother expected him to advance quickly, and within ten years to be Lord of the Camareen; and to have powerful sons within twenty years, with links forged to powerful houses.

Valko understood only part of his mother's plan. That she had a plan, he had no doubt, for she had raised no fool for a son. He knew that somewhere, sometime she would reveal herself to him again, and then he would learn exactly what was behind his training.

'Now,' said Hirea, 'we are going to a festival, in the city of Okora. There you will meet daughters and household females of rich and powerful men. Choose wisely, young warriors, for these shall be among the first to send you sons, sons who will return to your father's houses in years to come, and who those sons shall be is up to you.'

Silently, Valko thought, *Only in this one thing. After that, it is the mother who moulds the child.*

Pug strained against the urge to do something, anything, but willed himself to be as motionless as possible. They sat in a circle, Magnus to his right, Nakor to his left, Bek next to Nakor and opposite Pug, the Dasati named Martuch.

Martuch had spoken to Pug and Nakor on several occasions over the previous two days, asking questions that were clearly related to this undertaking, as well as seemingly making conversation about the mundane. Aspects of human existence fascinated him as much as everything Dasati fascinated Pug and Nakor; but without a frame of reference, it was difficult for Pug to put a name to his attitude towards the guide. If asked, he would have been inclined to say he found him to be an agreeable companion.

Martuch said, 'Be still, my friends. It is better that way. The more you struggle, the more uncomfortable the change.'

They were in the second week of practising magic in the city of Sushar. Martuch was, apparently, a practitioner of many trades, and magic was among them. He explained that on the Dasati worlds, 'spellmongers' were considered commoners of a trade no more elevated than that of a smith or carpenter. But he had reassured them that once they had mastered their arts on Delecordia, those arts would work on the Dasati worlds.

He had still not agreed to guide them. He had said he would give his decision when the time came, but as of yet he had said neither yes nor no. What he was seeking to understand about Pug and his companions wasn't clear, but he seemed in no particular hurry to come to a decision.

'You must be patient,' said Martuch. 'When this process is complete, you will be able to breathe the air, drink the water, eat the food of the Dasati, and to all appearances be Dasati. There is a glamour we shall employ that will make you seem one of us, though you will probably elicit odd glances from a Deathpriest if you happen to encounter one closely – I would avoid this, if I were you. In this one thing you have an advantage: the Ipiliac magicians are superior to the Deathpriests in that our magic does not depend entirely on necromancy. By various arcane means, we can ensure that your disguise bears close scrutiny.

'But that is the least of your worries. For in temper and nature you are as alien to the Dasati as they are to you, and there are a thousand ways of being, looking at life, and proceeding in the affairs of the everyday that will be lost upon you. Some you may learn quickly, while others will always elude you.'

He looked from face to face. 'We are a race of warriors, and I mean that without boast. It is not as if we are the only warrior people to exist; however, we are a race bred to struggle. We kill our young males, did you know that?'

Pug remembered a comment made by Kaspar. 'I had heard something like that.'

'Any boy may grow to be a threat, a rival, and as such must be obliterated before they can reach that state of existence.'

Nakor looked fascinated by this. 'How then did you endure as a race?'

'By being dangerous, even as a child. By being wily. By having mothers who dedicate themselves to sheltering their children until they are old enough to protect themselves.

'You will learn more about the Hiding and other things that are taken for granted among my people, but not all at once. For now, let us concentrate on how to keep you alive more than an hour once you set foot on any of the Twelve Worlds.'

'Not every member of your people can be a warrior, surely?' asked Magnus.

'No, there are warriors and their consorts, and their children and lesser brothers and sisters. That rank is not clearly labelled, much as you might think of the citizens of your nation as being "normal" while everyone else you meet is an "alien".' He looked from face to face. 'On my world you will be the aliens, so it is best if we find you a role that is somewhat suspect to the Dasati to begin with. Do you have any healing skills?'

Nakor said, 'I have some knowledge of herbs and how to dress wounds.'

Pug said, 'On my world, healing is done by chirurgeons and clerics, but I have some basic knowledge.'

'Then you shall be members of the Guild of Attenders.'

'Attenders?' asked Magnus.

'Everyone not part of the ruling class are known as "Lessers", said Martuch. 'Attenders are especially despised because of their impulse to take care of those not of their immediate family.'

'Yet you endure their presence?' asked Pug.

'Yes,' said Nakor. 'Because they are useful!'

Martuch smiled, and for a moment Pug felt there was a glimpse of something behind the stern exterior. 'Yes. You grasp the concept.

'Those you fear, you placate. Those who might be a threat, you destroy. But those who are neither fearsome or threatening, but who may be useful, you keep around. You make them clients and protect them from other rulers who might take a notion to obliterate them.'

Martuch waved his hand in a circle in the air. 'Beyond these walls lies a city which has much more in common with your worlds than with mine. While the people here are distant kin to mine, they have lived long enough in this twisted space, this place half-way between the first and second planes, that many of our . . . ways, are forgotten.

'Here you have merchants and traders and entertainers, much as you do on your world. By our standards, these distant cousins of our are carefree to the edge of madness – those of your world are surely mad.'

Pug said, 'So much to learn.'

Bek finally spoke. 'I don't understand any of this. I just want to do something.'

'Soon,' said Nakor, placating the restless young man.

Martuch said, 'Bek, we are done for now. Why don't you go outside and get some air?'

Bek looked at Nakor who nodded, and after the young man left, Nakor said, 'Why did you want him to leave?'

'Because so much of this is lost on him, yet in many ways he is more like a Dasati than any of you can imagine.' He looked at Nakor. 'He follows you?'

'He will do what I tell him to do, for at least a little while longer.'

'Keep an eye on him.' To Pug he said, 'Why did you bring him?'

Pug said, 'I was told to.'

Martuch nodded, as if that was all he needed to know. 'He may be important.'

Nakor looked at Magnus, then said, 'I need to ask you something, Martuch.'

'What?'

'Why are you helping us, without knowing our intent?'

Martuch said, 'I know more than you realize, Nakor the Isalani. Your coming was not unheralded. We received word some months ago that someone from the first plane of reality would be seeking access to my world.'

'Word?' asked Pug. 'From whom?'

'I only have a name,' said the guide. 'Kalkin.'

Pug sat stunned. Even Nakor's eyes widened. Magnus was the first to speak. 'It doesn't mean it *was* Kalkin, or Ban-ath. Just someone using that name.'

'But who would know?' asked Pug. 'Who besides the innermost circle of the Conclave even knows of Kaspar's vision on the roof of the Pavilion of the Gods?'

'And that, my friends, is why I may help you, if you show you're able to endure what needs to be done to get you to the Dasati worlds. For whether or not you're aware of it, we play a game of gods,

267

and the stakes at risk are far more than you can begin to imagine. It is not only your world that lies at risk; it is my world as well. Vast danger is circling: entire nations may die.'

CHAPTER 14

CELEBRATION

Pug lashed out.

Martuch put his hands up and a shimmering disc appeared in front of his crossed wrists, a virtual shield of energy. The blue energy dart Pug had cast was deflected harmlessly into the sky.

Pug, Nakor and Magnus had met earlier that afternoon with Martuch, who had escorted them to a relatively deserted meadow in the hills a short walk from the city. Pug observed that there were acres of cultivated land everywhere, but no farms.

'It is not our way,' Martuch had responded. He went on to explain that farmers were a caste of workers who laboured for associations of cultivators, millers, grain and produce exporters and who lived in clusters of rooms in large buildings he called 'apartments'. They drove wagons out every morning and returned at sundown. He said it was a legacy of their Dasati heritage, for on the Twelve Worlds strength in numbers was not merely a catchphrase, but an axiom to live by: the packs of predators on the Dasati worlds were such that a

269

farm family alone in a small house would not survive a year.

The other thing Pug noticed was his use of the term 'our way'. Whatever else he might think about the Ipiliac, he considered them one with the Dasati.

'Magic is often thought of as just another tool to the Dasati,' said Martuch, 'which of course means another weapon.

'I think once you comprehend the intricacies of working with magic in this environment, your mastery of the subject will make you supreme among magic users, Pug.' To Nakor and Magnus he said, 'Probably all three of you will rank highest.

'But do not underestimate the ferocity of those who you may encounter. A half-dozen Deathpriests may not equal you individually, but as a group they will overwhelm you. They are fanatics by your measure, as is every man, woman, and child in that realm.

'They live by a standard that can not even be called a "code" It is a set of unthinking responses honed over millennia of living in a world in which hesitation means obliteration.' He looked at the three magic-users and said, 'If you think, you die.'

Magnus said, 'You depict a grim reality.'

'It is all they know. It is not grim to them, for they are the living, ergo, they are the survivors, the victors – even the least among them – and in that they take pride and satisfaction. The lowest of the

Lessers, given the meanest tasks to perform, can feel superior to the failed son of the TeKarana himself. It is a sense of place you cannot begin to appreciate.'

Nakor said, 'I gathered as much hours ago, Martuch. What I would like to know is how you came to be different from your brothers?'

'That is something for another time, but that time approaches. I have decided today to let you know my choice: I will guide you where you wish to go. And, moreover, I will give you my pledge to do all in my power to bring you home again.'

'Speaking of which,' said Magnus, 'after we endure all these changes, how will we survive when we go home?'

'In good order, I should think,' said Martuch. 'It is the nature of the differences between the second and first plane of reality that as soon as you return home, you will start to revert to your old state. You may wish to take to your beds for a few days, and you'll no doubt feel like dying, but you will not. Think of it as a particularly bad flux or the result of far too much drink the night before, only far more worse, lasting a week or so. Then it will pass.

'There is an elegance in the order of nature, a stately progression of the universe which suggests that things should stay where they belong. As you seemed determined not to, the universe is inclined to forgive you and take you back once you return.' He squinted at Pug, a habit Pug had noticed usually meant he was very curious about whatever it was he was questioning. 'So, may I now know the reason you wish to venture somewhere no sane member of your race would ever wish to go?'

Pug glanced at Nakor, who nodded assent once. To Martuch he said, 'What do you know of the Talnoy?'

Martuch's eyes widened. 'First, that you should not even know that word, let alone what it is. Second, that it is a . . . blasphemy. Why?'

'We have one.'

Now Martuch looked openly shocked. 'Where? How?'

'It is the reason we must go to the Dasati world,' said Pug. 'I will tell you everything in time, but for now understand that it is the presence of the Talnoy on my world that is the cause of our concern.'

'Well it should be, human,' said Martuch. 'It is a thing to cause fear in even the bravest Dasati hero of yore, a monstrosity from the bloodiest days in the long and murderous history of my people.' He paused, then said, 'This changes things.'

'How?' asked Pug. 'You're not changing your mind?'

'No. To the contrary, I am now even more determined to take you where you wish to go. I was correct in telling you that you play the Game of Gods, but now you play at a much higher stake than you ever imagined.

'But I must go and speak to someone, and he

will in turn speak with someone else. When we have conferred I will return and when I do, we shall sit and talk of things no mortal, human or Dasati, should ever have to imagine, let alone face.' He looked around, as if suddenly concerned about being overheard. The gesture was almost humorous given their present location, but the implication was not lost on Pug. 'I will return as quickly as I can. It should be obvious that you must say nothing of this to anyone else, not even to Kastor. Now, let us get back to the city and I will be off.'

Pug and the others exchanged glances, then followed the obviously agitated Dasati.

Valko did not enjoy the festivities. They were odd and troubling to him, though his mother had described such social encounters before. It was as if he possessed an extraordinary ability to see what others could not, or perhaps had more ease in ignoring what blinded or gulled others. This was what his mother had called the 'social warfare' of the Dasati.

As Hirea had predicted, most of his fellow student warriors were making tavaks of themselves, save for Seeleth, who like Valko had retreated to a corner of the room to watch and appraise.

Several females had already made overtures to him, younger daughters of minor warriors, and one remarkably beautiful daughter of a Lesser Facilitator who specialized in wholesale arms and armour. Her father was an insect from what Valko could tell, but a very successful insect. And his daughter was extraordinarily attractive and using her beauty like a battering ram against a city gate. Valko had no doubt that given enough wine, several of his more foolish trainees would come to blows over her, perhaps even shed blood. Valko watched the way she moved, the way her otherwise very proper attire clung to every curve of her body suggestively, and the way she smiled. He reckoned she was easily the most dangerous person in the room.

He considered what Hirea had said earlier about the relationships between families and clans, houses and dynasties. He also remembered what his mother had taught him in contradiction to the conventional wisdom: that mating with a minor warrior's daughter was not necessarily a bad thing, if that coupling produced a successful offspring who might bind that warrior and his family to you as a vassal. Breeding 'up' was not the only way to success, she had taught him. Breeding 'down' to secure a broad foundation could bring many swords to any cause you took up.

In fact, he considered, looking around the room, there didn't seem to be much opportunity to breed up. Only one young female appeared to come close to Hirea's requirements, and she was surrounded by five of his companions.

Seeleth came to his side. 'You do not seek to couple tonight, brother?'

Valko cast him a sidelong glance and shook his

head. He saw that Seeleth had elected to wear the badge of Remalu on his armour. There was no prohibition against it, and Valko could have chosen the Camareen badge or the badge of the Sadharin. He chose neither. But to choose to reveal his society badge rather than his kinship badge, to name his father's associations rather than his family, that was strange. Valko was tempted to ask about it, but as with all things regarding Seeleth, he thought silence the better course. Valko had decided the opportunity for a mating for advantage was slim, and he thought Hirea knew this. The old warrior stood near the table of his host, listening to whatever conversation was underway, but his eyes were constantly seeking out his charges around the room, weighing their behaviour.

Valko knew that as the night wore on his comrades would get drunk and make foolish choices. What he didn't know was if this was something expected and that he should do the same, or whether it was something to be avoided. On one hand he did not wish to squander his time and energy on anything that was not advantageous, but on the other hand, he was mindful of Hirea's warning not to become too distinctive.

Weighing that choice, he said to his companion, 'And are you not seeking a female, "brother"?'

Seeleth grinned like a hungry zarkis. 'There is none here worthy of my attention, in truth. Don't you think so?'

Valko glanced sidelong at him, then turned his attention to the floor. His decision had been made. 'I think that female talking to Tokam might be.'

'Why? Her father is a lesser knight.'

'But her mother is the younger sister of someone placed high in the Bloodguard, Unkarlin.' Before Seeleth could speak, Valko stepped away and moved purposefully towards the female. She was attractive and he could feel his pulse starting to rise as he anticipated the possibility of coupling with her or battling with Tokam for her. He knew he would do neither, but by appearing to show interest, he acted predictably enough to avert any suspicion should he be observed, and he avoided wasting his time on a female who really wasn't ideally placed and therefore, in the end, a waste of time.

He glanced at Hirea, and saw the old warrior was watching him as he approached the pair who were speaking lowly, apparently lost in conversation. Could that be a hint of approval he saw in the old man's eyes?

Valko decided they must have that private talk, and soon.

Tad fidgeted, Zane stared, and Jommy grinned. The reception at the palace was nothing 'modest' by the boys' standards. At least two hundred courtiers stood along either side of the long carpet leading to the throne, and along the walls two dozen royal guardsmen, the King's First Dragoons, stood at attention in full gear – short round white fur cap with a black scarf that fell from the crown to the left shoulder, cream-coloured jackets with red piping, black straight-legged trousers tucked into knee-high black boots.

The boys were likewise turned out in their finest clothing, which they had to hurriedly purchase once the summons to the palace arrived. The monks were not happy to see their orderly schedule disrupted, but even the High Priest of La-Timsa couldn't ignore a royal summons.

Jommy, in particular, preened like a bantam rooster, wearing his first really fine jacket, of green corduroy with golden buttons worn open, a shirt Tad thought silly, but was now the fashion in Roldem – white linen with big ruffles down the front – tight black trousers and ankle-high boots.

Zane didn't like the boots, for as he observed, they were useless for anything that required real boots, but were not as comfortable as slippers.

Now the boys stood ready to be presented to the King of Roldem.

Servan appeared at Jommy's shoulder and whispered, 'This is what you get for saving a prince's life.'

'If you'd warned me,' said Jommy, not losing his grin, 'I'd have the little rotter still sitting up there.' Servan smiled and looked away.

Servan and Jommy had not become friends, but they had reached an accommodation. Servan and Godfrey had become civil with the three boys from

Sorcerer's Isle, and Jommy had stopped hitting them.

The Royal Master of Ceremonies struck the floor with the heel of a heavy wooden staff and the hall fell quiet. 'Your Majesties!' he announced, 'My lords, ladies, gentlemen, and all others assembled! Sir Jommy, Sir Tad and Sir Zane of the Royal House of Kesh!'

'"Sir"?' said Tad. 'When did that happen?'

Servan whispered. 'Well, they had to think of something to make you sound important. Now walk over to the King, bow the way I showed you, and don't trip!'

The three boys walked down the long carpet to the designated spot, six paces before the thrones, and bowed as they had been shown. Sitting on twin thrones were King Carol and Queen Gertrude. Standing at the Queen's side was a little girl of no more than eight or nine, Princess Stephané, and at the King's right hand stood three sons: the Crown Prince Constantine, a lad almost the same age as the three boys themselves; Prince Albér, a boy two years his junior, and of course Prince Grandy, who grinned at his friends. Constantine and Albér wore uniforms of the Royal Navy, while Grandy wore a simple tunic, as long as you considered that simple included gold threads and diamond buttons.

The King smiled and said, 'We owe you a great debt, my young friends, for saving the life of our youngest son.'

The three had been told not to speak until asked

a direct question, but Jommy couldn't help himself and blurted out, 'Not to dispute the honour, Majesty, but your son was really in little danger; he's an enterprising lad who can take care of himself. He was just in a spot of discomfort.'

For a moment the court fell silent, then the King laughed. Grandy rolled his eyes, but grinned at his classmate.

'As much as it pleases us to think our youngest boy can take care of himself, as you put it, we know from what was reported to us that his life was at risk and moreover you put yourself at even greater risk to save him.

'Therefore, it is with pleasure that we reward you with the following.' He waved to the Master of Ceremonies, who stepped forward.

'Henceforth,' cried the Master of Ceremonies, 'let it be known throughout the realm of Roldem that the three men presented here today shall be Knights of the Royal Court, vested with all the privilege and honour pertaining to that rank, with the gratitude of the court, for their heroic act in saving the life of our beloved son, Grandprey. Moreover they shall carry the title of Knight of the Royal Court throughout their lives. So proclaimed this day, by royal decree.'

Tad whispered, 'Grandprey?'

Zane glanced at the boy who looked skyward, as if to say he didn't pick his name, his mother did.

The boys said nothing else, while the royal court applauded politely. The royal family, however, seemed quite genuine in their warmth and thanks, which Jommy assumed meant that Grandy had given a colourful account of their heroics on the mountain.

The King stood up and descended the three steps to stand before the boys, while a page in royal livery appeared at his side, holding a large tray. The tray was covered in white velvet, upon which rested three golden pins with the royal crest of the nation on them. The King took the pins from the tray and personally pinned them on the collar of each of the three boys in turn, and then stepped back.

Jommy glanced over to where Servan stood. The young man motioned for them to bow, so Jommy did so, followed at once by Tad and Zane. The King returned to his throne and said, 'A reception will begin as soon as today's court is adjourned.'

Servan motioned for the boys to return the way they had come. They bowed as they stepped backwards, turned and walked to the entrance of the hall.

Once outside, Servan and Godfrey approached and Servan said, 'Well, that was good. You didn't trip, though keeping your mouth shut does seem a problem for you, doesn't it?'

Jommy had the good grace to look embarrassed. 'Well, I know, but it wasn't that difficult a situation, and you took a lot more risk saving my arse than I did with Grandy. They should have been giving you the honour.'

Servan shrugged. 'Well, I won't argue with you, but remember, they don't hand out honours for saving thick-headed peasant boys. Besides, I'm already a Knight of the Court.'

'What was all that, about, then?' asked Zane.

Godfrey said, 'What it means is you're knights until you die, but you can't pass along the title to your sons. They'll be peasants like you.'

Zane rolled his eyes. 'Fine.'

Tad laughed. Their relationship with Godfrey had also changed to one of guarded tolerance, if not friendship.

'Come along,' said Servan. 'You need to be at the reception before the royal family makes its entrance. Try not to spill wine on your new clothes. The gods know when you're ever going to dress this well again.'

Jommy clapped his hand on Servan's shoulder, just hard enough to make Servan's knees buckle ever so slightly, a semi-playful gesture. 'You're an intolerable twit. And just when I was beginning to think you were a tolerable twit.'

Tad, Zane, and Godfrey all laughed.

They entered the royal reception hall – a vaulted ceiling with floor-to-ceiling glass walls, through which a brilliant afternoon sun shone. The court was in full attendance, and Jommy nudged first Tad, then Zane at the number of pretty girls in attendance.

'Girls!' Zane said just loud enough for a few nobles nearby to overhear, causing a few odd glances and a few amused expressions.

'Behave,' said Godfrey. 'These are the finest daughters in the Kingdom and you're ill-educated louts.'

Tad said, 'That's ill-educated lout knights, thank you very much. Besides, who helped you pass that examination on geometry yesterday?'

Godfrey looked slightly embarrassed, but he said, 'Very well. You're well-educated louts.'

'Well-educated lout knights,' corrected Jommy.

The banter ceased when they reached their destined position, the centre of a circle of large round tables, each well laden. Servers waited nearby to ensure that the nobility of Roldem and honoured guests wouldn't have to actually secure their own food and drink.

The royal family entered and everyone bowed. When the King reached the three guests of honour, he signalled to the Master of Ceremonies who slammed his staff on the stone floor. 'At their Royal Majesties' pleasure, you are welcome!'

At once servers began loading up plates and filling cups. The boys had been instructed not to take any food or drink until after they left the King's company. Tad and Jommy waited, while Zane watched with badly-hidden alarm as the contents of the tables rapidly diminished.

The King spoke: 'Your modesty does you well, youngster, but never argue with a king in public when he's handing out rewards.'

Jommy blushed. 'My deepest apology, Majesty.'

The King motioned with his right hand and a

page appeared with a tray, upon which sat three small pouches. 'The offices you've been granted come with some minor properties attached, from which you'll derive an annual small stipend. This is your payment for this year.'

He looked at a royal courtier who stood nearby, and the man said, 'A hundred sovereigns, Majesty.'

The King nodded, picked up one bag and handed it to Jommy, then the other two to Tad and Zane. 'Your annuity can be picked up at the royal treasury each year on this date.'

The boys were speechless. A hundred Roldem sovereigns was worth well over three hundred common pieces of gold in the Vale of Dreams where they were raised. It was an income to match that of Miller Hodover at Stardock Town, the richest man Tad and Zane ever knew. Jommy had never known anyone who earned that sort of income. All three had the same thought at the same instant: they were rich!

The King said, 'Go and enjoy the attention. It's back to university for you this evening, and as I understand it, the monks are hardly impressed by titles and wealth.'

The boys bowed and retreated a step, then turned and moved into the crowd. Servan and Godfrey joined them, as Grandy made his way over to the five.

'Grandprey?' asked Tad.

Grandy shrugged. 'My mother's grandfather's name. I wasn't consulted.'

Jommy affected a bow. 'Your highness.'

Grandy said playfully, 'Sir Jommy.'

'Speaking of names,' said Servan. 'Just what sort of name is "Jommy"?'

Jommy shrugged. 'It's a family moniker. I'm really Jonathan, but my next older brother was a baby and couldn't say it, so he called me "Jommy" and it stuck. No one calls me Jonathan.'

Food appeared, carried by pages, and each young man helped himself to a plateful and a cup of ale. 'Enjoy,' said Servan. 'For at sundown, we're back to the tender mercies of the Brothers of La-Timsa.'

'Yes,' said Tad, with a smile, 'but until then we have food, drink and pretty girls to flirt with.'

Jommy's head came up like a startled deer. 'Girls!' he said as he glanced around the room. 'Damn me, and I'm now a knight!'

The other five boys laughed. Jommy grinned, and said, 'Until this morning I was a peasant lad with little to offer, but as of now I'm a handsome young knight with prospects, who happens to be a close friend of a royal prince. Now if you hooligans will excuse me, I'm going to see how many girls I can impress before we get dragged back to the university.'

'That's "Sir Hooligan", to you,' said Tad, but he handed his barely-started platter to a nearby page.

Zane started wolfing down the food and through a stuffed mouth said, 'I'll catch up to you in a minute!'

Zane finished the last bite then hurried off after

his foster-brothers. Godfrey glanced at Grandy and Servan. 'May the gods protect the daughters of Roldem.'

Servan chuckled. 'You've known those girls all your life, Godfrey. Feel sorry for the boys.'

Grandy laughed aloud.

CHAPTER 15

THE WHITE

Valko raised his sword.

From the distant parapet of the family castle, his father returned the salute, welcoming a surviving son home from training. Hirea rode at Valko's side. With training over, he had simply informed the son of the Camareen he would travel with him to his father's estates, then move on to his own home, Talidan, a town closer to the mountains to the east. At a suitable distance behind them rode Hirea's two retainers.

As they rode together, Hirea said, 'It is time for plain speaking, young Valko.'

'The talk you spoke of that afternoon on the training floor,' countered the young warrior, 'the one for which I waited in vain?'

'Such is the nature of time and circumstances,' said the old teacher. 'I have little to say, and your father will tell you more. For the time being let me tell you that your mother hid things from you to prevent you from betraying her or yourself before this day. She and I have met, and she is a remarkable female. This is what we need you to know: everything you have been taught by your mother is true; everything you've been shown since you emerged from the Hiding is false.'

Valko's head snapped around. He stared at the old man. 'What . . .?'

'The bloodlust we feel at certain times, the urge to kill young, all of this is false. All of this has been forced upon us, but it is not the true Dasati way.'

Valko's mouth hung open. No wonder the old warrior hadn't been able to tell him this in a public place. His heart beat wildly.

'Your father will have more to say to you soon. Speak to no one about what I've just said, and do not ask me more,' said the old teacher. 'Here we part ways, but believe me when I tell you the next day is crucial to your survival. When we meet again, you will understand why I've been so circumspect.' He waved once towards the distant castle, in salute of Valko's father, then turned his varnin away from the cut-off road to the castle and motioned for his two retainers to follow him, leaving Valko alone on the road.

Valko watched them go, nonplussed. He thought about the dire things Hirea had said. *The next day is crucial to your survival. . .* He wondered what this meant. Certainly a returning son, tested and now trained, might prove a danger to his father, and Valko was probably a more dangerous opponent than any his father had faced in years, but he also knew that his father was probably the most dangerous foe he would face any time soon. Hirea might be a fine instructor, but his prime days were past; Aruke still was a swordsman to be feared.

Valko rode at a sedate pace, not wishing to appear too anxious. He reached the gate of the castle, noting that both doors had been thrown wide for his return. He appreciated the gesture. Usually only one door would be opened for a single rider.

Inside the castle's main yard, he saw his father standing on the balcony, looking down at him. A Lesser, his father's estate manager, approached with eyes downcast and said, 'Master Valko, your father wishes you to retire and rest. He will see you in his private chamber after you've eaten.'

Dismounting, Valko asked, 'I'm not dining with him tonight?'

'No, master,' said the man with a slight cringe, as if expecting punishment for bearing what might be considered ill-tidings. 'He has other concerns for the moment, but wishes to see you as soon as circumstances permit. Food shall be brought to your room.'

Valko decided not to pursue the matter with the servant. He didn't relish dining alone: time spent with the other nine surviving warriors in training had given him an appreciation of company, something he had lacked for most of his childhood.

He let the Lessers take away his mount, and slowly walked into his father's great castle. Like all things Dasati, there was an assumption imbuing the style of the architecture that bigger meant more powerful. He realized that years of adding to the building, extending the coverage of the outer wall, and additional housing for retainers and Lessers, as well as housing for the other riders of the Sadharin should they be in residence, had created a position which was difficult to defend. As he entered the great double doors that dominated the courtyard below, he realized he could come up with at least three, if not more, sound plans to besiege or storm his father's estate.

He determined that when he ruled, his first order of business would be to correct these oversights and shortcomings of design.

He walked through the vast halls and everywhere he looked he saw nothing but Dasati tradition: massive, graceless columns, smooth walls with precisely-fitted stones stretching as far as the eye could see, which meant there were many blind spots along the walls because of the lack of archers' ports. It would by no means be easy to take this ancient castle, but it was far from impossible. As he mounted the stairway to the family quarters he decided that his best course of action would be to simply mount more guards and look-outs on the walls at strategic locations.

He reached his own quarters and wondered if every son saw his father's castle as both a place of haven and a prize to be taken. Pushing open the door, he found that his father had had his rooms refurbished. The simple bed he had last slept in here had been replaced by a large bed piled high with furs which dominated the room. Where there had been a plain chest in which he had kept his armour there was now an ornately carved blackwood chest and a mannequin upon which to place his armour. Brightly coloured tapestries adorned the walls, adding warmth both for the body and eye.

Lessers hurried in to help the young warrior remove his armour and others carried in a large tub in which he could bathe. He quickly stripped off his armour, realizing that he was sore, tired, and in need of the bath.

As he settled into the hot water, servants instantly set about applying sweet-smelling unguents to his hair and they started to wash his body with soft cloths. Valko had never been afforded such luxurious treatment in his life, and barely knew how to react.

After he had bathed, a selection of richly-appointed robes were presented, and he chose a dark blue one with white piping and abstract designs in golden thread that were very pleasing to his eye.

As the tub was carried away, food was carried into the room on a large table shouldered by four male Lessers. Upon it was a wide variety of fare, and several wines and ales.

Valko found himself ravenous from the long ride, and set to without hesitation. As he ate, the servants retired, leaving him with one attendant, a young female of unusual beauty, who waited, silent and patient until he had finished eating. Then she said softly, 'I am here for my young lord's pleasure. I have been instructed that I may not declare so that should I conceive, the child will have no right to claim kinship.'

Valko studied the young woman, and realized that as much as he desired to couple with her, his father's odd behaviour and Hirea's warning weighed on his mind. Finally he said, 'Not tonight . . . what is your name?'

'Naila, my lord.'

'I may send for you tomorrow night, but right now I need rest.'

'As the young lord wishes.' She bowed, then asked, 'Do you wish me to leave or stay?'

'Stay while I finish eating, and tell me about my father's household. What has occurred during my absence?'

'I'm sure there are others better able to tell you than I.'

'No doubt,' said Valko, indicating with a pat of his hand that the girl should sit next to him. 'But until then, I would prefer to listen to your words. Certainly you have eyes to see and ears to hear; what have you observed while I was away?'

Not entirely sure how to answer, the Lesser woman began to recite a long litany of castle gossip, rumours and speculation, most of which Valko found innocuous and boring. But once in a while she said something that piqued his interest, and after a few questions, she yielded up a few useful facts.

On balance, he considered, this was a far more profitable encounter than any mere coupling. He ignored his body's demand to take the girl, and kept asking questions late into the night, long after he finished eating.

The knock came in the middle of the night. Jommy was the first to rouse, as the door opened and Brother Kynan entered. 'Get dressed. Be silent,' he instructed the three young men.

Jommy glanced at Servan who shrugged. Godfrey blinked like a man coming out of a stupor.

By the time they were dressed, they discovered Tad, Zane and Grandy waiting silently outside the door, under the monk's watchful gaze. He held a finger to his lips then motioned for the six students to follow him.

They managed to reach their destination, the Proctor's office, without uttering a word, but once through the door, Godfrey couldn't restrain himself. 'What time is it?' he whispered to Servan.

Servan's eyes widened slightly in warning, but a voice from within the dark room said, 'An hour after midnight, I should think.'

Father Elias opened a shuttered lantern, and revealed himself behind the Proctor's desk. 'Wait outside, Brother, if you please,' he said to Brother Kynan.

Kynan nodded once and left the room.

The abbot stood and said, 'From what I've heard, it appears you six have sorted out your differences. Is this true?'

Jommy exchanged glances with Servan and nodded once, and Servan said, 'Yes, Father. We've come to an . . . accommodation.'

'Good. I was hoping for friendship, but I'll settle for a respectful truce. Now, the reason you're here is for me to say goodbye.'

The boys looked at one another, and Jommy said, 'Father, are you leaving?'

'No, you are,' the abbot said. 'There are things I am not free to tell you, but this you can know now.

'You six are knights of the Roldemish Court, and as such you have certain duties as well as the privileges that came with your rank.

'You also are six gifted young men with bright futures.'

To Grandy, he said, 'You above all the others, my prince, have greater responsibility and a higher duty.'

Jommy began to look uncomfortable and this didn't escape the abbot's notice. He smiled. 'Fear not, young Jonathan. I've had discussions with Turhan Bey regarding your future. He has agreed to your next assignment.'

At the word 'assignment' Jommy, Tad and Zane all got tense. The abbot hadn't said in so many words that these instructions were from the Conclave, but he might as well have done.

'You are all going to serve in the army for a while.'

The students displayed varying degrees of disbelief.

'The army?' said Grandy.

'Your father has two sons in the navy already, young prince. Roldem needs generals as much as she needs admirals, and you have done well.' To Jommy, Tad and Zane, he said, 'You three have done especially well in the short time you've been here, despite your lack of any previous education.

'It wasn't necessary for us to turn you into scholars, just make sure you were a little more refined when you left us than you were when you arrived. Your training in the army is another such exercise, where you will learn the military mindset and how to recognize true leadership.

'Towards that end, you are all commissioned as junior lieutenants in the First Army, the King's Own. A wagon awaits you outside, where you will be taken to the docks, where you will find a ship waiting to take you to Inaska. It seems some robber baron or another from Bardac's Holdfast has invaded Aranor, seeking to take advantage of the somewhat chaotic situation there since we annexed Olasko into the Kingdom.

'You're going to be fine young officers and help General Bertrand drive these raiders back across the border.' He bowed his head. 'May La-Timsa protect you. Long live Roldem.'

'Long live Roldem,' Servan, Godfrey and Grandy

responded, while the three boys from Sorcerer's Isle weakly joined in at the last.

Outside the door Brother Kynan was waiting for them. He showed them down the hall to the stabling yard, where a wagon waited.

'What about our things?' Servan asked.

'You will be given everything you need,' answered the taciturn monk, and when the six boys were in the wagon, he motioned for the driver to set off.

Pug awoke with a start in the small room in the back of Kastor's shop. Something was different: was it something outside? He couldn't hear any sound that should have awakened him. It was dark and no one else moved, though Bek occasionally tossed in his sleep, from dreams he never could remember.

Then Pug realized the difference he sensed wasn't anything outside, but rather from something inside. Inside himself. He had changed. He stood up and went to the window and looked out.

Suddenly he was seeing this world as a Dasati would see it! He didn't have words to describe what he witnessed. There were colours beyond the spectrum of violet and red, shimmering energies that now were visible; they were breathtaking.

In the night sky he saw stars that would be invisible to human eyes, their presence revealed by energies no man of Midkemia could apprehend.

They were without light, but he could see their heat, so many miles distant that no number could encompass it.

Suddenly a voice from behind him said, 'It's amazing, isn't it?'

Pug hadn't heard Ralan Bek stir, let alone wake and come to stand behind him. The fact that he couldn't detect the youngster's presence any more disturbed Pug. He kept his surprise under control and said instead, 'Yes, it's amazing.'

'I'm not going back,' said the young warrior.

'Where?'

'To our world, Midkemia. I . . . don't belong there.'

'You belong here?'

Bek said nothing for a while, staring up into the sky, then at last he said, 'No. Not here, either. I belong in the next place, where we're going.'

'How do you know that?' asked Pug.

'I don't know how,' Bek replied. 'I just know.'

Pug fell silent. He watched Bek gaze at the sky for a moment longer, then he returned to his pallet. Lying there in the dark, while Bek gazed out of the window, Pug wondered at his own mad plan. He knew it was his own, because those messages had all been in his handwriting, and for nearly fifty years not one had proven to be bad advice.

At times he wondered at his own cryptic style, the lack of information beyond a simple injunction or instruction. He knew he would think he had a good reason in the future to be cryptic, even if it frustrated him now . . . He felt the urge to groan aloud. Time paradoxes made his head swim.

He lay abed until dawn, wrestling with a hundred doubts, and a hundred more demons of the mind.

Valko awoke instantly. Someone was speaking. The voice was soft and unthreatening. He turned, to discover it was Naila. She had not left his side but had talked with him, then lain next to him as he drifted off into slumber, holding him as his mother had held him when he was a child. He had found the experience surprisingly pleasant and reassuring. 'Your father summons you,' she said quietly.

He donned his robe and followed her, until she paused outside the door that led to his father's private chamber. She knocked once then, without seeking Valko's permission, she hurried away, as if she had been instructed to do so.

The door opened, but instead of his father, another man waited there. Valko's hand went to his waist reflexively, but his armour and arms were bedecking a mannequin in his quarters: he was dead should this man prove to be an enemy.

But the man at the door made no threatening gestures. He merely waved Valko in saying, 'Your father awaits.'

Valko knew he had no choice but to enter. If it was destined that he would die here and now, he was helpless to postpone the inevitable.

Inside the room, four chairs had been arrayed in a semi-circle facing a single chair. Three of the chairs were in use, Aruke occupying the one directly opposite the solitary chair. Next to him sat a man in the garb of a Deathpriest. From the markings Valko assumed him to be of high rank. On the other side of Valko's father sat Hirea, who ventured the slightest of smiles as Valko's face betrayed his surprise. The man at the door was unknown to him, but dressed as a warrior, like his father, in armour and carrying a sword.

'Sit,' commanded his father, indicating the empty chair opposite him.

Valko did as instructed, and remained silent. The other warrior took the remaining seat, and Aruke finally spoke. 'You are at a crossroads, my son.' Slowly, he drew out his sword and placed it on his knees. 'One of us will die tonight.'

Valko jumped out of the chair and picked it up, ready to use the clumsy weapon as a last resort. The Deathpriest waved his hand, and suddenly Valko felt his body's strength begin to leach away. In a few seconds, he could not hold up the chair and it fell from his hands. The Deathpriest gestured and the boy's strength started to return.

'You cannot withstand us should we wish you dead, young warrior. But know it is our sincerest wish you stay alive.'

'How can that be?' asked Valko, leaning on the back of the dropped chair as he waited for his full strength to return. 'My father says one of us will die tonight. He cannot mean he feels his age and wishes an honourable death so soon.'

'He means exactly that,' said the Deathpriest.

Aruke again waved Valko to take his seat, and reluctantly the young fighter sat down. 'What you will hear tonight began centuries ago,' he started. 'On a day not unlike this, one of my many great-grandfathers was brought before his father in this very room, where four men sat, much as you see now. He was told things which he could barely credit, yet when the night turned to dawn, he was still alive and fully believed everything he had been taught. So it has gone for generations, for deep within the history of the Camareen lies a secret. It is a secret you will either keep within you for years to come, or take to your grave this night.

'I sat where you sit now, many years ago, as my father and his father before had done. We sat, we listened, we could not believe what was said, but when all was said and done, we came to understand. And when we understood, our lives were forever changed.

'Moreover, each of us has taken a pledge and embarked on a journey, from that ancestor to myself. My journey still takes place this day.'

'Journey?' asked Valko. 'To where?'

'To a place within the soul,' said the Deathpriest.

Valko's mind immediately turned calculating. His mother had warned him against listening to the Deathpriests, for they were highest in the regard of the Dark One, after the TeKarana. As such, they could decree that any deviation from accepted behaviour could be labelled blasphemy and bring instant destruction; although his mother had cautioned him that as often as not such accusations had more to do with property, rank, an old blood feud, or over a female advantageous to an alliance, and little to do with doctrine.

The Deathpriest read something in Valko's expression, for he said, 'I know your mother warned you against listening to those of us in the Brotherhood. But put aside what you think you know, and learn.'

'How do you know what my mother warned me of?' asked Valko, alarmed.

Aruke laughed. 'Because your mother is one of us, and if she could be, she would be sitting in the fifth chair. She is with us in spirit, if not in mind and body.'

Valko didn't understand, but he knew down to his marrow that for the next few minutes his life would be in the balance.

Aruke looked first to one side, then to the other, and the three men with him all nodded. 'My son, since long before you were conceived, plans were in place that required one such as yourself to be created.'

Valko wondered at the choice of the word 'created', but chose to remain silent.

'Like my father before me, I was raised with a single purpose, a purpose which I hope will be fulfilled this night.' He fell silent, either waiting to see if his son had a comment or question, or simply to gather his thoughts. 'You will either understand this or not and upon your understanding both our futures rest.

'Everything you know about our people, the Dasati, is false.'

Now Valko could not resist the urge to speak. 'False? What do you mean? In what way?'

'In every way,' said his father.

The Deathpriest spoke next. 'I am Father Juwon. As a child I knew I had a calling beyond that of being a warrior. When I returned to my father's estate and bested everyone he sent against me to test me and won, I left, seeking the nearest abbey.

'There I trained until I was elevated to the rank of lector, and then to deacon. At last I reached ordination as a priest, and am now High Priest of the Western Lands.

'But even from the first I knew my calling came not from the Dark One, but from somewhere else.'

The hair on the back of Valko's neck rose, for surely this highly placed Deathpriest could never utter such blasphemy? There was no other source for a calling, save the Dark One. That is what everyone he had ever known had said . . . everyone but his mother.

Valko said nothing.

The armoured man said, 'I am Denob, of the Jadmundier. I trained with your father, alongside Hirea. The three of us were chosen by fate to become as brothers, though this was not obvious to us at first.' He looked at Hirea.

'I have seen into you, young Valko,' said the old training instructor, 'deeper than you think. I have also spoken to your mother, and she told me what to seek within you.

'I have not found you wanting.'

'When we fought, and I bested you with my bare hands, why the deception?' cried Valko. 'Why did you act as if you didn't know my mother, and then tell me she was a Bloodwitch?'

Hirea smiled. 'Have you thought upon what I said?'

'Yes,' said Valko. 'I have.'

'And your conclusion?' asked the Deathpriest.

Valko was silent for a moment. Then, in a low voice, he said, 'I believe my mother is a Bloodwitch.'

'Then you've taken your first step,' said his father. 'When your mother and I coupled, it had been decided long before we had met that we should conceive a special child. Generations of Dasati were coupled and their offspring united in turn, in order that one day you would sit in that chair.'

'Auguries and portents had set us all on this path years ago,' said Father Juwon. He leaned forward and looked Valko directly in the eyes, a challenge in any other circumstance. 'You are that special child, and the prophecy has begun.'

'What prophecy?' Valko asked.

The Deathpriest sat back and began speaking, as if reciting a familiar old liturgy. 'In the beginning there was a balance, and within that balance all things resided. There was pleasure and pain, hope and despair, victory and defeat, the beginning and the end, and between them all things lived, bred, and died, and the order of things progressed as they should.

'But one day a struggle began and after epic battles and horrible sacrifice, the balance was destroyed.'

'I don't understand,' said Valko. 'What balance are you speaking of?'

'The balance between evil and good,' said the Deathpriest.

Valko blinked. 'I don't understand those words.'

'The words are lost because the basic concepts were lost,' said Aruke. 'Why do you think Attenders take up healing?'

Valko shrugged. 'They are weak. They are . . .' He let the thought trail off, for in truth, he had no understanding of why Attenders chose the lives they did.

'Why would any sane being choose a life of being despised by those they serve?' asked Hirea. 'They could just as easily be Mongers, Facilitators or Effectors. But instead they pick a trade that, while useful, earns them continuous contempt. Why?'

Again, Valko could not express a reason. He just had a deep feeling that something was wrong.

'They endure what they endure, because they

are good men and women,' said Father Juwon. 'They are good because they elect to help others, just for the satisfaction of healing, of helping, or repairing damage, of putting the needs of others ahead of their own.'

'I don't understand,' said Valko, but instead of a defiant tone, his tone was quietly reflective, as if he really did wish to comprehend what was being said to him. Deep within, he knew he was beginning to understand.

'In ancient days,' said the Deathpriest, 'there were two driving impulses within every man, woman, and child: the impulse to take what you wished, regardless of cost to others, to see and grab, to want and to kill, to live without regard for others. To live this life, there could be no progress, no growth, nothing but endless blood-shed and strife.'

'But that's how it has always been,' said Valko.

'No!' said Aruke to his son. 'The four of us here are living proof it is not always that way. Each of us would willingly lay down his life for the others.'

'But why?' asked Valko. 'He is a Jadmundier—' pointing to Denob. 'Hirea is of the Scourge, and he?' indicating Father Juwon, '—is a Deathpriest. You have no bond or loyalty to one another, no social alliances, no pacts or obligations.'

'Not true,' answered his father. 'Though Scourge might fight alongside Sadharin, or against Jadmundier, we three are as brothers.'

Father Juwon said, 'This is the other driving

impulse: the drive to band together, to share burdens, and to help one another; it's the very thing we now hold in contempt, yet some of us still feel it, or no one would ever become an Attender or Facilitator. Why choose a life that heaps scorn and hatred upon you?'

Valko now looked defeated. 'I don't understand.'

Aruke said, 'It's called "enlightened self-interest", my son. It's why warriors can put aside differences and aid one another, because it is to our mutual benefit. And we four, here in this room, are but a few of many who have come to understand that our people have become lost without the second impulse, the impulse to care for others. The only place in our people where that impulse is still pure is with a mother and her child. Think of your mother caring for you all those years in the Hiding, and wonder why that is the only time we Dasati exhibit that trait.'

Valko said, 'But you four have found it?'

'We have a higher calling,' said Aruke. 'We serve a different master than the Dark One.'

'Who?' cried Valko, now sitting forward on his seat.

Aruke said, 'We serve the White.'

Valko was stunned. The White was a tale told by mothers to frighten their young. Yet four men – three warriors and a Deathpriest – sat before him telling him they served a myth.

Silence dragged on, then Aruke said, 'You say nothing.'

Valko chose his words carefully. 'What I have been taught, above all else by my mother, is to question everything.' He shifted his weight in his chair, as if trying to make himself more comfortable as he wrestled with such difficult concepts. 'Until this moment, had you asked, I would have said what I assume every warrior of the Dasati would say: the White is a myth. It's a tale concocted by Deathpriests to keep the faithful in their place, or a fable created by the TeKarana's ancestors to give weight to the claim that his line was chosen by the Dark One to protect His Darkness's people from the harshest of light. Or perhaps simply a tale handed down from our ancestors that means nothing.

'It is said that the White is a being who lures the unfaithful into insanity and makes the weak perform irrational acts that mark them so that all Dasati can see their contamination. It is said that even to think overly long upon the White is dangerous. For me, the White always signified madness.

'Until tonight, I would not have believed such a thing as the White truly existed. Yet here you sit thus avowing, so I should assume that the four of you are mad, claiming as you do to be in the service of something that does not exist outside of myth. However, nothing I've seen in Hirea indicates irrationality, nor in you, my father.

'So I am forced to assume that the White is real and that the world is not what I have been told it is.'

Aruke sat back positively beaming with pride. He glanced at Father Juwon who said, 'You reasoned that well, young Valko. Assume the White is real. What do you suppose it is?'

Valko shook his head. 'I doubt I can even guess.'

'Guess,' commanded his father.

'The White is not a being,' Valko began slowly. 'Or there would have been more . . . believable stories. Witnesses, testimonies and the like. It would have to be immortal, for the legend has existed for centuries. I have never once heard of anyone who even knew anyone who had seen a manifestation of the White, so it cannot be a person or a being.'

Father Juwon nodded with approval.

'So,' continued Valko, 'it must be something abstract.' He looked at the four men, 'Perhaps a society, like the Sadharin or the Scourge.'

Aruke nodded. 'It is, but it is more.' He looked at Hirea.

Hirea said, 'I've watched you, young Valko, and I've seen you kill, yet you take no pleasure in it.'

Valko shrugged and said, 'I . . . no. I do not. I feel . . .'

'What do you feel?' asked Denob.

Valko said, 'I feel a sense of . . . waste. Even when I become enraged, or feel the hunger to spill blood, when it's over I feel . . . an emptiness.' He looked at his father. 'The young warrior I fought on my day of testing, Lord Kesko's son. . . I have seen those who would not stand against him

307

victorious in the training arena. It was chance that had him face me. Had he faced another, he would be serving his house and the Sadharin this very day. There is no advantage, but chance, and chance . . . it evens out eventually, doesn't it?'

Father Juwon nodded. 'It does. We lose many fine young warriors to mere chance, and keep lesser warriors alive.'

'It is a waste,' Valko repeated.

'It is wrong,' said Aruke. 'If you can come to understand this thing, then I am content to die this night.'

'Why should you wish to die tonight,' asked Valko. 'Why should either of us die? Is it because of this . . . secret you carry? I can scarcely believe it, but if you say the White is who you serve, then I will serve with you. You have much to teach me, Father, and there will be many years before I take your head.'

'No, you must take my head tonight.'

'But why?'

'So that when dawn comes, you will be Lord of the Camareen. You must install your mother as ruling female of this house and begin to sire sons. Your mother will pick those females who will give you strong, well-connected sons.

'And you must come to understand many things that I cannot teach you. Your mother must; for a time of change is soon upon us, and you must remain for many years the Lord of the Camareen, and come to fully understand your fate.'

'What is my fate,' asked Valko. 'That I must hear this and . . . believe it?'

'Your mother will tell you all, and she will be here within two days,' said Aruke. 'But before I go, I reserve the pleasure of telling you what you must know.

'You build an alliance unlike any seen since the Days of Forging, and you or your heir must take that alliance and ride across the Star Bridge to Omadrabar, and there you must do a thing that has never been done in the history of the Dasati.

'You must take the head of the TeKarana. You must destroy the Empire of the Twelve Worlds and save the Dasati from the Dark One.'

CHAPTER 16

LORD

Aruke made ready to die.

Valko again voiced his objection. 'This is wasteful, and unnecessary.'

'You are young,' said Father Juwon. 'You are powerful, talented, and perceptive beyond your years, but you are inexperienced.'

Kneeling before his son, Aruke said, 'Listen to them. Father Juwon will remain here, as your "spiritual advisor", and Hirea and Denob will visit regularly. Others will make themselves known to you.

'But it is to your mother you must look first, and then to Father Juwon, for they will be your heart and mind until you have matured to fulfil your destiny, my son. You must be the ruling lord of the Camareen, not any man's son. It is vital that you rise quickly, and that all recognize you, for a great struggle is coming, and you must be ready when it arrives. Your mother will be a fine mistress of this castle – it is to my everlasting sorrow she was never here long during my tenure as ruler; she taught me more than I imagined possible to learn from a female, and I regret that

I will not see her again – and with a prelate as powerful as Father Juwon acting as your personal advisor, you will begin with great prestige and influence.

'They will guide you, keep you safe from those who will seek to crush you, and shield you from those who wish to pull you down from below.'

He looked at Father Juwon, and nodded. 'I am ready.'

Father Juwon looked at his old friend, then at Valko, who saw a sheen of wetness in the Deathpriest's eyes. An open display of weakness from a Deathpriest? This, as much as anything he had heard, proved that what he had been told was true, or that it was at least the truth as these men knew it.

The High Priest of the Western Lands said, 'We are so far from the light, we who serve the White, that we do not even have a name for the One we seek to worship. Somewhere lost in time that being lived, and somewhere we pray goodness abides, until such time as the way is made to return it to our lost people. But we still wish for our brother that being's mercy and know that this sacrifice is all that can be asked of any man.' He looked at Valko. 'Make it swift, and with honour and respect.'

The Lord of the Camareen presented his sword hilt-first to his son and Valko took it from him. He took a deep breath, and then in one swift motion he brought it down in a slashing blow, cleanly severing his father's head from his shoulders.

Orange blood fountained up in a spurting arc as Aruke's head rolled across the floor and his body crumpled. Valko stood over his father's body, generations of Dasati breeding causing a feeling of triumph to rise up in him. He was now Lord of the Camareen! He was now . . . then another feeling intruded: a dark, cold sensation in the pit of the stomach, far more chilling than the mere sense of wastefulness he had felt before when seeing someone needlessly die. It was a lonely thing, a dull ache of the heart, and he had no name for it. He looked at Juwon with a silent question in his eyes.

'It is called sorrow,' said the Deathpriest. 'What you are feeling in your heart is called sorrow.'

Valko felt moisture gather in his eyes, and a cold grip seized his heart. He looked at the three remaining men in the room and said, 'Surely this cannot be what you seek to serve?' His voice was thick with unfamiliar emotions.

'It is,' said Hirea, also betraying sadness at seeing his old friend dead. 'Dying for a noble cause doesn't lessen the loss, my young friend. Your father was my oldest companion and the only brother of the heart I have known. I will think of him every day for the rest of my life.'

A single tear ran down Valko's cheek. 'I cannot welcome this,' he said.

Father Juwon put his hand on the young lord's

shoulder. 'You must. It is what will save you. And it will save our people. I know it is a great deal to understand, but in time you will. Just know that the most difficult task is now behind you.'

Looking down at the body of the man he barely knew, Valko said, 'Why do I feel such . . . sorrow? I . . . he was a stranger.'

'He was your father,' said Denob. 'In ages gone by he would have loved you as your mother has.'

'Can that be?'

'It is what we fight for,' said Juwon. 'Now, let us go forth and announce to the household that you are now the Lord of the Camareen, then send word to the courts of the Sadharin and the Karana. Then make this house ready for your mother, for she is sorely needed here, my young friend.'

Valko let his father's sword fall from his fingers. Staring at the headless corpse, he nodded. Yes, more than anyone, his mother was needed here.

In the distance the sounds of heavy siege engines being hauled over a ridge by mules echoed through the woodlands. Teamsters cracked whips and shouted at the fractious animals who laboured to get their burdens up a trail never intended for such use.

The wagon containing the six young knights of Roldem jostled and shook as it seemed to hit every rock, fallen branch and rut in the trail, ensuring that the passengers were completely road-sore and bruised by the time they arrived. They had taken a fast cutter from Roldem to the inland port of Olasko Gateway. From there they had gone by riverboat up to the town of Far Reaches, which nestled in a triangle of land formed by the confluence of two rivers, the Lor and the Aran, which formed the borders between the Duchy of Olasko, the Principality of Aranor, and the disputed lands to the south, which were claimed by no fewer than six different nations. To say the area was a trouble spot was an understatement, and since Kaspar's overthrow a few years earlier, things had become even more unsettled.

'Here you go, young officers,' said the driver, a cheerful little man named Alby, who puffed furiously and constantly on a pipe filled with the cheapest, most foul-smelling tabac. The cheerful teamster also had the annoying habit of talking all the time and not listening to a thing that was said by the boys, including two orders by Prince Grandy to stop smoking the tabac. To the best of their ability to judge, the boys concluded minutes after the ordeal began that Alby must be as deaf as a tree stump.

Barely able to move, they managed to get out of the wagon, and when all six stood firmly on the ground, Jommy said, 'Thanks for the ride.'

Without looking back, Alby said, 'You're more than welcome, young sir.'

Grandy said, 'You can hear?'

'Of course I can, young sir. Why did you think otherwise?'

'Because I ordered you to cease smoking that foul weed hours ago.'

The old man looked back and grinned. 'And I'm supposed to listen to a pup knight-lieutenant? This army's run by generals and sergeants, young sir. Best you learn that straight away. Have a good day.' He flicked the reins and his horses moved along, leaving six bruised and annoyed young officers standing before the command tent.

Looking at the guard, Servan said, 'We're to report to General Bertrand.'

'Sir,' said the guard, disappearing into the large command tent.

In a moment a familiar face appeared between the tent flaps as Kaspar of Olasko stuck his head outside to see who the new officers were. He smiled and said, 'Wait a minute, lads.'

'Kaspar,' said Tad.

'You know him?' asked Godfrey.

'That's the former Duke Kaspar of Olasko,' said Zane. 'I wonder what he's doing here.'

'I expect we'll find out soon enough,' said Servan.

As Servan predicted, a short time later Kaspar came out of the command tent in the company of a burly older man wearing a dirty, blood-stained tabard with the royal crest of Roldem on it. His hair was dishevelled and matted, as if he had recently removed his helmet. He looked at

315

the six boys and said, 'Gentlemen, welcome to the war.'

The boys saluted as they had been instructed, and it was Grandy who spoke first. 'How can we serve, General?'

General Bertrand smiled, his black beard parting to show even white teeth. 'Just don't get yourself killed, Highness, for a start. I have no idea why your father approved this notion to put you in harm's way, but if you're here to serve, then serve you will.

'Kaspar of Olasko is acting as a consultant on this march, as he is very familiar with the surrounding countryside.'

Kaspar said, 'I used to hunt around here.'

'Sir,' asked Tad. 'What are we to do?'

'Why, you are to observe, and learn,' said the General. 'And eventually, to lead. But for now, I need to know who among you is the fastest runner?'

None of the boys felt particularly swift after the long ride in the bouncing wagon, but without hesitation both Jommy and Godfrey said, 'Tad.'

The General nodded, and handed a rolled-up parchment to Tad. 'Up that trail and over that ridge, past where we're pulling up our siege engines, you'll find a company of infantry under the command of a Captain Beloit. Give these to him and wait for his reply. Now off with you.'

Tad hesitated for an instant, then saluted, and ran off.

Kaspar said, 'The rest of you come with me.'

When they were a short distance from the command tent, Kaspar stopped and said, 'We're at the end of routing some infantry from Bardac's who thought they'd raid down here and maybe even carve out a little private barony. As long as you follow orders, you should be safe, but don't assume for a moment there's not danger behind those trees.' He looked at Grandy. 'Especially you, young prince.' He shook his head. 'Last time I saw you I think you were cutting teeth.'

Grandy tried to look serious, but failed.

Kaspar said, 'Stay close to the command tent until I get the General to assign you to whichever companies need a raw lieutenant who has no idea what he's doing, and then we'll send you along.' He looked around, as if anticipating danger. 'Those dogs from Bardac's do have a company of light cavalry out there somewhere, and we have no idea where, so stay alert, because if those bastards show up, it's going to become very busy around here very suddenly.' He noticed they weren't carrying weapons. 'Whose notion was it to order you six into combat without weapons?'

They all exchanged glances, and Jommy said, 'Father Elias said we'd be given what we needed when we left the university. I guess he neglected that part of things.'

Kaspar shouted to a nearby guardsman. 'Take these young officers to the quartermaster's wagon!' To the five remaining boys he said, 'Each of you get a sword and an officer's breastplate. If they've got riding boots your size, trade in those gentleman's dainties you're wearing; if they don't, you'll have to make do with those. Some horses are being brought up from the remounts and should be here before sundown. You can each get yourself a ride then.'

The boys tried a collection of awkward salutes, and Kaspar had to restrain himself from laughing. After they were on their way down the hill to the provisioner's wagon, Kaspar groaned to himself, 'Pug, what are you thinking?'

Miranda could barely contain herself. 'What is your father thinking?' she demanded of Caleb.

Her younger son sat on a divan in his parent's private quarters in the villa on Sorcerer's Island, and held up his hands in surrender. 'I've never been good at anticipating the reasons why either of you do the things you do, Mother.'

Miranda paced. 'I've got a dead Talnoy in the halls of the Assembly, and we think there's a rogue rift somewhere on the planet that the most powerful magicians on two worlds can't seem to find. Your foster-children are off with Kaspar playing soldier, and your father is . . . somewhere.'

Caleb said, 'What would you like me to do?'

Miranda heaved a sigh and sat. 'Just . . . listen.'

'I can do that,' said her son with a rueful smile. He knew how frantic his mother became when his father was out of reach. She didn't mind most of the things he went off to do, no matter the danger,

318

as long as he could be contacted. It gave her the sense of reassurance that she seemed to need.

'Would it do any good to point out that Father is probably the most able man on two worlds to be where he is?'

'But there's so much back here that could use his attention,' she said, knowing as she said it that it was a petty complaint. 'And on Kelewan.'

'Like finding Leso Varen?'

She nodded. 'He's learned from his past mistakes, apparently. There's not been even the faintest whiff of his evil magic that anyone, Great One or Lesser Path, can detect. Fortunately, the Tsurani abhorrence for necromancy should make it easy enough to find him should he start murdering people for their life force.'

'Unless he's decided to take another tack.'

'Such as?'

'If he's duplicated his ruse in Kesh, and has insinuated himself within a high-ranking family, or even the imperial family, he could cause a great deal of harm that way.'

Miranda said, 'Let him try. Since the reforms of the last two emperors, the Game of the Council is about as deadly as a tussle between two underweight kittens. There hasn't been a political murder in ten years, and no outright armed conflict between clans or families in fifteen. It's become more sedate over there than it is here.'

'Still,' said Caleb, 'it might be the thing for you

to return to Kelewan and turn your abilities to finding Varen. You've not encountered him—'

'I was on the Island when he struck!' she reminded her son.

'And I was about to say, "except for that one time on the Island, but that makes you more likely to recognize him than anyone on Kelewan".'

'I could have been standing next to him, Caleb, and not known him. There may be some . . . quality of magic he uses that your father would recognize, but as for having any sense of him while standing and talking . . .'

'Perhaps there's another way.'

'What?'

'Ask around. Look for things that might give you a hint, such as who has been absent from the Assembly at odd times.'

'There are over four hundred members of the Assembly,' Miranda reminded her son. 'Accounting for the comings and goings of men who are used to having their every whim obeyed without question may prove a little difficult.'

'Then ask if anyone has been behaving oddly. Father says that it takes someone occupying another's body a while to adjust.'

'He's right,' said Miranda, as she stopped her pacing as something else struck her. 'My father had books on necromancy which are right here on this island.'

'Then might I suggest you consult them, for if you can't find the man, perhaps you can find the magic.'

'You've given me an idea,' said Miranda, quickly hurrying out of the room.

Caleb looked at the door his mother had just used and said quietly, 'You're welcome.'

Pug stood waiting as the Dasati Martuch stood next to Magnus, with a priest of some sort from a local temple on the other side of him. They were learning the dominant language of the Dasati, using 'tricks' Nakor had employed before – a type of magic Pug had witnessed during the Riftwar used by an Ishapian priest named Dominic. The local priest was necessary because Nakor's command of his 'tricks' was still tentative at best and would take more refinement before he would risk anything dealing with the mind.

All Pug knew was that it had taken the better part of an hour, but he now spoke fluent, idiomatic Dasati; and he had a throbbing headache. Magnus looked as if he was going to throw up his lunch.

'The discomfort will pass,' said Martuch.

The only one who appeared completely untroubled by the experience was Bek, who now seemed genuinely excited by the prospect of moving on to the second plane of reality.

Martuch said, 'Before we depart, there are things you must know for the journey, and things you need to know for when we arrive.

'Delecordia is a world that has somehow reached a balancing point between the first and second realms of reality. There have been many theories and speculations by great minds among the Ipiliac, but no one knows how, why, or when it happened. Nor do we have any knowledge of any place like it.'

'The Hall's a big place,' said Nakor with a grin. 'You'll find another one, some day, I bet.'

Pug knew better than to bet against Nakor.

Martuch went on, 'The people you see here are descendants of refugees. Ages ago when the ancestors of the current TeKarana rose to pre-eminence among the Dasati, there was a worldwide war and those who opposed his reign fled here. The details are lost in antiquity.' He looked around. 'The Ipiliac are people you could reason with, find common ground with, come to terms with, but we Dasati are less like the Ipiliac than you are.'

He studied Pug. Pug endured the gaze and understood. 'You fight every moment you're here, don't you?'

'More than you will ever know. It takes constant effort not to draw a sword and start a slaughter. The Ipiliac and other races are what I was taught to abhor: lesser beings, weaklings not worthy of existence.' He sighed. 'In time, I have been told, the struggle will be less overt, less conscious, and I believe that to be so.' He ventured what Pug had come to understand was a Dasati smile. 'I've gone entire minutes without wanting to take your heads, of late.' Then his tone turned serious. 'When we leave here, it will be unlike anything you've experienced, for there is no "door" into a Hall in the second realm, or at least no one has found anything like the Hall in the lower realms of reality.'

Pug interrupted. 'How do you know that?'

'In good time,' said Martuch, holding up his hand. 'There will be time for answers to such academic questions when we get to our destination.' He glanced around, and said, 'Right now, we need to concentrate on survival. Remember this: there is no escape. There is nowhere to which you can flee. Once you are on Kosridi, you are stuck there. And there you must remain until your mysterious mission is over. And always, every waking moment, you must remember that the most dangerous person among the Ipiliac is less of a threat to you than the gentlest soul among the Dasati.

'You are disguised as Attenders, which is both a risk and safety. Their moral position and impulse to help others makes them despised among most Dasati, yet it will help you mask any blunders you might make.' He held up his hand. 'I caution you, say or do nothing unless we speak first. There are countless ways you can get yourself killed, and I can not protect you until we reach our safe haven.

'I will be a warrior, a Rider of the Sadharin – that is one of the societies of warriors I've mentioned to you. You are under my protection because I find you useful, but should you make any blunders, I will be expected to kill you as quickly as a stranger might, so heed my warning:

if I must, I will kill one of you to save this mission. Do we understand one another?'

They looked at each other, and Pug knew what Magnus was thinking: that Martuch would have his hands full killing any of the four. No one said a word, just nodded in agreement.

'Lastly, speak to no one, under no circumstances, unless I instruct you to. We shall travel by thought alone to the world of Kosridi, and to the castle of an ally a few weeks' travel from the capital city. We shall rest there, and there you shall hone your deception, learning to be Dasati from other Dasati besides myself. After that we will travel to Kosridi City and take the Star Bridge to three worlds, until we reached Omadrabar.' Looking at Pug, he said, 'I trust by the time we do, we will both have a clear idea of what this mad quest is, and how it will benefit both our causes.'

Silently Pug thought, 'We can only hope.'

CHAPTER 17

WARRIORS

Jommy waved his sword.

From down at the bottom of the hill, Grandy returned the signal. The boys had been given a relatively safe post, overseeing a company of wounded soldiers behind the lines. Jommy, Servan and Tad were up on a ridge, scouting the best route out of the area of main conflict, while Grandy, Zane and Godfrey were down below with the three wagons of injured men. A few walking-wounded hobbled along beside the wagons, which were slowed enough by terrain for them to keep pace. They were wending their way through an alpine meadow cut by several game trails. The afternoon sun had turned the day warm and bright, but riddled the landscape with deep shadows, and keeping the slow-moving wagons on the correct path down the mountain was tricky. Without the three boys scouting ahead, the wagons could easily have wandered down a dry wash leading nowhere. Jommy knew that once over this last ridge it was a straight run down a trail that would take them to the waiting river-boats.

The conflict had reached a crescendo about five miles to the north-east, as General Bertrand's and Kaspar's forces had brought the infantry from Bardac's to bay. The invaders had holed up in an old frontier fortress, now half destroyed by the elements. Roldem's siege engines, two small trebuchets and two large ballistae, were being brought up to reduce the other half of the fortress to rubble. Of the Bardac cavalry, no sign had been seen, and speculation had run through the camp that they were already back across the border into the Holdfast.

Servan turned to Jommy. 'Once we're over this ridge I think we should see a fairly quiet run down to the river. The boats should still be there—' Suddenly he stopped.

Jommy heard it at the same instant. 'Horses!'

Neither boy had to be reminded that all the Roldemish cavalry was up at the front, providing a screen for the siege engines. Jommy was off down the hill, a half step behind Servan, and a step ahead of Tad who looked surprised to see his two companions racing down the hill. Then Jommy's shout penetrated, and Tad heard the sound of hooves on the rocks down a long draw.

Grandy, Zane and Godfrey had heard it as well. The injured men who were able to were helping the others out of the wagons. Any man caught in the open wagons when the cavalry struck would be dead.

Four archers and two swordsmen had been

detailed with the six young officers, and before Jommy could even think to consider what to do, Servan was giving orders. 'You, you, and you,' he said to the first three archers, pointing at each one in turn. 'Up on those rocks and shoot at the first head you see coming up that draw, man or horse, I don't care.' To the fourth archer, he said, 'I want you over there—' he pointed to an outcropping that rose up to the defender's right, '—and see if you can discourage them from turning towards you.' To the two fit guardsmen and the other boys he shouted, 'Unhitch these wagons and turn them on their sides! Let's go!'

Jommy saw no sense in debating who was supposed to be senior, for he had no idea what to do, and at least Servan had the men following orders. The young cousin to the Prince shouted, 'Any man who can wield a weapon, behind the wagons. The rest of you, up this trail—' he pointed to a game trail leading off over the ridge, '—and hide as best you can!'

Those who could helped those who couldn't move by themselves up the trail. A half-dozen wounded men joined the archers and the swordsmen.

Servan grabbed Grandy and said, 'Head up the trail with the wounded.' When the Prince hesitated, he shouted, 'Go! Protect them!'

Grandy nodded and did as instructed. Jommy knew he offered as much protection as a squirrel, but the order gave the boy a sense of purpose and saved his pride.

The wagons had been overturned and Jommy saw that everyone was ready as could be; and the freed horses were now scattering through the woods. 'Get ready!' he shouted, shifting his weight and looking to see where the charge would come from.

Then suddenly the air was full of war cries and arrows.

The three archers peppered the first riders, emptying at least four saddles, and when they tried to turn, the fourth archer killed the first two men who left the line of attack.

Those behind lowered themselves over the necks of their mounts and charged the wagons. Jommy judged them a rag-tag outfit, mostly mercenaries from what he could see, no uniforms, no organization. He knew that if they were offered an avenue of escape they'd take it, so he ran to stand next to Servan and said, 'If they break for the north, let them go.'

'Let them go?' said the young noble.

'Yes! These are swords-for-hire and will not die in a lost cause.'

Then the riders hit the wagons. Jommy saw Tad whirl and cut a rider from his horse, while Zane leapt up from his crouch behind one of the wagons to pull a Bardic man from his saddle. As Jommy expected, the riders needed less than a minute to get around the sides of the three overturned wagons, and now he faced two armed riders trying to turn in behind the defenders.

The wounded men were putting up the best fight they could, but Jommy knew they were over-matched. The archers would quickly run out of arrows and had no swords or shields, just trench knives. Jommy picked the closest rider and struck hard at the man, who caught Jommy's blade on his own. The man quickly began the short chopping blows favoured by cavalry that prevented an infantryman from getting in too close, and Jommy was forced to retreat. Another rider came at Jommy from his left, and the boy spun, bringing his sword around quickly as he ducked. The rider's sword passed harmlessly over Jommy's head, but Jommy's blade bit deep into the rider's leg. The man shouted in pain and couldn't keep his saddle with only one good leg.

Jommy saw the now riderless horse turn and without thought he made a two-step dash and leapt into the saddle before the first rider could turn and come at him. Jommy was a good swordsman, and a good rider, but he had never fought from horseback before, not even in practice. He knew from what Caleb, Kaspar and Talwin Hawkins had told him that an experienced warhorse would know what his rider wished because of leg pressure, but Jommy had no idea if this was an experienced animal or not; and he was not its usual rider. He quickly took the reins in his left hand and raised his right just in time to block a blow from the first rider.

Jommy lashed out with his right hand, a

sweeping sideways blow that almost took him out of his own saddle. And the horse turned in place! His leg pressure on the horse's left, along with the slight tug on the reins had caused the mount to follow the natural movement of Jommy's blow. He put his heels to the horse's barrel and was off, after the first rider. The man turned just as Jommy caught up with him and suddenly there was a tall red-headed rider swinging a murderous blow at him.

The man tried to lean back in the saddle, but he overbalanced and in that instant, Jommy had him. Jommy recovered from his forward sweep and dealt the man a lethal backhanded sword blow that took him completely out of the saddle.

Jommy turned his mount and saw that Servan, Tad, Godfrey and Zane were being hard pressed by half a dozen riders. Jommy charged.

He rode his horse like a madman, forcing the frantic animal to slam hard between two mounts. He ignored the rider on his left, hoping he wouldn't lose his head for doing so, and leapt from the saddle, dragging the rider on his right off his horse.

Suddenly Jommy was rolling on the ground, gouging, kicking, kneeing, biting, punching with the hilt of his sword, for he had no room to swing the blade. Horses were whinnying in alarm and stamping all around him, and the boy and the man he battled with rolled wildly. Jommy prayed he didn't get stepped on by a frightened horse.

He slammed the hilt of his sword into the man's jaw and saw the man's eyes lose focus. Jommy hit him again and the man's expression went slack, but only for an instant. He was an experienced warrior and no matter how strong Jommy was, the man had probably endured worse. The man shook his head to clear it and was about to draw back his own fist when a boot toe struck him in the temple. His eyes rolled up into his head.

A strong hand grabbed Jommy by the back of his uniform tunic and hauled him to his feet. Zane let go and said, 'Glad you could join us.'

Jommy turned and struck a blow at a rider who was trying to get away. The riders withdrew, heading up the north trail as Jommy had suspected they would.

He shouted, 'Let them go!' and then realized no one in this little company was in any shape to give chase. Jommy let the sword slip from his fingers and sat down hard on the ground, whatever strength he had left flowing out of him like water out of a cracked gourd.

Servan sat down next to him. 'That was a close thing.'

Jommy nodded. 'Very. You did well, the way you got everything organized. Very impressive.'

'Thanks,' said Servan.

Tad hurried over. 'I'm going after Grandy to see if he's all right.'

Jommy nodded and Godfrey said, 'I'll go with him.'

Servan said, 'I watched you when you rode your horse into the fray, you madman. You almost lost your head pulling that man from the saddle. The rider on your blind side barely missed you.'

'Well, you know what they say, "a miss is as good as a mile".'

'They do say that, don't they?' Servan smiled and then laughed. 'And the way you were rolling in the dirt. The biting, kicking, all that. Did you actually try to chew off his ear?'

'You bite anything you can,' said Jommy. 'It takes his mind off killing you.'

Servan laughed. 'I take your meaning now.'

'About what?'

'That practice bout, back at the Masters' Court. When you punched me in the face.'

'My meaning?'

'About how you do whatever you need to do to win,' said Servan. 'Duelling doesn't seem like much preparation for what we just went through.'

'I don't see any wounds on you, so I reckon you did well enough.'

Again Servan laughed. 'True. Is it always like this?'

'What?'

'This feeling? I'm almost giddy.'

Jommy nodded. 'Sometimes. You're damn glad to still be breathing. Not like those blokes.' He pointed to a half-dozen corpses nearby. 'It can make a man downright silly.'

'Ah,' said Servan leaning back against the over-turned wagon.

'Other times it makes you so sick to your heart you're certain you'll die from the ache,' said Jommy, remembering the torture of the captured Nighthawk Jomo Ketlami. He lowered his head for a minute. 'But most of the time you're just so tired you can't move.'

Servan took a deep breath. 'We'd better get these boys organized.' He stood and turned to offer Jommy a hand up.

The larger boy took it and when they were standing face to face, Jommy said, 'One thing.'

'What?'

'About that bout at the Masters' Court. So, then . . . what you're saying is, I won?'

Servan laughed, and put up his hands. 'No, that's not what I'm saying.'

'But you just said . . .' began Jommy; but the royal cousin turned his back and started giving orders to the men.

Valko stood motionless for a moment, then moved to the huge window overlooking the courtyard. His mother rode in on the back of a small varnin, dressed as he remembered her during the Hiding. He didn't know what he expected, perhaps to see her in some regal court attire, or being carried in a palanquin carried by Lessers. She dismounted and handed the reins to a lackey then quickly entered the keep.

Valko left the rooms he was using while his father's quarters were being made ready for him. He had chosen to remove all the personal items, having a bitter taste still from the killing. It had been nothing like the triumph he had imagined when he was a child, a moment of glory as he began building his own personal empire.

His mother entered the long hall leading to his father's quarters, and Valko called to her. 'Mother, over here!'

She hurried to him, looking exactly as he had remembered her. She was tall, commanding, and still beautiful, with only a touch of grey at the temples as her still-dark hair fell to her shoulders. He understood why many men desired her, but now he understood why he was her only child. It had all been part of a plan.

Her eyes were the most intense Valko had ever seen and her gaze filled him at once with a giddy feeling and dread. She was his mother, and the love between mother and son was unique among the Dasati. She would have died a hundred times over to save him.

She embraced him, a gentle hug which lasted an instant, then said, 'We must be alone.'

Valko indicated the quarters he had set aside for her, next to those used by his father. 'I will be taking the lord's quarters tomorrow,' he said as he walked her to her rooms.

She looked at him again, appraisingly, but said nothing until they were alone and the door closed. As he was about to speak, she held up her hand for silence, and years of obeying her took over and he went motionless. Those hand gestures had saved him in the Hiding more than once. She closed her eyes and muttered words he couldn't understand, then she opened them again.

'We are unwatched.'

'So it's true. You're Bloodwitch.'

She nodded. 'I am pleased to see you alive, my son: it proves my feelings for you; moreover, it means you have become the man I prayed you would become.'

'Prayed? To whom? Certainly not to His Darkness, from what I was told.'

She nodded, indicating he should sit in a chair by a dressing divan. She looked around the room, nodding her head in approval. The walls were of black stone like the rest of the castle, but Valko had ordered two women Lessers to bedeck it in a fashion suitable for the women of the Karana's household, and they had seen to it. The most beautiful tapestries in the castle had been moved to cover the walls, a richly woven rug made from ahasan wool lay across the floor, and her bed was piled high with rich furs. Scented candles burned and there were pots of flowers set around the room. 'I like how you've welcomed me, my son.' She sat on the bed.

He nodded. 'You are my mother,' he said, as if that explained everything.

'And you are my son.' She studied his face. 'You are also the son of an extraordinary man.'

Suddenly Valko felt an odd choking sensation in his chest. 'I know,' he said. 'And why do I feel this . . . strange . . . pain inside. . . I don't know what to call it, when I think of Aruke.'

'It's called regret,' she said. 'It is one of many feelings long lost to the Dasati.' She looked out of the window at the setting sun, glinting off the sea. 'You asked to whom I prayed. We have no name for that force, save "the White". We do not even know if it's a god or goddess.'

'I thought they all were destroyed by the Dark One in his rise.'

'So the Deathpriests would have you believe. It is the opposite of everything embodied by the Dark One.'

'So many questions . . .' began the young warrior.

'And we have time, but first there are things you must know to stay alive.

'The White is used as a children's bedtime tale, to frighten and gull, to lure Dasati everywhere into thinking it a myth of no significance, something you outgrow. This serves to make most Dasati disbelievers, and this ploy is far more effective than simple denial.

'Long ago the Bloodwitch Sisterhood ranked equal to the Deathpriests in Dasati society. The Deathpriest served all the gods, not just His Darkness, and the Sisterhood was more concerned with nature and the forces of life. Blood is not just something seen when you spill it on the arena sand, or on the battlefield, but the very stuff of life, pulsing through your veins. It embodies all the things that stand in opposition to the cult of the Dark One, and when he achieved primacy among the gods, we became anathema and were banished.

'The Bloodwitch Sisterhood has existed in secret for centuries, my son. We have served as best we can to stem the Dark One's might.'

'To me, it seems you failed.' He sat back on the chair. 'I know I am young, Mother, but I remember many things you taught me during the Hiding, and now I realize that you've given me many pieces to a puzzle. When they were put together one way it seemed one picture, but put together another way. . .'

She nodded and said, 'A sage insight for one so young. You are the one expected, Valko of the Camareen. For generations the Bloodwitch Sisterhood has been waiting for one such as you, for there is a prophecy, one which no one outside the Sisterhood knows fully. Those like your father and Hirea and Denob who serve the White, they only know part of it. You shall be the first outside the Sisterhood to know it all.' She paused, as if thinking of the best way to begin, then looked at her son and smiled briefly.

'In ages past a balance existed, and all things were as they were meant to be. But to sustain that balance, a struggle was required, for as with all struggles, the balance would shift from time to time.

'When the forces of the Dark One rose, they were opposed by those who worshipped gods and goddesses whose names are now lost to us, for even knowing their names is forbidden.

'At the time of the Great Purging, every Dasati was given the choice to worship the Dark One or die. Many chose death because they knew life under the Dark One's supremacy would be a life of hopelessness and despair.'

Valko interrupted. 'But the Dark One has always been supreme . . .' He hung his head. 'I spoke rashly.'

'It is what you were taught. And there were things I could not share with you while you were in the Hiding, against the risk you might say something to another child. So ingrained are these beliefs there were mothers who would have sacrificed their own children to alert a Deathpriest to what is considered blasphemy.'

Valko stood and walked to the window, shaking his head.

'We have much to discuss and much for you to learn,' his mother said. 'In a week's time you must invite the whole of the Sadharin here to celebrate your ascendance as Lord of the Camareen. Between then and now you must come to fully understand what it is you must do over the next few years. For you have an opportunity never afforded any Dasati since the dawn of our race.'

Valko looked away from the window, his expression troubled. 'This prophecy you spoke of?'

'Yes, my son. I will give it to you in detail, that and many other things you must learn. For if the prophecy is true, and we believe it is, soon change will come to the Twelve Worlds and we must be ready. We know one will rise to challenge the Dark One, and he will be known as the Godkiller.'

Valko's face drained of colour. 'Am I . . .'

'No, you are not the Godkiller, my son. But you must prepare the way for the Godkiller.'

'How am I to do that?'

'No one knows.' She rose and came to stand beside Valko as the sun sank behind dark clouds hovering over the horizon. 'Today was a beautiful day, but I think it will rain tomorrow.'

'I think so, too.' He looked at her. 'What shall I do until I know my task?'

'Play the role fate has given you, as Ruler of the Camareen. I have sent word and sisters of mine will be slowly making their way here, some young and beautiful, some with young and beautiful daughters. All will be wise and all will know more than any other woman you will meet.

'You will father many sons, Valko, and know there are other sons of the Sisterhood who are rising to rule in their fathers' stead, and when the time is at hand, when the Godkiller appears, we of the Sisterhood, and the men we love, we shall all rise up and destroy the Deathpriests and the

TeKarana and his twelve Karanas and we shall free the Dasati people.'

Valko felt overwhelmed. His mind could barely encompass such a concept, let alone embrace how it could be achieved. The boy fresh from the Hiding, the child within, knew the TeKarana was supreme among mortals, blessed by His Darkness, and his armies ruled the Twelve Worlds, and had crushed a dozen more over the centuries. This Empire had existed for more than a thousand years . . .

He put his arm against the wall and rested his forehead on it for a moment. 'It is all too much.'

'Then we shall go slowly, my son. We shall dine and speak after supper, and then have a good night's sleep.'

Valko took a deep breath and his head came up and he looked at his mother. 'There is one thing I would like to know now, Mother.'

'What is that?'

With an odd sheen in his eyes, Valko said, 'Tell me about my father.'

CHAPTER 18

FEAST

Grandy laughed.

The Prince of Roldem was drunk. It was the first celebration of any sort at which he had been permitted to eat and drink like his elders. And for a boy of fourteen a little ale went a long way.

The others were all two to three years his elder and the three boys from Sorcerer's Isle had been drinking like men for nearly two years. So they, along with Servan and Godfrey watched the young prince with thinly-veiled amusement. Grandy had been safe from most of the conflict that afternoon, but Servan's order for him to guard the fleeing wounded had given him a sense of participation far in excess of his real contribution. Still, he celebrated the routing of the invaders from Bardic's with as much gusto as the most battle-hardened soldier in the army.

They sat around a campfire a short stroll from the General's tent, listening to the stories being told by the veterans of the short assault on the old fortress. The commander of the Holdfast Brigade saw the inevitable before him after the first flight of stones from the trebuchet collapsed one of his key defensive positions, and sued for surrender. As was the case with such quick and relatively easy victories, the stories got funnier as the night wore on and the ale and wine flowed. Eventually, the last of the veterans got up, leaving the boys to amuse themselves.

Kaspar had helped General Bertrand negotiate the terms of the surrender, and the defeated invaders were now camped a half-mile up the road under guard. They would begin the long march home, without weapons or anything else the victorious soldiers could liberate from them, and their officers would be held for ransom to defray the cost of defending Aranor.

Roldem's newest province had long historical ties to Roldem, the principality having been part of the Kingdom before in ages past, but the speed of response had taken the invaders by surprise. Kaspar knew Bertrand, for he had served under the current Knight-Marshall in Opardum, Quentin Havrevulen, a man Kaspar had hand-picked to run the army when he had ruled Olasko.

Kaspar came out of the General's tent and walked over to sit down on a log next to Servan. 'Quite the little feast you've got going here,' he observed.

Jommy laughed, obviously intoxicated. 'The provisioner brought along enough food for a month, Kaspar. He didn't want to lug it all back to Opardum, I guess, so he's cooking everything.'

'Just as well,' said the former duke. 'Much of this would be simply thrown out back—' he was about to say 'home', as the capital of Olasko had been his home all his life, but it hadn't been for nearly three years, so instead he said, '—there.'

Kaspar looked at the six boys from university. 'You lads did well, today,' he said. 'Those bastards that hit you were a bunch of strays in a bad mood and looking to punish someone before they got run back across the border. You killed six of them, wounded another half-dozen and took the fight out of them.' He smiled at Servan. 'And the best part is you didn't lose a man. You've got two more with light wounds than you did before, but otherwise, it was a capital job.'

Jommy said, 'That was Servan. He organized everything, on the spot, like he'd been doing it all his life, Kaspar.'

Servan said, 'Everyone did their part. They jumped right to it and stood firm.'

'Well, it's good, because we're going to have need of field commanders and soon.'

'Why?' asked Godfrey. 'Is Roldem going to war with Bardic's?'

Kaspar shook his head. 'No, my young friend.' He looked out into the darkness and there was a sadness in his eyes. 'Soon everyone will be going to war.'

Godfrey looked as if he was going to ask another question, but a warning look from Jommy made him fall silent. Kaspar said, 'When I was a boy, my father brought me here to hunt. I've been back several times.'

'It must be strange to return,' said Tad. 'I mean, with you not being Duke any more.'

Kaspar smiled. 'Life has a habit of making changes without consulting you, Tad.' He looked from face to face. 'We make plans, but fate doesn't always listen to what we want.' He stood up, and looked at the beaming face of the young prince. 'And you, young sir, are going to have a very rough morning tomorrow if you don't stop drinking ale. May I suggest you drink some water before retiring?' Without waiting to hear the Prince's answer, Kaspar returned to the General's tent.

Jommy yawned and said, 'Well, we should probably bed down, as we'll be up early and on the march.'

Godfrey watched Kaspar disappear into the General's tent. 'I wonder what he meant, "everyone will be going to war"?'

Zane looked at Tad, who in turn looked at Jommy. Jommy shrugged, and suddenly it was silent, with Grandy sitting with a grin, looking up at companions suddenly gone quiet with concern. His grin faded, and finally Jommy looked down, put his hand on the Prince's shoulder and said, 'Let's get some water in you, youngster. Kaspar's right. You're going to be a sick puppy come morning if we don't.'

Without any further conversation, the other boys bedded down as best they could around the campfire while Jommy led Grandy off in search of a large bucket of drinking water.

Valko stood at the head of the table while the Riders of the Sadharin pounded their gloved fists on the ancient wood, shouting their approval. The new Lord of the Camareen had invited the other leaders of his society to a feast commemorating his rise to power.

Narueen had been very precise in instructing her son on the proper order of things once his father's body had been placed in the vault of his ancestors. A formal message was sent to the Karana in Kosridi City announcing his ascension to the mantle of the Camareen and begging acknowledgement, which she assured him was a formality only. Then messages had to go to every blood relative listed in the Hall of Ancestors, again a formality, and then the invitation to the Sadharin, which she made clear was far more than a formality. For the brotherhood of the Sadharin was more than mere family: it was a battle society that could influence imperial policy, even shift the balance of power between factions, topple clans, and destroy families. Narueen had already named four riders who had daughters who would make favourable matches. This very night Valko had to choose one to bear him his first child. Narueen had whispered in the darkness, before the morning sun arose, and the plans were now in motion. The Bloodwitch Sisterhood had arts unlike any other, and she would determine if there were sons or daughters born to the young Camareen lord. Two sons, she had told them, within a month would be conceived, then two daughters.

Their Hiding would be unlike any known in the history of the Dasati, for special arrangements had been made to include sympathetic Attenders, Bloodwitch sisters and a few trusted warriors, which would ensure that the location of this Hiding was never discovered, never purged. Within twenty years, a dozen strong sons and daughters would present themselves at Castle Camareen, and Valko's ascendancy would begin.

Valko rose and shouted, 'Long live the Sadharin!'

The fifty lords of the Sadharin pounded the table even harder, hooting their war chant. Lord Andarin of the Kabeskoo shouted, 'Long live Lord Valko!'

Valko picked up his flagon of wine and drained it. His mother had made sure it was heavily watered, for while every other lord of the Sadharin was falling drunk, she wanted her son to keep his wits about him.

At the tables below the massive wooden board that served the lords of the Sadharin, the wives and daughters sat observing their men with amused interest. More than one daughter tried to catch the eye of the young lord.

But Valko had eyes only for his mother, as she moved gracefully among her guests, ensuring that each was well cared for. She paused behind Lord

Makara's daughter, and let her hand fall to the girl's shoulder. Valko betrayed nothing, but he knew that this was his mother's clear instruction as to who he would bed tonight. He considered the girl. She was comely and regarded him with blatant hunger; he knew that she would rejoice should he allow her to declare. Her father would welcome becoming more closely allied with the rising young lord, for he would think of Valko as his client, though soon enough he would realize that the reverse was the case.

Valko looked around the room and smiled. The diners were becoming more raucous by the minute. He drank in their approbation and rejoined in his own youthful strength. Much of what his mother had taught him began to fade as his Dasati nature asserted itself, and he took a long drink from his flagon. He wanted wine!

As he turned to order another pitcher brought to the table, a gentle hand on his wrist restrained him. Somehow his mother had read his mood and anticipated his lost focus. 'It's time for the entertainment, my son,' she said in tones soft enough that none but he could hear.

Valko gazed at her for a moment, then nodded. 'My lords!' he shouted. 'For your amusement!'

The doors to the hall were opened and a dozen servants hurried in, bearing a huge earthenware pot. A struggling youth was carried in, bound hand and foot. Valko grinned as he announced, 'This youth sought to reach his father's castle, to challenge for a place within his household, and was caught last night in a vadoon snare!'

This announcement brought gales of laughter, for the stupid herbivore was easily caught – its primary value was as a source for fur, and its destruction of fruit trees was a nuisance for orchard-owners. The youth would have to have been very inattentive or very stupid to blunder into such a snare.

'Let me go!' he shouted as he was placed within the pot. He was ready to fight with his bare hands and feet if given the chance, but servants forced him downward, so that his knees were folded up under his chin. As hard as he might struggle, it was a position impossible to change without help, help no one was going to offer.

Valko shouted. 'You are an animal! Too stupid even to fight for your place among men. You will die like an animal!'

The youth began shouting, a series of enraged snarls and inarticulate screams. The guests at the feast laughed, for his frustration and rage was comical in its impotence. Valko signalled, and servants began pouring buckets of water over the youth's head. He spat and bellowed, and the laughter in the room mounted.

'In olden times,' said Valko, 'it was considered amusing to place a weakling in cold water, then slowly bring it to a boil.

'Now we need no fire, for there are agents that will do the same without heat.' He motioned and two servants emptied the content of the two bags into the water and stepped back.

The reagents began to react and the water began to bubble. The defiant youth's shouts quickly turned from rage to agony. Some of the mixture splashed on to a servant standing too close, and he clawed at his eyes in pain.

The guests began to laugh uncontrollably. The louder the prisoner screamed, the more the guests became lost in paroxysms of hilarity. The lad splashed liquid up on his own shoulders, neck and face and blisters and reddish-orange wounds began to form.

The screaming lasted nearly a quarter of an hour, and when the prisoner neared death, Valko could see the guests rising from their seats, staring with avid hunger. The women were ready, Valko could see, many of them running hands up and down their own bodies, and many of the men were showing obvious signs of lust.

His mother had been right. A single death, arranged at the proper moment, was more effective than the random slaughters usually orchestrated for these events. Watching half a dozen Lessers trampled by animals or eaten by starving zarkis caused too much distraction, but one death, artfully done, brought intense focus.

Valko signalled to a servant. 'Ask Lord Makara's daughter if she would join me.' The servant ran over to the indicated girl and whispered to her. Her head came around and her eyes were alight with hunger as her hands clutched at the fabric of her dress. Valko knew that if he wished, she would let him take her right now in front of the assembled company.

Several of the lords of the Sadharin had left the head table and were standing close to females they would bed tonight. Valko considered a great number of declarations would occur and in years to come, many sons would arrive at castles as a result of tonight's mating. Only Valko, his mother and a handful of the Riders of the Sadharin knew that every match was orchestrated by the Bloodwitches, and that every child born of tonight's mating who survived their Hidings would become servants of the White.

Thoughts of the White were difficult to entertain while caught up in the blood and lust of the moment. Valko smiled as the youth's last breath left his body and declared, 'Weakling.'

His mother whispered, 'He did not seek to cross Camareen lands, my son. He sought to come to this castle. He was Aruke's son. He was your brother.'

Valko felt an odd chill rise up within and his head snapped around. He locked eyes with his mother and at that moment his feelings were so confused he didn't know if he could keep from striking her. Yet her soft touch made him focus. 'Had you done anything other than what you did, you would have appeared fatally weak to your guests: you would have shown everyone that you are not worthy to rule the Camareen. Just know the price of what you do. You have just begun the struggle, my son, and the pain you now feel will return, many times in the years to come.' She caressed his cheek as she had when he was a baby. 'Go now,' she whispered. 'Put aside all thoughts of pain and suffering, blood and death. Go, make a powerful son this night.'

Valko forced his confusion aside, left the table and found the girl waiting for him at the door leading from the hall to his quarters. He put his arm around her waist and embraced her, violently, hungrily, and without tenderness. Then he took her hand and led her to his bedchamber.

The dinner was strange. Pug sat at the head of the table, Martuch across from him. Ipiliacs dressed in odd clothing moved silently around him, placing dishes and removing them, filling flagons and cups without a word.

Martuch insisted they dine this way every night for a week before leaving, for it was, he said, the best way in which they might become more attuned to all things Dasati.

'This food is not exactly what you will eat on Kosridi, but it is close. Enough so that if you're served a common dish you will not react to it in an unexpected fashion.

'Those serving you are acting in the fashion of Lessers, so watch them. You will almost certainly never find yourself at a table such as this, for this is how the warriors dine. The only time men and women dine at the same table is if they are alone, perhaps after coupling.'

Pug nodded. Martuch had been an exemplary teacher, his mind a repository of a million details of Dasati life. Pug could not imagine anyone better suited to prepare them for this expedition.

For weeks they had been practising the language, and a convincing story – that they were three Attenders, serving Martuch; and the young warrior Bek was the son of a distant noble in a minor society who was making a pilgrimage to the TeKarana's city of Omadrabar, which was not unheard of, especially if the young warrior was inclined towards becoming a Deathpriest. For in Omadrabar was the great temple of the Dark One, where Martuch claimed the living god resided, and from where all power emanated.

Pug worried about Bek, though Nakor said the young warrior would be kept under control. He seemed a different being here on Delecordia, and Pug wondered what change arriving on the second level of reality would bring about. He was becoming Dasati in many ways. He had to only be told once what was expected of him, and he complied, flawlessly.

Nakor had indicated from the first that he suspected that something alien, dangerous, maybe even something linked to the Nameless One, resided in Bek. But perhaps that darkness came from the Dark God of the Dasati. Pug hated that there were so many unknowns, yet he trusted that at least he must survive, or how would he otherwise have sent back the messages?

His big concern was for Magnus and Nakor, for he knew in his heart that Lims-Kragma's bargain with him, when he lay near death in her hall, was not an idle threat. He would watch everyone he loved die before him, including his children. But every day he prayed that this day would not be the day on which that pain began. Now, he wondered, was he fated to lose his son and Nakor on this mad mission?

Pug put aside his misgivings, knowing the worry over something he could not control was a waste of energy, both mental and emotional. Every member of the Conclave knowingly agreed to go in harm's way, risking their lives for a greater good. Even so, being aware of that didn't lessen Pug's concern.

Martuch would play the young Bek's mentor, a warrior pledged in alliance to Bek's mythical father. Dasati alliances were so complex, so multi-level in nature, that no one other than a Facilitator who worked at the Hall of Ancestors could possibly recognize every named lord, family, clan or battle society.

On that subject, Pug said, 'Martuch, you said you will be a Rider of the Sadharin. Is this a true position for you or a pose?'

The old warrior nodded. 'I am of that society.

You will find that among Dasati warriors, it is well respected and has a long and glorious history. It also numbers amongst its members many who are sympathetic to our cause.' He reached for a pomba fruit, tore it open with his thumbs, and bit deep into the pungent flesh. 'The agents of the Dark One would like nothing better than to know this, Pug. To reveal that any of the Sadharin are sympathetic to the White would guarantee its utter destruction.

'The TeKarana, in distant Omadrabar, might order the destruction of an entire region on Kosridi just to ensure that the "infection" was completely obliterated. Thousands would die.'

'The White?' asked Pug. 'Who or what is the White?'

Martuch said, 'It is a long story, or rather a series of long stories. But this you should know: in lost antiquity, there were two forces that ruled our universe, the Dark and the White.'

'Ah,' said Nakor. 'Evil and good.'

'So you call them.' Martuch shrugged. 'I still wrestle with the concepts, though I have accepted them as true. All our lives we hear of "the White" as if it is a thing to be feared, a disease within the body of Dasati society, and more than once my mother scolded me as a child in the Hiding with warnings that if I was disobedient I would go to the White.'

He laughed as he remembered. 'What would she think now?' He put down his knife and said,

'The White is an organization, but it is also a belief, a fervent hope, that there is more to existence than mindless slaughter and the Purgings. We have little of what you would think of as civilized ways – music, art, literature – things the Ipiliac take for granted, and I suspect you humans do as well. When I first encountered a book that wasn't religious doctrine or a cautionary fable of the Dark One's power I could scarcely believe my eyes. What madness would possess someone to sit and put meaningless words on paper for the entertainment of others? And music that is not battle songs or temple hymns. The Lessers have their work chants, but music that is there to be listened to for pleasure alone? Strange.

'I was sent here to learn these things, Pug, and as the Dasati best able to communicate with you, I was given the task of being your escort.'

Again, Pug had a tantalizing suspicion that there was more to it than Vordam merely finding a guide for them. 'Who sent you?'

Pug had asked that question before, and again got the same answer. 'Many things will be made known to you, but not that, not now.' Martuch's tone left no doubt the subject was not going to be discussed.

'Understood,' said Pug. Nothing about the Dasati were half-measured, he had concluded. They were the most dangerous mortal beings he had ever encountered. Not only were they faster than humans, more vicious than hunting trolls, and as courageous as the bravest Tsurani warrior; they possessed a mind set that could only be called murderous. Death was their answer to most social problems, and Pug wondered how such a society could come into being, or survive.

He remembered Nakor had often remarked that evil was by definition mad, and if that was true, the Dasati were the maddest beings in two universes. From what he had been told by the oracle, and what he had been able to glean from Martuch's talks, this society had not always been this way. The rise of the Dark God of the Dasati was shrouded in antiquity, confused by myth and legend, but it had occurred relatively late in this race's history. Until then, they had been much like the Ipiliac: complex, mostly peaceful, and productive.

Pug said to Martuch, 'In our history we have a time known as the Chaos Wars, when mortal beings and lesser gods rose against the greater gods. It is a time lost to us in history, but we know a little of it. Was the rise of the Dark One after such a conflict?'

'It was,' said Martuch. 'Winners write history, it is said, and the Deathpriests make no differentiation between canon and history. His Darkness's scriptures are history as far as we are concerned.

'The only reason I know of these differences is the Ipiliac records which go back to before their flight from Omadrabar.'

'I would like to see those records, if time permits.'

'It does, and it would be a wise use of your remaining time.'

'How is it you came to Delecordia?'

'That is a story for another time, to be told to you by another. But this much I am willing to share: until twenty-five years ago by your reckoning of time, I was much like any other young Dasati warrior. I had survived the Hiding, found my way to my father's castle, and killed in the Testing Hall to earn my place in his service. I was welcomed into the Sadharin and did all that a proper Dasati warrior could do. I hunted down children during the Purging, killed females who tried to protect them, mated with females for political advantage, and was always ready to answer the Karana's call to arms.

'Twice I helped crush rebellions, or so they were called by those who sought their enemies destroyed; and three times I served in campaigns against rival battle societies. Six great wounds I bear on my body and more light ones than I can number, but I had no doubt at my supremacy. Sons came and survived, and I found a female who pleased me enough that when our son arrived, I called her to join our household. We had what you would call "a family". That concept does not exist in the Dasati mind, but that is what I was: a happy family man in my world.

'Then something happened and life as I knew it changed. I would never again be able to judge myself by the standards of my race, and since that time I have worked to change my people.' He looked off into the distance, as if remembering. 'My female – wife if you will – misses me as she often reminds me. My sons do a reasonable job of ruling our small estate, and we live in a time of relative peace.' He put down the peel of the fruit he had eaten and wiped his hands on a cloth. 'Things are as they should be in the Dasati Empire,' he said with a wry, bitter tone. 'The only people to die are the innocent.'

Pug said nothing.

Martuch chuckled. 'Do you know that in the Dasati language there is no word for "innocent"? The closest we have is "unblooded", meaning someone who has yet to take a life.' He shook his head as he reached for a wine cup. 'To have innocence, you must explain the concept of "guilt". That's another word we do not possess. We speak of "responsibility". I think it's because the guilty are already dead . . . inside.' He stood up. 'Excuse me. I've had too much to drink.' To Pug he said, 'The archives are down the street outside, to our left. It is much like the other buildings, but there is a blue banner showing a circle of white hanging above the entrance. Go there and whatever you wish to see will be shown to you. I will return in the late afternoon tomorrow. I bid you good night.' And with that, he left.

Magnus turned to his father. 'Strange.'

'Yes, very,' said Pug. 'From the Dasati point of view . . .'

'You are weak and deserve death,' said Bek, matter-of-factly.

'My father is hardly weak,' said Magnus. 'None of us are.'

'I don't mean you or your father,' said the young fighter. 'I mean humans. You are weak and deserve death.'

Pug took note that Bek spoke of humans as 'you' and not 'we'. He glanced at Nakor who shook his head slightly.

Magnus said, 'Father, I think I will retire. I wish to meditate for a while before sleeping.'

Pug gave his assent and the younger magician left the room. The servants stood waiting, and Pug realized they would not leave until the table was vacant. He signalled to Nakor who said, 'Bek, let us go for a walk.'

Ralan Bek stood up smartly. 'Good. I like walking in this city. There are so many interesting things to see, Nakor.'

Pug and Nakor got up and followed Bek out of the door into the early evening air. Pug took a deep breath and said, 'I guess we are completely adapted, for now this smells much as the air would in Krondor or Kesh.'

'Better,' said Nakor. 'Not as much smoke and rubbish.'

Walking down the street, Pug said, 'The Ipiliac

are more fastidious than humans, from everything I can see.'

'Yes,' said Bek. 'This is a very nice city. It might be fun to see it burn.'

'It might not,' said Nakor quickly. 'One fire is pretty much like another.'

'But think how much bigger the fire would be, Nakor.'

Pug said quietly, 'Maybe it's a bit of Prandur inside?' making a reference to the fire god, known as 'the Burner of Cities'.

Nakor chuckled. 'Bek, would you like to see something new? Something marvellous?'

'Yes, Nakor, I would. This is a very interesting place, more than most I've been, but lately I've started to get bored with all the sitting around and talking.'

Pug glanced at Nakor who motioned for him to wait. 'You can go visit the archives tomorrow. This is something you should see, too.' They walked through the city, nodding politely to citizens who passed by, getting only the occasional odd glance; Martuch and Kastor had both mentioned that visitors from other worlds were a rarity on this world. They reached the eastern gate of the city and Nakor pointed. 'Up that hill.'

Pug said, 'What are you taking us to see?'

'Wait,' said the little gambler, with a delighted glint in his eye.

They climbed the hill and then Pug and Bek saw what Nakor had led them to see. Far in the

360

distance a shimmering line rose up out of the east, rising into the night sky to vanish into the distance.

'What is it?' asked Bek.

'The Star Bridge,' Nakor answered. 'Martuch told me we might see it on a clear night. That city is Desoctia, and the Ipiliac use that bridge to travel to a world called Jasmadine. It's the same magic we will use to travel between the Dasati worlds, I have been told.'

'How far is that city?' asked Pug.

'About two hundred miles if you flew there.'

'Then that bridge must be very big,' said Bek.

'Or very bright,' said Pug.

They stood silently for a time, merely watching the distant shimmer of a bridge of light that would take them into another realm of reality.

CHAPTER 19

KOSRIDI

Martuch raised his hand.

All eyes turned to him. The four humans and the Dasati warrior stood in the middle of a large vaulted chamber, in a place Pug could only think of as being like his Academy on Stardock, a place of study and learning. He had visited it, along with the archives in the last few days, learning as much as he could about the Dasati – which proved to be little, as most Ipiliac history seemed to deal with their history since reaching Delecordia.

The bits he had read were not heartening, as the Ipiliac perspective on the Dasati as a whole was what one would expect from a vanquished people speaking of their oppressors. Even so, Pug felt they were as ready as they would ever be to make this incredible journey.

The room was a hall used for meetings and social gatherings and big enough, he had been told by the Ipiliac wizard who was accommodating this move to the second realm, that they could do this in private and without distraction. Pug, Magnus and Nakor had listened eagerly to the wizard as he described what he would do to aid their journey, but even Pug felt he barely understood the arcane arts employed.

Martuch spoke. 'In a moment, the transition will begin. It will be unlike anything you have experienced, if you're lucky. I have made this transition a dozen times and each time I swear it will be my last. Are you ready?'

Pug stood with his arms linked to Nakor's, who in turn had linked his to Bek's. Magnus stood on his father's other side, one arm through his father's and the other through Martuch's. Martuch had warned they would be transitioning through a realm he thought of only as 'the grey', and that every sense would be confounded. The passage lasted brief moments, but felt as if time had stopped.

The Ipiliac wizard who had been summoned to oversee this transition had also taken great pains in informing Pug, Nakor and Magnus about what to expect. Bek was unconcerned and ignored the warnings. He seemed excited to be finally going to 'the next place'.

Pug took a deep breath, then said, 'Ready.'

Martuch nodded once to the wizard and he raised his staff above his head, in the final incantation of a spell he had begun almost an hour earlier.

Suddenly the room around them vanished. Pug tried to take in a breath, knowing that there was no air here, for he recognized this place! He was again in the place between! It was where Macros the Black had taken him when he had closed the first rift from Tsurani, at the end of the Riftwar. He knew exactly why Martuch had warned him. Pug reached out with his thoughts and quickly sheltered his companions as Macros had sheltered him.

Father, came Magnus's thoughts. *Where are we?*

We are in the space between moments, my son. We are in the very stuff of the universe, between those strands that Nakor calls 'stuff', in the void itself.

'You can speak,' said Nakor. 'Though I can see nothing.'

Pug and the others suddenly appeared, and Martuch said, 'How . . .?'

'I have been here before,' Pug said. He turned to Magnus. I was taken here by your grandfather. This is the realm of the void, where the gods fought in the Chaos Wars.'

Martuch said, 'It has never taken so long . . .'

'Perhaps it is because there are five of us,' suggested Bek, apparently fascinated by the total lack of any reference beyond them. The void was a sweeping nothingness: no light, no sound, no sensation.

'I thank you for this, Pug,' said Martuch. 'The passage has always been cold and painful.'

'It will not be pleasant when we arrive,' responded the magician. As if to prove the point of his words the transition to the second plane of reality was wrenching. The sensation was akin to having every particle of mind and body ripped apart. As Pug felt himself drawn into the Dasati world, something flickered past his field of vision. He tried to follow the movement, but he was physically yanked away from the void, and suddenly he was standing on a stone floor, in a room of black stone. He was on Kosridi.

Pain ran up and down every nerve of his body, leaving Pug standing and panting as if he had run a long race. Everyone was there, linking arms as they had been on Delecordia.

Pug staggered a little when he let go of Nakor and Magnus's arms. 'There was . . .' he started.

'What?' asked Nakor, his expression one of unusual concern.

'Something . . .' said Pug. 'I'll speak of it later.'

He turned his attention to his surroundings and had to blink several times, as if there was something wrong with his eyes. Then he realized that even more than on Delecordia he was seeing things the human mind was not conditioned to see. Shades of colour and pulsing energies were everywhere. The room in which they had appeared was finished in the black stone he had seen on Delecordia, but here any change appeared to make it shimmer with colour. The effect was almost overwhelming.

Then he realized they were not alone. In the room two figures waited, a man and a woman. Regal was the only word that Pug could conjure to describe the woman. Her high brow and straight nose gave her a striking look, despite her alien features. Her eyes were almost feline in shape and her lips were full.

The man was dressed in a warrior's armour, though something about his features led Pug to think of him as young. The woman looked at Magnus and her eyebrows rose slightly. She said, 'This one looks almost like a Dasati, my son. He is even handsome. Pity he's not a warrior.'

Pug looked at his son and realized that the glamour was upon them. He could see both Magnus as he knew him and a Magnus who looked Dasati, as if two images were laid one on top of the other. He could see that Magnus's height, slender features and long nose would be appealing to these people's sense of beauty.

The young man stepped forward and said, 'I am Lord Valko. This is my home. You are welcome, though I will confess it is difficult not to kill you. There is something about aliens being here that offends me. I will try to control this repulsion.'

Pug glanced at Martuch who said, 'Consider that as gracious a welcome as you will ever receive to a Dasati estate, my friend.' He turned to Valko. 'I am Martuch, Lord of the Setwala. I ride with the Sadharin.'

'Welcome, Rider of the Sadharin!' said Valko, in what Pug took as a genuinely warm greeting. They embraced each other with ritual backslapping and a gripping of each other's right wrist in their right hand. Then the young lord of the castle cast his eyes on Bek.

Ralan Bek stood with his head lowered, looking out from under his heavy black brows. His eyes burned like coals with the reflected firelight, and his face was set in an expression that could only be called hungry. He said, 'Martuch, can I kill him?'

Bek had been dressed as a Dasati warrior, and rehearsed in his role. Martuch shook his head. 'He is our host, Bek.'

As if he had spoken these words all his life, Ralan shouted, 'I am Bek! I serve Martuch of the Setwala and ride with the Sadharin!' He grinned like a demented wolf as he pointed to Valko. 'My master says I must not kill you, or take that woman behind you. I will honour his wishes and control my desire.'

'Is this one mad?' asked Valko.

His mother chuckled. 'He lacks manners, but he plays the part of a young Dasati warrior well.' She patted Valko on the shoulder. 'Most of the young men in the Hiding didn't have me as their teachers. His behaviour will serve these . . . persons, well.'

Pug understood her choice of words. Dasati meant 'people' but the word she used was obscure. Not quite Lessers, but certainly not Dasati.

'It is the middle of the night,' said Valko. 'Do you need rest?'

'No,' answered Martuch, 'but we are in need of

information. There is far more at stake here than we imagined.'

Pug took this to mean the Talnoy. No further discussion of the creation had been forthcoming, and when he had attempted to broach the subject, he had been rebuffed.

'Let us retire to a private room where we may discuss all that needs to be addressed,' said the woman.

Valko looked uncomfortable, and Pug was amazed at how quickly he had come to read Dasati facial expressions. He knew their training on Delecordia was partly responsible; but the rest was the result of the artful spells the Ipiliac wizard had used.

The young Lord of the Camareen said, 'It's just that . . . they look like Lessers, yet I must treat them like guests!'

He said it in such a way that Pug suddenly understood the implied insult. But the youth's mother replied, 'Do not be deceived by appearances. Each of these . . . persons is a master of great power, or they would not be here. Each is more powerful than the most puissant Deathpriest. Remember that.'

Without further word, Valko turned and walked, as if expecting everyone to follow him without question. Pug glanced at Martuch who indicated that he would follow with Bek behind him, and then the lady of the castle. Pug understood that it was imperative that they begin adopting their roles in this society.

368

To whatever gods could overhear him, Pug made a silent prayer that they might all survive this journey.

Nothing they had done on Delecordia prepared Pug and his companions for the experience of Kosridi. Even in the relatively sheltered castle of Lord Valko, the alien sense of this reality was nearly overwhelming. Pug ran his hand over a table and marvelled at the feel beneath his fingertips; it was wood, much like any dark, close grained wood that might be chosen by a furniture maker back in Midkemia, but it was not wood in any sense of what was real to Pug. It was the flesh of a thing that served the same purpose as a tree in this realm, just as the stones were something akin to granite and feldspar, dark flecked with colours, but here the stone had energies still trapped within, as if the making of it deep beneath the mantle of this world had never quite finished. And it hungered. Touching the table, Pug could feel it wanting to drain the energy of his body through his fingertips.

'Amazing,' he said softly as they waited in the chamber set aside for them by Lord Valko and his mother.

Martuch said, 'Yes, I had much the same reaction when I first went to Delecordia. When I visited my first world through the Hall, I almost couldn't move for the wonder of it. From our point of view, Pug, your reality is so terribly bright and warm.

It's almost too much unless you have the ability to focus. It can be like trying to listen to one conversation in a large hall full of many people speaking. It can be done, with concentration at first, then it becomes more easy.'

'Martuch,' asked Nakor. 'Why would anyone from this world wish to invade the first plane?'

'Why does any person, people, or nation do something we might consider mad?' He shrugged. 'They have their reasons. Is that why you are here? You fear an invasion of your world by the Dasati?'

Pug said, 'Perhaps. We are partially driven by that concern. We would just as soon discover we are incorrect and that your race is not a threat to my world.'

'Perhaps it is time for a little more plain speaking,' said the Dasati warrior. He was sitting on a stool, still dressed in his armour, while the others rested on a pair of divans replete with cushions. Bek sat staring out of the window, as if he could not get enough of the vista outside. Pug understood the fascination. The changing hues of the night as they became day provided a constant play of energies that were seductive to the eye. Even the tiniest detail of this realm could captivate the imagination. Earlier, Pug had caught himself being mesmerized by the view. In its alien way, it was beautiful, but Pug had to constantly remind himself that their adjustment to the Dasati plane of existence was illusory, and that even the most common thing they encountered could be dangerous, even lethal. Pug turned his attention to Martuch. 'I would welcome that.'

Martuch said, 'First, you must not mention the Talnoy on your world until you meet the Gardener.'

'Gardener?' asked Magnus. 'It is a name, or a title? In our world, that word is one who tends . . . plants, in a garden.'

'It is the same here,' said Martuch. 'It is a name we have for him so that others may not know who he really is.'

'Who is he?' asked Nakor, coming to the point.

'He is our leader, for lack of a better word, but rather than me telling you about him, Narueen should; she has met him. I have not.'

'He's your leader, but you haven't met him?'

'It is complicated. For years there have been among the Dasati those who could not bring themselves to embrace the teachings of His Darkness as being the totality of knowledge. Among your people I imagine there are those who question authority and challenge convention.'

'Absolutely,' said Pug, glancing at his son. 'It regularly occurs at the end of childhood. Ask any human parent.'

Magnus smiled slightly. He had been headstrong like his mother as a child, and when he had begun his training under his father, there had been many arguments between them before Magnus came to understand his father's wisdom, as well as his knowledge.

'We have no childhood, as you do,' said Martuch, 'so I will accept you understand my meaning. Those who question the teachings of the Dark One are put to death. So, those who have doubts learn quickly to keep quiet.

'But there have long been factions within our society, the Bloodwitch Sisterhood being the most . . . "notorious" or "infamous" would be the words in your tongue. They were rivals to the Deathpriests for centuries, each having their own influence. There was a balance.

'Then the Hierophants and priests began to fear the Sisterhood and, with the blessing of the TeKarana, named them apostate and had them hunted down and destroyed. A few escaped and kept the ancient lore alive, and now they have reappeared among us, though for most people they are beings of myth and legend.

'And there have been men, such as myself, who had no reason to question the order of things, but who did.' Martuch looked out the window, past Bek. 'This is a strange place to you, my friends, but to me it is my home. Here everything is as it should be, while your worlds are . . . odd and exotic. But even while this is my home, I sensed there was something wrong, something out of balance. It was a chance that made me who I am today.'

Martuch returned to his stool and sat down. 'I have seen worlds in the first plane, Pug. I have seen men step on insects, without thought, a habit perhaps, or a deeply ingrained abhorrence of vermin.

'That is as close as I can come in explaining to you how we Dasati males react when we see children. When I first saw males and females of other races carrying their children, holding them, going through crowded markets and leading them by their tiny hands, I could scarcely credit my senses.

'I don't know if I can make it any clearer, but it was as repellent to me as any perversity you can imagine witnessing in public.

'A mother scolding her child for wandering off in a crowd, that I could comprehend, for our mothers defend us to the death during the Hiding.' He paused. 'But when I saw a father lifting his child, merely to make it laugh . . .' He sighed. 'It troubled me more than you can begin to comprehend. It nearly made me physically ill.

'I think you might understand if you were suddenly whisked by magic to a place where you could observe a Purging. To see grown men in armour riding through the night, crashing through thickets in the woodlands, charging through camps of terrified children and enraged mothers, many of whom throw themselves on the points of spears and swords to permit their little ones a slight chance at survival, while, all the time the warriors were laughing and joking as babies died . . . what you might feel seeing that is how I felt watching a man kiss a baby's cheek.

'And yet, deep within, I knew the wrongness was

not in that father and child, but in me and my race.'

'How did you come to this insight?' asked Nakor. 'And how did you first get to the first circle?'

Martuch smiled, and looked at Nakor. 'All in good time, my friend.' He stood again and paced, as if trying to organize his thoughts. 'The first time I felt the wrongness, as I think of it, was during a great purge.

'Word had reached the riders of the Sadharin that a Facilitator – a trader, actually – had seen smoke at sunset in a deep woodland only a half-day's ride from this very castle.

'The mountains to the east of here begin with a series of foothills, and there are many caves and ancient mines in the region. It would be impossible for an organized force to explore every one in a year, let alone find moving camps of females and young.

'We rode at sundown so that we could strike the camp in the dead of night, and by the time we reached the camp, we could smell wood smoke on the air, and hear the soft sounds of mothers crooning to their young.

'We became filled with bloodlust, and wished to do nothing more than cleave and rend and trample these *things* beneath the hooves of our varnins. One female must have been alert, for we heard a warning scream moments before we overran the camp. Our women are clever, and dangerous when protecting their young. Several pulled warriors out of their saddles with their bare hands, dying to keep their children safe. One warrior had his throat torn out by a woman's teeth.

'I killed three females that night, to allow one of my brother riders to regain his mount, and when he had, the camp was empty. In the night I could hear the sounds of screams and cries, and the wailing of children cut off by the sound of swords striking flesh coming from all around me in the night.

'I could feel blood pounding in my ears, and my breathing was heavy. It is much the same feeling as we get when we are ready to couple. In my mind the pleasures are equal, making life or taking it.

'I rode into the underbrush around the camp, and when I had entered a thicket, I sensed something. I looked down and crouching under a low-hanging branch was a female, holding her young son. I never would have seen her had I kept riding or had I not looked down at that exact moment. She would have been behind the searches and could have made her way to freedom and safety but for chance.'

Martuch stopped his pacing and look at Pug. 'Then the amazing thing happened. I drew back my sword and made ready to kill the female first – she was the danger – and then the boy. But rather than leap to protect her child, she held him tightly to her chest and looked at me, eye to eye, Pug. She stared at me and said . . . "Please".'

Pug said, 'I take it that was . . . unexpected.'

'Unprecedented,' said Martuch, sitting on his stool once more. '"Please" is a word a Dasati rarely hears, except from a Lesser saying, "if it pleases you, master" or a warrior or priest saying, "this was pleasing", but as an entreaty, no, it is not our way.

'But something in that woman's eyes . . . there was strength and power there: this was not the pleading of a weak woman, but an appeal to something more profound than mindless killing.'

'What did you do?' asked Magnus.

'I let them go,' said Martuch. 'I put up my sword and rode off.'

Pug said, 'I can't begin to understand what that must have felt like.'

'I scarcely understood myself,' said Martuch. 'I rode after the others and by the time dawn arrived thirteen females and twenty-odd children had been butchered. The other riders laughed and joked on the way back to the great hall of the Sadharin, but I kept my own counsel.

'I had no sense of achievement or pride. I realized at that moment that I had changed within, and that there was nothing glorious in slaughtering those who were far less able to defend themselves.

'A woman with a knife is to be treated with respect, but I was mounted on a war-trained varnin, wearing full armour, carrying a sword and a dagger, and had a war-bow on my saddle. I should feel a sense of accomplishment because I killed her? I should feel triumph in slaughtering a child whose only defence is teeth and nails?' He shook his head. 'No, I knew there was something terribly wrong.

'But like many who come to this insight, I assume the wrongness was within me, that I had lost sight of His Darkness's truth, so I sought out a Deathpriest to counsel me.' Martuch looked at Pug with a half-smile. 'Fate conspired to bring me to a man named Juwon, a Deathpriest of the highest rank outside the Inner Temple, a High Priest, one who has jurisdiction over all this region of the Empire.

'He listened to my story, and later confided in me that the standing order in the Dark One's service is that any who comes with the doubts I expressed is to be instantly confined, interrogated, then put to death. I just happened to have confided in the highest-placed prelate in the region, who also worked secretly on behalf of the White.

'He listened, bid me keep silent on this matter, but asked me to return. We sat together many times, for hours, over a period of months, before he took me aside and said my calling was to serve the White.

'By the time he revealed this to me, I had already come to the conclusion that there was far more to this than my mere hesitation over killing one woman and one child. Since then I have spoken many times to him, to Narueen, and other wise men and women, to priests, Bloodwitch, and others. I have come to see so much more than I was taught as a boy.' Martuch leaned forward. 'That is how I came to serve the White. More, I have come to love the White, and hate everything about His Darkness.'

'How did you get to the first plane of reality?' asked Nakor.

'I was sent by the Gardener.'

'Why?' asked Pug.

'He is the one who works most closely with the White,' said a female voice from the door. 'We do not question his orders. If he tells us to go to another reality, Martuch, or I, or any other serving the White will go.'

Pug turned, and instantly stood, lowering his gaze to the floor. Magnus and Nakor were only a moment behind.

'Quicker,' said Narueen as she entered the room. 'A second's hesitation will make you remarkable. Remarkable Lessers are dead Lessers. Remember, Attenders are useful, but also despised for their helping ways.'

Pug stood motionless, and she came to sit on the spot on the divan he had just vacated. 'Sit beside me,' she said to him, and then to the others, 'you may drop your pose. It will almost certainly be the last chance to do so, and there is much we need to discuss before you leave.'

'Already?' asked Pug.

'Yes,' said Narueen. 'I received word that something extraordinary may be taking place on

Omadrabar. High Priest Juwon has been called to the Court of His Darkness, and if they are calling in the priests from the outer regions, then this is a meeting of importance.'

'Any idea why?' asked Martuch.

'When a Supreme Prelate dies, and there's a need to anoint his successor, this type of convocation is usual; but there has been no word of his illness. Besides, news of his untimely death would have accompanied any such order. In the past, the Supreme Prelate might convene such an assembly to announce new doctrine; but Juwon would know about such a theological movement in the hierarchy of the church.' She shook her head slightly: a very human gesture. 'No, it must be something else.' She looked at Pug. 'We always fear discovery. But one advantage we have is that the servants of the Dark One have no desire for the populace to know we are not a myth, that we exist.

Pug asked, 'When you say "we", do you mean the Bloodwitches or the White?'

'Both,' she replied, 'for in my mind the Bloodwitch Sisterhood and the White have been one for many, many years, long before we realized we served that force which stood in opposition to the Dark One.'

'Martuch told us the story of his sparing a woman and her son, do you know it?' asked Nakor.

Narueen nodded and her expression was revealing, the closest of a show of emotions Pug had seen from her. 'I know it well, for I was that woman and Valko was the boy I held. We had ventured out of the caves a short distance away and were cooking. Our fires were lit too early, obviously. The children were fractious, Valko was teething and angry. The cooling breezes of the evening soothed him.'

'Why did you simply say, "please"?' asked Magnus.

She sighed. 'I don't really know. An instinct that let me see something inside him. He was a vital warrior, the sort of man women seek out to father their children, at the height of his power. He had his blood lust up and was ready to kill, but there was a . . . look to him, something around the eyes under that fearsome black helm that made me just ask him to spare us.'

'And so lives change,' said Martuch. 'Valko doesn't know the story, and I would appreciate it if you didn't tell him yet. He will learn it soon enough, but what you must know is that our young Lord of the Camareen came to his office just this week. He beheaded his father only six days before you arrived. The celebration of his accession was two nights ago. Had we arrived then, most of us would likely be dead by now.'

Pug said, 'I often wonder at these small coincidences in life: that something that appears nothing more than a chance, but in the end turns out to be vital.'

Nakor had been unusually silent throughout all

380

of these discussions, content to watch and listen. He reached into his bag and pulled out an orange.

Pug's eyes widened. 'How did you do that?'

Nakor's ever-present bag had a small permanent two-way rift in it, which allowed him to reach through and pluck oranges and other items off a table in a produce shop in Kesh. By any magic Pug knew, it couldn't work here.

Nakor just grinned. 'Different bag. Looks the same, but it's not. I just put some oranges in it. This is the last one.'

He dug his thumb into it and peeled the skin, then took a bite. He made a face and said, 'Horrible. I guess how things taste to us has changed, too.' He put the orange back in the bag and said, 'I'd better get rid of this somewhere along the way.'

'Yes,' said Martuch, rising and holding out his hand. 'I'll see to it. I wouldn't want you to have to explain to a Deathpriest how you came by a fruit from the first plane of existence.'

Nakor handed over the fruit and turned to look at Bek who was sitting quietly, looking out of the window. 'What is it you find so fascinating, Ralan?'

Without turning, Bek said, 'It's just that I really like it here, Nakor. I want to stay.' He turned and his eyes were shining with emotion. 'I want you to fix what you did to me, that day outside the caves, because I think here I can be . . . happy. This is a good place, Nakor. I can kill and make people cry, and everyone thinks it's funny.' He looked out of the window again. 'And it's the most beautiful place I've ever seen.'

Nakor went to the window and looked out. 'It's unusually clear, today—'

The way his voice dropped caused Pug and the others to look at him. 'What is it?' asked Pug.

'Come here,' said Nakor.

Pug looked out past his two companions. The daylight of Kosridi had taken some getting used to, as there was little visible by Midkemian standards, but Pug had found that once his eyes had adjusted to a much broader spectrum, what Nakor had called 'the colours beyond violet, and under red', he could see a profound difference between night and day on this world. With the sun above, he could see heat and energy and more detail than at night. But even then, he saw far more with his 'Dasati eyes' as he thought of his new vision than he ever would have imagined possible. And he understood why he hadn't seen apparent signs on Delecordia or here: it had taken him a while to apprehend the energy signatures used on the stone above doors to indicate the purpose of the building.

Today was 'bright' as there were no clouds in the sky, and the sun shone down. Pug could see the rolling vista of the town beyond the castle, and the ocean below that. Then it struck him that there was something familiar about what he was seeing.

Nakor said, 'I've only been to a place like this

once before, years before when Prince Nicholas had to sail after—'

Pug cut him off. 'It's Crydee,' he said softly.

'It looks a lot like Crydee,' said Nakor.

Pug pointed out to the south-west. 'There are the Six Sisters.'

Narueen said, 'That is what those islands are called.'

Pug said, 'We're in Crydee.' He looked out again and said, 'This town is built . . . well, it's Dasati, all one continuous series of interlinking buildings, like the Ipiliac, but there, that bit of land jutting out north of the harbour . . . that's Longpoint!'

'What does it mean?' asked Magnus.

Pug turned and sat down on the window-seat next to Bek, who still stared outside. 'I don't know. In one sense, I guess it means we're back home, just on a different plane of reality.'

Pug began asking Narueen and Martuch questions about the geography of the region and quickly came to understand that Kosridi was Midkemia, only on the second plane of reality. After nearly half an hour of this, Pug said, 'Why would everything else be different, but the physical environment be the same?'

'A question for philosophers,' said Nakor. He grinned, 'But I do like a good question as much as I like a good answer.'

'So many mysteries,' said Magnus.

'We leave tomorrow for the city of Kosridi, by wagon,' said Martuch.

Pug placed the capital of this world roughly where Stardock would be on Midkemia, and asked, 'Wouldn't it be faster to travel by ship?'

'It would,' answered Martuch, 'if the winds were favourable, but this time of the year we'd be beating against them the entire way. Also, there's a series of dangerous places along the coast – I'm not a sailor so I don't know what they're properly called – rocks below the water where you can't see them.'

'Reefs,' said Pug, 'in our language.'

Narueen said, 'In any event, once we reach Ladsnawe, we can take a swift ship across the Diamond Sea to the river leading to Kosridi.'

Pug considered, and realized that the Bitter Sea was roughly diamond shape on the map. 'So, how long?' he asked.

'Three weeks, if we encounter no difficulty. We have already sent swift messengers ahead to carry word of our coming, so we will find safe haven along the route every night.'

'We have so many more things to discuss,' said Pug.

'We will have time. Everything we do is over-seen by the Gardener. You will travel with a surrounding cocoon of people who will protect your secrets, even if they themselves do not know what those secrets are. Act your part and all shall be well. We shall have time, ample time, trust me.'

Narueen stood and pointed to Magnus. 'You must come with me.'

Magnus appeared torn for a moment between

curiosity and his wish to appear the obedient servant, then he rose, bowed his head, and followed Valko's mother. Pug looked over at Martuch who stood with a faint smile on his face. 'What's all that?' he asked.

'She will take him to her bed tonight,' said Martuch. 'For a Dasati he is very handsome. Many women will wish to couple with him. I realize to your people our ways seem brazen and without . . . what is that word you humans use to explain your odd behaviour?'

Nakor said, 'Morality?'

'That is the word,' said Martuch. 'We have none of that when it comes to breeding.'

'But can he . . .?'

'I am no expert,' said Martuch, 'but I believe the essentials are basically the same, and while Narueen is indulging in some gratuitous pleasure, she's also ensuring that your son doesn't end up dead before we reach our goal.

'I do not overstate. He is very handsome, and many women will wish his company. And a few men, I expect. If he doesn't understand his role, how he must obey, when he can decline, or what to expect, you might never see him again.' He pointed to Bek. 'Likewise, I will have Lesser come to his bed tonight.' Lowering his voice, he added. 'I think he will have no problem convincing a Dasati woman he is a warrior.'

'I'm married,' Pug said quickly.

Martuch laughed. 'Do not worry, friend Pug. By

Dasati standards you are far too short and homely to attract that sort of attention.'

Nakor said, 'I like girls.'

Martuch laughed even harder, shook his head, and left the room.

CHAPTER 20

CRUCIBLE

The rain pounded down.

Six miserable junior knight-lieutenants of the army of Roldem hunkered down under the pitiful shelter of a canvas ground-cloth which had been hurriedly erected as a make-shift tent. The rain had been unceasing for three days now and they were chilled to the bone, footsore, and couldn't remember the last time they had slept.

After returning from the conflict with Bardic's Holdfast, the six had received instructions to head downriver to Olasko Gateway with the first and third Olaskan infantry, and report to General Devrees's staff. The boat ride had been uneventful and the boys had been full of their own sense of achievement.

The veterans in the first and third put up with the boys' boundless optimism. They had seen it before and knew it wouldn't last. Especially Sergeant Walenski, the senior sergeant given command of the first and third. The two units had been depleted below half the normal complement since the overthrow of Kaspar's rule three years before. They had been operating as a combined unit since, and Roldem seemed slow in assigning new recruits to the old Olaskan army.

The first and third had been ordered to help sweep the border with Salmater. The problem was chronic: the southern-most province in Olasko was a cluster of hundreds of islands, the home of pirates, smugglers, outlaws of every stripe, and a highway for raids into the region. Roldem had decided on a show of force and a warning to anyone else in the region who might wish to go adventuring in their two newest provinces.

'Why did they have to pick the rainy season?' asked Jommy, as he sat shivering under the tarp. All six wore the uniform of the Army of Roldem: dark blue tunics, dark grey trousers, and a belted tabard. Each had been given a conical metal helm with a nose guard. Grandy's was the smallest they could find and it was still slightly too large.

'To make sure we appreciate every possible aspect of the experience?' suggested Godfrey.

Tad said, 'Well, at least it's not a cold rain.'

'And the rain keeps the mosquitoes from biting,' Grandy offered.

'Ever the optimist,' said Servan. He reached out and rumpled Grandy's already wet head and said, 'It's good we have at least one of those around here.'

Zane said, 'I just wish they had something for us to do.'

Jommy said, 'Be careful what you wish for . . .' He hiked his thumb and everyone looked to see where he pointed. Sergeant Walenski was climbing the short trail from where the General's tent sat to where these most junior of officers huddled.

He came to stand before them and saluted in just a slow enough fashion to communicate clearly what he thought of these six 'children' who had been deposited in his care. 'If you young gentlemen would be so kind, the General would like a word with you.'

Jommy and the others came out from under the shelter and as the others followed, he said, 'I don't suppose you've had any luck in finding us a proper tent, now, have you Sergeant?'

'Sorry to say, no, sir,' he responded. The sergeant was a short, lantern-jawed man, who effected a large moustache that flowed out and curled up at the ends. He was still mostly dark-haired, but had just enough grey shot through to show his age. He had been a soldier – corporal, then sergeant – in the army of Olasko for twenty-five years and had little patience with junior officers, especially boys plucked from university who, from his point of view, were sent to play soldier while real men fought and died. He had been as close to insubordinate and insulting as he could get without actually breaking military protocols, but the boys had no doubt that he had rather these six lieutenants were anywhere in the army but here. 'Sorry to say the provisioner has not received any more supplies from Opardum . . . *sir.*'

Jommy threw him a sidelong look. 'Well, thank you for the effort, Sergeant. I'm sure it was heroic.'

'We try our best, young sir. Now, if you don't mind, the General is waiting.'

The boys trudged down the muddy hill to the command tent. As they passed a series of wagons, Jommy halted. 'Sergeant, what is that piled up on the second wagon there?'

The sergeant made a show of squinting at the wagon. At last he said, 'Why, I do believe that's a stack of tents, sir. I guess some came in that I missed.'

Glaring at the sergeant as he walked past him to enter the General's tent, Jommy said, 'I hope you don't miss the enemy when they turn up.'

The General's command tent was a large pavilion which housed a table with a set of maps on it, a pair of canvas-and-wooden chairs and a simple sleeping mat. Everything was damp or soaked depending on where in the leaky pavilion it rested. 'Miserable weather, isn't it?' said the General.

'Sir,' agreed Jommy.

'We've got a report of some smuggling down near a place called Isle Falkane on this map.' He pointed to it, and the six young officers gathered around. 'I'm in a bit of a predicament. We've also received a report that Salmater has mounted an expedition that's coming across the border somewhere in this vicinity. So, I've got to keep most of the first and third intact, but I want you six lads to take a company of twenty men down to this island and see if there's any truth to the rumour. I don't want you to go looking for a fight; the sight of more than

390

two dozen soldiers should be enough to send them scurrying off.

'I just don't want any problems on my south flank if Salmater does mount an offensive here.' He glanced at the six boys and said to the Prince, 'No disrespect to your family, Highness, but what are you doing here?'

Grandy shrugged. 'My brothers are both in the navy, sir. I guess my father decided it was time for me to start my military education.'

'Damned funny choice,' muttered the General. 'Still, it'll do you no good getting you killed. My aide got punctured by a smuggler's arrow, and when you get back, I'm detailing you to my command. The rest of you will be spread out among the first and third. I'll have a platoon designated for each of four of you, and the fifth will be working here at headquarters with the Prince.

'Now, meet your squad down at the dock and start rowing.'

Jommy took one last look at the map, as did Servan, both fixing the location in their minds. Then they saluted and left. Outside the tent they found the sergeant waiting for them. 'Sirs?'

'I expect you know the orders, already, Sergeant,' said Servan. 'Is the squad assembled?'

'Yes, sir, it is,' he said, still managing to make 'sir' sound like an insult.

They followed him down to the dock where a riverboat was tied up. Another half-dozen bobbed up and down as the rain-swollen river rushed south-east. Twenty soldiers waited there, sitting on sodden bales of grain.

Jommy looked at Servan and said, 'Oh, the gods wept.'

Servan sighed. 'Every malingerer, malcontent and thief in the army.'

'Ah, it's a good bunch of boys we have for you young officers,' said Sergeant Walenski. 'They've just had a bit of trouble, and I'm sure you six fine young officers will sort them out.'

Jommy looked at the twenty drenched men, as they sat staring at the six knight-lieutenants. Those that weren't scowling at them were appraising them and the rest were doing their best to look indifferent. All were dressed in the standard uniform of the Roldem army: blue gambeson jacket, grey trousers, boots, a yeoman's helm, and carried a sword and shield.

'Get to your feet!' shouted Walenski. 'Officers!'

The men made a show of getting to their feet as slowly as possible, a couple whispering and laughing.

Jommy said, 'Right, then.' He took off his helmet, unbuckled his sword, said, 'Sergeant, if you don't mind,' and handed it to him.

'Sir?' The Sergeant was taken aback.

Jommy turned to Servan and the others. 'Give me a bit of room, if you would.' He then took one step forward and unloaded a punishing blow to the point of the jaw of the biggest soldier in the group, knocking the man completely off his feet, sending him flying backwards into the two men behind him, who also fell down. Jommy then turned to Sergeant Walenski and said, 'Sword, please, Sergeant.'

The Sergeant handed it back, and Jommy re-buckled it while the two men who could got up; the one Jommy hit was still unconscious. Jommy retrieved his helmet, put it on, and turned to the soldiers. 'Right, then. Any question about who's in charge here?' When there was no answer, he raised his voice. '*Get on the boat!*'

'You heard the lieutenant! Get on the boat!' shouted Sergeant Walenski. 'You two, pick up that man and drag him!'

The twenty soldiers hurried to do as ordered, and as the six officers followed, the Sergeant said, 'A moment, sir,' to Jommy.

Jommy halted and the Sergeant said, 'If you don't mind the opinion, with a little work you have the makings of a fine sergeant, some day. It's a pity to see you wasting all that talent as an officer.'

Jommy said, 'I'll keep that in mind. And, Sergeant?'

'Sir?'

'When we get back, our tents will be ready, won't they?'

'You have my guarantee, sir.'

'Good,' said Jommy, joining the others on the deck of the riverboat.

Servan said, 'Jommy, one thing.'

'What?'

'That first day at the university?'

'Yes.'

'When you hit me? Thank you for going easy.'

Jommy laughed. 'No worries, mate.'

Pug watched in wonder as the boatmen poled up-river. Throughout the entire journey he had felt a terrible mix of the familiar and the alien. Although once they had realized that this planet was identical to Midkemia knowing where they were became relatively easy.

Pug's library held the most complete collection of maps in the world, and while some were out-of-date, and most incomplete, the collection had afforded him as good a view of the geography of the world as any one man could have. Nakor and Magnus had also reviewed most of the maps while on Sorcerer's Isle.

They had taken a trail over what would have been the Grey Tower Mountains, along the river called Boundary in Crydee. The ride through the forests and over the north pass evoked strong memories in Pug, from the time he and his boyhood friend, Tomas, had ridden with Lord Borric to warn the Prince of Krondor of the coming Tsurani invasion.

But now the trees were alien, almost like pines and balsams, but not quite. The birds were all predators, even the Dasati equivalent of sparrows, and only the size of the rider deterred the birds from attacking.

Nakor had observed that eons of learning who was food and who was hungry had created a murderous, but balanced world. As long as you were vigilant, you survived.

Once over the mountains, they came to a port that didn't exist on Midkemia: a large town called Larind here, but Pug knew the place, as it was close to the Free City of Bordon in his world. The town was a smaller version of the Ipiliac city: a series of interlinked buildings, as if the need for community against all the hostile forces of this world had created a group approach among a society that was murderously individualistic. Nakor expressed more than once along the way that he would love to stay and study these people. Magnus had observed that the Dasati would probably love to study him.

From there they sailed across the Diamond Sea – the Bitter Sea on Midkemia – and to the city of Deksa, where Port Vykor resided back home. Pug regretted that their course had taken them just out of sight of Sorcerer's Isle – or whatever it was called on this world – for he would have liked to have seen this otherworld version of his home.

Now they were on a large boat – what would have been called a keel boat back home, though it was longer than the Midkemian version, but with the same mode of propulsion: a team of men, six on each side of the boat, who planted poles in the bottom of the river and 'walked' towards the stern of the boat. In fact, they were standing still and the boat was moving under their feet, but the illusion was the same. When they reached the stern, they pulled up their pole, effortlessly shouldered it and walked towards the bow where they planted their poles and started again. It was a slow, but effective, mode of transportation and certainly meant they were more likely to arrive at their destination rested than if they had been in a bumpy wagon. Pug had not asked why magic hadn't been employed to get them to their destination. He assumed there must be a good reason.

On Midkemia the Sea of Dreams, which was really a very large salt-water lake than a true sea, was bordered on the north by the Kingdom city of Landreth, and on the south by the Keshian city of Shamata. Here the entire eastern half of the sea, on both shores, was occupied by the great city of Kosridi, the capital of this world.

They were still miles from their destination, but they could see signs of civilization on the north shore as the boat left the river and entered the lake. The polemen pushed out as deeply as they could, then put their poles in cradles along the roof of the centre cabin and raised the single sail. The boat was not really designed for sailing, but a bit of a breeze would get them wallowing along as best it could for a few hours, and eventually they would reach the nearest dock in the city.

The sound of bowstrings humming alerted Pug to the fact that another of this world's water-dwelling predators had come to close to the boat. He glanced over to see something large, black and serpent-like slip back below the chop. Within seconds the water began roiling as other predators swarmed to the scent of blood in the water.

'Mustn't go swimming,' Nakor said with a chuckle. The short gambler tended to find everything amusing, and Pug was relieved, for he was feeling quite enough worry for the entire group.

Given the Dasati habit of having all farms cultivated by a workforce that lived within the walls of the nearest city, Pug could only conclude that the city of Kosridi must be huge, larger than the city of Kesh or perhaps even the enormous Holy City of the Tsurani, Kentosani. Over a million people lived in that city, but judging from the signs of civilization rising up on all sides, Pug assumed that the capital city of this planet was at least three times as large.

Martuch said, 'We'll dock soon. We must ride the rest of the way.'

Pug nodded, preoccupied. He had been reassured that everyone on this boat had been selected for their ability to be both blind and deaf, and the captain was secretly a member of the White: no one aboard should be a danger to them.

Bek had been playing the role of Martuch's protégé to perfection. His ability to subsume himself into the Dasati mindset frightened Pug, as did Nakor's blind faith in his ability to control the youth. What Bek really was, who he was, and how he got to be this way were questions Pug had pondered since first meeting the young warrior. Nakor didn't have to tell him there was something unusual about him, for from the first Pug could sense the alien presence within him, and the yet-to-be-unleashed power. Nakor's description of the fight between Tomas and Bek had surprised Pug at the time; Tomas was undoubtedly the most dangerous mortal with a sword on the entire planet, but now that Pug had time to study Bek, he suspected that the day would come when Ralan Bek would surpass Tomas of Elvandar as the single most dangerous being on Midkemia.

If they ever got back to Midkemia.

Pug had asked Martuch how that was to be arranged, and the often taciturn warrior had merely said it was all arranged. But something in his tone left Pug wondering if he really thought any of them would survive whatever lay ahead of them.

They reached the docks as sundown approached, and by the time they had secured what passed for horses – varnin – Martuch said, 'I know an inn we can use. It will take us the better part of the day to reach the Star Bridge, so we'll rest in the city tonight.'

He assumed the role of Dasati warrior and motioned for Bek to follow. Neither paid any attention to the three Lessers who trailed behind them. Pug, Nakor and Magnus would walk behind their master's mounts, and Pug prayed everyone remembered his part, for now they were no longer in the relative safety of Lord Valko's castle.

Pug had wondered about that young Deathknight. Pug sensed that Valko was fighting a battle inside himself, and prayed his mother retained her influence over him. So many things about these people were repellent: but he reminded himself that this wasn't just an alien culture, it was an alien reality, and that similarities between Dasati and human were as often as not coincidental, and nothing more.

Magnus followed Nakor, who stayed close to Bek's mount, the better to monitor his behaviour. Pug was last in line.

Kosridi City was everything he had imagined from Kaspar's description of what he had seen in Kalkin's vision, and more. The city walls were massive, perhaps twenty storeys high in places, with gates that required a gigantic mechanical engine to open and close them. Pug could not even imagine those gates being shut by the labour of the heaviest draught animals. Either powerful magic was employed, or another source of power he didn't understand, because nothing he had seen humans devise would move those gates, short of a thousand men pulling on the ropes for hours on end.

They entered the city and Pug tried to etch every detail he could into his memory, yet so much of what he saw was inexplicable to him. Women swept along in groups of four or five, apparently shopping in stalls, merchants and stores.

He struggled to remember that these very same females, apparently carefree now, would the rest of the time be fugitives harbouring children from the very fathers and lovers in their lives who were trying to kill those children.

Pug found his mind swimming, and turned his attention away from these contradictions. He should know better than to attempt to force his own interpretation on what he saw. Just look, he chided himself. Just look, observe and evaluate later.

A group of four men in black robes with a circle of white around the waist and a line of white running down the front and back, were walking purposefully through the crowd. 'Praxis,' said Martuch. Pug knew the word meant 'standard behaviour or practice', but here it was an organization of laymen working for the Dark One's church. They were tasked constantly to remind Dasati citizens of His Darkness's presence, and to report any sign of blasphemous behaviour.

At a busy intersection, the two riders were forced to move slowly past a gathering of men and women who were listening to a man on a wooden stand. A lector was preaching to the Lessers, and his message was that every member of Dasati society had a role to play, and that it was their task to live their lives as joyously as they could in His Darkness's shadow.

Pug saw rapt expressions on the faces of those listening and again wondered how these people thought. It was clear that Martuch had grown and changed, and even the Lady Narueen, as Pug thought of her, seemed sophisticated enough for them to have a common basis for dialogue. But young Lord Valko could barely abide the sight of the human visitors, despite their Dasati appearance through magic, and Pug knew that he was sympathetic to their cause.

What would the average Dasati in the street think should the glamour fail and the humans be revealed? Pug had no doubt the most likely answer was that the four of them would be swarmed over and torn limb from limb by the bare hands of the Dasati Lessers long before any warriors could reach them. Whatever thought Pug had cherished that this world might have something in common with his own had been dispelled the morning of their departure, when he had seen a Lesser cook and her helpers fight what appeared to be domesticated barnyard fowl so she could get eggs for breakfast. Even the chickens here put up a fight, Nakor had observed.

They wended their way through the busy city, every sight and sound a distraction. Pug was forced not to stare, and had to prod Nakor several times for gawking.

Eventually they reached the inn where Martuch had said they would be safe as long as they maintained their pose as Lessers, and were quickly taken away from Martuch and Bek, to the quarters out at the back for servants of travelling warriors.

It was a barracks where three other Lesser men and a single woman were resting, while two other women were tending cooking fires. From the look of things, Pug realized they were going to have to manage on their own for food, but before he could tell Nakor and Magnus to dig rations out of their travel bags, one of the women cooking said, 'Two sus each for food. And another su if you wish something other than water to drink.'

Pug reached inside his bag, pulled out nine coins and put them on the table, unsure if he was supposed to say any-thing. He suspected 'thank you' would earn him nothing but trouble.

The woman scooped up the coins and put them in the purse that hung from a woven cord belt which cinched together her dress. Pug sat quietly down near the table, watching as they prepared a meal.

The two Dasati women were chattering about things for which Pug had no frame of reference, until he realized they were gossiping about a woman who wasn't present. The other three Dasati in the room were servants of others staying at the inn, and Pug decided that watching them for leads might be useful.

When food was placed on the table, the three Dasati who had arrived before Pug and his companions stood and took full bowls off the table, then returned to where they were resting. Pug nodded once to Nakor and Magnus, and they followed his lead.

As they sat eating, one of the Dasati women who had been cooking kept staring at Magnus. Pug leaned over and whispered to Magnus, 'You never said anything about your encounter with Narueen.'

Magnus looked down at his bowl. 'And I won't.'

Pug said, 'Difficult.'

'More than . . .' He smiled slightly. 'There are things a son doesn't want to share with his parents, even a father as . . . widely travelled as you.'

Suddenly Pug understood. The experience hadn't been entirely unpleasant for Magnus, and that disturbed him.

Magnus swallowed another mouthful of the stir-fried vegetables and a grain like rice with some sort of meat in it, and finally said, 'And, please, say nothing to Mother.'

Pug stifled a laugh.

Everyone ate in silence. Pug wondered if there was going to be a problem with women and Magnus. They just wanted to be ignored, but apparently Narueen was correct in her observation that Magnus was unusually handsome by Dasati standards. Unwarranted attention was unwelcome. Pug knew that he or his son could bring this entire inn down around the ears of anyone who might threaten them without difficulty. They could create enough confusion to escape. But escape to where? Pug wasn't entirely sure what this mission was, except to find out as much about these people as possible. So far he still had found no reason why these people would wish to invade the first plane of reality, beyond Nakor's oft-aired thesis that evil is by nature mad. On the other hand, Nakor also observed that even if evil was mad, it could act with purpose. That had certainly been proven repeatedly in the case of Leso Varen.

That made Pug think of Varen hiding somewhere on Kelewan, and that in turn made him miss his wife. He wished he had the means to speak with her, if only for a moment, just to know she was well. And ask her if there was any hint of Varen anywhere within the Empire of the Tsurani.

Wyntakata hobbled along as quickly as he could, attempting to keep up with Miranda, who was impatiently walking towards a hill overlooking a deep ravine. 'Please,' he said, and when she turned, he pointed to his staff. 'My leg,' he added.

'Sorry, but you were the one who said this was important.'

'It is, and I think you'll appreciate why I asked you to come alone with me. But I am not a well man, and a little more leisurely pace would be welcome.'

Miranda had received his message only hours before, and ignoring the time difference – it was just before dawn at Sorcerer's Isle, but late afternoon on this part of Kelewan – she had come at once.

They were moving across a meadow towards the hill, and when they reached the bottom, Wyntakata said, 'Another moment, please.' He paused to catch his breath, then said, 'You'd think with all the power . . . well, maybe one day we can do something about getting old.' He chuckled. 'It's odd, isn't it, that this man you're so eager to catch can move from body to body . . . a type of immortality, really.'

'From one point of view, I suppose so,' said Miranda, impatient to see what it was she had been summoned here to see.

The stout magician caught his breath and said, 'Let us go.' As they trudged up the hill, he said, 'Did you hear, old Sinboya was found dead last week?'

Miranda stopped. 'You knew him?'

'How could you not?' Wyntakata stopped for a moment, puffed, then said, 'He was perhaps the finest artificer of devices alive. Many of the Assembly had employed him to make his toys, useful as they were.'

Reaching the ridge, they could see down into a small valley, a half-mile depression between two rows of hills. Below them in the valley was a dome of energy, black as night and yet scintillating with colours, like irridescent oil floating on the surface of water. Miranda instantly recognized it as a barrier of some type; though what it was keeping in, she could only guess.

Wyntakata said, 'I hear Pug visited Sinboya just before his death.'

Miranda hesitated for an instant, then said, 'He hadn't told me.' Instantly, she knew she had been lured into a trap: the magician had referred to her husband as 'Pug' rather than his Tsurani name, Milamber.

She turned to gather energy, but suddenly a pain shot through her and her mind went numb. It was as if someone or something had sucked the air from her lungs, the blood from her veins, and all rational thought from her mind in an instant. She looked down and saw a faintly glowing latticework of lines in the soil beneath her feet. This spot had been the trap. The ward she stood upon negated her power and had stunned her like a blow to the head. She tried to move, and found her body disobedient.

Wyntakata smiled unpleasantly. 'Your mistake was assuming that your fugitive would conduct himself here as he did on your world, Miranda.

'You see,' said the man she knew now must be Leso Varen, 'you were so intent on looking for signs of necromancy that you neglected the obvious. These people—' he patted his rotund waist, '—are such powerful practitioners of magic that I could conduct myself as I saw fit and no one would notice, as long as I observed a few proprieties. "Your will, Great One," is such a wonderful phrase. I fly to "my" estates, and say, "I would like a meal", and people jump to getting it done. It's a great deal like being a king of a tiny little kingdom, really.

'These people do appreciate power. But they are nothing, compared to my new friends.'

Miranda fell to her knees, weakening by the minute. Wyntakata held up his hand and made a signal. He knelt, awkwardly, holding on to his staff. 'It's really too bad that I didn't have any say in whose body I grabbed, but this won't be my host much longer. I must confess I've been so busy since I found the first Dasati rift that I really haven't had time to make a new soul vessel. I plan on taking care of that as soon as possible, once I find a safe place to practise necromancy again without having a hundred angry Great Ones descending on me.' He glanced at the dome. 'I think it won't be too long before they're far too busy to worry about me.'

He reached out and took her chin in the cup of his hand. Her eyes were losing focus as he said, 'My goodness, but you are an attractive woman. I never really noticed that. I think I found you off-putting at first because you are so . . . determined. You walk around with that frown and your eyes . . . glaring. I see why Pug fell in love with you, though I do find I prefer women who are more . . . submissive. But it would be fun to nail you to a wall and see how determined you remained while I did things to you with all the toys the Tsurani have invented for inter- rogation. They have quite a collection in a museum at the Assembly, you know.'

Someone was coming up the hill behind her, but Miranda was too stupefied to move, let alone turn and look. Leso Varen used his staff to push himself to his feet as powerful hands gripped her shoulders and pulled her upright.

'I'd like you to meet two new friends of mine,' said Varen. 'These are, if I have it right, Desoddo and Mirab.'

Miranda was jerked around and found herself looking into the face of an alien, a being with a slender skull, greyish skin and black eyes. 'They are what the Dasati called "Deathpriests", and they are going to have a lot of fun with you, I think. Pity I won't be there, but I have other matters to arrange.

'You see, my new friends and I have come to an understanding. I'm going to help them seize Kelewan, and in exchange, they're going to help me conquer Midkemia. Isn't that a wonderful arrangement?'

Without a word, the two Dasati Deathpriests jerked Miranda around and began to drag her downhill towards the black energy dome. As she fell into unconsciousness, the last thing she heard was Varen humming an odd little tune.

'Oh, damn,' said Tad as he peered over the rise.

'Yes,' whispered Servan. 'Damn, indeed.'

'What are we going to do?' asked Zane, from a few feet behind.

Jommy squated. The four of them were hunkered down below a rise and at the bottom waited the twenty soldiers – now all grudgingly obedient – Grandy, and Godfrey.

'How fast can you get back to the General?' asked Jommy.

Tad thought. 'I can run to the boat. That should take no more than a half hour. If I go across the river, then run up the shore – that's got to be faster than rowing against the current – four, maybe three and a half hours if I can do it without stopping.'

Tad was unquestionably the best runner among

the six boys, perhaps the best in the entire Roldemish army. 'That will get you to him before nightfall. If he sends sixty men by boat at night, they can be here easily before sunrise. So all we have to do is keep them from moving before tomorrow.'

He glanced over the ridge one more time to look at the enemy and ducked back down. The Salmater offensive wasn't coming across the river where the General expected it; it was coming across the river here. Once that force was moving into Olasko proper, finding them among the hundreds of islands would be as big a problem as dislodging them once they were found. But if they could be kept on this beach, even for a few hours tomorrow, they could attempt a retreat back across the river. With sixty fresh soldiers holding this ridge, and the promise of more arriving soon after . . .

'How do we keep them from going around us?' Jommy asked Servan.

He motioned for the other boys to shimmy down the side of the ridge and at the bottom he said, 'If they think we're only holding this ridge, they'll flank us to the south. So, we have to make them think we've got soldiers everywhere.' He glanced upward. 'Wait a minute.' He crawled up on his elbows to the ridge, looked at the deploying Salmater soldiers, then headed back down again.

'They are still unloading,' said Servan. Looking at the afternoon sun, he said, 'I don't know if they're going to try to march across this island and set up on that next one over there—' he pointed to a distant island separated from the one they were on by a broad, shallow rill from the river, '—or camp here for the night. If they think they're undiscovered, they may not be in a hurry.'

Jommy looked at Tad. 'You'd better be off, no matter what. Tell the General to come down fast with every man he can spare.' As Tad started to move, Jommy reached out and grabbed his arm. 'Hey, tell the boat crew to head downstream. If they scout around the north side of the island, I don't think it would be a good thing for the boat to be seen. Have them hide somewhere.'

Tad said, 'I've got it.'

'And keep from getting killed,' said Zane.

Tan grinned and ran off without another word.

Jommy turned to Servan and said, 'So, how are we going to make them think there's an army over there if they decide to move?'

Servan said, 'I have no idea.'

CHAPTER 21

BETRAYAL

Miranda awoke in pain.

The two figures above her were speaking, but she could not understand what they said. Not only was the tongue foreign to her, but her senses were dulled: it sounded as if they were talking under water. She was tied to a table of some sort, unable to move anything but her head, and that only slightly.

She tried to breathe, but the effort taxed her: her lungs hurt as if she was suffering from too little air. She tried to focus her mind, to gather together enough energy to free herself, but something was making concentration difficult.

'She awakes.' She didn't need to know who spoke. The voice was that of Leso Varen, now in the body of the Tsurani magician Wyntakata.

The figure closest to her bent over her and spoke, in the Tsurani language, but with a strange accent. 'Do not move,' he instructed her calmly and without menace. 'You will feel pain for a while. It will pass.' He stood back up and motioned around him. 'This place is suitable for both our races, but you will need time to adapt.'

411

'What do you want here?' she asked, finding it difficult to speak.

'If I may?' Varen's voice came from just outside her field of vision. Then his face was hovering over hers. He spoke in the King's Tongue, which made Miranda certain he didn't want the Dasati Deathpriests understanding what he said. 'It's simple, really. The Dasati are a race of children, in a way; if you can imagine a few million two-year-olds running around with very sharp blades, powerful death-magic, and an urge to break everything in sight.

'But like toddlers everywhere, if they see something pretty and shining, they want it. And to them, the worlds of the first realm of reality are very pretty indeed; much brighter, much shinier than their worlds. So, in a short while there will be thousands of very tall children in armour running amok through this lovely empire shouting, "Mine! Mine! Mine!" as they kill, pillage and burn. Isn't that wonderful?'

'You're insane,' Miranda choked out.

'Almost certainly,' said Varen. He looked over to the two Deathpriests, and said, 'But compared to them, I am the soul of reason. You will long for these moments we've spent together when their priests are working on you.' He looked at the two Deathpriests and said, 'I've finished now.'

Miranda saw one of the two tall Dasati prelates put out his hand, placing something over her nose and mouth that was pungent and bitter, and suddenly she was swallowed up by darkness.

Some while later, Servan said, 'I have an idea.'

'Good,' whispered Jommy, 'because I certainly do not have one.'

'Take a peek and tell me what they're doing now.'

Jommy crawled up to the ridge and looked over. The Salmater forces were dressed as mercenaries, a ploy they had utilized on previous raids into the region, according to the General. But just one look at the way the camp was organized told Jommy all he needed to know.

He scrambled back down the slope and said, 'They're pitching camp. They're here for the night.'

'Good,' said Servan. 'Follow me.'

He made his way to the base of the slope and motioned for the men to follow. When he was certain they were far enough away from the new Salmater camp, he said, 'There are about two hundred regulars from Salmater over there. And there are twenty-five of us.'

'So let's get out of here,' said one of the soldiers.

'That's exactly what I want you to do,' said Servan. 'But I just want you to wade across that shallow there and lie low out of sight until morning.'

'What then . . . sir?' asked another soldier.

'When you hear shouting, I want you to rush to that beach over there, making as much noise as you can, but don't come across. Stir up as much dust as possible and run up and down the beach.'

'Huh?' said Jommy.

'The sun will be coming up right behind them,' said Servan, pointing east. 'If the Salmater sentries top that rise, they'll be blinded by the morning sunlight, or they'll only see shadows, and dust and men moving. They won't have any idea how many of us are here.'

'And what will we be doing while all this is going on?' asked Godfrey.

'Running around and making them think there are three different armies bearing down on them.'

Jommy said, 'And how are we going to do that?'

Servan knelt. He drew with his finger in the soil. 'Here's the ridge. We're on the other side of it.' He pointed. 'I'll take Zane. We'll head down south of them.' He touched a spot south of the line and west of it. 'You and Godfrey go up here to the north.' He glanced around. 'Stay back in the trees. Run around and shout orders. Make it sound like squads are coming at them from all sides.'

'That isn't going to keep them fooled for long,' said Jommy.

'It doesn't have to. We just need to make them think about not moving a while, until the General gets here with the first and third. If we can get them to just dig in a little, kill an hour or so, that should do it.

'When a company of real soldiers comes charging out of those north woods, and if we've done enough noise-making, those lads on the other side of the ridge should beat a fast enough retreat home.'

Jommy said, 'Well, as long as the General doesn't linger over his breakfast, we have a chance.' He let out a long breath. 'I hope this works, because I'm here to tell you I can face two men, maybe, but eight to one?'

Grandy said, 'What about me?'

'You,' said Servan, 'are to go across with these lads and make sure they do as they are told.' He looked at his cousin a moment, nodding once and said, 'Go along.' To the soldiers he was sending to the next island, he said with careful emphasis, 'Make sure the *Prince* stays safe.'

As if the point was made, the solder nearest said, 'Yes, sir.' He saluted once, smartly, and hurried off, Grandy at his side.

'Was that wise?' asked Zane when they had gone.

'Those lads are troublemakers, but not deserters,' said Servan. 'If they had been, they'd have been long gone by now. They'll take care of Grandy. It's one thing to be a foul-up in the army, quite another to get a royal killed.'

Jommy said, 'I hope you're right.

'Well, let's find a bit more cover for the night.' He motioned to Godfrey and said to Zane and

Servan, 'See you tomorrow,' and started north, keeping low behind the ridge.

Servan said, 'Tomorrow,' and turned south.

It was still dark when the call came. A breathless Lesser working for the innkeeper shook Pug, Nakor and Magnus awake. 'Your master calls.'

They dressed quickly, ignoring the still-sleeping Dasati on the floor. The travellers had been given rolled mats of rushes to sleep upon, using whatever they had with them for blankets and pillows. It had been a cool night, but not too uncomfortable.

Once in the courtyard, they found Martuch and Bek waiting, Bek looking skyward over the roof of the building Pug and his companions had exited. Pug looked over his shoulder to see what had the youth transfixed, and he almost stumbled at the sight.

Magnus whispered, 'Amazing.'

Nakor said, 'Now that is something to see.'

Rising up into the heavens was a pillar of light. It was far enough from where they stood to look slender, but Pug had no doubt it was massive. It rose apparently straight up into the night sky, pulsing with energy. The colours slipped subtly from blue-green to blue-purple and back, a slow shift through that spectrum. What appeared to be tiny bits of white energy flowed up and down its length.

'The Star Bridge,' said Martuch. 'It is now sending people to the homeworld.'

Pug knew that meant Omadrabar, the original Dasati homeworld.

'We must go. It will only be operating for the next two hours. I have secured our travel.' He leaned forward. 'So far, you have managed not to do anything foolish, but from this point forward, be even more alert.

'Nothing you have seen will prepare you for the TeKarana's world.'

He turned and motioned for them to follow, Bek one step behind him, the others trailing in a line, eyes down, hurrying to keep up with the two warriors.

They walked, Pug assumed, because the distance was not far from where they stood, and because varnin would not be taken on the Star Bridge. But Pug found himself rethinking this assumption as they walked briskly for nearly a quarter of an hour. They had traversed street after street, passing through massive plazas, all starting to show signs of life for the day to come. Lines of carts were moving along the streets, most empty from having unloaded the night before, and now heading out of the city to the distant farms and herds to pick up the next load of produce and meats needed to feed a city of millions.

Hundreds of Lessers hurried along, each engaged in a task considered beneath the notice of the warriors, but vital in its own way to the continued wellbeing of the city. Pug wondered if there was some way to reach them, to educate them in the potential of living in a society where the ability to murder wasn't the ultimate skill . . . Again, he chided himself, he kept thinking of these people as human in some way, despite all evidence to the contrary.

They continued to walk, and the Star Bridge loomed larger by the minute. It now appeared to be a huge tube or column, mostly transparent, but with a shimmering, pulsing nebula of light hugging the surface. Sparks of white energy twinkled along its entire length. As they approached the great central plaza, a deep thrumming sound accompanied by a tingling in the soles of the feet manifested itself, and Pug could sense energy on an enormous scale.

To Magnus he whispered, 'If they can harness energy like this . . .'

Magnus nodded. His father didn't have to finish the thought. *If they can do this, how would we ever stand against them?* For as powerful as Pug and Magnus might be, together, along with every student in Stardock and Sorcerer's Isle, they could never build a thing on the scale of this Star Bridge. The idea that somehow it spanned the space between worlds was even more impossible for Pug to fathom than the concept of rifts tearing holes in the fabric of space.

They reached a low fence of iron or some other dark metal, and a very ornate gate through which a long line of people moved in an orderly fashion.

This was the only time Pug had witnessed warriors and their ladies standing behind Lessers, for it was clear that everyone was lined up in order of arrival. Martuch put Bek and the others in line and walked to the gate where he presented a parchment to a pair of men in black robes, with a golden eye embroidered on their chests. Hierophants: those Deathpriests who were responsible for the secrets and mysteries of the order. Pug sensed that meant they were the Lesser Paths, so to speak, of these people, for this Star Bridge was a great engine, no matter how fantastic it looked.

Nakor whispered, 'This is a very impressive trick.'

Pug touched him lightly on the shoulder to remind him to be silent. Martuch returned and spoke as if only to Bek, but loud enough that the others could hear. 'Everything is in order. We leave now.'

They followed the line in front of them. When they reached the gate, Pug noticed that the two Hierophants were making each person pause for a moment. As Martuch and then Bek walked to the base of the column of light, Pug was held a moment, then heard one of the two dark-robed priests say, 'Step on quickly, step off quickly.' Then with a firm push they sent him along.

Pug hurried to keep the same interval with Bek he had before, and saw the young warrior step into the light. As Pug reached the boundary he hesitated for only an instant, but in that moment he reached out with his senses and caressed the Star Bridge.

He staggered a step, and only managed not to fall by an act of will he had not been forced to utilize in years. This *thing*, this Star Bridge . . . He could not encompass it. His mind rebelled.

Then he was inside. For an instant it was as if he was once more in the void, for his senses were taken from him, then abruptly he was speeding through another place, a dimension of alien beauty and unnameable sensations.

For a brief moment, Pug felt a part of this plane of reality, and felt there was an order to it, a system that he might understand if he could but linger and ponder it. Then, suddenly he was standing on solid ground, looking at Bek's retreating back. He remembered the warning to step off quickly and did so, and wondered what would happen had he waited until Nakor appeared after him. Probably something unpleasant.

He heard his two companions walking behind him. He wanted to glance back, but the images that flooded his senses now made him not just cautious, but fearful. For if Delecordia hadn't fully prepared him for the shock of going to Kosridi, then Kosridi had done nothing to prepare him for what was now before his eyes on Omadrabar.

Miranda regained consciousness to find that her arms and legs were still bound, but not as tightly

420

as before. She appeared to be in a bed chamber, tied by cords to four posts of a bed. A Dasati sat upon a stool near the bed, regarding her with cold, black eyes.

'Can you understand me?' he asked, and Miranda's mind wrestled with his words, for while she didn't understand the words, the meaning came to her. He was employing a magic unknown to her, but it was effective.

'Yes,' she said, and found she could barely speak. Her lips were parched and her throat dry. 'Could I have some water?' she asked, too sick and tired to display what would have been appropriate rage. Her head pounded and her body throbbed, and try as she might, using every mind skill and incantation she knew, she could not focus her thoughts nor find any sense of energy around her. The entire flow of magic was alien. It was impossible for her to come to grips with it.

The Dasati on the stool wore a black robe with a red death's head on the chest and an ornate purple trim around the hem, sleeves and hood. The hood was back, so Miranda could see his face.

She had no frame of reference for what Dasati were supposed to look like. She studied his features and found that they were not too unlike a human's, with two eyes, a nose and mouth where she would have expected them to be. The chin was long, the cheekbones high, and the skull thin, but apart from the grey cast to this man's skin, he was not that alien in appearance. Certainly he looked a great deal more like her than the Cho-ja magicians at Chaka-hal did. But she knew for a fact that the Cho-ja magicians were far more like her than this creature.

'Varen says you are dangerous,' said the Dasati, and again Miranda felt his words in her mind as much as heard them. 'I do not know how you could be, but I will not underestimate the possibility.' He stood up and towered over her as she lay helpless on the pallet. 'We shall study you, for if you are dangerous, and there are more like you on the world of Kelewan, we need to prepare for encountering such as you.

'It is His Darkness's pleasure that we take your world from you.'

Without another word the Dasati left the chamber, closing the door behind him. Miranda's mind raced; for while she had difficulty focusing, she knew Pug's worst fears were being realized: the Dasati were invading, and soon. If not Midkemia, it would be Kelewan; and she had no doubt they would not stop there. She examined her surroundings as best she could. She was in a room without windows. There was a torch in a sconce in the wall, no table or chair, one bed and one stool.

And she was tied firmly. Every time she tried to focus her energies, to use any of a number of spells to free her bonds or move to another location, her mind felt numb, as if something was interfering with her abilities. Perhaps they had drugged her.

She was considering what might be causing her lack of focus when she drifted off to unconsciousness again.

Jommy lay against a slight rise in the woods to the north of the encampment, watching while the hours dragged on. Their sentries were alert and posted far enough away from the campfires that Jommy couldn't see what, if anything, was occurring around the fires. The sounds that carried through the night were of men talking, at their ease, not worried in the least about being discovered.

Jommy glanced over to where Godfrey was hiding behind a tree. In the pre-dawn darkness, he could barely make him out. Jommy sniffed, his nose starting to run with the damp and cold. It would be a steam bath when the sun came up, but right now he was shivering. He wondered how Grandy was doing. Then he wondered, again, what Grandy was doing here.

'What are any of us doing here?' he whispered to himself. Since meeting Tad and Zane in Kesh, Jommy had found himself more-or-less adopted into a family that had its share of adventures and wonders – which included magicians living on an island, fighting assassins, travel everywhere in the world – but some of the things he was asked to do just didn't make much sense.

Still, it was better than farming, or working a teamster's wagon, and he knew what they were doing was important, even if he didn't understand half of what it was. He really liked Tad and Zane, as much as if they were his brothers – although remembering his older brothers and how they used to regularly smack him around, he amended that to he liked them better than his brothers; and while Caleb wasn't his dad, he treated Jommy the same as he did the others.

But what were they doing in the south of Olasko playing at soldiers? And why send a boy like Grandy along?

He was sure there was a reason, and he thought it had to do with Kaspar's remark the other day: that soon everyone would be going to war. Even so, they were not Roldemish, so why this army? Why now?

Jommy put aside his concerns, for the moment, as dawn was on its way, and with it, he hoped, General Devrees along with about sixty regular soldiers. Jommy glanced eastward, hoping for a sign of the rising sun. He had no idea of the time, and he wondered how much longer they'd be forced to wait.

A sound from behind him caused Jommy to turn and start drawing his sword. But a soft voice said, 'Don't.'

He found one of the men Servan had detailed to go with Grandy standing behind him, a sword pointed at him. Glancing over at Godfrey, he saw another soldier had him at sword's point as well. The soldier held out his left hand and Jommy slowly handed him his sword. When the man had it, he tossed it aside. 'Move,' he instructed.

Slowly Jommy moved from out of the trees and saw about sixteen men walking towards the camp with Grandy being escorted by two men with hands clamped firmly on his shoulders. 'Hello, the camp!' one shouted.

Instantly guards from Salmater were shouting alarm, and the Roldem soldier who had shouted, said, 'We're seeking parley!'

By the time Jommy and Godfrey reached the campsite, the full contingency of two hundred men were up, armed, and ready for a fight. Servan and Zane were herded in from the south. The leader of the Salmater force looked around and said, 'What is this, then?' He was a tall, dark-haired soldier, experienced from his appearance and an officer from his bearing.

The soldier who was leading the Roldemish contingency said, 'Look, I'll be quick. There's a Roldem general with a strong force heading down this way to thump you. We want no part of it. We're all Olasko men and hate having to serve in their army. We fought them at Opardum and we're not going to put up with wearing these Roldem monkey jackets any more.' As if to demonstrate, he started stripping his tunic. He was a stocky, blond-haired man with a couple of days of grey whiskers and a sunburnt, leathery face.

'You've got an army heading this way?'

'Yes,' said the soldier, throwing his jacket on the ground. 'We want to go to Salmater with you.'

'Why would we take you with us? We're going to be lucky to keep our heads once I report this raid as a total failure.'

'Not a failure,' said the soldier. He motioned and Grandy was pushed forward. 'This here is the son of the King, Prince Grandprey, out larking about, learning to soldier. Think of the ransom.'

'Prince?' said the officer. 'You expect me to believe that the son of the King of Roldem is mucking about in these islands?'

'Look,' said the Olaskan soldier. 'What have you to lose? If I'm lying, cut my head off back in Salmater. If I'm telling the truth, you're a hero and your king gets to dictate terms to Roldem.'

'Or bring the entire Roldem fleet down on us,' said the officer.

'But that's for your court and the court of Roldem to argue, isn't it? Here's what I know. They're expecting something big and the army is being pulled back to Roldem. That's why they haven't replenished the depleted Olasko divisions. My lads and I want nothing to do with that bit. We're Olasko men and we'll stay hidden in these islands if we have to, but if Roldem is expecting a war with Kesh or someone else, let someone else fight it. But if a big war is coming, the King of Roldem will just pay the ransom and be done with it, right?'

'What about the rest of these boys?'

'Officers, so they say. Might be worth something. These two—' he pointed to Zane and Jommy, '—got something to do with the court down in Kesh, and this other one—' he pointed at Servan, '—is the Prince's cousin. The other lad's his friend.'

'Bring them all,' said the officer. 'I'll let the generals sort it out back in Micel's Station.'

'You'll take us, then?' asked the blond soldier.

The Salmater officer said, 'What would I do with traitors? Kill them!'

Before the soldiers from Roldem could react, the Salmater raiders were on them, cutting throats and running them through with swords. When twenty dead or dying men lay in the sand, the officer shouted, 'Break camp! I want everyone back across the border by sunrise!' To Grandy and the others he said, 'Nobles or not, if you give me any trouble you'll end up like them.'

Four guards stood watch over the five boys while the raiders got ready to leave. Jommy looked at Servan and saw that bravado had gone out of him. Godfrey and Zane looked frightened, and Grandy was shivering from fear as much as from the cold.

All he could hope for was that Tad got through and was leading the General and men from Roldem down the river right now, and they'd get here before the Salmater raiders got back across the border. He glanced to the east and saw the sky was lightening.

Pug tried not to gawk, as it was clear that most Lessers kept their eyes down and attended to their own business. Nakor didn't seem to care, looking up at the lofty towers that rose hundreds of feet into the air. 'How do they climb those?' he asked.

Magnus said, 'Probably they have some device inside to lift and lower you.'

Omadrabar City was impossible to make sense of in human terms, thought Pug. There were no slums, no run-down sections of the city, no poor quarters, nothing remotely to indicate the class of citizen that one would find in every human city on two worlds.

Here, every building was connected by bridges that arched over wide boulevards or canals, or streets that went through tunnels in the middle of massive structures. Pug could only estimate, but in human terms it would probably take thousands of years to build a city like this, and he couldn't begin to imagine anyone in human history could ever have imagined a city as a single, interconnected structure.

They rode past one of the few open park areas, which was simply a plot of land left undeveloped, where trees and what appeared to be short ferns rather than true grass grew. Pug realized this passion for single, related structures, was probably triggered by the same drive that linked all social and political structures together within this culture.

Pug turned to his companions and said softly, 'Will we ever understand these beings?'

Nakor grinned, and even with his Dasati glamour on, it was clear to see he was delighted. 'Probably not, but we should be able to reach a mutually-beneficial accommodation if we can contact the right people.'

'And who are they?' whispered Magnus.

Nakor shrugged. 'The ones we are with now, we must hope.'

From the Star Bridge they had walked to where a wagon had waited, escorted by four hand-picked warriors of Martuch's society, the Sadharin. Even in this alien world Pug didn't have to be told something momentous was taking place.

Everywhere they went large numbers of armed men, Deathpriests and wagons were on the move. It was as if this city was making ready for an invasion, but that was impossible. This was the Dasati homeworld and no enemy existed within any imaginable distance.

Yes, Pug knew from his experiences during the Riftwar and the Serpentwar that invaders could reach anywhere with the right magic, but to attempt to invade this world . . . This wasn't a world of millions, like Kelewan; it was a world of billions. Moreover they were Dasati, a race where the warrior class consisted only of the survivors; the toughest, most dangerous men on this world. Each had been tested repeatedly by the time they were fifteen years old. And there were so many of them. This city alone was home to seven million people, according to Martuch, over a million of them warriors, members of a thousand battle societies. That was more than the entire population of the Kingdom of the Isles, and almost as many souls as resided in all of Great Kesh.

Souls, wondered Pug. Do these Dasati have them? If it hadn't been for the letters he had sent to tell himself to come here, Pug would have felt completely overwhelmed. He was riding in a wagon with his son and Nakor, on a world populated by billions of beings who would happily kill him as a minor part of their day's business, and he had no idea what he was doing here. Somewhere on this world was an answer, even if Pug didn't know the question at this moment.

One thing he would like to know, however, was why such a level of mobilization was apparently underway on Omadrabar. From what Pug had been told and what he had seen of the Twelve Worlds, the Dasati had no enemies left. One of the mandates the TeKarana had given the Order of Hierophants was to find more worlds to conquer. Martuch and Pug had spoken several times of the conditions within the Dasati realm, and yet nothing had been said about plans for mass travel beyond it.

They entered through a large gate into a relatively small yard above which rose a building – or another section of wall and bridges as Pug thought of them – that was Martuch's home on Omadrabar.

Pug waited as Martuch instructed his men to secure the house, though he wasn't sure if 'house' was the proper term. It was more a series of large apartments that were embedded into the wall of the city. Or rather, one of many walls in the city.

Pug's senses were reeling. Of all the worlds he had visited, none were as alien as Omadrabar. Delecordia had some elements in common with the first plane of reality, and the people were more pacific. Kosridi was an echo of Midkemia, and that had given him a sense of the familiar.

This place, though, was a different matter. The scale of things, the pace of life, the complete lack of anything familiar: he had no frame of reference for any of it. He had thought his introduction to the Tsurani culture, including the slave camps in the Great Swamp of Szetac Province, had been difficult. At least the Tsurani were human, and had families they loved. They prized heroism, loyalty and sacrifice. He didn't even know if the words the Dasati used for these concepts existed. He searched to express the concepts in a different way, and could only come up with bravery, fidelity and selflessness.

Pug, Nakor, and Magnus were given a single room in which to wait, and Martuch made it clear to the Lessers in his household that they were to be ignored. No one was to speak to them, nor were they to be given any tasks.

Hours dragged by and finally they were summoned to Martuch's private quarters, a huge series of rooms overlooking the central plaza of this region of the city.

They entered a room and found Martuch waiting with three others. Narueen and Valko stood near the door, the young warrior looking different to how Pug had ever seen him: tentative, unsure, perhaps even intimidated.

The figure standing next to Martuch was tall, with dark hair and a beard. He appeared to be Dasati, but there was something about him . . . Pug felt his world suddenly contract, as if his senses were betraying him. Before him stood a being who could not possibly exist. He was a Dasati, but he was someone well known to Pug.

That man stepped forward, and in a very familiar voice, speaking the King's Tongue, he said, 'Here I am called the Gardener.' He came to stand before the three visitors. He looked first at Pug. When he came to Nakor he nodded once, and Nakor stood in open-mouthed shock.

Then he stood before Magnus. 'Is this my grandson?' he asked.

Pug looked up into that Dasati face and whispered, 'Macros.'

CHAPTER 22

REVELATIONS

Jommy struggled.

His arms had been bound behind him and he and the other boys had been marched to the three boats pulled up on the shore. They were narrow boats which looked more like a ship's longboat than a true river craft. Jommy supposed they could have sailed up the mouth of the river, for this section of the river was broad and slow-flowing, so it would only take a few minutes to row across the shore.

The border between Salmater and Olasko was about a mile to the south-west of the river, so there was still a possibility of Roldem forces over-taking the raiders before they were back home. At least Jommy prayed there would be. Once he and Zane were interviewed the chances were good he would be disposed of: princes and nobles might fetch handsome ransoms, but the sons of farmers on the other side of the world were unlikely to be considered worth the bother.

As the last of the raiders approached the boat, a sentry on the ridge above them fell over. For a moment, Jommy and the other boys looked confused, as did the soldiers nearby, then suddenly they heard it: the whistling of arrows flying through the air.

'Down!' shouted Jommy and they flattened themselves, trying to keep below the gunwales. Three raiders had been detailed to watch the five boys in the boat; but they were also hunkering down and trying to see where the arrows were coming from.

'Push off!' shouted the raiders' commander, and two of the raiders slid over the gunwales. They had started pushing the boat into the river when one took an arrow in the back for his troubles. The other tried to clamber over the side and Jommy kicked him as hard as he could in the face. The man's eyes went unfocused and he fell into the water.

The one guard remaining in the boat drew his sword and raised it to strike Jommy, but Zane leapt up and shouldered him from behind. The man fell forward on top of Jommy and suddenly there was a writhing mass of bodies in a boat that was starting to drift downriver.

The guard tried to roll off Jommy, turning to find Zane landing on top of both of them. Zane head-butted the man while Godfrey bit his arm hard, and Jommy tried to move enough to breathe. Following Zane's example, Servan head-butted the man as well, and he slumped into uncon-sciousness.

'Thank the gods they're not wearing helmets,' said Zane.

'Get his knife,' said Servan.

Zane felt around behind him and managed to pull the dagger from the man's belt.

'Will you please get off me,' said Jommy, barely able to draw breath.

Zane held the knife behind him, while Godfrey positioned himself to get his bonds cut. 'Ow!' said the young noble. 'Hold that thing still.'

'It's a boat. It rocks!' said Zane. 'It's not my fault!'

'Get off me!' Jommy pleaded.

Finally Godfrey got his bonds cut, as well as his lower arm. He cut Zane, Servan, Grandy and Jommy loose, and they threw the unconscious soldier overboard.

Jommy sat up and took a deep breath. In the minute they had been struggling to get free, they had drifted a hundred yards down the river and were moving out towards the centre of the current, picking up speed.

'Where are the oars?' asked Servan.

'Still back on shore,' said Jommy looking around.

'Over we go,' said Zane, jumping into the water. He started swimming to the eastern shore. The others followed reluctantly: five drenched young officers came ashore almost out of sight of combat.

'Hurry,' Servan instructed, motioning them to move off the shore and into the trees. 'In case someone's coming after us.'

They got into the tree line and started back upriver. The sounds of men and combat reached them, and they ventured to look, but the site of the conflict was on the other side of a ridge. They reached an overhanging outcrop of rock that served as a barrier and Jommy said, 'I'll take a look.'

Still dripping, he scrambled up the rock-face and pulled himself up. In the distance he could see boats from Salmater still on the shore and a veritable wave of soldiers from Roldem running down the beach beyond, as well as sweeping up over the ridge to the east. 'Come on!' shouted Jommy, climbing back down. 'We've got them!'

He led the boys out of the trees and onto the shore and they started running towards the conflict. By the time they came into view the remaining Salmater forces were surrendering, standing there with their hands in the air, swords reversed, not putting up any resistance.

General Devrees approached the boys. Relief was etched on his face. 'Highness!' he exclaimed. 'You're safe!'

Tad came over to the boys, grinning. They were obviously exhausted, but he was happy to see his friends alive.

Grandy said, 'I'm glad to see you, General.'

'When this young man came running into our camp, I immediately ordered the entire first and third into a forced march.'

Servan said, 'Sir, you didn't think much of my idea of sixty men by boat?'

'It was a nice plan, if I didn't mind losing half

the forces down here; but when I heard that I had just sent two members of the royal court into a full-scale Salmater raid . . . I didn't relish the idea of explaining to either of your fathers—' he looked significantly at Grandy, '—especially yours, Highness, that I'd let their sons get killed. Our intelligence was faulty; I thought I was sending you lads as far from the real action as possible, not right into the teeth of the incursion.' He shrugged.

'We should certainly see an end to Salmater raids once word gets back to them we're willing to defend Olasko as if it's Roldem soil.'

'General, did you capture their leader?' Grandy asked.

'I think so,' said the General, leading the boys to where the Salmater prisoners were being guarded. 'See what you think.'

The prisoners sat on the ground, glaring at their captors.

Grandy looked from face to face then pointed to one man. 'Him.'

The General motioned for the prisoner to be brought forward. The young prince stared at him, then said to the General. 'This man killed twenty soldiers in cold blood.'

'They were deserters,' shot back the captive.

'Then they should have been left for Roldemish justice,' said Grandy. He looked at the General and said, 'Hang him.'

'I'm a prisoner of war!' shouted the Salmater

captain as two Roldemish soldiers grabbed him, thrust his arms behind him and tied them.

'You wear no uniform,' said the General. 'As far as I can tell, you're a common bandit. If his Highness says you are to be hanged, then hanged you shall be.' The General nodded to Sergeant Walenski who motioned for a group of soldiers to follow him into the trees. One carried a coil of rope.

'What about these others?' asked the General.

The young prince said, 'Send them home. Have them carry word that Roldem now regards these islands as being as sacred as the soil under my father's castle. Olasko is now Roldem, and we shall defend it to the last drop of our blood.' He turned to the General and said, 'I will ask my father to start recruiting to replenish the first and third and bring the garrison at Opardum up to full muster. We must ensure that this sort of thing stops.'

With a slight smile, the General said, 'Highness,' and motioned to the soldiers. 'Escort these men to the boats and let them go home.'

The soldiers did as ordered.

Servan moved over to his cousin. 'That was . . . impressive.'

'Yes,' agreed Jommy, then he added, 'Highness.'

All five boys looked at the young prince who now suddenly appeared years older than he had yesterday. Grandy looked at his friends. 'I think it's time for us to go home now.'

He turned and walked away, following the

General, and after a moment's hesitation, his friends trailed after him.

Miranda returned to consciousness and found herself on a bed, untied. She sat up and breathed deeply. Her chest hurt, but she could breathe without pain, and her mind was free of the clouding sensation that had gripped her the last time she had awoken.

She looked around, trying to make sense of her surroundings. She was no longer in the bedchamber where she had been tied up but instead appeared to be in something akin to a tent. However, when she touched the walls she felt hardness, like smooth stone, beneath her fingertips.

Suddenly a figure appeared before her – a Dasati in a black robe, but with a different device on his chest: a circle of yellow. She could see through the figure, so she recognized it for what it was: a sending. Trying to ascertain what she could and couldn't do, she reached out mentally and found her magic worked, but in a strange way.

'You are conscious,' the figure said, and she realized that he was speaking the Dasati language, which she now apparently understood. 'You have been here for three days. We have ensured that you may eat, drink and breathe without suffering. We have let you . . . regain your powers, but within limits.'

Miranda tried to will herself back to the Assembly

of Magicians, for she was the unquestioned mistress of that ability; but nothing happened.

'It has taken some work on our part,' said the Dasati image, 'but your power only works within the confines of this room.

'The creature who brought you to us says that you are a powerful practitioner of magic and we can learn much by studying you. We have watched you for some time now, Tsurani woman. It seems that your warriors are as children; but we do fear your black-robed ones.'

The figure vanished and a voice said, 'Rest. Many tests are coming. If you co-operate, you shall live.'

It left unsaid what would happen if she failed to cooperate.

Nakor said, 'This is really interesting.'

Pug could scarcely credit his senses. The Dasati who stood before him was Macros the Black, one-time owner of Sorcerer's Isle and Miranda's father. He probed with his own magical senses and ascertained this was not an illusion or some disguise glamour: this man he thought he had known *was* a Dasati. The last time Pug had seen him was battling a demon king on the Saaur world of Shila as a rift closed. 'You're dead,' said Pug.

'I was,' said Macros. 'Come, we have a great deal to discuss and little time in which to discuss it.'

Without apology or explanation for the others,

Macros led Pug out of a door into a small garden which was hidden from all eyes behind massive walls. Macros looked up and said, 'This poor little plot of soil only gets an hour or so of light, when the sun is directly overhead.' He was speaking the language of the Kingdom of the Isles, Pug's native tongue, and Pug realized that whatever he was about to say, he was taking every precaution not to be overheard.

Pug looked at the Dasati standing before him and said, 'I can think of nothing intelligent to say to you. I am completely confused.'

Macros motioned to a bench. 'Meditation is not a Dasati trait, so I had to have this space created to my own specifications.'

Pug was forced to smile. The bench looked exactly like one in the garden at Villa Beata. 'How is this possible?'

'I angered the gods,' said Macros, sitting down on the bench. Pug joined him. 'I fought Maarg with every magical weapon at my disposal while you attempted to seal the rift between the fifth circle and Shila.' He sighed. 'Obviously you succeeded, or you wouldn't be here.' He looked down. 'Some of my memories are still denied me, Pug. I do remember the first time we met, for example. I also remember the last time I met Nakor, but I don't remember the first time I met him.

'I don't remember much about my wife, or daughter, though I know I have one.'

'My wife, Miranda,' said Pug.

Macros nodded, and looked out at the wall opposite where he sat. There was pain in his eyes and Pug said, 'This is your punishment for angering the gods of Midkemia?'

'Yes,' said Macros. 'I fought Maarg, and suddenly the pain stopped and I was speeding towards a white light. Then I found myself before Lims-Kragma.' He paused, then asked, 'You've visited her?'

'Twice,' said Pug. 'A vast hall full of catafalques?'

'Endless, in every direction, and the dead would appear, rest for a while, then stand and walk to join a great line, where Lims-Kragma would judge them and direct them to the next turning of the Wheel of Life.' Macros sighed. 'But not for me.

'I appeared before her but I will spare you every detail of our exchange. I was, as you know, a vain man, given to a sense of my own importance. I thought my own judgment was better than any other's.'

Pug nodded. 'More often than not, you were right. Tomas never would have endured the transformation of the Dragon Lord's armour had you not taken a hand, and who knows where I would have ended up.'

'That was a minor transgression,' said Macros. He sat back, then said, 'I tried to become a god, remember?'

'Your attempted ascension when Nakor found you?'

'Yes, when I sought to hasten the return of Sarig, the lost God of Magic.'

'And for this you are punished?'

'More than anything, the gods hate hubris. They may urge us on to do great things, Pug, but without our worshipful devotion to them, they wither way. How would we worship them if we became like them?'

'Ah,' said Pug.

'Here's what you must know. Everything else can wait for another time. The Dasati have found Kelewan.'

'The Talnoy,' said Pug.

'That name is best not mentioned, for reasons I'll explain in a moment.'

Macros paused as if gathering his thoughts, then said, 'It's all connected, Pug. All the way back to the beginning.

'You've heard tales of the Chaos Wars, correct?'

'Tomas has memories, Ashen-Shugar's memories,' said Pug.

'Does he remember the triumph, when the Lifestone was hidden, and the Dragon Horde was banished from Midkemia?'

'Yes, at the end of the Chaos Wars. He's told me the story. It was something we discussed before his son Calis freed all the trapped energy from the Lifestone?'

'Ah,' said Macros. 'I have no memory of that. That's good. One less thing to worry about. But what you should know is that that wasn't the end of the Chaos Wars, Pug.' He looked at his heir. 'The Chaos Wars never stopped. The Riftwar and the battle with the demons on Shila and the invasion of the Saaur and the war of the Emerald Queen; all were battles in the Chaos Wars. And the most desperate struggle is yet to come.'

'The Dasati?'

'Yes,' said Macros. 'This world had its own Chaos Wars, or something much like them, but in that struggle one god emerged victorious over all the rest. That god is now simply known as His Darkness; but he is the Dasati god of evil. Look around you, Pug. This is what Midkemia might become in a thousand years if the Nameless One ever gains supremacy in Midkemia.'

'Incredible,' said Pug.

'The Dasati were not always as you see them, I believe. I will say that even at their best they would be unwelcome guests in Midkemia, for many reasons, not the least of which would be their ability to simply wilt grass by standing on it for too long a period of time.

'Moreover, they are aggressive to the point of making mountain trolls look mild-mannered.' Macros chuckled. 'Some of the things I do remember from my previous life . . .' He sighed. 'When I was reborn, I was allowed to keep some memories, enough so that I had a frame of reference for the work I need to do.

'I am the Gardener. I am tending a very delicate, very vulnerable flower.'

'The White?'

'Yes, the White. Nothing ever dies, Pug. It just changes. Nothing is destroyed. It is just changed to another state, from matter to energy, energy to mind, mind to spirit.

'It's vital you know that, because when this is over, you're going to feel a great sense of personal loss, I fear.'

Pug said only, 'So I have been warned.'

Macros stood and began to pace. 'Long ago, when this world's Dark God rose to permanence, the other gods were hunted down and imprisoned. These people, the Dasati, were warped and changed and perverted until all memory of good as we know it was lost.

'That is what the White does, it nurtures little pockets of good where it can. We have obvious members, like the Attenders who are despised for their tiny impulse to care for others, and some not so obvious members, including highly-placed Deathknights and a few prelates among the Deathpriests.'

'Macros, I came here because there is a threat to Midkemia. What is it?'

'There is no rational reason in two universes for the Dasati to wish to invade the first level of reality, Pug. You know that.'

'Nakor is of the opinion that evil is by nature insane, even if it acts with purpose.'

'In our realm . . .' Macros stopped. 'In your realm, that is most certainly true. Here?' He shrugged, a very human gesture. 'I have only been a Dasati for thirty years, Pug, as best I can judge – the time difference is difficult.'

'You've been gone closer to fifty,' said Pug.

Macros looked tired. 'I came to consciousness as a young Dasati boy, ready to do battle to claim his father's honours. For nearly a year I watched from within another's mind, and then gradually we blended, and his nature was subsumed into mine.

'I know relatively little of what the gods of Midkemia are capable of here. Which is why you are here, as their agents. But somehow an evil trick was played—'

'Ban-ath,' said Pug. 'Kalkin.'

'The Trickster?' Macros nodded. 'Yes, this sort of thing is what we might expect. I am Dasati, yet I am human. I have the mind of Macros the Black – who was I might say with some lack of modesty – one of the most powerful beings in Midkemia; yet here I found myself barely more than a boy, and most of my powers were gone.'

'But not all of them?'

'No. I've regained some of them, and retrained myself. It took all my abilities to hide that fact, or I would have become a Deathpriest, or a corpse.

'I've recruited others like myself; like Martuch, my first student and my best. Even though he is nearly ten years older than me, he looks to me for guidance. And he is the first Dasati who ever displayed what I would call compassion.'

'The story of Lady Narueen and Valko.'

'Yes,' said Macros. 'He is the one who with the help of an Ipiliac wizard readied us for this journey. When he contacted me, I had many questions, and some will have to wait, but first and foremost I must know: did you find the Talnoy?'

'Yes, we found them all.'

'Good, for here is the important part of what is coming.

'The Dark God is seeking to find his way into the first plane of reality, to extend his domain. The first rift into Kelewan was an accident, and the Deathpriests are not the researchers that you or the Tsurani are, but they persevered, using the experience of each rift formed to refine and improve their search for a way into the first circle. The Deathpriests sent . . . scouts, little homunculi, with wards to provide energy to stabilize their rifts. They were all closed, but one. Someone on the other side helped them, if you can imagine anyone mad enough to do such a thing.'

'Leso Varen,' said Pug with a sinking feeling. 'He's mad enough.'

'Tell me of him later. Now the Dasati have a foothold on Kelewan. The massed might of the Assembly may hold them at bay for a while, Pug, but eventually the Dasati will sweep into the first circle of reality and overrun that world; then they will find Midkemia, and from there, who knows how many other worlds?

'The balance between the first and second plane

of reality is already tipping – Delecordia shouldn't exist, at all, but it does. If the Dark God of the Dasati reaches Midkemia, the balance will be destroyed. The first and second planes of reality will collapse into . . . something else, and billions will die.'

'I'm not sure I fully understand, Macros. The Dasati are already there. The Dark God's agents have reached Kelewan. So if this dire event was to happen, wouldn't it have happened already?'

'You don't understand, Pug. The Dark God isn't a spiritual abstraction who can manifest his or her persona for a short period of time, like those you've encountered on Midkemia.

'The Dark God is a monstrous being living in a vast hall at the heart of this world. He is an eater of souls and the devourer of hundreds of sacrifices every day. He is real, corporeal, and he lives to destroy.' He looked at Pug. 'I have agents in high places, but not enough. I believe the Dasati are mustering for an invasion. There is much going on in this city and across the Twelve Worlds that tells me a massive mobilization is about to commence.'

Pug nodded slowly.

Macros sat down next to him. 'The Talnoy. What do you know of them?'

'Tomas remembers Ashen-Shugar facing them, when the Valheru tried to raid into the second realm. We were told by Kalkin that they contain the spirit of a Dasati who had been murdered in order to provide life energy to make it a killing machine.'

'Partially true,' said Macros. 'What should be obvious, but perhaps isn't, is that all Dasati magic is a form of necromancy. All their energy comes from killing. If you remember what Murmandamus did during the Great Uprising, that was but a hint of what the Dasati achieve every day.

'Thousands of children are killed in purges every year, and that energy is seized by Deathpriests when they can, and those souls are imprisoned.' Macros paused. 'But the Talnoy are not what you think. There are "Talnoy" in the service of the TeKarana and his princes, the Karanas, but they are there to keep the battle societies in check. They are really hand-picked soldiers in false armour, and they only appear on specific days for special events.'

'But the ones on Midkemia?'

'Those were hidden there. They are the real Talnoy.'

'Who hid them?'

'That is a mystery. If I knew in the past, I do not seem to know now. Perhaps that memory will return. Or perhaps we will find out in the future, but for the moment this is what you must know about those creatures: the Talnoy are not machines powered by the spirits or souls of slain Dasati. They are slaves, confined in bondage that has lasted millennia; for the spirits that inhabit them are not Dasati, but rather are the ten thousand lost Dasati gods.'

Pug was rendered almost speechless. 'Gods?'

'Like the Midkemian gods, they do not die easily. And even when they are dead, they seem intent on not staying that way.

'There are many hours ahead in which we can speculate, but for now this is what I believe: the Dark One wishes to get to Midkemia for the sole purpose of destroying them, and he will think nothing of obliterating the entire planet to do so.'

Pug whispered, 'And we must stop him.'

Macros nodded. 'Yes.'